Book II

The Dark Masters

The Tales of Nevaeh: Book II

DAVID WIND

ISBN-13:978-0-9900035-4-0
ISBN-10:099000354X

Cover design by Erin Dameron-Hill
© Copyright 2015 by David Wind
First Edition May 2015

◇◇◇

A listing of David Wind's previous novels are at the end of this book.

◇◇◇

ACKNOWLEDGEMENTS

I would like to thank everyone who has helped me on this journey into the future. To Bonnie Wind for all her support and love, and to my fabulous Beta readers, Terry Vanlandingham, Effrosyni Moschoudi, Nicholas Rossis, Amanda Tibbets & Mike Kaufman.

This book is dedicated to
Bonnie Marilyn

◇◇◇

"…what people call magic is but the witnessing of a science they cannot comprehend…"

—Areenna of Freemorn, Age twelve, 5267

PROLOGUE

SHE LAY ON the cavern floor, unmoving, her twisted limbs spread awkwardly as *she* stared at the high ceiling above. *She* had failed, and with failure came fear. Her masters would soon know of this failure, if they did not already have the knowledge.

Trembling on the rock floor, exhausted from the battle fought with the forces *she* had never encountered before, *she* pleaded with her masters even as *she* built the message of her failure to them.

She was explicit within the message, sparing no detail of what had happened and filled the mist-carried winged messenger with her impression of the powers that had defeated her creations and herself. At the end of the woeful tale, *she* added her plea for mercy, knowing well the answer might never come.

There was no choice. There was no one other than her dark masters, the rulers of her world, the ones who had entrusted this part of the world to her with the most important task of all. To destroy Roth, his woman, his child and the woman-child called Areenna, just as *she* had killed the woman child's mother with a lingering painful death.

She dragged herself from the floor and half-walked half-scuttled to where the winged mist awaited outside the cavern. *She* drew into herself, all the strength *she* could muster and once her message was complete, and the mist swirled about her impatiently, *she* would either live or die at their whim. Yet, until that day came, *she* would not cease her attempts to finish what her masters had decreed.

"I will destroy them, I will do as you have commanded. Or I will give my life in the attempt."

A rush of confidence filled her when *she* swirled her hands and called up the formula to send the message on its winged way.

She completed the message and the mist disappeared. *She* saw not the cloud-filled heavens above, but the faces of the four *she* had sworn to destroy. From within the black remnants of what once was her soul came a haunting laugh, for she knew what was coming.

I

AREENNA OF FREEMORN sat stone still: her breathing soundless, her senses ranging, searching. Hidden by the branches of a low hanging gazebow tree, she eased her tense muscles before making her next move.

Challenging her inner strength while willing her body to rest and recover, she could not help but marvel at how much had happened in the few months following their testing on the Island.

She had changed in so many ways there were times when she barely recognized herself. Her strength and her powers had increased more than she'd ever imagined possible—far more than the short eighteen years she'd lived. Her ability to meld her mind with his was as if they were one person. Harder though, was the knowledge that the emotions within her could not rise to the barest of thoughts—not yet.

From above, Gaalrie's warning tugged within her mind and she stopped thinking. *He comes.* She stood, let her senses expand, and shot off into the thicker woods.

Racing through the forest, zigzagging between trees like a mad weaver creating a bewildering drapery, Areenna moved with the swiftness of a rantor on hunt. Above her, the foundling treygone she had rescued and bonded with four years before, flew in pace with her running, its six foot wingspread rode the currents above the treetops. The thickness of the forest prevented her from seeing her pursuer through her aoutem's eyes, yet she knew he was close and coming fast; exactly where she wasn't sure for he had blocked himself well. She paused for a breath.

To her left was another giant gazebow tree, its long and heavy branches curved downward to kiss the ground, offering her a degree of protection. To her right stood a tall pine, hundreds of years old, its trunk almost as wide as the gazebow.

Standing between the two trees, Areenna sought him with her mind. *There!* He was close. She could not read him through the block, but recognized the complete absence of anything as the block he'd raised around himself. She closed her eyes and drew on her inner power, seeking one of the new abilities gifted to her on the Island. When the heat roared through her abdomen, she created a mind picture of herself and set it under the gazebow tree. She positioned the vision so only the barest glimpse of her arm and shoulder was visible. She moved behind the bole of the tall pine and drew her short-sword. Gaalrie settled on a branch above her. She slowed her breathing, knowing she could not hold this ability for long.

Thirty seconds later came the faint echoes of dead twigs and old leaves crunching beneath boots. She drew in a slow breath.

Emerging from behind a small cluster of trees to her left, tall and broad, black hair hanging to his shoulders and gray eyes searching everywhere, Mikaal of Tolemac stepped between the gazebow and the pine, took three steps, and turned. He spotted the mind picture hidden by the branches.

When he moved toward the gazebow, she launched herself from behind the tree. She was on him in three strides, her shortsword swinging in a deadly killing stroke.

Before the blade reached him, he spun and caught her sword on his longsword. The ring of metal upon metal echoed loudly in the quiet forest. A smile broke across his face. *Good*!

"Good*?* Is that all it was?" she asked aloud, lowering her sword and sheathing it. "Anyone else would not have known I was behind them."

I am not anyone else, Mikaal told her in their wordless way.

True, she replied, returning his smile with her own. "Let's rest for a minute. We've been at this for hours."

Mikaal lowered himself to the mossy grass and Areenna did the same. Sighing pleasantly, she looked at the sky. The sun had crested three hours earlier and was deep into its western descent. Rays of staggered sunlight, filtered beams of yellow and white, slipped through the tree branches of the forest near the border of Tolemac, at the edge of the Southern Outlands. These shafts of light, like fences separating the trees, marked the boundaries of the training field Areenna and Mikaal had been using for the past months. Here, away from prying eyes, and for days at a time, they worked on their abilities, sharpening them, practicing each until they were available at the merest hint of a thought.

Here, they worked on their physical fighting abilities—sword work, bow work and knife training. Mikaal, halfway through his twentieth year, was the equal of any warrior of Nevaeh; at eighteen, Areenna, under his tutelage was not far behind.

Yet more potent than the training of blade and shaft was the understanding of their special abilities. Areenna's abilities had grown twenty fold since the Island. Still her most powerful weapon was the blue-white light she could wield to stop or destroy an opponent. While Mikaal's ability with fire had grown into a weapon both fierce and fearful.

"My father's Sixes will be here shortly," Mikaal said, offering her water from his gourd. The 'Six groups' were his father's specially trained guards—trained in the same manner Roth had been trained in the twenty-second century, before boarding the starship that had kept him alive and in stasis for three thousand years.

Our final training, yes? she asked, using thought rather than word as she removed her padded leather tunic to allow her skin to cool in the chilled air. The short-sleeved undergarment was damp with sweat. While the weather in Tolemac was never too cold, this winter had been one of the coldest in many years. For them, it was beneficial, as they had spent the past months acclimating themselves to the cold, in preparation for the Frozen Mountains of the northwest.

The only bad part of the winter was that instead of leaving for the northwest when they had planned to, the heavy blizzards in the northwest and western dominions caused them a month long delay.

Watching her, Mikaal traced her features, taking in the smooth lines of her cheekbones set beneath sea green eyes and hesitated only momentarily on her full mouth before dropping to her exposed arms. The lean muscles of her upper arms glowed in the afternoon light. "If we are to leave in three days, today will be our last here," Mikaal agreed.

"Are you sure about the Six?"

Mikaal's smile was gentle, his nod emphatic. "They will be a good test. We must know if we can handle fighters of their level, individually and as a team."

"But we already know this."

His smile faded, his voice turned low and serious. "We are, you and I, good against one or two, but there are no fighters in Nevaeh who are their equal. If we can hold our own against six of them, we will know we are ready, physically, to do what we must."

We cannot use our abilities with them. It will not be easy.

True. Then, aloud, he said, "Today isn't about how we combine our powers; it's about how we blend together in physical battle." He sat straighter, the water skein in his hand forgotten. His eyes glazed momentarily. *They come. Put on your leather, they are near.*

Areenna put on her padded leather tunic, closed her eyes and pushed out with her mind. Gaalrie left her roost and flew low through the trees. She joined with Gaalrie and through her aoutem's eyes, saw the 'Six' moving silently through the woods. She watched their progress while she closed her padded leather tunic, which she would wear beneath the special armor Roth created for her as he had Mikaal.

Join with me, she asked.

Mikaal immediately connected with her. Since their testing on the Island, their joining had become fast and natural. He settled within her thoughts, and watched through Gaalrie's eyes as the six warriors wove toward them in silent passage.

Charka's warning came as a tweak to their shared minds when the men passed the kraal and closed in on them. When Mikaal stood, Areenna did the same.

Leave your sword sheathed until the last second. Let them think us unprepared.

"Your father said he will have my armor ready tomorrow," Areenna said aloud. *They have surrounded us*, she added silently.

"I know," he responded, to both her voice words and the silent ones as well. *Now!*

They spun, drawing their weapons and ending up back to back, as the six men charged from behind trees, racing toward Areenna and Mikaal with their swords held high.

Like all Nevaen men, they were tall, broad, and powerful. Today they wore full battle armor—their bodies encased within hammered metal, the joints of subtle leather. A moment later, they broke into two packs of three and charged.

Areenna eyed the three who veered toward her. She set herself, her stance solid, just before the first man reached her. Tall and broad-shouldered, the soldier's sword glinted in the waning sun, its long blade blurring toward her. She moved fast, ducking low and weaving to the left while reaching out with her sword. She struck him hard across his thighs with the flat of her blade, recovered quickly, and blocked the second man's sword when he attacked from behind.

The third man swung. She summersaulted forward beneath his blade, rose to her feet and, in a smooth and swift movement, blocked the descending blade of the second man who had recovered and followed her move. The two warriors backed away from her, one in front, the other behind her.

<><><>

Mikaal, having taken out the first of his attackers, was backing away from the other two when they struck simultaneously at him. Flashes of sunlight reflected from his sword as he wove a defensible figure eight over and over, deflecting their blades and, instead of back stepping moved toward them. He sensed Areenna's battle behind him, but kept his concentration fixed upon his attackers.

Mikaal watched the two carefully as he parried their thrusts and saw, in a quick exchange, when their eyes met and the one on the left nodded imperceptibly. Something inside him flashed and he saw, to the very last detail, every movement they would make. The man on the right shifted slightly and side stepped. When he did, the one on the left lunged forward in an attempt to push Mikaal toward the other. Instead, Mikaal moved directly to the man on his left, caught his sword with his own blade and spun. The tip of his blade reached the attacker's cross guard and with a flick of his wrist, tore the sword from the man's hand.

While the sword arced, Mikaal followed through and placed the tip of his sword on the man's neck. The instant it touched skin, Mikaal lowered the sword and spun to catch the swing from the third man. Behind him, the clash of metal rang loud. The light touch of her mind whispered across his senses and he knew she was holding her own while he dodged a killing blow aimed at his head.

Mikaal's eyes locked on his attacker's, their blades met and held. Just when the man began to withdraw his sword, Mikaal sidestepped, lashed out with his right leg and swept his opponent's feet from under him. The warrior hit the ground hard and the same instant, Mikaal placed his sword at his throat.

The fighter released his word. "Well done My Prince."

Mikaal lowered his sword and turned to watch Areenna, who was holding off the other two. He started forward to aid her, but the man he'd just defeated grabbed his leg. "Hold. Let her deal."

<><><>

The two men separated just far enough so Areenna had to face one while the other edged close behind her. Sensing what was about to happen, Areenna let instincts take over—there was only one chance and it had to be used right. When the second man edged past her peripheral vision, she turned to face the first. She feinted with a lunge; the man raised his sword defensively. Twisting in the opposite direction, Areenna dove toward the ground and rolled forward. Like flowing water, she rose behind him even as the other fighter swung at the space she'd been standing in a half second earlier.

Gaining her feet before the man could turn; she slammed the flat of her blade against his head and faced the third, who was regaining his balance from his swing. In the heartbeat before he could plant his feet, Areenna pulled her knife from its scabbard and lunged. The knife caught the man just above the groin, slipping into the exact spot between the joining of upper and lower armor. The tip of the blade did not break skin.

The man dropped his sword, took off his helmet and stared at the blade, which was slightly above the joining of his legs. "Good choice, Princess" he said, eyeing her knife.

II

THE EVENING MEAL was long over and, in a clear, crisp and cloudless night, a slice of crescent moon hung a quarter way above Tolemac's main keep. Beneath it, Roth, High King of Nevaeh walked alone on the parapets, his fingers tracing along the smooth stone surface of the surrounding balustrade while he worked out his troubled thoughts. He had a decision to make, and although his wife had urged him toward it, he wasn't sure if the weight of what was required was worth so much.

Ten minutes later, his mind made up, he started down. When he reached the second level, he found Enaid waiting for him. Her gray eyes, awash with a mixture of silver and green flecks, stared openly in question.

When Roth nodded, she reached out and stroked his cheek. "It is for the best. They must know the depth of what they face."

"I'm not so sure," he said as he took her hand in his and held it tight. "Too much knowledge can be as harmful as too little."

"In certain situations, I disagree not, but for this it is important they know the true magnitude of those who they will face. They must know what those who created this have done and what they remain capable of doing."

Roth tried to smile, but failed. "Call them," he whispered.

<><><>

Areenna sat before the flowing fountain in the center of the keep. She saw not the movement of water; rather, she flew on Gaalrie's wings as her treygone circled the outer reaches of Tolemac on her nightly patrol.

Ever since returning from the Island, she had followed the same routine as she had since gaining her abilities and finding her aoutem four years ago. Tonight, like all the nights before, the giant treygone flew in search of what might be about. The only difference between now and before, was Areenna's understanding of how insidiously deceptive the Black Sorceress was, and of how desperate *she* had become since failing to kill Mikaal and her at the Island.

Over the past few months, there had been a few attempts on them. While none had succeeded, one stood out for her. It had been a month ago, when she'd gone home to visit her father and to make sure all was well in Freemorn. It had been a wonderful homecoming, and being with her father had eased the tensions she had been under for too long.

Her cousin Tissel had come to act as King Advisor while Areenna was at Tolemac. The daughter of her father's eldest sister, Tissel was—at almost thirty and an unmarried woman of moderate powers—acting in Areenna's place as advisor during her absence.

After spending two days with her father and Tissel, she had gone with Gaalrie to the Blue Desert in search of certain herbs, which grew only there.

Although cool, winter in Freemorn was warmer than in Tolemac. The Blue Desert was usually even warmer than Freemorn itself, but this season it was not. Areenna wore her padded leather tunic, not because she expected trouble, but because it was both warm and flexible. Three hours after entering the forest leading to the Blue Desert, she finished gathering the herbs and returned to where she had left Hero, her kraal.

Relaxed and happy, even with the troubling thoughts about Mikaal and the future that lay before them, Areenna felt safe in this place she had known all her life and had no need to maintain any defenses. When she stepped through a grouping of trees, and saw Hero grazing not fifty feet away, a warning flashed through her mind, sent by Gaalrie, who flew above.

Dropping the bags of herbs when Gaalrie's mind push hit her, she spun.

Before completing the turn, she was seeing through Gaalrie's eyes as the treygone dove at a low branch and struck the back of the man straddling it: one hand rested on to the branch, the other gripped a long knife. The man screamed out in pain when the treygone's three inch talons ripped across his back. He tried to hold on to the branch with his free hand but his desperate one handed grasp slipped and he crashed to the ground where he lay unmoving, the long bladed knife embedded in his chest.

From a tree across from the first, a man jumped to the ground, his sword held in both hands and charged at her. Her power flared instantly—an explosion of heat burst through her body, encasing her hands with crystal blue light.

The man ran toward her and she sensed darkness swirling about him. She released her power without hesitation. Twin spheres of blue light arrowed at him. He'd stopped as if he'd hit a wall. His sword flew from his hand. His body lifted into the air and, with a flick of her wrist, Areenna sent him flying backwards, where he struck the bole of a tree and lay unmoving.

Gaalrie landed lightly on Areenna's shoulder. *Thank you my sister*.

In answer, Gaalrie ducked her head and nestled it against Areenna's before gently lifting skyward.

Foul traces of the Black Sorceress lingered and Areenna knew *she* had taken over the two men. It would have been easy for her, as they were exiles living in the wastelands and badlands who believed their physical mutation too severe for them to stay within a dominion of Nevaeh. Although no man or woman, no matter how badly mutated, was ever exiled or cast out of their home dominion because of a physical mutation, most left of their own accord rather than stay among others who were not so unlucky.

She went to the man. He was unconscious but still lived. The other, the one Gaalrie had knocked from the tree was dead; his knife had been forced through his heart when he'd struck the ground. A wave of sadness struck her as sharply as had Gaalrie's warning. She understood well how these men could think themselves unwanted by the Nevaens who were not malformed, but to have to live beneath the thumb of one so evil was in itself an undeserved horror.

She could do nothing for the one who had died, but for the other, there was hope. Kneeling over him, she closed her eyes and grasped both sides of his head. She ignored his badly deformed mouth and unevenly set eyes and concentrated on her ability to heal, and gently pushed her power to him.

While she worked in the blind darkness of her healing ability, seeing only where he was injured, a stream of memory images flowed into her mind. Rather than fight them and stop helping the man, she let the images play out. Within them, she saw the ugly malformed witch, one handless arm moving before the man's face. The sorceress' mouth moved, but Areenna heard no words. A dark mist grew around the evil entity, enveloping her and like a swarm of bees; it shot from her and entered the man and his companion.

The man stirred and the images faded. Areenna stepped back, her sight fully returned. His eyes, one set an inch higher than the other, flickered open to stare at her. He stiffened and pushed back, his face rigid with fear.

"Easy," she whispered. "The fighting is done. How feel you?"

He blinked several times, his face puzzled. "I...I feel like myself."

"You were taken over," she said.

"I tried to kill you."

Areenna smiled. "Yes, but it is done with. Do you know what happened to you?"

The puzzled expression returned. He shook his head. "The last I remember before this morning is when Orlon and I were in the outlands and we met a beautiful woman. She took us to a cavern above the ocean and.... That's all I remember."

"She was beautiful you say?"

"She was and it surprised us that she was nice to us. We are—"

"—you are men, nothing more, and nothing less."

"We are exiles. We are not fit to be with others."

"By your own choice," Areenna stated, dismissing his words with a wave of her hand. "Can you stand?"

He nodded and stood. His torso was average, but his legs were not. One was thick, the other thin. His skin had the look of old tanned leather but Areenna sensed he had not yet lived thirty years.

“Return not to the badlands: find someplace else, perhaps further south.”

“I am in your debt, Lady.”

“Your friend is dead by his own blade,” she said, motioning to the other. “Will you give him burial?”

He looked to the man and back, his eyes troubled. “I will.”

“If ever you seek dominion, call on Freemorn and ask for King Nosaj. Tell him I offered you welcome.”

The man smiled, his oddly shaped mouth twisted. “You tell me to speak to the King? He would not see me.”

“He will. Tell him his daughter Areenna, bid you welcome. That is all you need do. Your name?”

“Elyl,” he said.

“Elyl, will you allow me to try and prevent the sorceress from taking you again?”

His pale eyes never wavered from hers, “Yes, My Lady.”

She closed her eyes, built a block within her, and pushed it at him. Like a door closing, it fell securely into place. “It will help, but you have to keep your mind strong as well.”

“I will,” he said.

When he turned to go to his companion, Areenna retrieved her herbs and walked to Hero. Halfway to her kraal she heard him call out, “My Lady.”

She turned. “I thank you My Lady, for sparing my life. I will not forget.” With his words said, he went to the body where he squatted and, lifting the man effortlessly, carried him into the deep woods.

Angered by the Black Sorceresses use of these defenseless men, Areenna watched him disappear into the trees. She stared at an unseen distance. “You will not win, you rotten—”

Areenna shook away the memory, but she was thankful for it, because the memory served as a reminder that no matter where she was, no matter what she was doing, she would never again let her guard down, never.

“A lesson well learned,” Mikaal said from behind her.

Areenna smiled and turned to look at him, she had been so lost in the memory of the day in the Blue Desert that she had been unaware of

Mikaal's presence, either behind her or in her mind. "Indeed it was, My Prince."

Mikaal returned the smile. "My father wants to see us."

<><><>

Ten minutes later Areenna and Mikaal were in the library sitting across from Roth and Enaid. The light from the illuminating nightmoss filled the room with a warm glow. On the low table, separating Areenna and Mikaal from Mikaal's mother and father lay several hand drawn maps. The maps were highly detailed with notations written in Roth's neat lettering. Before each of them were the traditional glasses of wine and water.

Roth's face was set in edgy lines: he sat stiffly. Although Enaid appeared more relaxed, Areenna sensed her tension as well. Next to her, she knew Mikaal was aware of their strain in the same way. *They're worried*, she told him silently.

In answer, he took her hand and gave it a gentle squeeze. Releasing it, he looked at his father. "Are these the routes to the Frozen Mountains?"

Roth nodded, bent toward the table and pointed to the top map. He touched his forefinger to the spot marked Tolemac. "The trip is well over two thousand miles. In my time, we called the Frozen Mountains the Canadian Rockies. They were not as they are today."

Areenna and Mikaal studied the map. A moment later, they exchanged glances. "Something is wrong," Mikaal said without turning from Areenna. When she nodded, he turned to his father. "When they told us what we had to do, they put a picture in our minds. This—"

"—isn't where the mountain is," Areenna finished Mikaal's statement. "It's further."

"You're sure?" Roth asked.

"Very," Mikaal responded. "It is beyond these mountains, and it is by itself. It is also taller than any of these, and has two peaks."

"Two," Roth whispered. He stood and went to the bookcase behind Areenna and Mikaal. He reached up to a high shelf and pulled down another rolled sheet. He placed it on the table on top of the others and spread it open.

"The tallest mountain I know of on Nevaeh is in what used to be called Alaska. Your journey," he said, looking up from the map and staring at them, "will be longer than I thought. You'll have to cross the Frozen Mountains, and from there move north and west to the interior, the center of Alaska. The mountain you seek, McKinley is its name from my time, is unpopulated wastelands. What could possibly be there?" he asked, knowing there would be no answer.

Listening to him speak, Enaid followed his finger while he detailed the route they would have to take when something began vibrating within her. The chamber faded when she entered a vision. The vision built before her; her breathing deepened and she found herself floating just above the peak of a mountain—a frozen mountain. Looking around, she saw ice and a few outcroppings of rock. Thick layers of hazy fog, cast like a quilt over the ground, prevented her from seeing it. She could make out only the desolation of snow and ice. To her left, she spied an unnatural curve in the side of the mountain, near the top.

She floated closer and saw within the curve a faint outline that was long and high, and knew this was where Mikaal and Areenna were to go. As soon as she understood the vision, she was back in the library chamber where she found the three staring at her.

What was that? Areenna asked silently.

You saw?

Areenna shook her head and said aloud, "Only the last of it."

Enaid took a deep breath, reached over and grasped Roth's hand to ground her to the room. "I have seen where they must go," she said to Roth before turning to the others. "As you face the mountain, high on the northern side, you will find a spot, carved out, not natural. There is an entry there: how to open it, I know not. It is the place you seek."

"May we join you?" Areenna asked aloud.

Enaid nodded and opened herself. The three joined instantly. Moments later, they separated and all turned to Roth. Mikaal leaned forward and placed his finger on the map at the north side of the mountain. "This is where we go."

Roth did the calculations in his head and exhaled sibilantly. "You will need a lot of supplies. I doubt there will be much game if any, where you travel. Once you leave the northern border of Welkold, you will need everything you can carry. Water can be drawn from the ice and snow, but food will be a problem."

Areenna thought back to her day on the Island and the eight sorceresses who had given them their mission. She shook her head. "We will take all the supplies we can manage, but *they* would not send us to this place only to have us die of starvation. No, there will be something."

She glanced at Enaid, who still gripped Roth's hand. Enaid nodded slowly. "It must be so."

Roth held adamant. "Still, you will re-supply at Welkold, take everything the kralets can carry without overburdening them. You may take much on faith, but preparation is the wisest way."

When Mikaal and Areenna nodded their assent, Roth drew his hand from Enaid and stood. "I have no idea what you will be facing, but I have no doubt it will be dangerous and not from the ice and cold, but from *them*." He paused to fix the two younger ones with an intense stare.

After a minute of silence, he said, "I have told you both many things about the Dark Circle, but there is so much more. It is time you learned the rest, for you must prepare for anything and everything. It was in the year two thousand and one, when the first of the massive attacks began and war was born…."

III

"THE ATTACK CAME in the morning. The terrorists took over four flying machines—in my time, we had many types of machines," Roth explained, pacing around the library in tight steps. "The flying machines were called airplanes. People used them to travel to different parts of the world. We could fly from a place such as Northcrom to Fainhall in only a few hours…in the time between morning and mid-day."

He saw their expressions of disbelief and smiled. "Oh, it's true. Our sciences were amazing, but our science was the weapon that killed our world.

"That morning, which was remembered by the numbers 9-11, was the true beginning. Two airplanes were taken and flown toward Manhattan—*The Island*—a third and a forth were flown to a place called Washington. The first two airplanes struck the two tallest buildings on the Island and killed thousands of people. The third was flying toward its target when the passengers rose up against the terrorists and the plane crashed in what we now call Aldimore. The fourth reached its target in Washington…Dees as you know it now."

Roth paused for a breath and saw the questions flowing across Areenna and Mikaal's faces. He held up a forestalling hand. "That was the beginning of the war, which was started by religious fanatics. Following the attacks, small wars erupted in places called Iraq and

Afghanistan, Syria and Iran, Israel and Palestine. These wars went on for many years, until finally a sort of peace was drawn."

When he saw the puzzled look on their faces, he understood why. "You've never heard the word religion before, have you?"

When they shook their heads, Roth exhaled. "Religion is a belief in a...higher power, a power that oversees all. There were many philosophies about religion: my own personal belief is religion was a way to show people what is right and what is wrong. However, these religions were controlled by people, not by any higher...authority. Because people are diverse, religions were diverse. In much of the world, there was what we called religious freedom, where people could believe in whatever they chose. Most people used religion to help guide them in their lives, to bring value and faith and to follow their conscience; but others used religion for their own benefits and to control others. Such were the fanatics of the Middle East. A few bad people, who could make others think in the same way as themselves, controlled them. These fanatics had one goal, to make everyone in the world believe as they did. They refused to tolerate anyone who thought differently and so they waged war on everyone who did not believe in their way. They treated women as property...slaves. They believed that only they had the right to rule."

"Religion is bad?" Areenna asked.

Roth smiled. "Religion was meant to be good. It helped people to understand what was right and wrong, but people, bad people, would subvert religion to use it for their own power. The belief in a higher being protecting and helping them, especially in the worst of times, was something people needed."

Areenna glanced from Enaid and to Mikaal. "This higher power, what did it do?"

Roth had to think of a way to explain. It took a few moments. "The people believed this higher power created life, brought all that lived and grew on the world to life. They believed this higher power gave them life, and when it was time, took them back again. It controlled all, saw all, and was above all other things."

Areenna saw Enaid's shadowy smile. She studied Roth for a few seconds and said, "I understand. We too believe in a higher power."

Roth was startled. Never once in twenty-four years had he heard of this. “You believe in God?”

Areenna’s features turned puzzled. “I know not such a word. We believe Nevaeh itself, the world we walk on, created all. All life springs from her and all life returns to her. She gives us many gifts and asks only for us to nurture life.”

Roth took this in. He had heard Enaid say many times how the earth was where she gained her powers. “I have never heard this before.”

“Why would we speak of it? It is part of us. It is the way we are, it is how we have always been.”

Enaid smiled. “The story,” she reminded him.

“The story, yes,” he said and continued. “For a hundred years the fundamentalists battled everyone who was not a believer. As their doctrines spread, they began to take over their part of the world. The fundamentalists—the terrorist groups—joined together and when they did, they grew in power, grasping for more and more as their ranks swelled, spreading their beliefs to all who would listen. But much of our world resisted. Soon they began to fight with weapons powerful enough to kill thousands, and then hundreds of thousands. In their mad quest to control the world, they poisoned it.”

Roth stopped, his body pulsed with the emotions his words had drawn forth, emotions he had thought himself well past. Enaid grasped his hand and drew him closer to her. She put his hand to her face and pressed it to her cheek to help calm him.

Releasing her hand, he turned back to his son and Areenna. “In their drive to conquer, they used what are called nuclear bombs: weapons so powerful they destroyed entire cities, cities of which the whole population of all the dominions of Nevaeh could fit within. This war of terrorism went on for another decade. Most of what we called Europe and the Middle East and Asia were engulfed in radioactive fallout, hundreds of millions of people died because these people, who were known as the Circle of Afzal, wanted to convert everyone to their beliefs.”

“And the world was changed,” he whispered. “I…I can’t describe what happened, I don’t have the words to make you understand everything.”

From within her, Areenna knew instinctively she could reach him. "My Lord," she said in a voice so low it barely reached his ears, "would you allow me to join with your mind?"

Enaid, startled by Areenna's words, turned to her. *You can do this? I have never been able to do so.*

I believe so. I...my abilities have grown and changed since the Island.

"Solomon?"

Roth turned to Enaid. His voice was deep and solemn. "Someone must know the whole truth. What happened, the truth of what they did must be carried on." To Areenna he said, "No woman has ever been able to do this with me."

"My Lord," Areenna said, "If you allow it, I think we can join with you."

"We?"

"Yes, Father," Mikaal said, meeting his father's eyes. "Areenna and I, we...we can become one."

Roth looked from Areenna to Mikaal. "How is this possible? You know I am different from everyone else." His eyes swept across his son's face before moving on to Areenna. He saw that while she was still so young, her eyes were those of a woman ages older than the woman-child seated before him.

"We are as well. I don't know why, but after we left the Island, we were different. Were you here when the silver...lance destroyed the Island?" Mikaal asked.

"Silver lance?"

"It came from the sky and when it struck the ground, the Island was destroyed," Mikaal said.

Roth closed his eyes and shook his head. "The silver lance is called a missile. No, it happened after I left."

"It landed in the meadowland in the middle of the Island. There were people there who were unlike any we have ever known. They had white, yellow, brown, and black skin. They all died."

"How could you know this," Roth whispered.

The memory of the glass tunnel rose swiftly in her mind's eye. She again experienced standing in the tube of glass and seeing it all. "We were shown," Areenna spoke this time. "We were underground, in a…tunnel of glass. Trapped inside the glass were animals and people. It was a terrible sight for most were not whole but only shards of what they once were. We were told it happened when the…the missile came."

Roth picked up his glass of wine and drank deeply. "Yes," Roth said.

"Yes?"

"Yes, try to see my memories." His voice was low, and Enaid, sitting next to him, stared in question.

"What bothers you?"

"I have never done this. There are memories no one should have to know, memories of my…time to here."

"Think of only what you want known. This is not the reading of minds, only of what you want to share," Enaid said.

Looking into his wife's gray eyes, flecks of green and gold floating within, he nodded and turned to Areenna.

Areenna reached for Mikaal's hand. With their fingers interlocked, she said, "Think of what you want us to know. Start with your early memories and tell us the story with your thoughts." She paused. "Nod when you are ready."

Enaid took his hand in hers. She smiled gently at him. Slowly, he thought about the old files he'd watched as he'd grown up, the old newscasts showing the destruction of the attacks of 9-11, and the terrible aftermath.

A pale light built within the room, emanating from both Areenna and Mikaal's hands. It built from a soft glow into a stronger light, which soon engulfed the four, and, suddenly, Roth was watching the first plane crash into the World Trade Center, on the eleventh of September, two thousand and one.

Dreamlike, his memories came forth, some of which surprised him with their detail. He led them forward from that terrible day, his memories sweeping the others along.

They witnessed the destruction and deaths caused by the two airplanes: they watched a third crash in a field and the fourth dive at the Pentagon building. They saw the wars in Iraq and Afghanistan. As the years flew across Roth's mind, they saw different groups of fanatics battle each other while destroying the countries they fought over until Afzal Mahmud Tarek united all the fundamentalist groups at the end of the Twenty-First century and created the Circle of the Afzareen—the disciples of Afzal as they became known.

At this point, everything changed. Afzal Mahmud Tarek organized his followers into an army of destruction. Wave after wave of fanatical soldiers battled everyone they met, fighting them into submission. Nuclear weapons rained horror on those able to resist their armies. By the twentieth year of the new century, the world had begun to change. The nuclear weapons caused massive land shifts; the earth's plates moved and radioactive clouds turned the inhabitants of the earth, its people and animals, into something far different than they had been.

They watched millions of people die and witnessed the deaths of countries. Roth guided them through his memories until he reached the point when the starship left Earth's orbit and started on its three thousand year voyage. From his memories of the messages from Earth to the starship, they watched land masses shift, new mountains rise from the oceans, and continents change. Then his memories became leapfrogging visions of himself watching the giant screens on the bridge of the starship, during the duty periods, when he had watched the dwindling reports sent to the ship during the first three hundred years of their travels.

They lived Roth's memories and learned what Nevaeh had once been. There were images of earthquakes cracking open the Earth's crust. They saw the western part of the American continent sheared off by earthquakes and consumed by the fast rising oceans and saw too, how Europe and Asia disappeared beneath dark clouds refusing light to pass through.

Roth stopped.

Areenna's gasp was loud in the quiet room and following the sound, the light died. Still caught within Roth's memories, Areenna could only stare blankly ahead.

Mikaal, holding Areenna's hand, shook his head slowly. "I feel sick," he whispered.

"Hold that feeling. Never, ever lose it! Your enemy will never stop and if we do not end this, Nevaeh will not survive—not as we know it."

He echoes the eight, Areenna said silently to Mikaal.

"We understand," Mikaal said.

"Good," Roth said. Shifting and shaking off the grip of his memories, he leaned forward and pointed to a map. "There is another route, if necessary, but it makes a wide swing through the frozen badlands and adds more distance. Even taking into account the time you will have to spend crossing the Frozen Mountains, the mountain crossing will be faster than going around them." When he paused, Areenna leaned forward.

Mikaal's brows knitted. "It also depends on the terrain, does it not? When we go uphill, we will make less time and put more strain on us but traveling downhill will be easier."

Roth waited a moment before shaking his head. "Not on snow and ice. Going downhill will be even more strenuous than uphill because of the footing." He shifted the maps, drawing out one that had been beneath the others. This one was different, almost as if it were not hand-drawn. The lines were thin and complicated. "This is the mountain range."

The intricately drawn map held many swirls, lines, and varying numbers. While Roth did his best to explain about how the mountains were geologically set, Areenna studied the lines and numbers.

"Can we not simply follow along the eastern side of the mountains, here, where they are the lowest?" She traced the range with her finger, showing him the path she meant.

Roth watched the path her finger took and after a moment shook his head. "This," he said, showing her a broken line, "is a deep canyon. It's most likely a trench created by an earthquake. You'll not be able to cross it; but," he hesitated, "if you go this way, and then go into the mountains here," he added, pointing to a spot just before the trench, "you can cross to the western side to here," he said, his finger tracing from the trench to the other side of the range. "You will only be in the high mountains for a short time, perhaps a week. It is narrow at the western tip and the mountains touch just before the sea. There, I believe you will find a way across."

"The first leg of the journey, from Tolemac to the Frozen Mountains will take at least two to three weeks. The next leg through the mountains can take triple the time or longer. It will take another week, possibly two to reach your final destination."

Silence followed his last words as Areenna and Mikaal digested his words. A few moments later, with Areenna's hand still entwined with

Mikaal's, she said, "It matters not how long it takes; what matters is our reaching the mountain and accomplishing what we must. In this there is no choice."

IV

THE STARS FILLED the sky with pinpoints of light so strong moonlight was not needed. With only a few pale gray strings of clouds floating above, Areenna leaned on the balustrade and gazed upon the houses and lands of Tolemac.

The night sped by, yet she could not sleep. So much had happened in the past months and she was constantly wrestling with herself, trying her best to understand why everything was falling on her shoulders. *Had it only been a few months since they had gone to the Island?*

So much had changed in so short a time. She missed her home and her father and the people who lived in Freemorn. *When will I be there again*? she wondered, already knowing the answer. *Possibly never*. The future was not open to her, and the knowledge of what she must do was the only future she could allow herself to consider.

Her complement, as the Eight called Mikaal, was the only other person who could understand. What of her and Mikaal? A burning grew deep within her, not of her powers but of a need she could not define, which twisted inside with a fire unlike those created from her abilities. She pushed the feeling away, knowing such emotions could not be allowed to grow, not yet, even though she knew he had the same emotions as she. All she could hope for was that they would both be alive when the right time came.

A call from Gaalrie interrupted her thoughts. She opened her eyes just as the giant treygone appeared near the keep, her wings spread wide, the triangular head held high and her narrow tail flowing behind her. The giant bird landed on the stone in front of her. *Welcome sister*.

Gaalrie pushed forward and pressed her beak to Areenna's cheek. She stroked the bird's head with two fingers and received a rush of warmth. As she had done every night since Gaalrie reached full growth, four years before, Gaalrie had flown the night patrol. Now was her time.

Go little sister, hunt.

Gaalrie gave vent to a short cry before lifting from the stone and darting high into the night sky. Moments later, she was gone.

Areenna searched the cloudless late winter sky until she found the constellation Mikaal had taught her about, the Belt of Orion. She gazed at the belt, wondering how so much beauty could be contained in such perfect order.

Staring at the stars, she asked the question she had asked herself a thousand times already, *why me*?

The stars wavered as a shimmering mist grew before her eyes. *The answer will you find, daughter of Nevaeh, when the time is right*, came the too well remembered single voice of the sorceresses of the Eight.

<><><>

Mikaal awoke an hour before sunrise. Ten minutes later, he entered the stables and went to Charka's stall. His aoutem welcomed him by pushing and nuzzling his chest. Mikaal led the kraal out of the stables and, without saddle, mounted him. He rode to the southern gate, where two guards stood on the last hour of their shift. The gate was open, except at times of conflict.

When they saw him approach, they stood straighter. "Your Highness," said the guard on the left, a man Mikaal knew well for they had grown up together. "A long night, Tomsa?" Mikaal asked the guard.

"And almost done, my Lord," Tomsa replied. "It is early for a ride, you go alone?"

"I do."

"I—"

"It is alright, I will not go far."

"Yes, My Lord."

Mikaal shook his head. "Tomsa, we grew up together, we are friends and now all you can call me is My Lord?"

The guard favored him with a momentary smile. "Yes, My Lord. I am on watch, not at play."

"Have you put your name in for the 'Six'?

Tomsa nodded. "It was done a month ago. I wait to hear word."

"Do not be concerned about the selection. You will make a good Six, Tomsa, of such I am certain."

"Thank you, My Lord. Ride safely," he said, stepping aside and motioning the other guard to do the same.

When he was far enough away from the outer walls of Tolemac, he turned south and rode for another ten minutes until he reached a small grove of trees he had long ago claimed as his own. Not by ownership, for no one owned the open unoccupied lands of Tolemac. Anyone could build upon it and grow food there, for all Nevaeh owned the lands of Tolemac.

He dismounted and let Charka range on the tall grasses within the grove. He walked to the center, removed his sword, laid it on the ground, and sat cross-legged. He closed his eyes and drew in a deep breath of the cool dawn air. Bands of pink blended into the dark purple of the horizon as the day rose upon Nevaeh. He lost himself in the quiet of the grove, with only the sounds of insects welcoming the new day.

When he at last opened his eyes, he drew in several deep breaths, stood and removed his shirt. The cool air flowed across his skin; the muscles of his abdomen and chest tightened in response.

He exhaled sharply. He was troubled by all that had happened and even more so by their future. A sense of danger lingered in a corner of his mind, so cloying he could never quite shake it away. Had it been only six months since Areenna had arrived at Tolemac for the council meeting that had changed everything?

Since that day, they had been apart only once. Her absence of only a few weeks had reinforced his understanding of how much Areenna meant to him. Moreover, as much as he had taught her of swordplay and fighting, she had taught him how to access and use his abilities and even more so, of who he was and who he would become. But beneath all, hung the emotions of which he must constantly keep locked away.

Shaking his head, he bent and picked up his sword. He inhaled deeply and set his legs in preparation for the exercises he had learned as a young boy. He lifted the sword up and out, lunged forward, turned and repeated the movements. Then he stepped sideways, holding the sword cross body, bending his knees and striking with a curved blow as if there was an opponent to his left.

He repeated the same set of movements for a quarter hour until a sheen of sweat covered his chest, arms and face. Then he moved next into the set of movements, his sword flying so fast the metal blurred in the light.

Moving, weaving, striking, feinting and defending, he repeated it until his labored breathing forced him to stop, his head bent, his hands resting atop the sword's pommel for support.

So lost was Mikaal in what he had been doing it took until he regained his breath to realize he was not alone. Turning, he found a rider astride a kraal. Recognition was instantaneous. "Your Highness," he said.

"My Prince," Areenna's father, King Nosaj replied as he dismounted and started toward Mikaal. "That was a treat to watch."

Mikaal smiled, "Have you been there long?"

"A few minutes. Long enough to know my daughter will be well protected."

Mikaal laughed as he stepped forward to meet Nosaj and grip his forearm in greeting. "Trust me Highness; it is usually she who protects me."

Nosaj echoed Mikaal's laugh with a short one of his own. "Yes, she does seem to have that ability well mastered."

When they released each other's arms, Mikaal bent and picked up his discarded shirt, drew the sword from the ground and sheathed it. "I am surprised to see you here."

"I could not let my daughter leave on this…quest without saying goodbye. You go when?"

Mikaal held King Nosaj's gaze and said, "The day after tomorrow."

"Then I am in time. I was afraid I might miss her. I had planned to be here two days ago, but there were problems at home."

"Bad?"

Nosaj shook his head. His silver hair flowed with the movement. "Nothing bad, just issues within the domain. My niece watches over Freemorn in my absence."

"It is good you are here," Mikaal said as he pulled on his shirt. "Areenna has missed you and Freemorn."

"As I have missed her. She is well?"

"She is. Come, it's time I returned and supervised the supplies." He paused. "You came alone, no guards?"

"Should I need such between our borders?"

"No, but the times are strange… The line between friend and foe is wavering."

"Perhaps," Nosaj said, "but not badly, not yet."

<><><>

Sunlight streaming through the windows of the bedchamber awakened Areenna, who had slept later than usual. As she lay in bed, she became aware of Mikaal's absence from his chamber. *Where?*

Sitting up, she used her senses to search for him. As soon as she found him, and knew he was safe, she withdrew. Leaving the bed, she began to prepare herself for the day. Her maid entered a few minutes later carrying a simple long tunic, at which Areenna shook her head.

"I have too much to do today," she said, "pants and a short tunic."

By the time she finished brushing her hair, the girl had returned with the right clothing. Minutes later, she descended to the lower level of the keep where she found Enaid entering the small dining hall.

"Good morning," Enaid said, dressed almost the same as Areenna. "You slept late, that's good."

"It was not intentional," Areenna replied, "and yes, it was good—one of my few dreamless nights."

Enaid flashed a warm smile. "Ah, the plague of we women with abilities."

Areenna sat down a few seconds before Enaid, and when the High Queen sat, two servants entered the room. One carried a tray of food, the other a steaming teapot.

The women were quiet until the servants left. "Have you seen Mikaal this morning?" Enaid asked.

"No, he is at his grove, exercising."

Enaid studied her for a moment before saying, "He told you?"

Areenna shook her head. "No, I…I know."

"Is it difficult?" Enaid asked as she poured tea for both of them.

Areenna knew exactly what Enaid meant. "I didn't think it would be so. We cannot allow it to be, but yes, for me it is becoming difficult."

"There is nothing I can tell you, nothing I can say to make it easier, but both of you are strong. It will work out."

"I hope. But, My Lady, I fear for what might happen if we give in now."

"Child, you and Mikaal are meant to be. There is no need to do anything but wait until the time is right—and when it is time, you will know."

"If we survive whatever is to come."

Reaching out, Enaid rested her forearms on the table, her palms up and open. Areenna accepted the unvoiced invitation and gripped Enaid's hands. When their skin met, a rush of warmth spread from her hands through her body. "In the entire world, with all the people living upon Nevaeh and beyond, I am absolutely clear on this: you and Mikaal are two people destined to be together, but not yet, not in that way."

"Because we must first accomplish what the Eight have sent us to do?"

"Not quite…and yes. In order to do what is necessary, you cannot burden yourself with the emotions that would follow if you and Mikaal take each other as mates. You must remain as the two of you are until this is finished."

"I do understand but am afraid it will never be."

Enaid gently squeezed her hands briefly. "It will, but only in the manner it must. Your focus cannot be on yourselves. Such will lead to defeat and death, for you and for everyone else."

"I know," Areenna admitted. Drawing back her hands, she picked up her tea. As she raised the cup, Gaalrie's thought pushed into her mind. "They return."

"They?"

Areenna's smile widened and she nodded. "Mikaal and my father…I saw that not before. They will be here soon." With that, the conversation ended and Areenna quickly downed some food and raced outside to greet them.

Alone, Enaid sat back and closed her eyes. *Strength child, you are the key whom we have been so long awaiting.*

V

THE WARM MID-AFTERNOON sun lent gentleness to the day as Areenna and Enaid rode their kraals out the northern gate. They stayed on the road for almost three-quarters of an hour before turning on a narrow hidden path leading to a secluded place within the surrounding woodlands. As always, the beauty of the area captivated Areenna.

They guided their mounts a hundred yards down the path, to where a curving and seemingly impenetrable wall of trees and vines blocked their way; the vegetation so thickly interlaced it appeared carved and painted upon a solid wall of wood.

Enaid stopped her kraal and dismounted. Taking the kraal's reins, she tied it to the bole of a young pine while Areenna did the same for Hero. Gaalrie dropped from the sky to alight on Areenna's shoulder. Irii, Enaid's white gorlon padded next to the High Queen. They walked to a spot a dozen feet away and stood before the living wall.

Grasping hands, Areenna and Enaid stepped forward together and disappeared into the solid wall of vines and trees. Two steps later, they emerged within a small grove.

As she had each time she entered Enaid's 'Haven', Areenna gasped. They stood in a field of flowers, surrounded by a circle of trees, their branches and vines as thickly interwoven within as they had been on the other side. To her right was an oval pond, perhaps thirty yards across, and its water sparkled iridescently in the midday sun. Gaalrie lifted from Areenna's shoulder and flew above the meadow; Irii padded to a sunlit patch of grass and after stretching, rolled several times on the blanket of grass ending on her back.

"Peace, finally," Enaid whispered with a hint of a smile.

Areenna breathed deeply of the floral scented air. Finally, her mind and body were calm and relaxed. She thought not on the quest she would be undertaking, only of the peacefulness of this place.

Without a word, both women undressed and went to the pond. Not for the first time did Areenna think how perfect Enaid was. Enaid's body was lean and well muscled, her nutty mocha shaded skin taut, her breasts high and her stomach flat. The scars on her back and legs, the faded remnants of battles fought two decades earlier, detracted not from her. She walked with the grace of a warrior and the presence of a queen. Her face, framed by long raven hair, glowed in the sunlight and appeared more like a young woman's than a woman of forty-six.

Enaid stopped walking. "What is it?"

A flush warmed Areenna's face. "I was thinking how beautiful you are, how young you always appear."

Enaid smiled. "The women in our family have been gifted with long lives and a youthful appearance. Nevertheless, Areenna, I feel every year that I have lived. Here," she said, pointing to her heart. "And, here too," she added, tapping her temple. Then she turned toward the pool and dove in.

Areenna laughed and followed. Slicing the water like a knife, she swam under the surface until she had to come up for air. "I will miss this place."

"You will be back," Enaid replied. Her face turned serious. "Your father is worried for you."

Paddling close to Enaid, Areenna said, "I know. I wish there was a way to ease his worry."

Enaid reached out and stroked Areenna's cheek with the back of her hand. "I know child, but it is a parent's...duty to be concerned for their child. And while your father is a King, he is also a father."

He has lost so much already—

—then it is up to you to see he loses no more, Enaid stated. She added aloud, "You leave in two days, going into such dangers I cannot

imagine. It is up to you to make certain you return. And, it is up to you to make certain as well, my son returns."

"To me? Why is such my responsibility?" she asked, already knowing the truth of Enaid's words but refuting them even as they were voiced.

"Deny not what you know to be true. I have known since your birth. Your mother knew, and others as well."

A sudden memory rose. It was of she and Mikaal in Northcrom, sitting with Queen Ilsraeth, who had said, '*Because of what you and Areenna, represent...the legends. Your presence here makes them real*'. "Ilsraeth had spoken of a legend, but never explained it to me," Areenna said.

"Come, let us dry on the grass and talk."

Enaid spun in the water and swam to the edge of the pond, Areenna following behind. When they were laying on the mossy grass the sun drying their bodies, Enaid said, "When the time comes for ...Mothers of daughters to hand down lore, the daughters are told of many things, but of one there is absolute certainty. Your mother could not tell you because her life was cut far too short and you were too young."

She paused to offer Areenna a wistful smile. "This responsibility now falls to me. Usually this lore is past down near the end of a woman's life, but for you, it is essential to know. Your mother was the daughter of the Duke of Lokinhold; your mother's mother was the daughter of the King and Queen of Fainhall. Of this you know."

Areenna nodded. "And her mother was the daughter of Northcrom, but further back I do not know."

"I do. Areenna, what you know not is that your female lineage is descended from all dominions. Within your body flows the blood of every dominion of Nevaeh."

"As do many others," Areenna said.

"No, child. While logical, such is not reality. Because a woman child is born to a ruler of a domain does not mean such a child will become queen. It means only her parents rule. Bloodlines break because of love, not obligation. Love controls us as much as does any other power. The right to choose whom you love is a woman's right; the right to choose your life's path is your right as well.... But you, child, unlike all other women, have been chosen."

Areenna shook her head in an effort to decipher the meaning of Enaid's words but could not find any. "I still do not understand."

Enaid sat up and said, "One of our pieces of lore concerns a legend. This legend, passed down for so long, no one remembers its origins. The legend speaks of the birth of a woman of power who will be born with all the blood of Nevaeh and who will unite Nevaeh and lead to the defeat of the Dark Ones from across the sea. It is said, when the dark ones begin their final conquest of Nevaeh, this woman will have the power to stop them."

"How can one woman do so?" Areenna asked, her heart barely beating as the words sank deep within her mind.

"The legend speaks of how, when this woman-child meets her complement, she will become the most powerful woman ever born to Nevaeh. She, with her complement, will defeat the Dark Ones."

"Mikaal—"

"—you are she. He is your complement. But there is more. The legend speaks of your complement as part of you. If something should happen to him, you will fail."

"Bekar," Areenna whispered. "When we met Bekar on the old highway, she said I had no choice! If I failed, everyone and everything I love will be destroyed, forever." Areenna's eyes went wide as she gasped. "My mother told me stories about Bekar of the Woods. She knew I would meet her one day."

"Yes, she was blessed with vision. Areenna, what I speak of is the oldest legend we have, older even than the legend of Bekar. The frightening truth is that you were born for a purpose. Your powers you have been given are stronger than any woman of Nevaeh has ever possessed. They continue to grow stronger every day do they not?"

There could be no denial of Enaid's words and Areenna nodded her head.

"And the women of the Island …you sense them even when you are away from of the Island, have you not?"

"Yes," she admitted, thinking of last night and the words she had heard. "But what you speak of…how can I do such an unbelievable thing as defeat the dark ones?"

Enaid smiled and took Areenna's hand in hers. "Because you must. If you do not find your strength, if you believe yourself not capable, my son's life is lost as well."

Enaid's words drilled deep within the very core of her powers. She put her hands on Enaid's shoulders and locked her eyes with the queen's. "I will never let that happen," she whispered.

<><><>

Hundreds of miles away, a squall streamed over the Southern Palisades. Dark clouds let forth sheets of rain while churning winds ripped across the rocks, howling through the crevices. Yet at the very edge of a palisade cliff, the deformed shape of the Black Sorceress stood untouched by the storm.

On her shoulder rested a black-feathered carrion eater. The dangelore listened to the words *she* whispered into its ears. A few minutes later, the bird flew into the storm. It too was unaffected by the eddying winds as it headed northwest toward Tolemac.

"Find them," *she* called after the winged messenger in farewell. Then *she* laughed as a vision of Areenna, Mikaal, Roth and Enaid rose before her eyes. *Think you I am defeated? Think you I know not what you attempt? You will die by my hand, of this I promise!* Then *she* turned seaward looking for the sign she had been waiting for.

As the whirlwind surrounded her, *she* raised her arms toward the sea. "Come soon Master, all is in readiness."

VI

THE PALE AND waxing crescent moon floated above Areenna's shoulder as she walked with her father in the central garden of Tolemac. Illuminating nightmoss cast a soft whisper of light along the walkway. Nosaj's silver hair shimmered in the low light, which served to emphasize the drawn lines of his face.

"Solomon and I think you should take one of his Six groups with you."

"I understand your concern, but they would be more hindrance than help, Father. Mikaal and I…we do not need bodyguards. Others cannot see what we do, not yet. Both you and the High King know the truth of this."

Nosaj stopped walking and Areenna turned to him. The worry in his eyes cloaked her as if it were her own and she reached into herself to draw on her abilities. She took his hands into hers, enjoying the strong touch and the feel of calloused skin. Although he was the king of his dominion, Nosaj had never missed a chance to work beside his people.

"Father, I need you to trust in me, to believe in me. I cannot do what is required without your support. I cannot take away your worry, but I promise you I will do whatever is necessary to come back to you, and with Mikaal." Then she pushed a small bit of her own energy to her father, letting it settle through him until she sensed his tension ease.

He bobbed his head in reluctant consent and drew her close. He wrapped his arms around her and smiled down at her. "I trust you, Areenna, I trust you to know your strengths, your weaknesses and your abilities, but my concern is not for the woman of power you have become; it is for the child I watched grow to womanhood, and the woman I hold now in my arms." He paused for a moment but did not release her. "And your mother, wherever she is in the life after life, trusts you as well."

Releasing her, he took back her hand and said, "let us walk more, for we have been apart for too long and another separation is coming."

<><><>

When the midday meal ended, Roth, Enaid and Mikaal left to oversee the final gathering of supplies, leaving Areenna and Nosaj at the table. After a few moments of silence, Nosaj said, "Mikaal tells me you have become well adept with the sword."

"I have learned a great deal from him as I have from you," she replied.

Nosaj nodded, his eyes fixed on hers. Just as he was about to speak, Areenna smiled and said, "Would you like to work with me? It's been a long time since we last sparred."

"It would be my pleasure," he replied.

"So sure are you?"

He held her challenging gaze. "Yes."

"Then come, My King, let us play. I have to get my sword. I will meet you at the training grounds."

Ten minutes later, dressed in her leathers, she met her father at the wooden fence surrounding the training grounds. The sword pit was empty, but twenty feet away, two Six groups, were training. They fought barehanded, using movements Areenna had never seen before coming to Tolemac. They did not fight using fists; rather, they used their entire bodies, kicking in smooth arcs, hitting open handed with their fingers straight and stiff, chopping at their opponents instead of punching. They wrestled and fought, the sounds of flesh meeting flesh was loud.

"Mikaal calls this hand-to-hand fighting," she told her father.

"I have seen it before, when we fought the dark ones. Roth is a master of this fighting."

They watched for a few more minutes until Nosaj turned to Areenna. "Shall we?" he asked, a single eyebrow rising with the question.

"We shall," Areenna replied and led him into the sword pit. The brown earth was dotted with boot prints, the evidence of much training. She went to the center, where she turned, drew her shortsword and cocked her head at her father. "At your command, My Lord."

Nosaj drew his sword, nodded to his daughter and shifted his stance. "Now," he said in a low voice, his eyes locked on Areenna.

Each held their sword on a two-handed grip and began circling to the left. The grunts, slaps and noise coming from the adjacent training area faded from Areenna's ears as she concentrated solely on her father' eyes, waiting for a tell-tale sign of attack.

It came perhaps thirty seconds later. A slight narrowing of his eyes told her he would attack. When he did, she parried, slid from beneath the attack and spun, her sword held defensively ready.

Nosaj came again, this time swinging from the opposite direction. She caught the blade on the flat of her own; the force of the blow sent a numbing shockwave along her arm. She back-pedaled quickly, and circled to the right to give her arm time to recover.

When the feeling returned to her arm and hand, she twisted beneath another sudden attack and spun again, her sword slicing toward her father's head. Nosaj caught the blade at the last instant and flicked his wrist to separate them. Then he charged.

She caught the first blow easily and separated. He came again, this time with an arcing attack. She stopped his blade before he could finish the swing, slipped beneath it and pushed him back.

Spinning, he reversed and attacked again, faster than she expected. In the midst of his attack, she saw his eyes flick to the right and she backed quickly away. He came at her an instant later in a full out charge.

Instead of back-pedaling, as she knew he expected, she pushed forward, her blade moving in the figure eight Mikaal had taught her, her arms and wrists weaving so fast the blade blurred as she counter attacked and threw him off balance.

Nosaj was barely able to keep up with her, but a few seconds later, he fell into her pattern of weaves and faints. Once settled in the defense of her attack, he changed pace and began to push her back, his sword hammering steadily in short swift strokes.

They were so locked in their battle they didn't notice the two groups training nearby had stopped to watch them. All they saw was each other.

Father and daughter maneuvered in tight battle, their blades gleaming, the sound of metal upon metal echoing loud and crisp in the cool afternoon until, finally, Areenna spotted an opening in Nosaj's defensive pattern. She dipped beneath one swing, stepped closer and an instant later, touched the tip of her sword to the side of his neck.

Nosaj lowered his sword and stepped back. He gave Areenna a slow bow of his head. "Well done, Daughter."

Areenna smiled and sheathed her short sword. "Thank you, Father."

Behind them, the twelve men returned to their training, but only after raising their swords against their palms in a salute of silent applause to the swordplay they had witnessed.

<><><>

Mikaal and Roth inspected the kralets Roth had chosen as the pack animals for the journey. The three were young, barely four years old, strong, well-muscled and healthy. Combined, the pack animals would carry enough supplies to keep them fed for a long while.

"You will need to hunt until you reach the Frozen Mountains. There will be little game there, and what you find will more likely hunt you than you will them. Roth paused in thought. "Do you remember the stories I used to tell you of the animals from my time?"

Mikaal chuckled. "I remember the nightmares I had about them—one in particular. Giant animals weighing five times more than a man, with huge paws and long claws and covered with brown and black and even white thick fur. I think you called them bears."

Roth nodded. "Yes, the brown ones are grizzly bears, the white, polar bears. They are mean tempered killers. I can only imagine what they have become with the changes from the radiation."

"You also said you had not seen even one since returning to Nevaeh."

"True, but you can never be certain. There are other animals as well, dangerous ones near the frozen regions. These are not game for you; rather, you would be game for them."

"And we will be watchful, Father."

"You will have to conserve," Roth advised.

"We will be careful with the supplies," Mikaal promised. "My concern is more of the cold than the animals."

"As it should be. There is a trick I learned when I was younger: always wear several layers of clothing; it helps retain your body heat. Do not wear armor unless necessary in the Frozen Mountains. The metal retains cold and will hamper your movements."

"Understood," Mikaal replied, concerned more by his father's unvoiced worries than the preparation for the trip. "What really bothers you?" he asked.

Roth took in every line, of his son's face; each shaded plane before saying, "Everything about what you face worries me. You go to a place where no one we know had travelled. Even I know little of the area. Yet what I do know is, somehow life goes on. Whatever species of animals were there before the world changed may still be there, but by changed by the radiation mutated too, as was all life on Nevaeh. Besides the bears, there may be the descendants of what we called wolves," he added. "They are like…gorlons—larger and more predatory. They thrive in the cold, run in packs and are vicious. But I know not for sure their breed survived. So much has changed. So much mutation…. You must be watchful of everything."

"The Eight would not send us if we could not do what is necessary."

Roth's smile echoed with the cynicism of his next words. "The Eight, as you call the witc…sorceresses of the Island, are not omniscient. I trust them not."

Mikaal grasped his father's shoulder and squeezed gently. "But I do. I have been in their mind, and they have been in mine. They survive for a single reason; to defeat the dark ones."

"You are certain?"

"Absolutely," Mikaal responded, "But, Father, I doubt not they would sacrifice us should it become necessary to defeat the Dark Masters. In such I believe—absolutely."

"Good. Being prepared for any outcome is always the way to survival." Turning, Roth signaled to the men standing by the supplies. "Dunnel, have the kralets ready by sunrise."

The man called Dunnel, taller than the others by half a foot and slim, with a frizzy halo of black hair surrounding his head, nodded. "They will be ready at sunrise, My Lord."

"And now?" Mikaal asked.

Roth turned to a groom and called him over. The boy came running. "My Lord?"

"Find Queen Enaid, King Nosaj and Princess Areenna and tell them to meet us at the shop of Halan."

The boy sped off on his errand and Roth turned to Mikaal. "I have asked Halan to make a few items for you and Areenna."

Halan's, which was more a small foundry than a shop, was on the opposite side of the keep, and as they walked through the center of Tolemac, they replied to the greetings of the people on the streets. Roth, by virtue of where he came from, and Mikaal, by his father's example, never sought the formality of royalty and expected nothing more than a casual nod or wave from the men and women who had chosen to live in Tolemac under the High King's rule.

By the time they reached Halan's, Enaid had arrived and moments later, Nosaj and Areenna appeared from around a corner. Together, the five entered the shop. The Weapons Master and his wife gave them a simple head bow before Halan said, "Welcome My Lord."

"Good afternoon, Halan," Roth said. "Salinar," he added to the Arms Master's wife. "All is ready?"

"It is," Halan replied and nodded to his wife.

Turning, Salinar took two cloth-wrapped items from a shelf behind her: one long, the other smaller. She slid them on the counter and opened the smaller one to reveal two identical knives.

Areenna, looking at the knives, drew in a sharp breath. The workmanship was amazing. "I have never seen such knives," she whispered.

Smiling at the complement, Halan picked one up and held it aloft. The knife was nine inches long; the top of the blade had two inches of serration. A center-grooved channel ran the length of the blade. He turned kit over twice. "I crafted these knives from the special metal you gave me, My Lord. I made each knife from a single slice of metal, the handle molded to fit each of your hands. I bound the leather to the handle while the metal cooled so it would become part of the handle. It will wear down over the years but it will never separate from the metal."

He paused for a breath. "Salinar has blessed each blade, and the knife's strength will never be in doubt. The blade is sharp and the metal never dulls. This is yours, Prince Mikaal," he said and extended the knife handle to Mikaal.

When Mikaal took the knife, his fingers curled around the handle and it settled in as comfortably as if the knife had always been his. He opened his palm and laid the knife cross-wise. The balance was perfect and its weight so light it was as if he held nothing. "Magnificent," he whispered.

Halan lifted the second knife, which was almost but not quite a duplicate of the first. The handle was slightly smaller and the blade that much longer. He offered it to Areenna, who hesitated a moment before taking it from Halan's hand. When she touched it, a spark of energy skipped across her fingertips. Salinar smiled and nodded.

When she grasped the handle, it fit snugly within her grip and molded to her hand. "It's wonderful. Thank you, Master Halan, Mistress Salinar."

Both bowed to her.

"There is one more piece, My Princess," Halan said and nodded to his wife.

Salinar opened the second wrapped weapon to reveal a bow carved from the wood of a white gazebow tree. "On a journey to Northcrom, at the farthest northern border before the tar fields, I found a white gazebow struck by lightning. I was able to harvest a small and unharmed section of the tree and brought it to Tolemac. I created the bow by carving it whole. It is powerful yet the draw is deceptively easy. I hope you will find it to be a weapon and a tool of value," he said, handing the bow to Areenna.

When the bow touched her hands, a gentle warmth flowed from the wood, which gleamed with a light coat of oil. "It is beautiful," she said. She hefted the bow in her left hand and with her right, drew back the gut. The bow's power vibrated through her and she knew this weapon would serve her well.

Before she could speak, Halan reached behind and, when he turned back, offered her a wrapped bundle. "Arrows of acont wood," he said handing her the package.

Looking at the weapon maker and his wife, she said, "Thank you again, both of you. I have not the words."

Halan smiled. “Your face and eyes tell me all I need. Go safely on your travels.”

When they left Halan’s foundry, Enaid said, “We have one more stop.”

Mikaal and Areenna stayed still. “Come,” was all she would say.

Now what? she asked Mikaal silently.

He gave a mental shrug. *My mother likes surprises.*

They followed Enaid for three short streets until they reached a small shop. Areenna read the lettering on the glass window, which informed all that this was a seamstress’ shop. Inside, behind a small counter amidst the scent of perfumed candles and bolts of cloth piled high on a myriad of tables stood a tall and very thin woman.

“Welcome, My Lords, My Ladies.” The woman bowed slightly to the five. “I am honored.”

“Thank you Etina, all is ready?”

“Yes, My Lady.” Turning, she lifted a long cloak and held it high. “I used the pelts of rabts, and sewed them to well-tanned and thin beaten dar hide. There are no warmer garments in all of Nevaeh than these two cloaks.”

“They are beautiful, but they seem…so heavy.”

“Come, see if the weight is too much,” Etina said, motioning Areenna to her.

The seamstress draped the cloak over her shoulders, placed the hood over her head, and stepped back. “How feels it?”

Areenna accepted the weight of the cloak and was surprised that it did not weigh her down. “Comfortable.”

“While it is heavy, it is not overly so, and the pelts are balanced in weight. After a short time, you will adjust to its feel.”

“Thank you.” With Areenna’s smile and a nod, the seamstress picked up the second coat and handed it to Mikaal.

He slipped it on and adjusted the fur to his shoulders. “Thank you, Mistress Etina, it is perfect.”

The seamstress smiled. “Wear it in warmth, My Prince.”

“Come,” Enaid said as she smiled at the two wrapped in fur cloaks. “The day is ending and there is still much to be done.”

VII

SITTING AT THE table in the small hall, their plates and only two glasses remained before each of them: one of wine the other water. The mood was somber. Everyone knew this had been the last shared meal for a long time. The musicians who had been playing behind a sheer curtain had left a quarter hour before.

Talk was over. What remained was to sit and enjoy each other's company. Although outwardly calm, a strange edginess filled Areenna—not born of fear but of anticipation for what lay ahead.

She glanced at Mikaal, who was looking at Roth. A smile tweaked the corners of his lips. "Try to relax, Father," Mikaal said, breaking the silence that had fallen when Roth finished speaking, "we will do what is needed."

Roth did not smile. "If it were only so easy as saying the words…I wish I could be with you."

"But none of us can," Enaid said in a low voice. "We each have our own paths to walk. Neither does it mean we will not be of help when the time comes." *I will be there when you need me*, she added silently to Areenna and Mikaal.

Areenna nodded at her mentor's words. She understood exactly what Enaid meant, and the thought from the High Queen brought her comfort. "When we know what it is we seek, I shall find a way to notify you," Areenna said to the three.

"And Mikaal," Enaid said pointedly, "your father's worries are justified. You…you and Areenna are still children—" Enaid held up a hand to forestall Mikaal from speaking.

"—I know you no longer consider yourself such," she added, turning to look at Areenna as well, "but you are only twenty and eighteen. Old enough to have to do what is necessary, but you are too young to have the experience we have gained; too young to know the depths of evil you face."

Before either Areenna or Mikaal could speak, a Tolemac guardsman entered the dining chamber followed by a guardsman wearing the markings of Fainhall. The two walked directly to Roth, and bowed their heads. "My Lord, a message from King Nomis." he announced and motioned for the other to hand Roth the message.

Roth took the message, broke the seal and opened it. "Tell me exactly what happened." he asked the guardsman after finishing the message.

"Two villages were attacked, one was destroyed, twenty men and eight women were taken prisoner. Prince Samot has been injured."

"The injury?"

"He will live, but he may lose the use of his left arm," the guardsman said.

"See this man is fed and rested," Roth instructed his guardsman. "Send in the Captain of the Watch."

The two left and within moments, Stamel, the Watch Captain appeared. "My Lord?"

"There is trouble in Fainhall. Have the main guard company ready to go tomorrow. Full armor. Send Noslen to me," he added.

Without a word, Captain Stamel left the chamber.

"*She* knows," Enaid said. "I sense this is her work."

Everyone knew Enaid spoke of the Black Sorceress.

"Why?" Areenna asked. "What purpose does it serve?"

Before Enaid could speak, Roth said, "Disruption. It splits our forces and if I understand the way *she* thinks, *she* believes it will weaken us."

"But it will not," Enaid said. "*She* baits us, trying to see what it is we do. That is what this attack on Fainhall was about."

"You are certain?" Nosaj asked.

Enaid turned to Areenna's father. "It's nothing more than *she* has been doing for these past twenty years. Only this time fear motivates her. *She* senses the coming changes and fights for survival. *Her* defeat at the Island pushes her. *She* is afraid."

She turned to Roth. "You will need me for this."

"Understood," Roth responded as Noslen appeared in the chamber. The Captain of the Six was tall and broad and although he wore no armor, there could be no doubt he was the embodiment of a warrior.

"My Lord?"

"Fainhall has been attacked. I have ordered preparations. Pick two Six groups to lead us. We leave in the morning. We travel light and fast."

"Yes, My Lord."

"You go as well."

Noslen smiled. "Thank you."

Alone again, King Nosaj turned to Roth. "I will bring a small force and join you on the road to Fainhall."

Roth shook his head. "No, old friend. It is more important for you to ready your people for what is coming." He paused and glanced at each in turn. "We have spoken our hopes and fears tonight. Sunrise will come soon enough. It is time to rest and ready ourselves for tomorrow."

Standing, Roth held out his hand for Enaid. She grasped it and let him pull her to her feet.

As they left the chamber, Areenna caught the thought Enaid sent to her. *Worry not of this. It is a diversion meant to confuse us. Do not stray from your path.*

<><><>

Less than an hour after going to bed, Areenna lay staring at the dark ceiling. After leaving the small hall, she had gone to the parapets and set Gaalrie free to hunt. Then she'd returned to her bedchamber and prepared for her last night of sleep in Tolemac.

The anxiety humming through her since the meal had prevented sleep. Enaid's earlier words rose to taunt her. She and Mikaal were children, it was true, but they were so much more. And so many people depended on them. *Can I do this?*

A tear slid from the corner of her eye. *Oh, Mother, how I wish you were here.* In the two years since her mother's death, there was not a day she did not miss her, but tonight was different for tomorrow signaled the start of another chapter in her life and, above all else, she craved the comfort of her mother's arms and words.

The single tear turned into more and as she lay crying silently, she brought up a picture of her mother as she remembered her, so full of life that everyone around her could do nothing but feel the warmth Queen Inaria of Freemorn had radiated. She saw again, the white blond hair framing her oval face and the green eyes—identical to her own—awash with silver motes and a small straight nose above full lips.

With her tears still falling, she wrapped the well-remembered sensation of her mother's arms around her and slipped into a dreamless sleep broken only when bands of light rose in the east and Gaalrie's always gentle push rolled into her mind, showing her the beauty of the coming day and the gathering of Roth's soldiers preparing to leave for Fainhall.

Rising from the bed, she moved quickly. She took care of her needs and dressed in her traveling clothes, a pair of leggings and a short tunic. She strapped her shortsword to her side, where it hung against her left hip. The knife Roth had given her sat in its sheath on her right hip. Then she put on a light traveling cloak, for the day promised more warmth than chill, and went downstairs.

An hour later, with the sun above the eastern horizon, Areenna, Mikaal and their parents stood by their kraals. At the south gate, ninety guardsmen and two Six groups awaited Roth and Enaid. At the north gate, three sure-footed pack kralets loaded with every ounce they could carry awaited Areenna and Mikaal. Only their goodbyes remained.

Enaid laughed. When everyone turned to her, she shook her head slowly. "It was just a thought. As I stood here, I thought how this morning must seem to those who watch us. An army goes southwest, while two young ones go north. Who would think it was the two northbound who carry the hope of Nevaeh upon their backs."

"We will not let you down," Areenna promised aloud.

"We know," her father said, stepping close to her and drawing her into his arms. "Do nothing foolish, I want you back," he whispered, his mouth touching her ear.

She smiled softly. "I do only what I am meant to, Father. I will come back to you, I promise."

"A promise I will hold you to," he said, his words as intense as the gaze he favored her with.

In turn, each said their own farewells and mounted their kraals. When Mikaal and Areenna turned their mounts north, Roth, Enaid and Nosaj turned west. The most direct route to Fainhall lay through Freemorn. Nosaj would journey with the fast moving force until reaching home.

At the north gate, with the kralets' lead tied to Mikaal's saddle, they went through the gate. As soon as they crossed out, Areenna sensed something nearby. She searched further, but found everything was calm and peaceful, yet there was a cloying within her head of something…off.

<><><>

On the third day of travel, wrapped in their fur cloaks against the cold, Areenna and Mikaal crested a long rolling hill and saw Brumwall's capital, Apolis, sitting on a plateau ten miles away. From the distance, it appeared smaller than it was; but awash in the afternoon sun, it sparkled like a crystal sculpture. In the hazy distance beyond Apolis, the blue water of the great northern lake lent the scene an aura of peacefulness she only wished she could feel. Areenna drew Hero to a halt and, twisting in the saddle, cast a glance behind her.

From the moment they'd left Tolemac, and throughout the three days of travel, she had been unable to shed the sensation of something being wrong—of something *off*. She spotted Gaalrie flying above, her cinnamon and silver feathers aglow in the morning sun, and asked her aoutem to scout the road behind them.

Gaalrie flew over their back trail while Areenna spread her senses in all directions, again seeking the cause of the low and cloying emanations. At first, there was nothing; but she pressed on, pushing the distance further, until she found a flicker of gray emptiness hanging in the air.

Directing Gaalrie to the spot, she watched through the treygone's eyes, but saw only earth, trees, and grass. Yet the gray patchiness remained in her senses.

"What is it?" Mikaal asked, fully aware of Areenna's concern.

"Nothing…something...I don't know. I see it not, yet I feel it at the edge of my thoughts."

"Are we being followed?"

"I can't tell. It does not have the feel of…her, yet it might be possible. You feel it not?"

"No," he said.

She pushed into his mind and drew him to the sensation she was hunting.

I feel it, but… "Shielded? Some sort of a blocking?"

"No. It's something else."

"If it continues to stay with us, we will eventually know what it is and will be prepared."

Areenna recalled Gaalrie and they started toward Apolis. A few minutes later she asked, "Be prepared for what?"

VIII

FROM HER VANTAGE point high in the keep, Areenna stood at the window and watched as Apolis, bathed in the morning sun, came alive. Shops were opening and farmers were setting their goods on display in the small stalls lining the outer walls of the keep.

Sounds of life emanated everywhere. While she loved the peace and quiet of the country, she also treasured the bustle of multitudes of people going about their lives. Then a wash of sadness gripped her. *If they only knew...*

We should be glad they do not, came Mikaal's thought.

She smiled at the warmth contained within his thought. *True.*

When are you joining us?

Now, she replied and left the bedchamber.

By the time she reached the dining chamber, King Ecorah and Queen Enna were there. Mikaal's grandparents were a regal pair, and despite his seventy odd years, Ecorah was physically fit. His head, completely devoid of hair, emphasized alert blue eyes. The color of his skin was the same nutty mocha shade as Enaid. Queen Enna, the same age as her husband, was slim, tall and regal. The queen's face, carved with lines of wisdom, held the matured beauty of her youth. Her hair was straight and white and contrasted with the golden oak of her skin. The powers stemming from her were strong and Areenna drew comfort from them.

"A good day to you, Areenna," Enna said with a smile.

"And to you, My Lady."

"Enna, only, Cousin" she told Areenna.

Smiling, Areenna sat next to Mikaal.

"I'm glad we are together this morning," Ecorah said. He reached across and patted Mikaal's shoulder. "I'm concerned about this journey of yours. The Frozen Mountains are not a place friendly to us and your grandmother tells me you must be on this…mission because we may soon be facing the dark ones again."

"A pleasant way to start our day," Enna said with a hard glance at her husband.

"Said now or later, this discussion must be had."

"Grandfather, Areenna has been charged with a duty, and I as well. There is no point in discussion. We have no choice," Mikaal said, in a vain hope to end the conversation.

"Everyone has a choice," Ecorah said.

"Yes, and ours was to go to the Island for Areenna's final training. That choice is why we are here now."

He worries for you, Areenna said silently.

I know, but he needs to understand we must do this.

Ecorah smiled. "Spoken like a true warrior."

The conversation ended as two serving women brought their food. They ate silently and when they were finished, Ecorah cleared his throat. "I have a gift for you, Grandson." With that, he pushed an old and faded rolled dar hide across the table to Mikaal.

Picking it up, Mikaal untied the strings holding the hide closed, and opened the leather to reveal a carved bone-handle knife.

Mikaal picked it up and tested its weight and balance, Ecorah said, "When I was your age, perhaps a year or two younger, I made this knife. The bone came from the foreleg of a rantor I hunted down after it attacked a farmer. The blade is of the finest metal and blessed by your grandmother. It has served me well and will do the same for you when you have need of it."

Mikaal studied the knife for several seconds. "Thank you, Grandfather," he said without mentioning the knife his father had given him three days before.

Pushing from the table, Ecorah stood. "And now I tend to my people. Come, Mikaal, join me like you did when you used to visit."

Mikaal stood. "With pleasure."

He paused to look at Areenna. "Do you—"

She shook her head. *Go with your grandfather.* "I will be fine. I need to speak with your grandmother."

When Mikaal and Ecorah left the chamber, Queen Enna stood. "Let us go to my chambers." The queen turned to one of the servers and said, "Notify the stable that Princess Areenna and I will be riding."

"My Lady," the young woman said with a slight bow of her head as she moved to the door.

Once in the queen's antechamber, and alone, Enna stepped close to Areenna. "Kneel."

Without question, Areenna went to her knees at the feet of Queen Enna, who placed both hands on Areenna's head. A spark leapt from Enna's hands and centered deep within Areenna's mind. It grew strong and traveled to every part of her body, fading away a half minute later.

"Rise," Enna said.

Standing, Areenna took a deep breath. "With what have you gifted me?"

"Divining and the ability to manipulate water is my gift. Powerful abilities when used correctly. Very few women can hold this ability. I sense such strength in you, Child."

Areenna could not stop her laugh.

"Is this gift funny?" Enna asked, her eyes narrowing with puzzlement.

"No, My Lady, it was what you called me. Enaid calls me child all the time. Child I only wish I could be again. My childhood is past."

Enna raised her arm and cupped Areenna's cheek. "You are so wrong. A woman you are, make no mistake, but a child as well. Your innocence is evidence of such."

Areenna shook her head. "Of what innocence do you speak? I lost that at the Island."

"You have become powerful Areenna, more so than I believe any suspect. I feel it. Yet I feel the other…the innocence as well. You may see it not, but shed it not, for it is a part of you."

"I...I don't understand," she whispered. "What I have seen, what I have done. It is not possible to have any innocence."

It is not something to dwell on; accept it as the part of you that makes you Areenna. Like a caress, Enna's silent thought was soft, warm and gentle. "Come, there is not much time to teach you how to use this ability before you leave for the mountains."

<><><>

The air was cold as they drew their kraals to a stop before a grove of trees. As soon as she saw the entwined wall of trees, she knew what they represented. Turning to Enna, she said, "Your Haven?"

Enna smiled and nodded. "Enaid?"

"She took me into hers."

Nodding, Enna dismounted and tied her kraal to a sapling, turned to the trees and raised her palms toward them. When she lowered her hands she said, "You have invitation." Without another word, she stepped into the trees and disappeared.

Dismounting, Areenna tied Hero to a different sapling. She walked up to the trees, envisioned herself stepping through the wall of tangled trees, and followed Enna in.

When she emerged on the other side, she was within a moderate size circle of trees. There was an ice-crusted pool, smaller than the pool within Enaid's haven, shimmering with reflected sunlight. The ground was clear and green; the temperature within Enna's Haven was much warmer than without.

"It is beautiful," she said.

"Yes, even now in the cold, but when warm weather comes it is truly magnificent. Look at the water and tell me what you sense."

Areenna focused on the pond. It took only a heartbeat for her mind to flow into the water. The instant she did, her eyes snapped open. "It has the same source as Enaid's haven, the same water as in Tolemac." She turned to Enna. "It comes from the high mountain at the far northern edge of Brumwall."

"How do you know this so quickly? You…"

"Before I went to the Island, I was in the center courtyard of Tolemac's keep. Somehow I melded with the water and traveled to its source."

"Before you went to the Island?"

"Before," Areenna said.

Enna's eyes reflected more than a little surprise. "How powerful are you?"

Areenna shrugged. "I don't know. Enaid said I am more powerful than she, but I do not believe it to be so."

"When we're finished here, I want to know of all your abilities."

"All I know of, of course."

Then we begin. Look into the water, meld with it and create a fountain in the middle of the pond. A fountain of water.

She thought about a fountain, not the one at Tolemac; rather she pictured the one her father had carved himself for her mother. It was small, only a few feet tall, but intricately worked with figures of rantors and gorlons at each point of waterfall, as if the water sprang from between their legs.

The water bubbled and rose as she called it forth with her new ability. Soon the water took on the shape of the picture in her mind. It was hard to maintain the picture and to will the water to follow her commands, but after a few minutes the fountain blossomed and water poured from between the legs of the rantors and gorlons. She held it for another minute before releasing it, her strength drained.

Enna's expression was one of disbelief. "I expected to see some water rise. What you did, I expected not." *Who are you Areenna? Who are you to command such strength and power?*

Areenna sensed much in the thought, but held herself back when the Queen of Brumwall's face changed from disbelief to scrutiny and Enna said, "We have much to do today. I will skip the manipulation. You know it already. Water has many uses; one of its unexpected uses is as a weapon. This is what we will concentrate on."

She paused, took Areenna's hand, and her closed eyes in thought. "First, find the underground path of the water feeding this pond. Search for it; seek its path beneath the ground. Join with me so I can show you…."

<><><>

Exhausted from Enna's teachings, Areenna and Brumwall's queen returned to the Apolis keep just after sundown. In the west, deep pink and purple bands chased each other beneath the horizon by the coming of night, while above and in the north, blackening clouds massed. They had spent the entire afternoon in training. In-between the bouts of work, she had explained her abilities to Mikaal's grandmother.

When they reached the stables, two men raced out to take their kraals. As they started toward the keep, Areenna sensed the older queen's fatigue and grasped her arm to give her support.

Before they reached the entrance to the keep, Mikaal came through the doorway. Areenna saw concern carved on his features as he walked toward them.

What?

A storm comes. Worry laced his thoughts. "It looks bad," he said aloud.

The gathering clouds swarmed above in dark and menacingly thick strands. Too tired to have taken notice on the ride back, she realized this was not a simple evening of clouded skies; rather, it was the foretelling of a massive storm.

At her side, Enna gazed in the same direction as Areenna and Mikaal. "You will not be leaving in the morning. While unexpected at this time of year, storms have come. This one will be bad. Has warning been issued?"

Mikaal nodded. "Men have been sent to the outlying areas. Prince Darb returned earlier with the news of the storm's path. My uncle said it is a monstrous one and warned the King to have the people brought into Apolis."

"Darb is home, good," Enna said and stood straighter, somehow shrugging off the fatigue. "We must make preparation. Where is my husband?"

"He's been working with his guardsmen, setting up the Great Hall with supplies for the people. They are just about finished."

"Then we go there," she said and, slipping from Areenna's support, started inside.

Without another word, Queen Enna led the way to the Great Hall. She walked tall and straight, her tiredness cast off. When they entered the hall, they found it bustling with people. Long tables filled with platters of food and pitchers of wine and water were set against one wall,

There were already two dozen of Brumwall's citizens in the hall, and another hundred or so would eventually arrive. The outlying region around Apolis consisted of vegetable and animal farms. Most of the farmers, especially the carna breeding farms, would not seek safety in Apolis; rather they would gather and tend their herds during the storm to protect them as much as possible. The King dispatched guardsmen from Apolis to help the farmers staying on their lands. The vegetable and fruit farmers would come to Apolis, as only a few farms grew winter produce. The farmers and tree harvesters who lived further out would have no choice but to fend for themselves.

"We're done here," Ecorah said when they entered the Great Hall. "All that is left is for the rest of our people to arrive. We have a few hours before the storm strikes."

"It is a harsh storm, Mother," said Prince Darb, Enaid's brother and the heir to Brumwall.

"Welcome home." Queen Enna clasped Darb to her. "Your trip was fruitful?"

"It was, Mother. The rogue Free-Blades have returned to the outlands. They left many in the ground as they ran."

"As it should be. We cannot allow them to roam Brumwall without response. Our losses?"

"Two mother. They fought well."

"Make sure their families are told of this."

"It has been done. Princess Areenna, it is good to see you."

Areenna smiled at Darb. "And you, My Prince," she said and yawned. "My pardon," she whispered. "I am more tired than I realized."

She caught Mikaal's concerned thought and shook her head. *I was training with your grandmother.*

We'll talk later, came Mikaal's response.

"If all is done, we must get some food into Areenna before she can no longer stay upright," Enna said.

"And you as well," Areenna replied to the queen.

<><><>

The food did its job and Areenna was less tired. The meal had ended two hours earlier and, at this point, the hall held many of Apolis' outlying citizens. She had pleaded exhaustion shortly after dinner and had gone to her chamber. Now she stood on the parapet of the keep. She wore the rabt fur cloak and stood beneath the falling snow, which had started a short time before.

Watching the clouds blot out the stars, she realized the clouds were not moving in a single direction; rather, they came from every direction and swirled together directly above Apolis.

The pattern was strange; one she had never seen before.

"Are you testing the warmth of the cloak?" Mikaal said from behind.

Turning, she found him a foot away. *I did not sense you.*

"You were concentrating on the sky. What bothers you?" he asked aloud.

"You know me well."

"I know you as well as I know myself." He reached a hand toward hers and she took it in his. As always, a tingle spread between them followed by a flow of warmth. "What is it?" he asked.

"Look at the clouds. Tell me what you see."

His brow furrowed before he turned his eyes skyward. "I see storm clouds swirling, snow falling."

Look closer.

He did as she asked and, a moment later said, "They come from all directions to spin above us. It is…wrong."

Gaalrie's cry broke his concentration. He turned toward the sound as the giant treygone descended madly toward them. Ice coated the bird's wings, hampering its ability to fly.

Areenna released Mikaal's hands and raised her arms toward the treygone. *Join me*!

It took no longer than an instant to join with her, and to feel the deep cold filling the treygone.

Areenna released a stream of energy toward Gaalrie, wrapping her aoutem with it, lending it the strength to fly to her. The energy formed a block around the giant bird, warming her just enough for the treygone to move her wings and keep flying. A half minute later, she landed in Areenna's outstretched arms, the treygone's weight almost knocking Areenna from her feet. She drew the giant bird close to her, accepting its weight and size without thought.

Pressing the treygone to her chest, she wrapped the cloak over her to add warmth. "I have never seen a treygone affected by the cold in this way."

Mikaal lifted the cloak to look at Gaalrie. He reached out with his hand and stroked Gaalrie's head. "Nor I."

"This storm has a target," Areenna said.

Us, Mikaal shot back.

"*She* is tracking us," Areenna whispered. *I was stupid not to see it.* "The feeling…the emptiness I showed you yesterday. It is the Black Witch's magic."

"I did not feel her presence in it," Mikaal admitted. "I missed it."

"Nor I. *She* found a way to hide it from us. But this storm is of her doing."

"What can we do?" he asked. It was not a question of helplessness but one of action.

Areenna drew Gaalrie even tighter against her chest. The treygone's body heat soon grew and she knew her aoutem would be fine. *How can I stop this? What ability can fight a storm? What have you given me*? she asked the eight of the Island. *What?*

"I have never heard of an ability to control the weather, but there must be a way," Mikaal said.

Areenna thought about it. "She is not controlling the weather; she is using the air currents. Pushing them from every direction to us."

"Can you fight that?"

"No, but she has to continually use her powers. She will tire."

"Look at the amount of snow. I have never seen snow fall this fast."

Areenna bent over the Balustrade. The snow was at least a foot high on the ground below, and in less than two hours. *There has to be something.* She shook her head in frustration. Anger boiled up within her, fueling the frustration. "Snow is water," she whispered.

"Frozen water, yes," Mikaal responded, wondering at the path she was taking.

"Take Gaalrie." She extended the treygone to him. When he drew the bird beneath his cloak, Areenna turned back. Holding her hands palms down, she forced away her exhaustion and called forth her powers. The burning sensation in the pit of her body exploded instantly and power raced through her. She focused on the snow and, as Enna had shown her earlier in the afternoon, began to call forth the gift the Queen of Brumwall placed within her. Watching the snow on the ground directly beneath her begin to whirl in circles, she directed it to form a column. She stopped the manipulation and watched the seven-foot column fall apart.

"There may be a way," she told Mikaal after turning to him. *It will be hard. I am tired. I need your strength. Yours and Charkas. Can you join with your aoutem?*

Mikaal closed his eyes and reached out to Charka. An instant later, he tasted the grain his aoutem was eating. He closed off the taste of the food and opened his eyes. *I am ready.*

She pushed to Gaalrie, who responded instantly. Her aoutem's strength was returning rapidly and she knew Gaalrie would be of help. "I am not sure," she began hesitantly, "but I believe I can manipulate the snow as if it was running water—push it back to the clouds even as it falls. Perhaps this will work…"

Areenna opened her mind and drew Mikaal in. His strength, combined with Charka's, amplified within her. Her fatigue faded and she pushed her power higher. Deep inside, at the very core of what made her female, the power flowed strong and hot. She tilted her head toward the swirling center of the storm and raised her hands. An instant later, Gaalrie pulled free from Mikaal's grip and jumped to Areenna, one taloned leg upon each shoulder.

Areenna released her powers, concentrating not on the clouds but on the falling snow. She drew on Mikaal, Charka, and Gaalrie as she fought the Black Sorceress. The snow continued to fall, but instead of reaching the ground it swirled, reversed, and returned to the clouds. She stood tall, her arms outstretched, her concentration absolute as she fought the power above.

The battle went on, Areenna forcing the snow to remain aloft while the black one fought for the snow's release. Midnight passed and the three on the parapet stood as one. Then something changed. A tentative search through the clouds directed downward at her. She blocked it quickly and it retreated. Holding her manipulation strong, she chased after it.

Areenna caught the stink of the Black Sorceress and followed the scent through the clouds, through the night and toward its origination. The scent trail ended abruptly and the emanation disappeared. A scream ripped through her mind, a cry of rage that rocked her badly. She fought it away. The clouds were shifting, changing, and a moment later began to drift slowly east.

The snow lessened as the clouds moved away, and Areenna knew the worst of the storm was over.

She turned to Mikaal and started to say something, but as she did, blackness curtained her mind, and she fell unconscious to the stone floor of the parapet. The last sound she heard was of Gaalrie's loud cry.

IX

A WARNING WITHIN awakened Areenna—a light pressure at the center of her forehead. Her last memory of being on the parapet surfaced. She became aware of a presence, opened her eyes and blinked twice.

Sitting in the chair across from her, and staring at her was Queen Enna. "Last night was strange. I had many dreams. One was of a young girl standing on the parapet above my chambers fighting a storm. With her was another woman of power. There were two aoutems as well, a treygone with you and a kraal in the stables. Only it wasn't a woman of power with you, was it Areenna?"

"I—"

"Be careful what you next say, Child."

Areenna moistened her sleep-dried lips with the tip of her tongue. She shook her head, never losing eye contact with the Queen. "I would not lie. You dreamed true."

"How is this possible? How can Mikaal have power?"

Areenna sat up. Behind Enna, Gaalrie rested on the stone sill of the window, watching them both. She realized Mikaal must have brought her aoutem to the chamber when he carried her here last night. "Because he is the son of Roth."

"And the son of my daughter as well. But that is no explanation."

"What more can there be? You know who Roth is, do you not?"

"I do," Enna said in a low voice. "He came to us from the past, as if he were an 'Old One'. He brought us peace and he showed us how to live together and to protect ourselves from *them*. But it explains nothing."

"You will have to trust me and trust Mikaal. Enaid will explain it to you."

Her shoulders stiffened and she shook her head once, sharply. "No, you will explain it to me. I am far too old to have use for patience."

Areenna took a deep breath and sought the right words, but could not find them. "Can you join with me?"

Enna reached out and grasped both of Areenna's hands. Gripping them tightly, she nodded. An instant later they were connected. *Find what you seek.*

Their eyes locked on each other's, their hands gripped tightly. They stayed together for several long minutes before Enna released Areenna, leaned back and took two long and deep breaths.

A few seconds later, Enna said, "So much for someone so young. It seems impossible."

"Yet it is fact," Areenna responded.

"He survived the Island.... Call Mikaal to us."

She sent the silent call to Mikaal, who responded quickly. She sensed his surprise but cut the question off. "He is on the way."

"There is much danger in this," Enna whispered.

"Of which we are all too aware."

"How long has he...been with power?"

"He discovered it during his thirteenth year, but told no one, not even Enaid or Roth."

Enna nodded. "It must have been very hard for him, to be so alone. His abilities?"

"He has all of mine, all the gifts I was given as well, except for those only a woman can hold. Healing is one such. On the Island, he received others. He has the ability to see ahead for a few seconds at a time." Areenna paused and shook her head. "It is a gift I cannot understand."

"It is difficult. I only knew one woman with such an ability. She tried to pass it to me, but could not. Yet, she taught me its control, should I find it alive within me in the future—" Enna fell silent, her eyes went distant and her breathing all but stopped.

Areenna reached out and grasped her shoulder. "Enna," she called softly, shaking the queen's shoulder gently.

The queen blinked, twice. "I…I am sorry. I just realized why she trained me in a power I could never use. She saw this," Enna finished, her voice a bare whisper in Areenna's ears.

"Saw this?"

Enna looked down at her hands. "Of course," she said almost to herself. "She knew this would happen. She saw it with her ability and knew I would have to train Mikaal. I…I saw this as well but did not know it. He is the complement to your power."

"I—" Areenna stopped herself. Enna's words called up what Enaid had told her when she and Mikaal had left for the Island.

Before she could ask more, Mikaal entered the bedchamber. Outside, the first light of day was breaking in the east. "What's wrong?" he asked, looking from Areenna to his grandmother.

"You, obviously," Queen Enna said.

"I—"

"Say nothing until I'm finished. Did you think I would not discover your powers?"

Mikaal held his grandmother's stare for several seconds before shaking his head.

"Never before has this happened—a man with a woman's power." *How long did you think you could hide this from me?* she asked, using thought instead of words.

Mikaal held her stare. *I did not know how you would take it. If anyone learns of this…*

"It will go badly for you, both of you!" she said. "Areenna has told me you have command of many abilities. And you have the foreseeing as well."

Mikaal nodded. "But it seems to come only a bare instant before something is to happen."

"Of course it does," Enna said. Then she glanced at Areenna for a moment before saying, "Let Areenna prepare for the day ahead." She turned to her. "Meet us for the morning meal as soon as you are ready. Mikaal, come with me."

Without waiting for a reply, she stood and walked out. Mikaal gave Areenna a shrug and followed his grandmother, leaving her alone for the first time since waking. Areenna sat in the bed, staring at the door. Everything that had happened seemed dreamlike.

She left the bed, went to the window and lifted Gaalrie into her arms. A heartbeat later, their minds melded and as Areenna drew on the warmth and closeness of her aoutem, her mind settled.

She opened the window by pushing it on its pivot and gave Gaalrie the command to fly and hunt. Then, she turned to face the day ahead.

<><><>

"When plan you to leave?" King Ecorah asked after finishing his food.

"Later this morning," Mikaal answered for both of them. "We have lost time because of the storm."

Prince Darb looked at his nephew. "Only a short time."

Areenna nodded. "But valuable time. Every hour is important." She studied Darb as she spoke. He was a duplicate of Enaid, a male version, handsome almost to a fault. Four years younger than his sister, his dark hair and pale eyes were the same as Enaid's, and there was an aura of wisdom about him as well.

Darb held Areenna's eyes for another few seconds before nodding. "There is a way to gain back the hours you lose this morning." He turned to his father. "With your permission, I would show them a shorter way to Farg, through the upper passage into Lokinhold."

When Ecorah nodded his permission, Darb turned back to Areenna and Mikaal. "When do you want to leave?"

Before either could respond, Enna said, "I need time, a few hours with both of them. There are things…women's work I must do." She paused in thought. "Have their supplies filled and their kralets readied. You can leave by late morning."

"As you say," Darb responded.

Enna rose. "Come, there is not much time," she said to Areenna and Mikaal.

<><><>

The sun was midway between its zenith and the horizon when Prince Darb pulled his kraal to a halt. "Follow this road for another two hours. You will come to a triple fork. Take the first road to the left. It leads directly to Farg. A half mile after the fork, there will be a stand of trees; three burned white by lightning and. Turn there. A half mile into the woods you will find a safe place to camp within a small grove of gazebow trees."

Darb paused a moment in thought. "Be wary between here and Farg and throughout Lokinhold. There are renegade Free-Blades roaming the outer territories, pillaging the smaller settlements."

Mikaal studied his uncle. "Free-Blades pillaging? Why, when there is always employment at the dominions?"

"They are turncoats from their own bands of mercenaries. They prefer raiding and looting to serving a dominion with honest work. But we have been controlling them so far."

"Has this been going on a while?" Areenna asked.

Darb shook his head. "It started a few months ago. But it is not unheard of."

"I wonder," Areenna began, but stopped.

"Of what?" Darb pushed.

"If it is connected to the darkness…to the dark circle."

"How could that be? They are but mercenaries."

Areenna exhaled slowly. "Believe it not, My Prince, just because these renegade blades are traitors to their own kind, does not mean they cannot be controlled by the Dark Ones."

"Listen to her, Uncle," Mikaal cautioned.

"Tell your mother of this," Areenna added. "Tell her I ask she be wary."

Darb nodded. "As you say," he said. "Now, be off with you. Stay watchful."

<><><>

Mad shadows flickered on the sides and the ceiling of the huge cavern, buried within the Southern Palisades. The distorted shadows seemed to dance along the rocky walls, flickering in time with the vacillating flames while the deformed woman-thing danced about the fire, driving herself into a frenzied fugue.

She turned and raced out of the cavern, running like a wobbly three-legged coor until *she* reached the very edge of the high palisade. There *she* stopped, her eyes staring upward at the sky, searching, searching, until at last *she* spotted the dark and misty messenger. Not a living thing, this flying bird-like apparition; rather, it was the embodiment of evil.

It dropped lower, circled around the Black Witch, descending in a sheet of mist to envelope the sorceress within a bubble of vacillating darkness. Then, when it held *her* enclosed within, the sorceress opened *her* mind.

Into the dark void of *her* mind came the words of her Master, loud and sharp, slicing through *her* like a keen edged sword until *she* stood trembling within the darkness. After a while, the mists fell away and the night returned.

She staggered away from the ledge and back into the depths of her cavern where *she* sat near the fire and took in deep breaths. *She* began to laugh. The sound built to a fever pitch as *she* replayed her Master's words.

We travel across the waters. Be ready. I bring many with me. I want the girl and the boy. Find them, capture them, and we will take Nevaeh!

She laughed again, the dry cackle echoing out from the cavern walls as *she* sent a thought. It took only a few seconds to find what *she* sought and knew exactly where the two were. *Follow, stay hidden, she* commanded.

X

THE FIRE GLOWED softly in the night. The scent of rabt clung to the air, although the meat was long gone. Areenna sat within the fire-lit circle, Mikaal to her left. The kraals grazed freely and Gaalrie had settled on the highest branch of a gazebow tree after hunting and eating her fill.

While it should have been an easy and relaxing time, Areenna could not shake off the feeling of someone or something following them. It was the same sensation she'd gotten when leaving Tolemac and just before arriving in Apolis.

What is it? Mikaal asked, sensing her unease.

I don't know. "A feeling," she said aloud. "Something *she* sent follows us."

"But not near?"

No, it tracks us only. Of that, I am sure, she responded. "Tell me, how did it go with your grandmother after I left you?"

He gazed at the sky before saying, "It was strange. Not like when you and I join, not like with my mother, either. It is hard to explain. The training was difficult. She kept pressing me to feel for what would happen."

"And?"

He shrugged. "Nothing happened at the beginning, but later she told me to concentrate on nothing. It was the hardest thing I have ever tried. How do you concentrate on nothing?"

Areenna laughed. "I haven't any idea."

"Neither did I, until I realized nothing itself is an impossible thought, so I focused on a color." He said the last with a smile.

Areenna sensed he was waiting for a question. "What color?"

His smile grew wider as his eyes roamed her face. “The green of your eyes.”

Her stomach twisted. “And?”

“I answered my grandmother’s question before she asked it.”

“Then you can call up this ability?”

His smile faded. “Maybe, if needed, but I discovered this ability has its own way of working. It comes without asking…if there is danger.”

Areenna’s brows knitted together. “How is this possible?”

“I don’t know. What I do know is when I was leaving my grandmother’s chamber; she drew a knife and attacked me. I saw it happen before she drew the weapon and turned to face her. Her hand was on the knife.”

Areenna gazed at him. “This is good. It will help keep you safe.”

“I hope,” Mikaal said as Areenna gave in to a yawn.

“I’m more tired than I thought,” she admitted.

We should both get some sleep, Mikaal pushed to her. “I will check the kralets.”

They stood and when Mikaal walked toward the kralets, Areenna called to Gaalrie, who rested on the high branches of the tree. Their minds joined and she accepted the warmth the cinnamon and silver bird showered upon her. *Scout, hunt, be watchful, My Sister.*

Five minutes after Gaalrie left her roost, Mikaal secured the pack animals and said goodnight to Charka. Finally, he joined Areenna in the lean-to, where he slipped into his sleeping silks. “We should reach Farg by late afternoon tomorrow.”

“We will be on schedule,” Areenna added. “Sleep gently,” she whispered as her eyes closed and sleep claimed her.

◇◇◇

Areenna was high in the heavens, flying gracefully above everything, as free as if she were Gaalrie. She knew she was dreaming, but reality held no bonds on her; rather, she embraced the freedom of being aloft, of flying. An instant later, she saw dark storm clouds beneath her. In the next breath she was beneath the clouds of a mad storm, yet she was unaffected by the weather.

Below her, the stormy waters of the ocean rose and fell while torrents of rain cascaded downward in slanting wind-driven sheets. She saw ships—ungainly and strange ships, long and box-like, sailing in a formation like birds flying south; their sails billowing under the strain of harsh winds, the ships rising and falling upon the waves. Powerful winds were pushing them toward their destination much faster than was natural.

On the flagship stood a tall figure in the center of the bow, surrounded by a swirling mist, arms raised and palms facing skyward. His features, obscured by the mist, seemed unaffected by the rain, as if a bubble surrounded and protected the figure.

Sounds came from his strangely shaped oval and almost round mouth yet she heard no words. Behind this figure stood hundreds of malformed beings with the shapes of men but so deformed as to be almost unrecognizable as such. Despite the storm-ravaged sea, the ships and those within them moved in a straight line. Fifteen hundred miles ahead rose the southwestern palisades of Nevaeh, their destination.

Areenna descended toward the strange figure in the lead ship. As she neared it, a wave of rotting darkness swept over her, so evil, so vile and so repugnant that even in her dream, she choked.

Then she was above it, close to it. Yet, she could see no feature through the swirling mist, only that of the shape. She willed herself to see what stood there until she knew not only what it was, but its plans as well.

She awoke that instant, sat up and hugged herself. She sucked in deep gulps of air in an effort to cast the dream vision from her mind, wanting only to have never having seen it, for she knew exactly who the vileness was—one of the Masters of the Circle of Afzal. How she knew, she could not be sure, but know it she did.

Laying back, her breathing calmed while she listened to the soothing sound of Mikaal's steady breathing, grateful for not having woken him. She would tell him in the morning, but for now, she needed to work the dream vision, replay it until she understood the full meaning of what she had seen.

Only after she relived the vision again, and slowly came to the full understanding of its meaning, was she able to fall into a restless sleep.

◇◇◇

Mikaal watched Areenna emerge from the woods. When she walked toward him, he sensed a change about her. Something had happened during the night, of what he could not ascertain. He tightened the cinch on the last kralet and went to meet Areenna near the dying embers of the fire.

Two small bowls rested on the ground. Two cups were set next to them. Tendrils of steam from the tea rose in the cold air of the morning. "Fruit and tea," he said as she approached. Her long pale hair was untied and hung below her shoulders. She wore a leather tunic with leggings. Tall boots graced her feet. However, when he stared into the green pools of her eyes, he knew something had changed.

"What is it?" he asked, handing her a cup of the hot dark tea.

She took the cup in both hands, raised it to scent the drink and blew across its surface. She took a sip before saying, "A dream…a vision. They are coming. They will be here soon."

"A foretelling? Who?"

"Not a foretelling, a vision within a dream. A Dark Master. He comes with hundreds, maybe thousands of his slaves. He comes to begin war. He comes to destroy us."

"You are certain?"

Areenna nodded. "I don't know when, but they are on the sea. He is…evil."

"Sit, eat and tell me what you saw." She spoke, taking small bites of fruit as she did.

When both the fruit and her story were finished, Mikaal said, "We must warn them."

Areenna closed her eyes and began to seek. High above them, near the top of a tall gazebow tree she found a family of craves. The male was standing guard while the female fed her chicks. She reached out to the male—perhaps an eighth the size of Gaalrie—and sent a gentle request. A few seconds later, the bird dropped to the ground before Areenna.

She smiled at the silver-tinged white bird, drew a small piece of cloth from her pocket and, in the manner she had been trained, wrote a message on the cloth and tied it to its leg. She reached out with her mind, seeking a sense of where Enaid was and a moment later, sent the crave to her.

"Your mother has just reached the border of Fainhall. The crave will find her, but we must go now. There is no more time for delay."

"Agreed. Still, we can go only as fast as the kralets."

They reached the outskirts of Lokinhold's capitol, an hour before sundown. They had ridden the entire day at a steady mile-eating pace and had stopped only to relieve themselves. During the ten hours of riding, they had discussed many things. Nevertheless, the need to find a way to reach their ultimate goal while the dark forces tracked them was paramount.

Do we warn them? Mikaal asked, using their silent means of talking. *I have been thinking about it. The warning will create fear.*

Areenna, caught off guard by his question, turned to him. *We must. They must begin preparations. War is coming. I saw such last night. If we…if Nevaeh is not prepared, all will be lost.*

You said a small fleet…they cannot carry enough fighters to overtake us.

The ships were large, meant only to carry men, weapons and food. They are but the first Mikaal. Many more will come. Tens of thousands will cross the water to us.

"You're certain?" Mikaal asked as they entered the more populated area surrounding Farg's main keep.

"As certain as I breathe. The Master wants us. He wants me…and you."

Mikaal's gray eyes narrowed. "Which is something that shall never happen."

She welcomed his comforting words but said nothing. Instead, she called to Gaalrie, who flew above them and sent her aoutem to Farg, to fly over the keep.

A few minutes later, through Gaalrie's eyes, she saw Queen Ammie standing in the courtyard, looking up at Gaalrie. The Queen, tall and thin with long flowing red hair veined with silver, waved. Beside her was a small tan Gorlon, barely older than a puppy.

When they entered the streets of Farg a short time later, they found the shops closed and the streets emptying of people. Dressed as simple travelers and wearing their cloaks for warmth, they drew few curious glances on the way to the main keep.

They passed through the gate and reached the courtyard where Queen Ammie, two stable boys and a woman-servant waited. Without a word, one of the boys took the reins of the kraals while the other went to the kralets. Mikaal stiffened slightly when the stable boy took Charka's reins but forced himself to relax. It was always hard to allow someone else to handle Charka.

"Welcome, Areenna, Prince Mikaal," the tall woman said with a head bow toward both of them.

"Thank you, My Lady." Mikaal returned the formality with a head bow of his own while Areenna stepped closer to the queen and embraced her.

"Enaid sent word of your journey. I expected you yesterday, but I knew the storm the other would delay you. The evening meal has been prepared. Let me show you to your rooms and then please join us in the dining chamber. Give Yemmat whatever you wish brought to your chambers."

Areenna and Mikaal pointed to the lead kralets, which held two woven bags near the front. With that, the queen nodded to them and started away while the servant went to the kraals. Next to her, Mikaal cast another quick glance over his shoulder toward Charka, before following the two women.

After showing Mikaal to his bedchamber, queen Ammie led Areenna to hers. There, Areenna turned to Ammie. She was about to speak when the Queen said, "I sense much anxiety in you. Why?"

Areenna closed her eyes for a moment. When she opened them, she gazed deeply into the Queen's eyes, building on the story Enaid and she had worked out. "There is much danger coming," she whispered. "Mikaal and I.... We have been sent on a mission of which I cannot speak, My Lady, but I know the Dark Ones are coming from across the sea and Nevaeh must prepare."

Ammie's eyes widened. She took in a sharp breath and said, "There are rumors flying everywhere about you. About your powers. Are they true?"

"Rumors?" Areenna asked, continuing to hold Ammie's eyes with her own. "What say they?"

"That you came away from the Island with abilities more powerful than any woman of Nevaeh. Is this true?"

Areenna digested the words, worried them through her mind and came to the only answer she could give. "I don't know. Enaid believes this is true, but I…I do not know. So much has happened since I returned from the Island I am still trying to understand it all."

"This danger from the Dark Ones after so long…. You are sure?"

"Yes," Areenna said simply.

"We will talk later."

"You must prepare King Esnal."

"I will speak with him now," she said as a knock sounded at the door. When Ammie opened it, a servant came in with Areenna's bag. "I'll leave you to change. Yemmat is at your service."

A half hour later found them seated around a long table centered within an ornate chamber. The walls, lined with colorfully woven artistic tapestries, served as pleasant backgrounds of faraway vistas. Nightmoss lit the room with a soft glow. Lokinhold's King, Esnal, sat at the head of the oval table. Queen Ammie sat on his right, and to his left was Trebor. Areenna sat next to the queen, while Mikaal sat by Trebor. Plates of Dar and vegetables had been set out, and each had glasses of wine and water. Trebor's younger brother Nahtan was visiting an outlying village and their daughter Likala was in her last year at school.

Esnal lifted his wine and took a drink. The King was large in all directions. He stood taller than most and broader, a powerful man with a large stomach and a voice to match. His brown hair, two shades darker than his skin, reached his shoulders. He sported a full beard peppered with gray. Light blue eyes sat above a prominent nose, which worked well with his size.

When he put down the wine, he turned to Areenna and said, "Ammie has told me of the reason for your visit. She says you bring word of the Dark Ones—that they are coming to Nevaeh."

Areenna glanced at Mikaal quickly before saying, "They are, and all of Nevaeh must prepare."

"To cross the open sea…Why? We drove their minions out twenty years ago. It makes no sense."

"As long as we of Nevaeh live freely, they will never stop."

"Then we will drive them out, again."

"My Lord," Areenna began, seeking the right words to make him understand. "When you, my father and the High King drove the dark forces out, their armies were but the slaves of the Dark Ones taken from the people of Nevaeh. They do not use such now. They bring with them tens of thousands of their creatures. They intend to take Nevaeh and turn it into their own darkness."

"Tens of thousands? I do not see such happening."

"Then you will end up as a slave. My father is at Fainhall as we speak, fighting the exiles from the southwestern outlands. The exiles are under the control of the Dark Ones. Prince Samot was badly injured. Do you think these exiles would have the courage to attack a dominion on their own? The Dark Ones are sending their…slaves to make forays against us. To attack and kill Nevaeh's leaders and take our women as breeding slaves."

Esnal lifted his glass and drained it. "No," he said, "I would not think they act on their own, they are not capable of such."

"There are other signs as well," Areenna said. When everyone turned to her, she went on. "Prince Darb told us of Free-Blades attacking travelers, taking their valuables and wounding and killing some. Think you they do this on their own too? Have you ever heard of such happening?"

Again, King Esnal remained silent for several breaths before speaking. When he spoke at last, his words came out slowly. "To do so makes them outlaws, even among their own kind. No dominion would seek their service. Not since Roth became High King have I heard of such happening."

"They are being controlled by the Black Sorceress, the one defeated by Roth. They know it not, but it is so."

"This is what Roth warned us of at the last council. What asks the High King of us?"

"For now," Mikaal said, "you must begin to prepare your people. Rebuild your army as quickly as possible. They will be here soon."

Esnal nodded slowly. "It shall be done." He paused thoughtfully. "You go to Welkold next?" Esnal asked.

"We do," Mikaal answered.

"Perhaps you could do us an accommodation?"

Careful, Areenna warned Mikaal silently.

"If possible, Highness."

"So cautious, like your father. It is nothing more than to let Trebor ride with you to Welkold. Despite what may be happening, there is a wedding to prepare for. Trebor is needed in Welkold for the month of betrothing."

"Of course," Areenna answered for her and Mikaal.

Trebor looked from his father to Mikaal. "We should postpone the wedding. This…danger is too great."

His silent plea to the High Prince touched her heart. She saw his words had startled Esnal and Ammie. "Is this match not one you desire?" she asked Trebor.

He shook his head vehemently. "Why would you ask? This is not an arrangement. Akassia and I…we chose each other. But I should be here to help my father."

Areenna sensed his emotions were at war within him. He wanted to stay but he wanted to be in Welkold as well. "One day you will be King here, and Akassia your queen. King Libon is young, only three years older than you. Your brother will be here to help your father. Libon will need your help to prepare his people for what is coming, do you not see this?"

With her words, everyone looked at her. She saw their faces filled with surprise at her answer, but she said nothing more. *What did I do*? She asked Mikaal silently.

The right thing. Your words were perfect.

"Areenna has spoken wisely," Ammie said, looking at Trebor. "And it unites our dominions even tighter."

"Then it is settled," King Esnal declared, "You leave in the morning with the Prince and Princess. Trebor, Mikaal, let us walk and discuss what needs to be done. Ladies, if you will allow us?"

Ammie and Areenna nodded formally. The three men stood and left the room. The moment they were gone, Ammie turned to Areenna. "Now, we go as well, to talk in my chambers. I want to know exactly what is happening, everything!"

Her stomach tightened with Queen Ammie's words.

.

XI

"I VISITED MY sister a few months ago, in Aldimor," Ammie said after the maids left the room and they relaxed on a cushioned bench beneath a large window. Moonlight filtered in as pale streaks, accenting the glow of nightmoss from the wall sconces. Fire burned in the fireplace, casting warmth through the room. She caught a tug from Gaalrie, who flew above. It was a sensation of concern. Her aoutem had picked up Areenna's tension.

The light framed Queen Ammie, surrounding her within a low haze. The queen's eyes were deep blue, and her irises wide. Areenna knew she was a woman of power, not fully as strong as her older sister Atir, Queen of Aldimor, but strong nonetheless. While the queen formed her next words, Areenna sent a thought to Mikaal. His response was immediate.

Be careful. She must not know about me.

Stay with me through this, she asked. His answer came with a rush of warmth.

"My sister told me about the time you went to the Island." On the last word, Ammie directed a probe at Areenna.

Expecting and blocking the probe effortlessly, Areenna held Ammie's eyes and slowly forced the probe back.

Without a mention of what she'd attempted, Ammie continued. "She told me of the wraiths, of the crossing to the Island and of your return from the Island. She told me how you used your abilities to destroy the wraiths. She told me something happened to you on the Island, something far more than any other woman experienced, ever. She told me you are more powerful than is any woman of power. Is this truth?"

"I don't know," Areenna whispered. She saw a flash of surprise cross the queen's face.

Ammie's shoulders stiffened. "How can you not?"

A stomach-wrenching emotion ripped through her at the queen's words. Her throat tightened and her pulse quickened. She pushed Mikaal from her, cutting their bond instantly. She was flooded with such powerful emotions she was unsure of how to control them and was afraid of what Mikaal might see.

She took in a deep breath and released the flood of emotions. "Ammie, I don't know what was given to me on the Island. I am eighteen; I have had powers for only a few years. I don't know how to find whatever it was, or if there is anything to find. What have I done to deserve this…honor? Why me?" she whispered, barely able to get the words out. Her eyes blurred and she closed them to prevent any tears from escaping.

A second later, Ammie's arms wrapped about her, the queen drawing her tight. "I'm sorry, Areenna, forgive me for pushing you so hard. The talk at the table tonight has frightened me. Another war. I…I had to know."

Areenna drew back and, ignoring the tears streaking her face. "Last night I received a vision within a dream; this will give you the truth you ask for. Will you join with me?"

When the queen nodded, Areenna placed her right hand on Ammie's chest and her left on the queen's temple. She closed her eyes and carefully opened her mind and brought forth her dream.

Ammie's sharp intake of air was loud in the silent chamber. The queen, caught in the dream, watched the ships travel upon stormy seas. When Areenna ended the stream of images, she released Ammie's mind and lowered her hands from the queen.

"Such wickedness," she said, "such horror coming to us. I understand more now, Areenna, thank you. I will do whatever is necessary." Then Ammie smiled. "Your block, it's very powerful."

"Thank you."

"I apologize, Princess. It was…rude."

"It's all right. Your sister did the same thing."

"It must be a family trait," Ammie said with a short laugh. Then her face turned serious. "How long do we have, does anyone know?"

"The ones coming now are but the first wave. There will be many more. A few months if we are lucky."

"So soon." She paused and nodded. "And you've been riding all day as well. Perhaps it's time for sleep."

"Almost," Areenna said. They rose together and started toward the door. "I must go to the parapets and to my aoutem."

"Of course." She paused at the door. "Areenna, this mission you are on to the Frozen Mountains, what is it you seek?"

"Like those powers I may or may not have, I have no answer because I know not what's there."

"It seems to always be the same for a woman; we are given gifts and must discover ourselves what they are for. Goodnight Areenna."

<><><>

Mikaal walked with Esnal and Trebor, listening to the King's preparations for calling in his people and warning them about the future.

Esnal asked not advice from the two young princes; rather, he spoke with the experience of his years and, Mikaal realized, he was adding to his son's education and to Mikaal's as well. When Esnal finished his walk, Mikaal sensed the King wanted to talk to his son privately.

"If you'll excuse me, Highness, it's been a tiring day."

Esnal turned and nodded to Mikaal. "Of that I am sure. Rest well."

"Thank you, Highness, Trebor," he nodded to the prince and left them talking. He went to the stable even as Areenna and Ammie were talking. Before he got there, he lost mental touch with Areenna. An instant before, he had sensed her sudden anxiety; now there was nothing. He tried reaching out to her, but there was only a blank space in his mind. At Charka's stall, his aoutem pushed his snout against Mikaal's chest. He melded with the kraal and took in the soothing sensations Charka washed over him. Charka's mind touch assured him Areenna was all right. If there were something wrong, the kraal would know.

When he left the stable, he was certain where Areenna would go when she finished with Ammie. The parapets and Gaalrie.

◇◇◇

I knew you would be here, she whispered into his mind when she stepped on the parapet.

As I knew you would.

"I am sorry Mikaal. I was wrong asking you to stay with me; I needed my thoughts kept to myself."

Mikaal reached up and cupped her cheek. "As long as you are safe."

She did her best to ignore the spark between them when his fingers touched her skin. "We have been hiding in Tolemac too long. There are many rumors about me floating through Nevaeh."

He lowered his hand. "I was with you then. I know. There is nothing to do about rumors. Just be prepared for whatever people ask."

When he finished speaking, a flutter of wings announced Gaalrie's arrival. The giant treygone landed smoothly on the parapet wall and Areenna went to her. Gaalrie laid her head on Areenna's shoulder in greeting. She stroked the treygone gently for a moment before the bird rose and flew off toward the woods in the North.

"She hunts," Areenna said.

"As we will soon, in the mountains. We must be careful when Trebor is with us."

"We have become good in that, these past months."

"We have," Areenna agreed. "It is but two and a half days."

"A lot can happen in two days," Mikaal said in a half-whisper.

◇◇◇

The first day and a half of travel had been smooth, the three keeping a steady pace throughout the first day, while they talked and rode. Areenna and Trebor had brought up many of the memories of their time at the school while Mikaal had listened and laughed at the stories.

When they finished their noon meal by the side of the old road to Ontan, the capital of Welkold, a warning sense caught Areenna. "Men are coming," she said.

Who? Mikaal asked silently.

She shook her head. *I know not. There are at least six.* "They are not friendly."

"Free-Blades?" Trebor asked, gripping his sword but not drawing it. His red hair splayed fan-like as he looked around.

"Possibly," Areenna whispered. "They come from the north." She sent a command to Gaalrie, who circled above and flew north. Through Gaalrie's sharp eyes, she saw the men. There were seven, not six. Each was dressed and armed as a free-blade. They were on foot.

"There are seven. They come straight toward us on this road. Trebor, do not refer to Mikaal as prince."

Trebor's eyes flicked from Areenna to Mikaal. He nodded. "Of course I can't hide who I am." He ran a hand down his chest, emphasizing the royal emblem of Lokinhold on his tunic. His cloak bore the same emblem as well.

"I am your guard, Areenna, your servant," Mikaal said.

"I understand."

Areenna wrapped her cloak about her, hiding both dagger and sword. Then she closed her eyes and sent her thoughts to Gaalrie, who flew high above the band of Free-Blades. They were a quarter mile away and walking swiftly toward them.

Mikaal turned and repacked the supply bag they'd opened for the meal and tied it to a kralet. He removed his cloak and placed it across the kralet's back. He walked to the other two, drawing and re-sheathing his sword several times to make certain it moved freely—the cold had a way of making metal stick in its scabbard and cause a delay in drawing the weapon. He turned his back to Trebor and closed his eyes. An instant later, he saw through Gaalrie's eyes. The Free-Blades were about to crest the rise ahead.

"Areenna, play your part, bring Hero and Trebor's kraal to us."

"They are here," Areenna said as the first of the men appeared on the rise. "Be ready." Then she turned and went to the kraals as Mikaal had asked.

It took the Free-Blades only another few minutes to reach them. As they came closer, Mikaal studied them. The seven were rugged men, tall and strong, wearing simple leather tunics beneath light metal torso armor. Each carried a sword and a knife at their hips; three had bows slung over their shoulders. Two worn-looking kralets trailed with their supplies and equipment.

When the first reached Mikaal, he sized him up and nodded. "A good day to you," he said simply.

"And to you, Free-Blade."

"I am Leinad, leader of this small band," he said in introduction and offered his arm in the traditional greeting of men.

Mikaal accepted the greeting and placed his hand on the other's arm. Leinad gripped Mikaal's forearm. "I am Siwel, guard to Prince Trebor of Welkold."

Releasing Mikaal's arm, the free-blade turned to Trebor. "My Lord," he said with a head bow. He looked over Trebor's shoulder to where Areenna stood with the two kraals but said nothing.

"You are pledged to a dominion?" Mikaal asked.

"We are on our way to Llawnroc where we have been called."

"A long distance yet to go," Mikaal said, sensing the lie easily.

"True, but a worthwhile venture. You go to Ontan?"

"We do," Mikaal responded.

"Then I wish you good speed. There is a fine place to camp a half day north; clear water and strong trees to break the night winds."

"My thanks for the information. We will make use of it."

"A good day," Leinad offered and started forward with another head bow to Trebor and a furtive glance at Areenna as he led his men past them.

He is already making plans to follow us. We must be careful.

And watchful, Mikaal added to their silent conversation. *He has his eyes on you.*

"That went well," Trebor said with a relieved sigh.

"With luck," Mikaal responded as he called Charka to him. "Let us put distance between them and ourselves."

◇◇◇

An hour before sunset found the three at the exact spot the leader of which the Free-Blades had spoken. "This is where they want us," Mikaal said.

"Yes, it would be perfect. The trees are thick enough to hide them until they are ready," Trebor said.

Areenna gazed around, studying the trees, the ground and the stream flowing through the left side of the grove. "It is a peaceful place, good to lull one into a sense of security."

"Let the kralets graze. We will secure them near us after dark. It will be safer that way. We don't want them stolen.

"I think they want to steal more than the kralets," Areenna said, looking at Trebor.

"Me? Why would they want me?" the young prince asked, startled.

"Ransom," Mikaal said simply.

"They would not be so stupid," Trebor said.

Mikaal studied the prince for a moment. "They are Free-Blades, mercenaries without dominion. They care not for dominion nor how we live. They do what they want, not what is right."

They are under the influence of the Black Witch, Areenna added to Mikaal.

Mikaal did not respond to Areenna's thought; instead, he freed Charka of the saddle and let him graze. Behind him, the other animals did the same.

"See if there is game nearby," Mikaal asked Areenna.

Areenna sent a thought to Gaalrie, who wheeled above them and began to search. The three set up their camp, erecting two lean-tos and placing their sleeping silks within.

Areenna set her white bow and the quiver against the inside slant of the lean-to, to be easily available when needed. Gaalrie's call came when she left the lean-to. Closing her eyes, she joined the treygone and saw a small wild klirt, pushing its snout through the ground hunting for shrooms.

"There is a klirt to the southwest, small enough for the three of us. It's about a quarter mile away."

Mikaal turned and smiled. "Perfect. Trebor, keep a watchful eye out. Areenna, your bow?"

I can do it.

I need you here in case they come early, he replied in their way.

Areenna retrieved the bow and a single arrow. When she handed it to him, he raised his eyebrows at the arrow.

"I could do it in a single shot."

"I know. But that isn't the issue, is it?"

Trebor watched them from a short distance, puzzled by their words. "If it's a problem, I will hunt it."

They turned and said, "No."

Trebor frowned, shaking his head when Areenna and Mikaal laughed. Then, without a word, Mikaal walked in the direction of the klirt.

When he disappeared through the surrounding gazebow trees, Trebor said to Areenna. "Are you in love with him?"

Her jaw dropped. "Why would you think such?"

He shrugged, eloquently. "I don't think it, I see it…I hear it. The two of you talk as if you have been together…forever. Does he feel the same?"

"Does it matter?" she snapped.

"I'm sorry, Areenna, I did not mean to pry."

"No," she whispered, "you and I have been friends for a long time, Trebor. I...I'm just sensitive to it. He will be High King one day, and I am destined to rule Freemorn. The High King cannot be farther guardian to another dominion."

"Why is that?" Trebor asked. "It doesn't seem to make much sense. There has been but one High King. There is no tradition, no rule about such."

"No, there is not, but I sense it will go badly with the other dominions if such happens."

"I do not share that, and Roth is still young and strong. He has many years ahead of him—"

"—Depending on what comes," Areenna cut in.

Trebor nodded. "Yes. But," he said, pausing for a moment before saying, "Does Mikaal feel the same as you about that?"

Areenna shrugged. "I sense he does, but we don't speak of it. We have too much to face without dwelling on it."

"We are, you and I, the same age. Yet, I think I know more about emotion than you. I have loved Akassia since we were together at school. I know how I feel and I know how she feels, and I see that you and Mikaal are no different."

“You are sweet, Trebor, and you have grown into a good man, but what Mikaal and I face in the time ahead prevents anything from happening between us. Perhaps when it is over…”

Trebor reached out and took her hand. He held it tight. “I understand, Areenna.”

When he released her hand, she smiled at him. “Not a word.”

“Of course not. I will gather wood for the fire.”

“Stay close,” she warned.

By the time Mikaal returned with the klirt and prepared it for cooking, the fire had burned down to a cooking glow and they set the klirt above it. While it cooked, Mikaal walked the boundaries of the grove, looking for the various ways the Free-Blades would use. Not that he was worried about the renegade surprising them; Gaalrie and Charka would sense their coming long before they attacked. He and Areenna would as well.

Yet, worry tugged at him. His concern was for Trebor. The focus of the attack would be to capture the prince. They would not expect Areenna, as a servant girl, to play any part in it. Mikaal knew that would be their downfall. Protecting Trebor was his ultimate responsibility; the Prince was but one man and would have no chance against two or three experienced Free-Blades. Using his abilities around Trebor was not an option either.

He lost track of time walking through the trees, looking at the distances between the boles, charting the pathways in his mind until Areenna’s call to return broke into his thoughts. Suddenly, heat spread through his stomach. He started back and froze as a vision crossed his eyes. He saw the Free-Blades moving through the trees. The moon was already high in the sky above as he watched them come noiselessly through the grove of trees. His vision faded and he knew his grandmother had been right. His ability of foretelling came when needed.

He gazed skyward. The moon had not risen; the sky was dark but not black. The stars were pinpoints of pale light waiting patiently to show their true brightness. It was in that moment when he knew the seven would come just after midnight.

XII

GAALRIE'S WARNING CAME just as Areenna and Mikaal sensed the Free-Blades approach. From behind, Charka called out with the low-pitched cry of a kraal. "They come," Areenna said aloud for Trebor's benefit.

She joined with Gaalrie and watched the men slip into the trees. Their weapons were at the ready and their faces determined. In the lean-tos, each of the three had their swords lying next to them. Areenna and Mikaal wore the special armor Roth had made for them, while Trebor wore a leather-quilted vest.

When the Free-Blades disappeared from Gaalrie's sight, Areenna called her treygone to circle above the clearing. Her aoutem flew up and over and began circling. The instant the first of the men came through the woods, the bird dipped lower, floating on the currents and holding her position as if she were not moving.

Areenna watched and as she did, Mikaal joined with her. The Free-Blades moved noiselessly through the trees. When they emerged, there were only six. "Six only," Mikaal whispered, "One is in the trees. Be watchful."

Trebor stirred. He grasped his sword and started to rise.

"Not yet," Areenna whispered. "Wait."

Areenna called up her powers, which had already begun to stir. Mikaal, lying next to her, did the same. The burning within the depths of his insides spread like fire through his body. Time slowed; seconds became minutes until, finally, Mikaal said, "Now."

The three rose quickly, swords in hand, stepping out of the lean-tos. The six men stood in the light of the dying campfire. The leader, his face half-hidden by his helmet, shouted, "Take the Prince and the woman. Kill the guardsman."

The six surrounded them, their swords held high. They moved inward. In that instant, Mikaal saw a flash of what was to come. From his left, sitting on a branch of the tallest gazebow tree, the seventh man was drawing his bow back.

Seconds later, the man released his arrow. Prepared, his power soaring through him, Mikaal lifted his left palm and, as the arrow sped toward him, called up his own powers and deflected it. The arrow veered to his left. One of the Free-Blades cried out when the arrow buried itself in his neck. Blood spurted in pulsing jets from the wound and the man fell.

Areenna sent a command to Gaalrie to attack the archer and hefted her sword to face the oncoming men.

"Now!" the leader shouted. The five charged.

Mikaal faced the leader, who charged with a mad cry. Their blades met with a loud clash and then they separated. Behind him, he sensed a second man about to strike. He ducked, spun, and with both hands on the sword, sliced across the man's chest. His armor split and blood gushed from his chest as he fell. Whirling his sword in a figure eight, Mikaal turned back to the leader and struck. The man deflected his blade. They stepped back and circled each other.

Behind him, another man screamed and he knew Areenna had taken the man down. He concentrated on the Free-Blade before him, attacking swiftly, seeking an opening while listening to the sounds of the fighting around him. The man was a good swordsman and defended well against Mikaal's attack.

From the trees came a scream and the sound of a body falling through the branches. A second scream of pain followed the loud cry of a treygone. The leader hesitated momentarily before charging Mikaal.

Areenna had taken out one Blade, but the other was charging her, using strokes that blurred before her eyes. To her right, Trebor fought the fifth man, who was bigger and heavier than Trebor and the Prince was losing ground quickly.

Areenna called forth her powers and as they raged through her, drew up a ball of energy within her hand and shot it at the man before her. It hit him hard, knocking him back a dozen feet where he lay unmoving.

She ran to where Trebor back-stepped under a deluge of blows he was barely able to turn away. She stepped to his side and together they attacked the man. They drove him back until he made one mistake and Trebor reached past his guard, putting the blade through the man's leather armor, piercing the thick leather as if it were merely skin.

When the free-blade fell, they both turned to Mikaal. The two men were circling each other again, slowly, carefully. Then Mikaal feinted and struck. The Free-Blade barely countered and when their blades met, the man staggered back but did not go down. Again, they circled each other.

"Your men are lost," Mikaal told him. "This is over. Take your life and go."

He hesitated, as if thinking over the offer. Then, strangely, his face changed. His body stiffened and his eyes turned dark. A mist floated out from his skin and his lips turned into a smile.

Areenna, watching what was happening reacted instantly. *It is she! She possesses him!* A burst of blue light from the palms of her hands followed her silent warning to Mikaal. It struck the man, but did not affect him. Laughing, he turned to Areenna and raised his hands. "You think yourself more but you are still a child!"

Mikaal reacted instinctively. A split second after the man lifted his hands, Mikaal dropped his sword and palms forward, released the weapon Areenna had gifted him. Two beams of light erupted from his palms and shot straight at the man. The light enveloped the free-blade leader and exploded. When the light died, the man lay dead, his body twisted unnaturally, thirty feet distant.

Trebor! Mikaal and Areenna turned at the same instant and saw the prince staring at them, his face filled with disbelief. *I had no choice,* was Mikaal's thought to Areenna. *I tried not to use my ability.*

I know. This is bad.

"Trebor," Mikaal called to the prince.

Trebor shook his head as if trying to clear it. "How is this possible?" he half-whispered.

"This isn't the place to discuss it," Areenna said, her voice low and gentle as she swept her hand gesturing to the unmoving bodies.

"This is the very place," Trebor stated. "How is this possible? How can you make magic?" he asked Mikaal.

"The archer is in the woods. Come with me to check on him. We will talk."

His eyes filled with question, his face tense with suspicion.

"Go with Mikaal, he will explain everything. Then we'll talk." As she finished, she pushed a sense of calm to him and saw his facial muscles ease, a moment before he nodded.

Reluctantly, Trebor went with Mikaal. As they walked toward the woods, she went to the man she had last fought to see if he still lived. When she knelt next to him, she saw the rise and fall of his chest.

Standing, she went to the kralets and took down a coil of rope. She cut enough to tie his hands and feet. When she finished, she checked the others. All were dead. She returned to the survivor and, drawing up all her strength, dragged him to where the kralets stood. With another piece of rope, she tied him to the same stake as the pack animals.

She finished just as Mikaal and Trebor returned, carrying the unconscious archer. "He lives. His leg is broken."

"One lives. He is tied by the kralets."

Mikaal studied their attackers. "We need to move the bodies away."

"We should leave," Areenna countered.

"And go where? It is safer here. Trebor, work with me."

They took the archer to where the other one lay and tied him as well. Then Areenna sent Trebor off for a strong and straight branch for the man's leg. While he was gone, Mikaal and Areenna went to the bodies and dragged them away.

What did you tell him?

What he needed to hear. I told him some truth, some falsehoods. I explained how my mother charged me to accompany you to the Island, to protect you. When you went to the Island, I accompanied you to the far landing. While I waited for your return, the Black Witch attacked me. Before she could kill me, something from the Island stopped her and, whatever saved me, whatever force lives on the Island, changed me. When we left the Island, I discovered I had a power.

He believed this?

He seems to. Perhaps he wants to, I don't know, but we must be sure he speaks nothing of this night.

Not now. The morning will be a better time.

In this, I defer to you. His eyes raced across her face, seeking something within her.

A half hour later, with the archer still unconscious but his leg splinted, Areenna pushed calming energy to Trebor. With the area around their lean-tos cleaned of the bodies, the three travelers returned to their sleeping silks. The prisoners lay unmoving by the kralets.

Above them, on a branch close enough for Areenna to see her perched Gaalrie. Charka, still uneasy after the battle, rested next to the lean-to, his head against the silks. Long after Mikaal and Trebor had fallen to sleep, Areenna lay awake; worrying about how to be sure Trebor would not speak about Mikaal's powers.

Thankfully, all he'd seen was the last battle. He had not realized that Mikaal had deflected the arrow. If he had, Mikaal's explanation would have sounded false. *What to say? How to say it?* Those were her last thoughts before sleep claimed her.

<><><>

An hour before dawn, Charka woke Mikaal with a mind picture of the unhurt Blade trying to free himself. He rose silently, slipped from the lean-to with his knife and went over to the man who he found contorted, trying to untie his feet with his hands by bending his body backwards like an inverted bow.

"Stop. It's useless."

The man froze at the sound of Mikaal's voice. He pulled his legs from under him and turned to face the prince. His eyes were hard, his mouth pulled tight. "Why keep us alive? What will you have of me?"

"You seek death?"

"I am not afraid of it."

"Such is more than obvious for you attacked us without knowing us. Why?"

"Why not? What fight could a single guardsman, a woman and a boy prince put against the seven of us?"

"You found not what you expected, eh?"

The man shook his head. "A sorceress, no."

"Talk to me truthfully and I will let you free when we leave."

"And I am to believe that?" the Free-Blade asked sarcastically.

"You have the word of Mikaal of Tolemac, son of Roth, High King of Nevaeh."

The man's eyes widened in surprise. Then they narrowed. "Why release me?"

"I bargain for information, but if you prefer..." Mikaal drew his knife.

The man's eyes locked on the blade. "All right," he whispered.

"Why did you and the others turn renegade and leave the Free-Blades?"

"What does it matter?"

"It matters," Mikaal said, "much more than you know. Why?"

The man shrugged. "There was something wrong with our Free-Blade company. I don't know what, but it was wrong."

He sent a thought to Areenna to waken her so she would be a part of this. *I have been here,* came her replying thought.

I felt you not.

I did not want you to be disturbed.

"Wrong in what way?" he asked the man.

"I don't know. All I know was one day I was with them, the next day there were seven of us on our own. We have been roaming ever since, taking what we could, where we could."

"Why attack us? What would we have?"

"The prince."

"To what purpose? You would never survive King Esnal and his men."

The man shook his head. "You would not believe me."

"Try me."

"All I can tell you is that it seemed the right thing, to take the prince...and I had to do so. The others were of the same mind."

"The purpose? Feeling right is not a purpose."

The man's eyes seem to be pleading for understanding. Then they changed. They became hard and opaque, as had the eyes of the leader before he died. Smoke rose from the ropes on his wrists and ankles and a moment later the bonds fell free.

Instantly, Areenna's energy flowed into him and he exhaled slowly and allowed her through. As her energy surged, it spread across to the man. His eyes cleared and he shook his head. He stared at Mikaal as if he had never seen him before.

"What…"

"Who are you?" Mikaal asked.

"I am Nivram of Marlot's Free-Blades." His voice was different from moments before. His tone was smoother, the sound higher.

"Do you remember what happened last night?" Areenna asked from behind Mikaal. She stepped next to him and knelt. "Do you?"

The man nodded. "I remember it, but I… It was not me. I don't understand."

Mikaal turned to Areenna. "It is like the man you told me of in the Blue Desert. The one *she* had taken over."

"Yes," she replied. "Do you remember anything of the day you left the Free-Blades?"

He nodded. "I remember feeling that I had something important to do and they were holding me back."

"What was so important?" Areenna asked.

"To capture him," he said, nodding toward the lean-to where Trebor slept.

"To take Prince Trebor?"

He shook his head. "To take any Prince or King if I could. All of us had to do this."

She is trying to weaken Nevaeh for the benefit of her Masters, Areenna told Mikaal.

I see that. "Nivram, you may not understand this but the darkness, the Dark Ones have been using you. If I release you, will you return to your Free-Blades?"

The man nodded slowly.

"There is a war coming. Nevaeh will need everyone. I charge you with that message to your commander. Make him understand the words come from the High King Roth, Prince Mikaal and Areenna of Freemorn, daughter of King Nosaj. Can you do that?"

"I will try."

Areenna leaned toward him. "Your mind, the way you thought things were wrong with the Free-Blades, a sorceress with dark powers did that to you. She was controlling you. I can help protect you from the Dark Ones. Will you allow it?"

A small light of understanding built on his face. "You can stop them?"

"From taking you again, yes."

"I am willing."

She reached out with both hands and put one to each side of his head. When she released him, the block was firmly in place. Then she turned to the man lying next to them and saw his eyes were open. "You have heard everything?"

The man nodded. "Are you willing to be protected?" When he nodded again, she repeated the blocking on the injured man but offered no healing. There was no time.

"We leave at dawn. You are free. Bury your fellows. They deserve not to become food for the danglores," Mikaal said, looking up at the large carrion-eating birds circling above, waiting patiently for the people below to leave so they could feed.

"I shall do so," the man promised.

"You have been tied all night. Relieve yourself, drink some water and do what you have promised. Help your comrade as well."

"Thank you, My Lord, My Lady, I will keep my word."

"I am certain you will, Nivram," Areenna replied.

She and Mikaal rose together and returned to the lean-to where they saw Trebor awake and watching. When they reached him, he raised his brows in question. "Tell him while I start to break camp," Mikaal said. "We eat as we ride. I need to be away from this place."

XIII

THE COLD MOUNTAIN air washed across their faces. After leaving the campsite, they had climbed steadily into the higher mountains of Welkold. The temperature dropped with each mile traveled. All three wore their heavier cloaks. Trebor's was thick and quilted; Mikaal and Areenna wore their rabt fur cloaks.

Two hours earlier, Areenna had sent Gaalrie to Akassia, letting the Princess know of their arrival. They had talked throughout the morning, explaining more to Trebor about what Nevaeh would be facing and deflecting questions about Mikaal.

As noon approached, and with less than an hour's ride before they reached Ontan, Welkold's capital, Areenna knew it was time to speak to Trebor about Mikaal's magic. She glanced at the young prince, who was the same age as she, and wondered why she felt so much older.

"Trebor, we must talk about last night."

He turned to her, a question on his face. "What more is there to say?"

"You understand nothing of what you witnessed of Mikaal can be told, do you not?"

He shook his head slowly. "No. Why?"

"Think of how it affected you when you realized Mikaal had a woman's ability. What was your first reaction?"

His eyes locked on hers. "At first I could not believe my eyes. When I realized what I had seen was real, my first thought was of dark magic. No man can have a woman's magic."

"You know Mikaal's gift is not of the dark powers now, yes?"

"Yes. I...." He shook his head; his eyes were troubled. "It seems wrong somehow."

"I know it seems that way, which is why no mention can be made. The people of Nevaeh will not understand, not at first. All they will see is dark magic. They will cast Mikaal out, and by doing so weaken Nevaeh. If this happens, Nevaeh will be lost to the Dark Ones."

"You are so certain?" Trebor asked, his eyes laden with doubt.

"As certain as my ability to breathe. Do you trust me?"

"Of course," Trebor responded. "I have known you all my life."

"Then you must believe I would not ask this of you if it were not so important. Trebor, when we...when I was on the Island, the forces there, the powers that give women their magic charged me with a mission, and they charged Mikaal the same. The ability they gave him was to help protect Nevaeh and me. We go to do our best to defend all our people from what is coming. But if Mikaal's ability to do magic is known, we will not complete our task and..."

Trebor turned from Areenna to glance at Mikaal, and then he looked straight ahead. Areenna sensed his conflicting emotions and remained silent.

Mikaal, slightly ahead of them, stayed silent as well, intuitively knowing it had to be Areenna, who convinced Trebor of the need for his silence. He also understood the prince had to be convinced. If they forced him to keep the secret through their abilities, they would be no better than the Dark Ones who sought to dominate Nevaeh.

Several minutes later, Trebor turned back to Areenna. "You have my pledge. I will speak nothing of what I witnessed."

"Thank you." A weight lifted from her shoulders.

Watching them, Mikaal heard Trebor's promise but sensed the young man's troubling thoughts of Mikaal and the unnatural gift he had seen at work during the fight.

A half hour later, the top of the center tower of Ontan's keep came into view. It was a magnificent sight. Nestled high in the mountains, the capital of Welkold sat on a wide plateau, the clouds so low their white trailing tendrils surrounded the keep's high tower. A ring of snow-capped mountains— undulating slopes filled with tall green pines, slumbering gazebow trees and the most important trees on Nevaeh, the acont tree, whose wood was the rarest and valued above all, encircled

Ontan. The only passage through the protective mountains was this very road.

Unlike the other dominions of Nevaeh, Welkold had no outer wall for defense. The mountains were barrier enough. The keep itself had a high wall, as did all castle keeps. Surrounding the keep wall was a ring of shops where merchants sold and traded their goods. Across from them were the stands of the farmers. Further back from the merchant shops, and in concentric rings, were the homes of the citizens of Welkold. Far from Ontan, at the base of the mountains next to a fast-flowing river, spread the warehouses and mills of the wood merchants.

Welkold was a trading dominion. They bartered wood, lumber and game for whatever the dominion needed. The wood of Welkold was the strongest and best in Nevaeh for the acont tree only grew in the local mountains.

High above them and directly overhead, Gaalrie soared on warm currents of mountain air while Areenna watched through her eyes. A few moments later she saw herself, Mikaal and Trebor—three small spots on the road.

"Go," she told the giant treygone and built a mind picture of Gaalrie flying over Ontan.

The bird dove downward for hundreds of feet before straightening and flying toward Ontan. Still melded with her aoutem, Areenna watched the road below. Halfway to the keep, the road grew busy with people going to and from the capital. Smoke filtered upward from hundreds of chimneys and life abounded.

While Gaalrie circled the keep, Areenna noticed there was much activity in the courtyards. Soldiers were at their duties, and the staff of the keep was hard at work. In the center courtyard, Areenna saw Akassia walking with another woman. The Princess paused, smiled and waved to Gaalrie, who dipped once before returning to the road and Areenna.

"Akassia knows we are near," she said aloud. In reaction, Trebor pushed his kraal slightly faster. Areenna smiled.

A quarter hour later, they passed through the keep's main gate, where both Akassia and King Lebon waited. Dismounting, Areenna drew Akassia into an embrace and Mikaal greeted the King with a bow and a gripped arm. Trebor did the same.

Stepping back, Areenna studied Akassia. It had been a year since she had last seen her. In that year, her friend had become a beautiful woman. Thick wavy black hair flowed halfway down her back; her face, which had been unusually thin, had filled out. Her deep copper skin glowed with life. The umber eyes set beneath narrow arching brows had matured to womanhood.

The stable hands came to take the kralets and the kraals to the stable, and the three followed Lebon and his sister into the keep, and to an already prepared chamber where platters of food and pitchers of wine and water awaited.

Seated, Libon turned to Mikaal. "How long will you stay?"

"The night only," Mikaal responded. "We have considerable distance to cover and not much time. I wish it were not so. It has been a while since I spent time in Ontan." Mikaal paused for a moment. "We grieved on the passing of your mother. She was a powerful woman and a good queen."

He watched the young King as he spoke. Libon appeared the same as he had at the council meeting in Tolemac, a little more than a half-year before. He was tall and reed thin, with the same copper skin as his sister and identical black wavy hair. The only change to his face were new lines at the corners of his eyes. Being King matured one quickly.

"We thank you," Libon said. "We miss her counsel, my sister and I."

"I understand, Highness," Mikaal responded.

"The messages we have received from your father, he is certain of what is happening?"

"Sadly, yes. The Dark Ones are preparing for war. They use whatever minions they can find to disrupt life in Nevaeh, and they are coming from across the sea. Have you started preparing your people?"

"I have, and I've also given instruction to the merchants for weapons. Arrows and spears from acont trees will be made, not just for us, but as much as we can produce for where they are needed."

"You are generous, Highness," Areenna said.

"I do only what I know my mother and father would have done. We have always stood with Nevaeh. We shall continue to do so as long as I am King. Now tell me more of this journey you take."

Mikaal exchanged glances with Areenna before saying; "When Princess Areenna went to the east, to the Island, at her time of the woman's calling she was—" he searched for the right words. "—charged with mission to the Frozen Mountains."

"Charged with a mission? By whom?" Libon asked, looking from Mikaal to Areenna to Akassia, his brows pulling together in question.

"We are…women are called to the east when it is their time to learn if their abilities will remain the same or grow. There are ancient powers on the Island. It was these powers that charged me with this responsibility," Areenna said in a low voice. "These powers are trying to save Nevaeh from the Dark Masters across the sea."

While she spoke, a burning built within her. When she stopped speaking, she sought out its source and realized it was Akassia. She glanced at the girl, who nodded imperceptibly.

Libon exhaled softly. "Then we must make the most of your time here. We must talk more of the preparations necessary. Trebor, you will join us?"

Trebor drew his eyes from Akassia and nodded. "Of course, Highness."

Libon smiled at him. "There will be much time to spend with my sister." His smile widened and he added, "Many years."

When they finished their meal, Libon took Mikaal and Trebor to the King's administration chamber, leaving Akassia and Areenna alone. When the voices of the men faded away, Areenna asked, "What bothers you?"

The young Princess reached across the table to grasp Areenna's hands. She sighed softly. "It has been hard, these past months since mother's death. There are no women of strong power, and I feel alone."

"I understand," she said, giving her friend's hands a gentle squeeze. "It was the same for me after my mother… Akassia, it will get better. You will soon be in Lokinhold and have Ammie to work with you."

Akassia nodded. "But not until Libon marries. I cannot leave him without advisor or my powers, as weak and untested as they are."

"Sanna of Kashold has grown strong. She will be a good advisor, as you will be to Trebor."

Akassia smiled. "Was it so short a time ago when we were in the school? It seems longer somehow. I remember how you and I would play in the trees behind the school, go exploring the caves nearby and Master Thrumweld would come to chase us back inside. It was a time I hold close."

"And I," admitted Areenna. Of all the children at the school, all the sons and daughters of the ten dominions of Nevaeh, she and Akassia had shared many adventures, some of which had landed them in trouble. "It has been only a few years since school; but, yes, it feels like a very long time since we were there," Areenna admitted thinking how her life had changed in the past six months.

"Areenna, I… I have been having dreams, visions I think."

Looking into the troubled girl's eyes, Areenna sensed fear coming from her. "What visions?"

"They started about… ten days ago. At first I thought them only disturbing dreams, but meaningless. Anxiety perhaps about the coming bonding with Trebor, but they kept coming, stronger and clearer each night. Last night was the strongest and I have been unable to understand it."

"Tell me."

"I… It is hard to speak about this. It seems not real."

Areenna held Akassia's trembling hands. "Will you join with me; show me instead of speaking the words?"

The Princess's eyes widened into deep brown islands surrounded by pure white. "You can do so, now?"

"I can."

"Then you have my permission."

Areenna's hands tightened around Akassia's and she closed her eyes. "Think of the visions, and bring them into your mind."

Akassia brought out the vision and Areenna was suddenly watching everything as if it were happening to her. The vision began with a vista of open grasslands, the blades of grass weaving at the whims of the breezes. She moved forward, riding a kraal and covering huge distances. A short time later, the kraal drew to a halt, and she saw before her the wastelands of the east, the barren brown gravel with its odd vegetation growing randomly in all directions.

The vision carried her onward and all too soon she was in the old ruins, the rusting metal and destroyed bricks of the past as clear and present as when she had been there. She moved forward again. Above her flew a traimore, which she realized was Akassia's aoutem. Smaller by a third than a treygone, the swift flying bird was a skilled hunter.

She could hear the scuttling of the strange and deformed creatures, who lived within the ancient ruins and pushed the vision kraal faster until she was free and on the black surface of the road leading to the landing.

When she broke free of Akassia's thoughts, she exhaled slowly and favored her friend with a soft smile. "Ease your mind. This is nothing of the Dark Forces. It is your summoning to the Island. What you saw was the way to go. The path you must ride to reach the Landing and cross to the Island. They call you…"

Akassia blinked. "Mother told me this would happen, I…I am not prepared. And why now, just when Trebor comes for the betrothal period?"

"There is no set way of this. Every woman is different. When you are called, there are but two choices: go to the Island and become who you are meant to be; or, give up the abilities you have not yet discovered."

"I could not do such to Trebor. He needs a strong woman to rule Lokinhold."

"Akassia, the time coming is filled with trouble. The dark forces, the Masters controlling them, are coming to Nevaeh. You are being called because of what is happening, I feel it deep inside myself," she said and realized another truth. "Every woman of power will be needed to protect and save Nevaeh. You are one of such, I know this!"

Akassia studied a painting of her mother and father, which hung on the far wall. Several long seconds later, she turned back to Areenna. "You are right. I will go. I just hope I shall be able to return."

"You will—" Her words cut off as her mind twisted and left the chamber. She saw the Island as clearly, as if she were there. She saw Akassia walking the same streets she had trod. She even saw her face the black half-woman, the speaker for the eight, and watched as she passed the first test. Suddenly, she was back in the chamber, her mind once again her own.

Releasing Akassia's hands, she smiled again. "You will return. You and the powers to be gifted are needed."

"Can you talk about what it was like there?"

"I cannot. Each woman must experience the Island for herself. That is important. Just be watchful, ever alert. And be open."

They fell a silent for moment. When she spoke again, it was in a low voice. "You must go to Enaid, in Tolemac. She will explain how you are to proceed to the Island. There will be instructions you must follow, things you must do before you reach the Island. Take Trebor with you to Tolemac. When you leave Tolemac, he should return here, to Ontan, to help your brother and await your return."

Akassia nodded. "It shall be done as you say. I will begin preparations. There is much to do before I go."

"No. You must leave soon, tomorrow even. There is no time to waste. Have you a messenger to send to Enaid?"

"We keep craves on the tower."

"Good. Let us go and do this."

"Why is this happening now?"

"Because you are needed. Akassia, I think not that you will be alone in this. I think many who will be true women of power are being called."

"Because of the Dark Forces?"

There was no reason to answer the Princess. All Areenna had to do was look at her.

XIV

ALONE FOR THE first time that day, Areenna and Mikaal stood on the wide parapets of Ontan's keep, thirty feet below the high tower. Gaalrie rested on the stone ledge of the parapet wall, her eyes locked on Areenna. "It has been a strange day. A good one too," Areenna said as she reached out to stroke Gaalrie's triangular head. On the horizon, the sun descended behind the tall snowcapped peaks.

"That it has," admitted Mikaal. "Libon will be a strong King. He has grown much since his mother's passing. He took us to the warehouses where they produce their weapons. He may be young, but he is smart. He requested only half of each warehouse be used for weapon making and storage. The other half to continue as usual."

"Wise. Preparing for something that has not happened in two decades will not sit easily with the people, not without proof. There is something else," she said, looking directly at him. "Akassia has been called."

"Called?" he began before understanding came. "To the Island? Now?"

"Now. I think too, there will be more. I sent a message to your mother, asking her to prepare Akassia as she did for me. I also told her I sensed Akassia was but the first of many."

"The Eight are preparing as well." A picture of the eight Black Sorceresses, half-woman half-snuck, rose in his mind. "They call all whom they believe will be have help."

"Yes, I see it so. I told her to take Trebor with her to Tolemac but advised her to have him return here, not home."

"Trebor will be a great help to Libon, but it leaves Welkold without a king advisor or a woman of power to be at Libon's side. This can be a danger should *she* seek him out."

"Is he not bound to Sanna of Kashold?"

"He is, but the bonding is not for six months and betrothal is not set."

"Does that matter right now? Kashold has Queen Kali, who has great strength and much experience. I was told she stood with Enaid and my mother in many battles."

"We will talk with Libon later."

Do you still feel the presence following us?

At the instant of his mind touch, a flow of warmth rushed through her. She raised her arm, extended her hand and fingers and gently stroked his cheek. The strength of his willpower, when he did not cover her hand, as he so desperately wanted to do, made her emotions tug at her heart. Hesitantly, she lowered her hand.

I feel it still, distant, but it is there.

We have to find a way to throw it off our trail.

We will find a way, she promised.

"I know. Come, we should prepare for our last meal of real food before we leave."

Areenna shook her head. "How can you eat so much? I still feel the afternoon meal within me."

"Trust me, My Princess; you will regret not eating tonight. Tomorrow we head to the Frozen Mountains."

She breathed deeply and exhaled slowly. The thought makes me even less hungry."

<><><>

The cavern walls flickered with the light and shadow of the ever-present fire. Sitting before the flames, bent over a bowl of liquid, the Black Sorceress watched the surface vibrate with the force of pressure *she* exerted upon it as *she* called up the image of the spirit *she* had sent after them.

Behind her, outside the opening of the cavern, waves crashed upon the rocky walls of the palisades. The sun was down, the pitch black of night cast its deep spell over the entire southern coastline while *she* pushed harder and harder until *she* finally broke through the night and reached it.

Her grimace almost passed for a smile; peeking out from behind taut lips, three remaining teeth gleamed black in the firelight, but there was no one to see them.

She pushed her mind toward the emptiness hanging among the trees, miles outside of Ontan, and joined with the spirit's presence. *She* issued a command to keep following, closed her thoughts and withdrew. *She* laughed; the sound, low and unpleasant, echoed emptily against the rock walls.

It was just as *she had* expected. The two were at the keep. *She* would not lose them, they would never know. It was better this way. The useless, weak-minded men, who had tried to take them and had failed, had only added to her need to keep track of the two. When the time was right, she would take them for her Masters.

She stared deep into the bowl, watching the way the liquid shimmered in the firelight. Then *she* spoke, her voice rising and falling in waves of meaningless sounds. The water whirled, circling within the bowl and spinning madly until it exploded in all directions. The instant the water sprayed from the bowl, a vision rose before her. *She* saw the two, the child of Roth and the woman-child who had defeated her at the Island. *She* saw them riding upon kraals, moving through the deserted badlands, the last band of brown scorched earth before the rise of the Frozen Mountains.

When the vision faded, a low guttural twisting groan issued from between her lips, and *she* knew what *she* must do next. Their crossing was an opportunity to stop them from reaching the Frozen Mountains.

Standing and moving in her crab-like hobbling way, *she* prepared the necessary things to create the destruction of the two who dared defy her Masters. Within her mind, pictures of strangely distorted animals, gorlon-like but not gorlon rose in her mind. Larger than gorlons, with long fur and sharp faces, their mouths were filled with huge fangs and razor-sharp teeth. *She* would not let them kill the two…perhaps *she* would injure them, immobilize them for her Masters.

She stopped working for a moment, knowing it would take a long time to create the magic to control the beasts that roamed the wasteland and the foothills of the Frozen Mountains. *She* touched each of the objects *she* had collected, and her thoughts returned to the hated one.

He had defied her again. Roth had come and attacked the ones *she* had taken over and sent to kill the young prince of Fainhall. *She* had planned everything to perfection. *She* had raised a small army of mindless fools and sent them to attack the villages near the outlands of Fainhall, knowing the old king would send his soldiers and with them his son, the prince, to command. He had done as *she* had foreseen, and in a preset ambush, attacked them. While they had failed to kill the prince, they had wounded him gravely. But Roth had come with his soldiers to chase and destroy her small band. With him was the woman, Enaid of Tolemac, Enaid who was also the daughter of Brumwall. Enaid who had fought beside Roth in the final battle…

"I will have my revenge yet!" *she* screamed to the fire. You will die beneath my hands!" *They will all die: the bitch sorceress Enaid and the hated one Roth and the two children who had defied her, she* promised the unseen dark forces that filled her with purpose.

<><><>

The stars hung in massive proportions in the sky above the main road to Tolemac. Beneath the widespread pinpoints of light, forty-eight men and fourteen women rode behind Roth and Enaid. They were two-thirds of the way between Freemorn and Tolemac, returning from the fighting at Fainhall. They had left thirty of their troop to reinforce the battered soldiers of Fainhall and help train those new recruits, who would be joining Fainhall's ranks.

What they had found there was enough to create deep concern in Roth and Enaid. Prince Samot was severely injured and it had taken

Enaid and Fainhall's Queen Eetak a full day of ministration to hold back the oncoming death and to begin the healing process.

By the second day, he had improved and had been able to drink a little soup. While she had been tending the prince, Roth had taken his men and gone after the exiles in the wastelands, the ones who had attacked the outlying villages. They had fought and defeated them without losing anyone under Roth's command and had returned most of the kidnapped women.

There was more to what was happening, Enaid thought as she rode next to her husband. *Much more.* Looking up, she saw the moon had crested the sky. They had been riding the full day and half the night. Thankfully, they would reach Tolemac in another hour.

Something touched her shoulder. She found a white and silver crave trying its best to keep pace with her. Lifting her arm, she let the bird grasp it as a perch. She saw the message and, releasing the string holding it, let the bird free. *Home.* She pushed the thought to it as she read the message written on both sides of the cloth. She read it again to make sure of what she was seeing. When she finished, and the words faded from the cloth, she turned to Roth.

"Mikaal and Areenna are in Welkold. They leave for the Frozen Mountains in the morning. There was an attack by Free-Blades. They were after Trebor."

"Trebor?" Roth echoed. "First Samot, now Trebor? Do they mean to kill all our leaders?"

"It is one way to defeat us. Without leaders, the people have no direction. They become easy to defeat and enslave."

"We must send word to all dominions."

"Yes. There is more. Akassia has had visions of the Island. She and Trebor ride to Tolemac in the morning. Areenna asks me to mentor her for the Island. She says she senses there will be many women called so."

"It is because of the coming of the Dark Ones, is it not?" Roth ventured.

"It seems so. We will know soon enough."

"We have much preparation to attend to."

"We do, My Lord. I only hope we have enough time to do so."

XV

LATE ON THE third day after leaving Welkold's capital, Areenna and Mikaal reached the edge of the badlands. The foothills of the Frozen Mountains were but a short distance away. Above the foothills, the white coated mountains rose to massive heights.

The air was crisp and cold; the ground had become harder as they approached the mountains. Ahead, Gaalrie flew scout over the foothills, rising and falling with the shifting currents. The sharp-eyed treygone searched everywhere while Areenna comfortably joined within her aoutem's mind.

"All appears quiet," she told Mikaal as she drew her thoughts from the treygone. "Like these badlands, there is no game ahead, not yet."

"Cooked meat would have been nice," Mikaal said, wistfully.

She smiled. "The smoked dar we carry will be sufficient."

"Sufficient yes, but tasty? Still, we do not have an inexhaustible supply. We must find game."

"They would not have sent us here to starve," she said, repeating what she had said two weeks before in Tolemac. "What point would that serve?"

"Do you think they even eat food?" Mikaal wondered aloud.

Areenna knew he meant the eight sorceresses of the Island. "They are alive, we know that. Of course they eat. What kind of a question is that?"

Mikaal laughed. "It was a thought. We know nothing about them. We take what they say as truth, yet we know not if they are whom they proclaim themselves to be."

Areenna twisted on the saddle to stare at Mikaal, her thoughts disturbed. "You were there with me. You spoke, heard and watched everything. How can you doubt?"

"How can you not? We blindly follow their directions without as much as a thought for what comes."

She drew Hero to a halt. Mikaal did the same. "What is it? What disturbs you?"

He gazed at her, taking in the soft curves of her lips, the smooth line of her nose and the green eyes staring back. He shook his head. "It is…I don't know. I feel something is wrong."

Areenna used her senses, but found nothing disturbing. *May I join with you*?

He opened his mind to her and they melded instantly. The moment she was with him, she caught the disturbance. She pushed slightly, searching for its cause, and withdrew.

You are thinking wrong. Look for the disturbance within you. Seek its source. It is not what you perceive. Use your abilities.

Thinking wrong... He drew into himself, pushed through his mind, seeking the elusive feeling until he found the cause within a darkness set in a corner of his mind. His eyes flew open and he turned to look at the foothills. *Danger, there is danger ahead. I cannot see what...*

"It was not doubt of them. It is your ability to see ahead," she said aloud. "Try to force it," she suggested.

He pushed himself hard, sought for a vision of what waited, and failed. "I can't," he whispered.

"It will come," she said. "In the meantime, we are warned." She freed her bow from the saddle hitch, slung her quiver over her head and settled it on the fur cloak. At her side, Mikaal drew his sword and laid it cross-wise on the saddle before urging Charka forward.

Forty minutes later, with the sun sinking and darkness rising, they entered the foothills of the Frozen Mountains. When they crossed from the badlands, the temperature dropped quickly. Cold winds plunged down from the higher mountains, wrapping chilled fingers around the two riders.

Several twisted trees rose on the rocky ground ahead. Mikaal looked higher along the mountainside and saw more trees peppered throughout. "At least we will have firewood."

They moved forward in the gathering darkness: Gaalrie scouted the foothills ahead. Through Gaalrie's eyes, Areenna saw a small level area past the next rise. "There is a small ravine and place to camp just after."

They crested the rise as she finished speaking. Mikaal eyed the ravine. Its sight made him uneasy. Two hundred feet long, the ravine dipped between two rocky outcroppings before rising to the clearing.

"I do not like the looks of this," he said.

"You see something?"

He shook his head. "No."

Calling to Gaalrie, she asked the treygone to search the ravine. The giant bird dropped into the ravine. Areenna, accompanying her aoutem, saw all through her eyes.

"Nothing," she said when Gaalrie rose into the sky at the far end of the ravine.

Mikaal gripped the handle of the sword tightly. His body tensed, his muscles vibrating. "There's something."

Areenna did not dismiss his words. Instead, she lifted her bow and notched an arrow. Mikaal hefted his sword and started Charka into the ravine.

As they rode, the walls grew higher on each side. Just enough twilight filtered through for them to see clearly. Halfway through, their bodies taunt, their eyes watchful, they stopped. "Has the feeling left?" Areenna asked, searching his face, trying to sense what he did.

He shook his head. As he started to speak, Charka let free a low cry and back stepped.

The disturbance in his mind grew strong. His vision wavered and cleared. On a ledge, hidden by the taller rocky outcropping he saw a pack of gorlons…yet they were larger than gorlons, dark, with shaggy coats. They were about to attack them. He remembered his father's words about the animals Roth had called wolves.

He cleared his vision and said, "Be ready, we are in danger. A pack of gorlons…no, not gorlons, things…"

Charka rose suddenly to his back legs, emitting a loud cry and kicking the empty air before him as two of the darkly menacing animals appeared. From above them, growls emanated.

Dismounting quickly, Areenna shed the confining cloak and braced her back against the wall. On the ledge above, a half dozen sets of eyes glowered down at her. Her power flared instantly. She sent a probe toward one of the beasts. At the same time came a sharp inner warning to hold back—something about the animals was wrong. Her pushed thought hit something and died. She contained her power—protected! She had to concentrate on defending herself…she could build either magic or fight. She chose fight.

The first of the strange gorlon-like creatures moved forward. It was huge, almost twice the size of a gorlon. Unlike a gorlon whose coat was short and smooth, this beast had a long coat with patches of dark tufts hanging shaggily. Orange yellow eyes glared angrily, spittle drooled down the sides of its mouth in long stretching threads. Fangs the size of a man's hand curved downward from its wide snout. Puffs of condensing moisture shot from its nostrils like smoke from a chimney.

"What are they?" Mikaal asked as he drew his knife with his left hand and held his sword in his right. He too shrugged off the cloak, letting it fall on Charka's back and dismounted.

"I know only that black magic surrounds them," Areenna whispered as she looked at the gorlon-like creature, hatred and bloodlust flowing from it. *Her creatures. Protected.* She ignored her regret at not defending with her powers, but there had not been time enough to understand what she faced. Her powers continued to swirl hot within her.

She reached inward, drawing on her abilities but as she did, Mikaal shouted a warning, spun toward her and jumped, his sword arcing inches above her head. An unearthly scream resounded when his blade sliced through the neck of a creature who had launched itself at her back.

The animal fell dead at Areenna's feet. When it hit the ground, the leader of the devil-like pack leapt toward Mikaal. Charka rose and kicked out, striking the beast on its side. The animal screamed and fell while a second beast slipped past the kraal and charged Mikaal.

The abomination of an animal jumped upward, its mouth wide. Before it could reach him, Mikaal crouched and in one fluid movement turned, swung his sword in a long arcing movement and sliced through the beast's abdomen.

At the same instant the leader attacked, Areenna let fly her arrow at one of the mutated wolf creatures when it leapt from the ledge toward her. The arrow pierced its chest and it fell dead at her feet. From the corner of her eyes, even as she notched another arrow, she saw the lead creature rise and slip past Charka's frantic kicks and move toward Mikaal.

Above him, another of the huge animals launched itself at Mikaal's head.

Areenna released the arrow, which embedded itself in the charging creature's shoulder but did not stop it. Mikaal caught the jumping beast from above on his sword, but the weight of the animal tore the sword from his grip. It lay unmoving between them, with Mikaal's sword out of reach.

Behind you! Areenna warned.

Mikaal spun, his knife at the ready, as the lead beast struck. Snapping jaws and huge fangs reached for his neck. Mikaal stepped forward, not back, and buried his blade deep in the beast's chest. The rush and weight of the creature slammed him down, pinning him to the ground. His right hand grasped the animal's neck, holding back the large fangs, which tried to tear at his jugular. He twisted the knife, pushed harder and sliced upward. The creature shivered and died atop him, spewing its vile odorous blood everywhere.

Areenna's back was against the rock wall as more of the beasts surrounded her. With an arrow notched in the bow, and more shafts curled inside the hand holding the powerful wooden weapon, she faced the oncoming creatures. They padded forward, low growls coming from their throats. Six yellow eyes glared at her as they inched closer. *Mikaal,* she called silently.

Mikaal struggled beneath the dead creature until he was able to push it from him. He gained his feet even as Areenna called to him. Tearing his knife free, he raced forward, covering the distance quickly to launch himself at the first beast. Seeing him come toward them, Areenna released the readied arrow and buried it in the eye of the black beast before her.

Mikaal landed on the back of the closest one, his knife going deep into its chest. He rolled from the dead thing as another fell from Areenna's arrow. The third leapt at Areenna before she could set an arrow. As it flew at her, Mikaal grabbed the creature in midair. They fell to the ground rolling, the mutated beast growling and snapping while Mikaal sought a place for his knife.

A lance of pain ripped through him when the black thing sank its fangs into the heavy muscles of his shoulder. He roared out in anger and rolled to his back in an effort to dislodge the beast. He rolled again, pressing the thing between himself and the ground and raised his knife.

Above him, Areenna fought for a clear shot, but they were moving too fast, wrestling and twisting on the ground, the onrushing darkness overshadowing everything. She saw the beast curl within Mikaal's grasp. Twisting and growling, it drew its hind legs inward and raked them down his thighs.

Mikaal cried out but did not loosen his grip. In a swift movement, he rolled over, freed his arm and slid the blade between two ribs, puncturing its heart.

The animal stiffened and died. Areenna raced to Mikaal, pushed the heavy monstrosity from him and knelt at his side. Blood was flowing from his thighs, his leggings were in shreds, and there were deep punctures and a huge tear on his shoulder.

She saw the pain in his eyes. She stroked his face as he struggled to move. "Stay still," she commanded.

Charka came to them, lowered his head and pressed it to Mikaal's chest, pinning him to the ground. Mikaal did not fight. Gaalrie, who had been hovering over everything, unable to find a way to help, dropped to the ground next to Mikaal. She lowered her beak to his forehead. Both aoutems pushed their essences to him.

While they did so, Areenna raced to the kralets, who were shaking with fright. She grabbed the first one and pulled down a bag, opened it and took out one of her tunics. While she returned to Mikaal, she drew her knife and sliced the tunic into strips.

She knelt at his side. *Hold tight,* she pleaded.

"I am not badly injured," he said and tried to sit.

"You are. Hold still, this will hurt." She balled one of the smaller pieces, pressed it into his torn and punctured shoulder. She tied it with another piece to stem the flow of blood. Then she inspected his ripped thighs. One had seriously deep slashes through the muscles; the other was not as bad. She wrapped the lacerated thigh with the largest piece of her tunic, tying it tightly to stop the bleeding.

Finally, she took a deep shuddering breath. "I…" she began.

Mikaal, looking up at her and seeing her eyes fill with tears as she held his eyes, raised his good arm and cupped her cheek. "You are untouched?"

When she nodded, he exhaled slowly and lowered his arm. "I will be fine by tomorrow. We need shelter tonight."

"Yes." She called to Gaalrie, asking her to find a place for them. The treygone pressed her beak gently against Mikaal's forehead once again before rising into the air and beginning her search.

Areenna grasped his uninjured arm and pulled him to his feet. He clenched his jaws to stop from crying out.

His shoulder burned and his legs flared with fiery slices of pain. With Areenna's help, he made it to Charka, who went to his knees for Mikaal to struggle onto his back. He stayed down a moment longer while Areenna pulled the cloak over Mikaal's shoulders, who winced when the heavy fur pressed against the wound.

She took his sword from the chest of the dead beast and pulled his knife free from the side of the other. The dead animals, created from darkest of black magic, made her stomach twist with revulsion.

Gaalrie's tug within her mind came a few minutes later. She saw a place, not too distant. A cave opening within a high ridge where the foothills and the first high-slanting slope of the mountains met.

Turning to Mikaal, she said, "A half mile at most, there is a cave and safety."

Mikaal nodded. "We should go, now."

She turned, rose and started toward the kralets but stopped after three steps as more orange yellow eyes gleamed in the distance ahead. This time there was no hesitation. She drew up her power instantly, the burning in her depths turning volcanic.

Leaning forward, she released every bit of her energy. Silver blue light spewed from her upheld hands, and she sent it at the first beast. Impossibly, the blue stream of killing power flared a foot before the creatures as if a wall had risen to stop it. The animals stood there defiantly for several seconds before turning and walking into the oncoming night.

"*She* protects them," Areenna whispered. Only when she sensed the beasts were gone did she turn back, gather the kralets and tie them to

Hero. They rode slowly out of the ravine. Charka walked carefully, doing his best to keep Mikaal steady on his broad back.

Nightfall was complete, and Areenna was aware of everything. She heard scuttling in the rocks and sensed small rock dwelling animals running back and forth, tracking them as they moved. Still, she knew it was from curiosity only that these animals trailed them. There was no animosity, no sense of danger. Nor was there a 'feel' of the other beasts.

It took them twenty minutes to reach the cave opening on the side of the mountain. Dismounting, Areenna went to Mikaal. She checked his shoulder and saw the blood seeping through the makeshift bandage. "Wait here, hold on," she whispered, turned and stepped into the opening. She called forth her powers, easily accepting the swift rise and the burn always accompanying them. She concentrated on one ability and a heartbeat later, two glowing spheres appeared on her palms. Light flowed from them, encircling her and spreading forward. She walked carefully and slowly for almost twenty feet until the tunnel she was in began to widen. Ten feet further found her in a huge cavern, the walls high, and the rock ceiling a good fifty feet above.

Holding her palms upward she sent the balls of light deeper into the cavern. They rose slowly until they were midway between the floor and ceiling. She pushed hard and the light grew brighter.

She gasped. The sound echoed from the walls a dozen times before it came back to her. Before her, centered within the huge cavern, stood a wooden structure the likes of which she had never before seen. It was two stories high, its width twice its height. Two sets of stairways led to the top level while the first one had two huge closed doors.

She froze for a moment. Her senses told her the building was old, perhaps as old as Nevaeh itself. The wood appeared petrified and glowed under the floating balls of light. Windows of smooth glass were everywhere. There were strange words painted on the door, words she could not read.

There was no sign of life.

A powerful cry hit her mind. There was no sound, but she knew it was Charka. "Mikaal," she cried, seeking his mind, his thoughts, but all she found was a blank space where he should have been.

XVI

"MIKAAL IS INJURED," Enaid cried out, sitting up straight in the bed. Next to her, Roth rose as well.

Turning to her, he wrapped an arm about her and drew her to him. "Tell me," he whispered.

She drew on his physical being, absorbing his strength. "I saw it as if I were there. Strange creatures attacked them, bigger than gorlons, but gorlons of some sort. They had long shaggy coats and huge fangs. Pointed snouts, not like a gorlon. Their eyes were yellow, an evil deep-glowing yellow and orange. Mikaal and Areenna fought them off, killed six, but one wounded Mikaal. It is serious. The Black Bitch...*she* controlled them. *She* protected them. They could not use their powers against the creatures, only bow and blade. *She* took no chances and did not use her energy against them; *she* used it only to protect the animals, which made her block stronger."

"Wolves, mutated... What can we do?" he asked, his stomach knotting impotently.

Enaid shook her head. "There is nothing. He is too far from us. Areenna cares for him. She will heal him. But they will lose much time and will be exposed to even more danger."

"There has to be something," Roth insisted.

Earlier in the day, Queen Lyra of Morvene, Queen Ilsraeth of Northcrom and Queen Atir of Aldimore had arrived after receiving the messages Enaid had sent before she and Roth left for Fainhall. With Ilsraeth had come Timon, who was now father guardian of Aldimore following King Maslow's death. Atir's daughter, Princess Laira, had come as well. She had already foreseen the troubles ahead and knew she must join them.

Enaid nodded slowly. “Perhaps there is.” She rose from the bed and put on a robe. Turning to Roth, she said, “Stay abed. We will do what we can. I will let you know what happens.” With that, she turned and started out, already sending a call to the four women of power within Tolemac’s keep.

Minutes later, sensing Enaid’s urgent calling, the four women encircled the High Queen. “Mikaal is hurt. That black she-snuck sent beasts to attack them. He is badly injured. Areenna works to heal him. We must find a way to help.”

“Her powers are strong,” said Atir, “the healing power will be well used in her hands.”

Enaid shook her head even as she agreed. “We cannot take the chance. We must try to aid her.”

Laira stepped forward. The youngest present, she was the same eighteen years as Areenna. She cleared her throat and spoke in a low voice. “On the Island, when I was lost inside a black room, I had many visions, so many I still work to understand most of them even now, after almost six months. The one I know best was the first one. It showed me here, in this very chamber, the five of us in a circle, our hands entwined, our minds one.”

“You saw such on the Island,” Ilsraeth whispered. “I saw such not a week prior. I was in my garden, tending a sickly stand of flowers when I received the vision.”

Enaid, standing in the center of the room, sank to the floor, pulling her legs under her. “Come,” she said.

The five formed a perfect circle on the floor, each holding the hand of the woman next to her. When they were ready, Enaid sent her core essence toward each. They followed suit and gave their own essences to each. Unexpectedly, Laira took charge of their thoughts. When she had control, she drew a mind picture of Areenna and pushed everything toward her. The five women opened themselves completely and gave forth all the energy and power they possessed.

<><><>

Mikaal was unconscious. She couldn't reach him. He was drifting from her, his body dying as the blood flowed from him, his mind following. She stoked his face, unwilling to give up.

You will not leave me! You will not die! Come back! She pushed her determination, her desperation directly at him.

Areenna called up her healing abilities and fell into the blindness accompanying the power. She saw nothing except the glowing of her hands and the pulsing aura surrounding his injuries.

Working carefully, she pressed her hands to the wounds on his shoulder, funneling every bit of her healing gift into him, but the wounds were grave, and the blood would not stop flowing.

What? How? Her thoughts whirled frantically. *I cannot lose you! I will not lose you!*

A memory filled her mind. She had been fifteen. She and her mother had been walking in the courtyard when a woman came running to them, tears streaking her face. Her husband had been pinned under a fallen beam he had been repairing. It had fallen across his legs, severing one at the knee.

They had run with the woman and when they saw the man, Inaria, her mother had gone to him and inspected the wound. Then she removed the leather belt from his waist and tied a tourniquet. When the blood slowed, she created fire in the palm of her hand and, when it grew hot, cupped the torn bottom of his leg and cauterized the wound. The man had lost part of one leg but lived for many years afterward.

Flames rose instantly from Areenna's palms. These flames were not the gentle flames of her mother but Mikaal's powerful fire. She damped the fire, controlling it carefully, and held her hands over Mikaal's shoulder. *How can I do this? How do I close the punctures*?

A sudden surge of power caught her off guard. The flames in her hands rose two feet into the air. Her powers grow past anything she had known before. Then came the vision of the five women, locked together, swaying in rhythm. Areenna caught Laira's thought, *Use us.*

Closing her eyes, she let the five enter her. A breath later, she knew what to do. With their abilities supporting her own, she manipulated the fire into two small streams the size of the punctures. She moved the flames to the tip of each index finger and, staying fully melded with Mikaal, forced the fire into the open wounds.

Unconscious, Mikaal's body arched upward with the pain of the fire. Areenna, so closely connected, screamed out as her body arched and her shoulder burst with pain. Fighting the burning agony, she held her fingers to the wounds for five full seconds before drawing them back. The pain in her shoulder did not lessen when she put out the fire.

The flow of blood had finally stopped. She ignored the pain, cast it from her and separated from Mikaal's mind. There was more to do. She could not consider herself. Turning to his legs, blind to his naked body, she bent over the most damaged thigh and again, with the aid of the five women, began to run her hands over his mutilated skin.

Giving no thought to time, she held her hands a hairsbreadth over his skin and channeled all the healing power she could raise. She worked slowly and carefully on first one thigh and then the other. The bleeding stopped, the skin reacted to her healing power and finally—how many hours later she could not imagine—his skin began to knit together. There would be scars, but no permanent damage.

Thank you, she thought, pushing the words to the five. An instant later, they were gone and she was alone.

She withdrew her hands from his skin and her vision returned. She rose and went to where she had thrown his rabt skin cloak and, returning, covered him.

She was tired, exhausted, but knew she could not yet stop. She went to Charka, and removed his saddle and Mikaal's sword. Then did the same for Hero. When she turned to where the kralets stood, she saw Charka go to Mikaal and maneuver his bulk to the ground next to him. She knew Charka would not move until Mikaal awoke.

She went to the kralets, untied them and removed the supplies. She opened a bag and tossed grain on the ground before them so they could eat. She searched for Gaalrie, whom she found perched on a nook-like ledge near her. *Watch*, she asked the treygone, nodding to the kralets. Gaalrie would not let them stray from the cavern.

Exhaustion claimed her. She staggered, regained her balance and grabbing her cloak, lay on Mikaal's other side. Wrapped in the furs, she turned to him, placed a hand on his chest and felt his heart beating steadily. She pushed into his mind and found him sleeping, unbothered by the pain. She fell asleep a few moments later, her mind and his still locked together.

<><><>

The hours dragged by until Roth was unable to wait any longer. He went to Enaid's personal chamber, took three steps inside and froze. The five women lay in a circle, their hands locked to each other, none of them conscious.

Slowly, carefully, he knelt by Enaid's side. He reached down, stroked her cheek, and her eyes opened. "It is done," she whispered, her voice thick. She rose, releasing the hands of the two women on either side. "Mikaal lives. Areenna has done everything she can. But they will not be able to move on for several days."

She stood slowly, holding on to Roth for support. When she faced him, she whispered, "Those…the powers of the Island, they have gifted Laira with much. Solomon, I… They are using our children to fight the Dark Ones. They send our children to war."

He put his hands to each side of her face. "Were you not fighting them when you were their age? Their youth combined with their power gives them strength."

"And puts them in even greater danger. I fear for them, not just Mikaal, not only Areenna, but for the young ones. They have not had a chance to live yet, and many will die before they can."

Roth exhaled and drew his wife closer. "Then we must do our best to stop that from happening."

"My Lord, how do we do such?"

He shook his head. "I don't know...yet, but we will not lose our children."

Enaid looked at the sleeping women. "I must wake them. Leave now, I will join you shortly."

Roth followed Enaid's bidding, and a moment later, she woke the four. Each rose, hugged the others and returned to their chambers. Each knew what they had accomplished.

They paused at the door, waiting for Enaid to speak.

"Tomorrow, be ready to begin work on what we must do."

XVII

RISE, WALK, EAT, her hand rested firmly on Charka's powerful neck. The kraal had lain next to Mikaal throughout the long night and into the late afternoon. Areenna knew the aoutem had to move soon. To lay on the ground for so long was dangerous for an animal, who always stood upright.

She concentrated on Charka, urging him to stand. Finally, he gave in to her asking and began to struggle up. She rose quickly and stood next to him, helping him with her thoughts, pressing her hands to him to add what strength she could to his efforts. When the large kraal finally stood on all fours, he lowered his head and pressed his snout to Mikaal. Then he walked to where Hero and the kralets were gathered. He drank from one of the pots they'd brought with them and ate some of the grain spread on the floor.

Areenna sank next to Mikaal. She had slept a few hours after the healing but only fitfully and had woken up often to check on him. His sleep was still that of deep healing and she sensed it would be days before he would be able to travel. For now, their supplies would hold, but they had not planned for this, which meant the food they'd brought would run out sooner than anticipated.

Her shoulder still ached. She did not need to look to know there were two patches of burnt skin in the exact same spots on her shoulder as on Mikaal.

With her hand resting on his chest, feeling the steady rhythm of his heart, she turned to look at the ancient building. Earlier in the morning, she had followed Gaalrie outside, and the treygone had led her to an old long-dead tree. Using her short sword effectively, she had chopped as much wood as she physically could. She'd made three trips from the tree to the cavern and when she was satisfied with the amount of wood, she'd built a fire.

Gathering snow and ice, she filled the pot and melted it, boiling the water as she did. Then, using dried meat, grains and herbs from her supplies, she made a thin soup. She ate first. Then, carefully supporting Mikaal's unconscious head, she dripped as much soup as she could get him to swallow.

With Mikaal sleeping easier, knowing Charka would warn her if Mikaal stirred, she decided to go to the old building and explore. When she reached the first step of the structure, she cast her senses throughout and found nothing of the dark powers or its creatures.

She used her ability to create a floating ball of light and moved through the first level of the edifice. The floor was strong, the wood was solid and not a single plank showed any signs of rotting. She moved slowly, exploring each of the many areas. As she moved from room to room, she found the furniture seemed to have been made of the same solid and strong wood used to build the structure.

Entering one of the rooms near the rear, she found the frame of what she was certain had been a large bed and, next to it was a wide chair of which only the frame and the seat of metal weaving remained. Beneath each were piles of undisturbed dust. Intuitively, she knew it was the disintegrated fabrics and cushions of the chair and bed.

She knelt beside a pile of thick white dust and blew a breath at it. Tiny specs of material lifted and floated randomly before settling back down. *How old was the structure*? *How many centuries had it stood thus*?

She leaned toward the bedframe and grasped it tightly, trying to sense its age. Its feel had been unnatural. All she had been able to glean was it was older than anything she had ever known and while it seemed to be wood, it was not. She bent and ran her hands over the floor and realized all of it, the floor and walls and ceilings of the structure were the same strange substance that imitated wood, but was not wood.

She stood, the light floating over her left shoulder, and continued with her exploration. She roamed the rooms randomly until coming into what she sensed was a kitchen. In the center, she found a strange contraption. She unable to come up with a word to describe it. It was about three feet tall, wider than it was deep, with four rusted metal circles on the top. Metal knobs, disintegrated into rust but holding their shape, were next to each circle. She knew if she touched them, they would crumble. On the front of it was a door with a glass window in its center. Through the door, she saw a shiny metal rack stood in the middle. Beneath it was a draw. When she pulled it out, she found a pile of ashes, which as soon as the air touched them, folded into themselves and all but dissolved before her eyes. It took another second for her to understand the ashes signified the metal box was for cooking.

Rising, she continued to look around. Hanging from the ceiling were several pans. Upon closer inspection, most were only shells, rotted with rust. However, two were different. They were of a metal that did not rust; rather, they held a high sheen beneath the soft glow of her floating light.

She spent another half hour exploring the structure but found nothing of importance. In one room, she discovered a pile of long bluish metal tubes sitting atop of what must have once been deteriorated wood. The metal rods were long and hollow and at the ends of each, which lay in the remains, were strange metal objects—rectangular boxes with a smaller circle of metal attached beneath it and inside the circle was a curved lever.

Areenna shrugged. She could not come up with any idea of what they had been. Then, sensing she was too long gone from Mikaal, she took the two metal pots and returned to his side.

<><><>

With Mikaal's breathing softer and easier, and the long day ending, Areenna knew she needed to find game and water while there was still some light. Mikaal needed meat to heal—not the dried meats and grains they carried, which were good enough for survival when healthy, but for healing, he needed more.

She called Gaalrie to her. The treygone flew from its perch on the wall to her shoulders. Together, they left the cavern and went into the cold. Areenna stopped two feet later, and projected her senses in every direction. When she found no darkness, no threatening dark entities, she opened her eyes and asked Gaalrie to search for game.

Gaalrie rose into the sky, where the treygone flew in ever widening circles. A short time later, Areenna heard Gaalrie's call. Instantly, she was with her aoutem, looking through her eyes and saw a small tarq on the upslope of the mountain, grazing on a few straggly growths of grass. She sought for any others but found no emanations and returned her attention to the mountain tarq. The tarq, small and dwarf-like, was full-grown. Two horns sat atop its head. A long twisted beard hung from its lower jaw and its fur was a shaggy black and white.

She judged the distance to the slope at just under two hundred yards. Pressing her back to the rocky crevice where she stood, she unslung her bow, drew an arrow and notched it in preparation. She moved swiftly toward the place Gaalrie was showing her, while making sure she stepped only on solid rocks to avoid any noise. When she reached the area Gaalrie found, she hid behind an outcropping and drew the gut back. She aimed at a spot on the tarq between its belly and shoulder, exactly where the heart sat.

She released the arrow. The shaft flew straight to its target, pierced the tarq's skin and slipped between two ribs. The animal stiffened, and a few seconds later, fell. Areenna went to it, her knife drawn ready to finish the animal if it still lived. When she knelt beside it, she saw there was no need for a finishing stroke as the arrow had struck true.

She pushed a thought to Gaalrie. The giant bird wheeled and flew to the cavern where she landed on Charka's back. The kraal left the cavern, pausing near Mikaal before going to Areenna. By the time Charka and Gaalrie reached her, she had bled and cleaned the tarq.

Areenna lifted the dead animal and slung it across Charka's back. She was pleased there would be enough meat to last several days, if she kept it packed with ice.

She walked next to the kraal on the return to the cavern and thought back to the gift from Queen Enna. Using what Mikaal's grandmother had shown her, she searched for signs of water.

It took only a few minutes for her to find an underground stream. The only problem was it was beneath the very path they trod. She followed the water's flow but sensed it rose not to the surface anywhere nearby, yet the flowing water led in the same direction as the cavern.

Just when she reached the entrance, a dark tendril touched at the edge of her mind. She froze at its tentative touch, her hand on Charka's neck. Closing her eyes, she reached toward the darkness and recoiled instantly. The feel of it was repulsive and she realized it was some sort of spirit creation of the Black Sorceress.

That it had not sensed her, she was hopeful, as she built a strong block, hiding her and Mikaal as best she could. The knowledge that a creation of hers was nearby unsettled Areenna, especially with Mikaal in so serious a condition.

Kneeling at the opening to the cavern, Areenna closed her eyes. She concentrated on constructing a more powerful shield, building it block by block, solidifying it slowly and surrounding the entrance, setting it into the mountainside itself to hide the cavern. It took her almost a quarter hour of intense focus but the resulting shield was solid and she was confident the shield would block anyone or anything from finding them.

<><><>

Like a cloak made of a hundred thousand buzzing flies, a shimmering black mist surrounded her, clinging to every inch of her body. *She* stood on the cliff overlooking the sea, watching the tossing waters crash against the high rocks. *She* could not stop shaking. Fear gripped her. She had failed, and she cowered within the buzz of the mist.

There was no moon this night, but the stars poured forth enough light to cast a low glow to the palisades. Summoned moments before, *she'd* scrambled out of her cave to stand on the ledge above the ocean, where the black swarm of mist had covered her.

You have failed to secure the two, came the thoughts of her Master with a mind picture of the Dark One.

Within her mind, the Master stood on the prow of the ship, taller than any other being *she* had ever seen. He was wide and slightly hunched. The cloak he wore, which fluttered madly in the winds, had a tightly drawn hood shielding most of his face. What *she* could see showed the skin of his face to be a dark gray and almost as black as a starless night; his eyes burned with an amber glow.

Secured them, no, Master, slowed them for you I have. They are powerful… She brought up a mind picture of the attack by her creatures and the wounding of the boy.

His anger lashed at her, sweeping her from her feet and slamming her against the rocks behind her. *I said to capture them not to harm them. Why have you done such?*

I did what I thought you wanted, Master. I…

You did what you wanted. You allowed your anger at them to go too far. You will not do this again. We want them alive and uninjured. Find them! Capture them!

She fell to her knees. *Master, I but do wh—*

—Silence! You do what I command. Only what I command. The Master released a lash of whip-like anger at her. Fire burned her abdomen and *she* cried out.

If your creations harm them, the same will happen to you. Go now. Prepare for our arrival in two days. Gather those you control. Find the two of power. Capture them!

◇◇◇

While the tarq meat cooked in a high spit over the flames, Areenna explored the cavern. It was far deeper than she had expected, stretching out behind the ancient building for hundreds of feet. As she walked deeper into the darkness, lit only by the floating spheres of light she had created, she began to scent moisture.

Looking up, she sent the light higher. The spheres rose toward the high ceiling and a shimmering began the closer they came to the top. Moments after they reached the top, the cavern's stone ceiling began to glow.

Areenna's breathing all but stopped when a rainbow of color appeared on the dome-like ceiling. She traced the glowing as far as she could, until the light began to dim at its far reaches.

It took but a moment for her to understand what she was seeing. When she did, she smiled. Encased within the stones were pieces of crystal. Each piece reflected light with a slightly different color and, together, they created an iridescence of magnificent beauty from the light of Areenna's glowing spheres.

She recalled the spheres of light until they floated above her head and the shimmering faded into blackness. *Water*, she reminded herself and again took up the search.

Beneath her feet, she sensed the rushing water she had found running under the outside pathway. A short time later, she heard the sound of water and sent the spheres of light toward the sound.

Her breath was stolen for the second time as the light revealed a pool of water, perhaps twenty feet wide, surrounded by rocks. To her left, coming from the rocks themselves, three small streams of water cascaded over the stone in miniature waterfalls.

Staring at the unexpected pool, she sensed the rocks around it were not a natural formation. Everything was too perfect. The rocks closest to her were more like flat-topped boulders. There were no small stones; the large ones seemed strategically placed, almost as if they were benches created for sitting on at the edge of the water.

The longer she gazed at the pool, the more certain she was that the same people who had built the old building had created this pool. She knelt between two large bench-like rocks and dipped her hand into the water, cupping it to capture some. Lifting it to her mouth, she smelled the clean scent and sipped. The water was fresh and cool.

She looked for signs of life, but found only water.

Areenna...

She heard his mind-call and turned from the water. *I'm coming*. She raced back to where Mikaal was struggling to sit upright and moved quickly to his side, where she gently pushed him back. "Lay still," she said, her face inches above his. "Be easy."

"I...where are we?" His voice, more a dried croak than spoken words made her heart beat faster.

"In the cavern, hidden." She reached across him and lifted a skein of water, held it to his lips and let him drink. When he pulled away, she set the leather container down. Before he could ask his next question, she answered it.

A night and day since the creatures attacked. It is the second night.

"Help me sit," he asked.

Gently, she pulled him to a sitting position. He looked at the cloth wrapped around his shoulder. He moved it and tried to raise his arm. He grimaced with the attempt.

"Rest," Areenna said. "It is healing well. I checked the bandages earlier. Can you eat?"

Mikaal nodded. "My stomach feels as though it is pressing against my backbone."

Areenna smiled for the first time since the attack. She exhaled, reached out and stroked his cheek. "Then you are healing well."

He covered her hand with his before she could withdraw it. Looking into her eyes, he said, "Thank you."

She smiled again as she pulled her hand free. A flush had streamed to her face at his look and touch. "Let me get you some tarq meat."

"You were hunting," he said, ignoring her quick retreat, overly aware of the cause.

"I was." She knelt before the fire and using her knife, cut a slice of the tender meat.

"Mountain tarq," he said, sniffing the air as she brought the meat to him. "Good meat if young enough. Tough if too old." He took a bit and chewed. "Good," he said after swallowing. "Tell me what has happened since the attack."

She went over every detail, from arriving at the cavern, to the help she had received from the other women, to Charka's refusal to do anything but lay at his side. Then she told him about the building. "The wood it is built with is not wood, but something I have never seen."

"I will look at it when…when I can." His eyes started to close on the last word and she knew he needed to sleep.

She eased him back and when his head touched the balled silks, he sighed. "Sleep," she whispered. *Rest.*

"Tomorrow," he whispered. "Tomorrow you show me the building." Then he was asleep.

Areenna gazed at him for several long minutes, her emotions fluttering within her. She had not thought of what might happen should the healing not work. It was unimaginable. Without being able to stop it, tears rose. Two of them dropped to his check and trailed downward. She wiped them from his skin.

"You will get strong," she whispered before bending to kiss him. When she drew her mouth from his, she stood and walked to Charka. The kraal nuzzled her, and she drew warmth from him.

Her lips tingled still from the kiss, and she realized it was the first time she had kissed him. She closed her eyes, thankful he had been asleep when she had done so. Then, taking a deep breath, her emotions firmly under control, she went back to Mikaal, knelt and drew on the healing powers within her. Blind, her hands flowing over him, she concentrated the force first on his shoulder and then his thighs.

When she stopped, she realized several hours had passed. She tried to stand, but a wave of dizziness caught her. Slowly, easily, she dropped to Mikaal's side, curled against him and fell into a deep and dreamless sleep.

<><><>

Enaid stood upon the parapet, her hands on the stone balustrade. Her aoutem, Iiri, pressed against her hip, the gorlon's warmth a welcome touch. She had been standing silently for an hour, watching the northwestern skyline, which was deep and black on this moonless hour before dawn. She had ranged with her senses as far as possible, but found no sign of Areenna or Mikaal in the distance. Either they were too far away or…she cut off her thought. Her emotions swirled. All she knew was that the healing may have worked, but without sensing, without being able to know, it was hard for her.

"Mikaal heals," Laira said from behind.

Turning to the girl, Enaid tried to smile. "You are so certain."

"I am. I sensed her earlier, just as night was settling. Areenna is strong, and Mikaal is healing."

"So much power you have."

Laira nodded. "Now, not before the Island. She…they," Laira corrected herself. "They gave me such gifts as I could not have imagined. My foretelling, the ability I was born with, has become stronger. It is no longer random."

Laira's eyes wandered past Enaid. Even without a moon, and only with stars for illumination, Tolemac spread out in a magnificent display of shadowed earth. "They come, the first of the Dark Ones. A Master rides with them. They will be at the southwestern palisades in two days. The Dark Master brings thousands of his…creatures."

"You have seen this?"

"On the Island, they showed me this vision. I saw it again when I awoke a few minutes ago. I saw you here as well."

"And Areenna and Mikaal? I cannot sense them."

"She created a shield and a block against the Black Witch who tracks them."

"A strong block for I could not feel it."

"They are safe for now," Laira said.

"Did they give more instructions?"

Laira shook her head. "Just to prepare for the coming of the Dark Ones. All of Nevaeh is at risk and we must stop them."

"Akassia arrives today. She has been called to the Island."

"I know. I will accompany her."

A silver and brown ret, Laira's aoutem, stuck its head out from beneath her cloak.

The High Queen of Nevaeh smiled and ran a finger over the animal's small head. "That will be good. Akassia will need you. She is not as strong as you and Areenna. It will be a hard time for her. She was to start the period of betrothal. The marriage is a month away. But I think such ceremonies will not be so important over the coming months."

"She will understand the delay and will come away much stronger. She too is needed." Laira added.

Enaid gazed toward the mountains she could not see, and the son she could not sense. "We will all be strong. We must be to save Nevaeh."

XVIII

MIKAAL AWOKE TO find his pain had subsided greatly since last night. Turning, his body stiff from laying on the stone floor, he looked at Areenna, who slept next to him.

He gazed at her and for the first time, realized he was naked and that she had undressed him to heal and bandage him. Without disturbing her, he slid out of the sleeping silks and rose carefully. A sharp pain lanced through his thigh when he stood. Bending, he removed the bandage of tied strips of silks to look at the damage. There were a dozen long scratches and by their look, they had been deep. The skin had closed around them and only a barely visible red showed at their seams. His other thigh had just a few remaining scratches.

Looking around, he spotted the packs from the kralets and went to the one he knew was his. He removed a leather tunic and leather pants and dressed as quickly as his sore muscles allowed. Then put on his boots to cut off the cold stone floor from his skin.

There was a nudge on his back and he turned to find Charka standing there. He smiled, leaned against the kraal's large head and stroked his neck. "I'm better," he said, melding with his aoutem and sharing the warmth of their feelings.

A low probing touched his mind. He turned to where Gaalrie perched on the stone ledge above Areenna. He smiled at the bird and walked toward the tunnel leading to the cavern exit. He went to the opening. The edge of the sun peeked out from behind a bank of gray and white clouds, showing it to be early afternoon.

He went back inside. *Had it been two days or three*?

When he walked to where Areenna lay, he saw her eyes were open. "You slept deeply."

"I did," she said, stretching and sitting up. "How are you feeling?"

"Stiff, sore, but better. Much better." But as he spoke the words, he grew tired. He sat on the silks and shook his head. "I am still weak. I like this not."

"There is no more to do to speed your recovery. We must wait until you are ready."

"Spoken like a true sorceress. Nevertheless, we lose time. We must move on."

To do so would endanger everything. What if there is another attack? "No, we cannot risk it. Mikaal, without all your strength, without your abilities, we will not survive. I need you to heal. I need you. Not the Eight, *I* need you."

He held her eyes, saw her determination, but it was her words, not her determination that caught him so heavily. He nodded slowly. "As you wish."

His response twisted within her. She stared at him, her eyes moving back and forth across his features. "There is much I wish. Perhaps one day those wishes will become reality."

He held her gaze. "They will, but until then…" He smiled. "I need food. I am starving again."

She pointed toward the cooking fire, moved her fingers in a weaving pattern, and the fire grew taller. "I found a large pot in the…building and filled it with water. It's chilly but wet. Perhaps you might want to ah…wash yourself." She decided not to tell him about the water she had found until she was certain nothing dangerous lived in it.

He bent his head, sniffed, and turned to Charka. "You didn't tell me I smelled like you."

Areenna laughed aloud. "Be careful of the wounds."

Perhaps you should wash me.

She cocked her head to the side. *One day, perhaps, but you seem capable enough now.*

His eyes narrowed. "I look forward to that day."

For the second time, Areenna blushed.

Mikaal moved to the side and used the pan of water and a cloth to wash himself. When he was finished and dressed again, he returned to the fire and sat next to Areenna.

"I'd like to see the building now," he said.

"You feel strong enough?"

He smiled at her and extended his hand. "Yes."

They went to the ancient structure, where Mikaal inspected everything from floor to ceiling, room by room, until he finally admitted he did not know what the building was made of or who could have possibly lived there, other than the 'Old Ones', who had survived in the earliest days of Nevaeh.

An hour into the inspection, he'd weakened enough to know he had to stop. They returned to the campsite and, after eating more of the tarq meat, looked over Roth's maps, tracing the trail the High King had suggested.

Mikaal's finger moved along the lines of the mountains. "We take this route here," he said, moving his finger to the eastern side. He traced forward until stopping at what appeared to be a valley. "If it is as level as my father believes, we can make up some of the time we have lost."

When Areenna nodded her agreement, he went on. "With luck we will find game in the area. And here," he added moving to a point a few inches further along on the map, "is where we cross to the western side. It appears to be of lower elevation, which will make it easier, but it will still be a hard crossing."

"Easier than if we went across now and had to go over the mountains at their tallest spots."

"Yes," he said, yawning.

Areenna glanced at him in concern. "It's time to stop. You need to rest and I need to work my healing. Lay on your silks, I will be there in a moment."

"I wish it was not so." After rolling up the map, he went to the silks, took off his tunic and lay down. As he did, the effects of the hours he had been up and moving caught up.

He watched Areenna kneeling by the fire, take a pot from it and pour its contents into a small cup. "What is it?"

She reached into the pot and with two fingers pulled out a strangely shaped thing. "Farna root," she said. "It helps with the healing."

He made a face, remembering the times his mother had made him drink the ugly tasting herb.

"It's not that bad," Areenna said, reading his face as she walked up to him. Kneeling at his side, she handed him the cup. "Sip it slowly. Do not rush it."

"I know." He raised the cup, took a sip, and grimaced.

Bending over him, Areenna put her hands on the badly injured thigh. The leather he wore was as hot as his skin. She called her power and the familiar heat rushed upward, through her chest, into her shoulders and downward through her arms to her hands. Then, came the loss of sight of anything but the wounds. She held her hands lightly above the leather, barely touching it and concentrated only on healing.

When she finished his thighs, she broke off the healing powers and sat up. She saw he had put the almost empty cup down and although he was sitting, he was asleep. Gently and carefully, she laid him back and began the healing process on his shoulder.

<><><>

Morning came faster than Areenna wanted, as Gaalrie woke her from a disturbing dream with a warning cry. She opened her eyes and looked around before realizing it was the dream Gaalrie had reacted to, not any danger.

She slowed her breathing. Everything was as it had been last night. Morning light brightened the short tunnel leading to the outside. Enough light filtered in to illuminate Mikaal.

As she studied him, his chest rose and fell smoothly. She reached out using her mind-touch and found his body relaxed. She sensed no pain. Then she remembered her dream and why she had been so disturbed. She had been reliving the ambush and attack of the wolf creatures.

Laying there, she realized she had failed in protecting them by not finding a way to use the powers she had been given. She was responsible for what had happened to him.

You are wrong, came Mikaal's sharp thought, breaking into her concentration.

Wrong? Of course I am not. If I had used my abilities, if only to shield us properly—

—to do what?

To stop them from reaching us. To protect us.

You are not thinking straight. These were not spirits created by the Black Witch; they were animals, mutated animals, living things, not projections of her dark magic. She controlled their minds. Nevertheless, they bled and died at our hands. You have told me often enough that a shielding can stop magic but rarely flesh and blood.

I should have found a way to use my abilities. I have the powers.

Perhaps. Mikaal's next thoughts seemed louder than words. *She had shielded them from your weapon. Areenna, we did what was necessary. They came at us fast, we chose to fight, and we survived. That's what matters, nothing else. You did not cause this. You did nothing wrong!*

"Then why do I feel like I have?" she snapped.

He smiled at her and sat up. "Because you are Areenna, daughter of Nosaj, King of Freemorn. And you have no choice…you were born to be this way, born and taught responsibility for others."

"And you know this for a fact?" she challenged.

His smile stayed in place when he said, "absolutely."

Before she could reply, Gaalrie screamed and dove toward the side of the cavern. A loud squeal resounded when she struck whatever she had attacked. Areenna flew from the sleeping silks, grabbing the knife that lay within reach and raced to where Gaalrie was fighting.

Behind her, Mikaal tried to do the same but could not rise quickly as the pain ripped through his shoulder. He squinted into the hazy dimness of the cavern and saw Areenna reach Gaalrie and bend. She stood, holding a large traat by its tail. The rodent was dead and Gaalrie was off again, chasing another of the rodents.

Rising slowly, and not bothering to put on his tunic yet, he went to where Areenna stood. He followed her gaze to the ice-packed carcass of the Tarq. "They feasted, eh?" Mikaal asked.

"They did. I will have to hunt again."

While he did not like the thought of her going without him, he knew he was not yet strong enough. "We can survive on what we have. Another day and I will be ready to move," he added as he lifted his arm and rotated it smoothly without allowing the pain to show on his face.

"We will see about your wounds—I am aware of the pain you tried to hide," Areenna added, "And I will hunt. We cannot afford to use up our supplies."

He started to argue but stopped at the look in her eyes. He laughed. "As I said, you are the daughter of a king and you have no choice in taking on the responsibility for everyone around you."

She shook her head and walked to the cavern's opening. The dead traat, suspended by two fingers, hung by its tail. "But traat we shall not eat." She paused, shifting her gaze to Mikaal. "At least not yet…"

<><><>

Early afternoon found Areenna outside the cavern, Gaalrie flying low above her. She had spent the morning inventorying their supplies and working her ability on Mikaal's wounds, which were healing more rapidly than she had hoped. With luck, they would be able to resume their journey in the morning.

A half hour outside the cavern and with Gaalrie scouting ahead, she climbed upward on the slope, seeking a good vantage point to hide and wait. As she climbed, she let her senses range. Then she turned a corner along the rising pathway and sensed darkness. Stopping, she knelt, closed her eyes and concentrated.

Her eyes flew open. Below, perhaps a hundred yards away and moving along another pathway were three of the wolf-creatures. She watched them sniffing the ground, hunting for a scent. Her scent, she realized as a putrid wave of malevolence washed over her, pushed by the Black Sorceress's mind with *her* desperate need to find Areenna and Mikaal.

She called Gaalrie, who came quickly, sensing her alarm. The treygone landed on the rocks next to her and held still. Areenna watched the creatures below stop and turn. Within seconds, another half dozen of the huge deformed things joined the first three and turning, headed back.

She knew they had picked up the scent and were heading to the cave. She rose, pulling her bow and notching an arrow. Then she stopped as she sensed something else. It was the Black Sorceress' spirit. It had found her shielding block. It had called the four-legged creatures.

Moving quickly, Areenna sent out a warning to Mikaal and before releasing the powers within her, calling up more of her abilities as she ran. Heat erupted, the bands of fiery energy uncoiling within her depths to spread through her like lightning. In that instant, the 'spirit' caught her emanations and stopped.

Areenna froze in mid-stride. Far below, hundreds of yards ahead of the pack of vile animals was a shadowy wavering. As her power welled up, she brought forth Ilsraeth's gift of hiding and an instant later, she disappeared.

At almost the same moment, Mikaal's mind touched hers. She sent the images of what she had seen to him. *They are coming*, she told him. *Stay inside, stay within me.*

There was a second of resistance before he agreed.

She watched the spirit move closer. She knew it sensed her, could feel its frustration when it could not find her. Then the spirit reversed itself and continued toward the cavern.

Invisible to the spirit and the mutated animals following it, Areenna raced ahead, the advantage of height in her favor. When she found a level spot where she could kneel, she raised the bow and fired. The first animal fell, a howl spewing from its mouth before it died. The others stopped. With blurring speed, Areenna released two more shafts and the first three animals lay dead on the rocks below her, their blood turning the rocks dark.

The spirit solidified into a curtain of dark misty air, which began to whirl madly. Dust and rocks kicked up, but it moved neither forward nor back. The pack of creatures following the dead ones raced forward. Weakening, Areenna realized the hiding was draining her too fast and released it. The moment she did, the spirit stopped its whirling and settled down. It had found her.

Use me, came Mikaal's command.

She drew on his strength, and as low as it was, it helped her. Then she saw the wolf-creatures turn from their path and climb toward her. Without thinking, she dropped the bow and called up more of her power. Her hands glowed white and then blue. She stood as the animals drew near. She knew her weapon would not penetrate the shield protecting the wolves but remembered the time in the journey to the Island, when she had discovered the ability with which Bekar had gifted her. Her anger at herself for not having used this power rose furiously, burning through her body like a fever gone mad.

When the creatures were within a dozen feet, their eyes a glowing orange-red, fangs dripping strings of saliva in anticipation of her flesh, she slammed her hands together. The shockwave of power exploded, bursting the Black Witch's shield apart. It caught the animals in midstride, sent them flying backwards and down.

As they fell, Gaalrie sent her a frantic warning. She turned and looked up, hearing her aoutem's screaming charge as it flew toward a small wraith above her she had not sensed. Reacting without thought, Areenna raised her right hand toward the wraith and released a stream of silver white light. The wraith was trapped within it a second before Gaalrie was able to pull up and barely avoid the stream of energy.

She encircled the wraith within the globe of white energy. It fought wildly to break free, while Areenna drew on the reserves of her strength to hold the wraith prisoner within the globe.

Stunned at how the wraith had appeared without her sensing it, Areenna pulled the globe toward her. *Careful,* came Mikaal's warning.

I need to learn about it, she responded. When it was close, she pushed her thoughts at it. She gagged when she touched the edge of its mind. When she pushed harder, she found nothing other than an overpowering need to find and take Areenna and Mikaal.

"Never," she said and closed her hand into a tightly balled fist. The white globe began to collapse into itself.

Turning quickly, her chest heaving from her efforts, she sent a stream of energy at the still visible spirit. A flash of blackness met the white of Areenna's light. The spirit deflected her power and spun again. Seconds later, it shot up and away.

She followed its path, seeing not the sky, not the dark spirit, but the shadowed form of the Black Witch herself. "You will not stop us!"

She picked up the white wood bow, slung it over her shoulder and started back toward the cavern with Mikaal still firmly lodged within her mind. *We eat from our supplies tonight. We leave in the morning,* she told him.

Yes, he replied, pushing as much of his waning strength to her in an effort to help her exhausted body move faster.

She walked to the cavern with one terrible thought burning deeply in her mind. The brief contact with the repulsive spirit had gained her an important piece of information. They had been wrong. The Black Sorceress' creatures were not trying to kill them…not any more. *Mikaal, she seeks to capture us.*

<><><>

The great hall of Tolemac's keep echoed with the voices of those gathered within. Roth and Enaid sat on one cushioned bench while Akassia and Trebor sat on another. Across from them were Ilsraeth and Timon and next to them were Atir, Layra and Laira.

Never was there a stranger council, nor a more powerful one, thought Roth as he observed everyone's reactions. "Then it is settled. Akassia and Laira leave for the east in the morning. The rest of us go to Fainhall. Messengers have been sent to all dominions, warning them of the coming invasion and with instructions to prepare their people." He paused to look at Trebor.

"I have sent another message to Kashold to build their army quickly and join us in Fainhall. If I am right, they will use a spot between Fainhall and Kashold as a landing area for their ships. Trebor, you must travel first to Lokinhold and warn your father about what is happening and urge him to gather his forces. Then to Welkold—Libon will need your help to raise his army and prepare. We must also protect the weapon stores you've said he is building,"

Roth turned to Timon and the queens. "Fainhall, Welkold and Kashold will be the most strategic places. They will start there."

Timon shook his head. "They bring only a few thousand. I don't see how they can hope to conquer any dominion."

"If I am right," Roth said, pacing his words slowly, "this first wave seeks only to gain a foothold they can maintain until the rest of their forces arrive. With such a foothold, they can safely bring in the full force of their armies."

Timon nodded. "We must send word to Llawnroc and Aldimore to prepare their vessels. They will be useful for attacking from the water."

Roth nodded. "Most are fishing boats; others are built for carrying supplies. Small boats."

"And maneuverable. They will be hard targets for bowman. They will outmaneuver the large ships. With the right men, we can burn many of their ships before they reach the shore."

"You're right," Roth agreed, "but the gathering of the boats must not be seen. We want no dark spies to know our plan."

"Such is wise. Shall I go and oversee the preparations?" asked the Master Boatsman.

"Yes, and I will send messages to the two dominions to do this quietly. I will have my men ready to leave as soon as possible." Roth looked at the others. "As soon as we can be ready, we ride to Fainhall and hope Areenna and Mikaal are nearing their destination."

Enaid stiffened at the mention of their names. She was very aware that the other three queens were staring at her. *They must*, Enaid said silently to them. *If they do not…*

XIX

"THIS IS THE spot," Mikaal said, looking at the high slopes of the mountains from the center of the junction of two paths. "We need to make a decision."

Areenna glanced from the split trail to Mikaal's questioning eyes. They had been on the move for three days since leaving the cavern. The lower trail, the one Roth had said would be their best way to go but the longest, had proven accommodating at times and difficult at others. There had been a lot of ice on the trail where the mountains shaded the sun on the narrow passage but overall, they had made good time by pushing themselves as fast and far as possible each day.

The remaining wolf-creatures were trailing them by a half day.

Within moments of awakening earlier that morning, Areenna had become aware of the beasts following them. It had been just after nightfall, last night, when they'd made camp on a level spot. There was no need to stand watch, as both Gaalrie and Charka would handle that chore easily. Nothing had disturbed their sleep except for the cold surface of the rocks beneath their sleeping silks.

She had woken Mikaal and told him of the wolf creatures. They'd risen, gathered their things and moved on. They had eaten on their kraals and pushed as fast as the sure-footed mounts could navigate the icy patches. At the worst parts, they'd dismounted and walked. Mikaal spoke rarely and Areenna had sensed there was something disturbing him that he was not yet ready to bring up.

Areenna had spent a good part of the day keeping track of their followers. The creatures had gained ground during the day and were only a few hours behind.

Areenna, Mikaal called silently.

Areenna shook away her thoughts of the last days and refocused on Mikaal. "We need to find a way to mislead them," she said and turned to look at the second pathway.

"Too bad there aren't any rabts or slungks to help us out," he responded with a slight twist of his lips. "The way you used them against *her* in Northcrom."

His words sent her mind veering in a different direction. An idea formed and she toyed with it for a few minutes. "There is a way, but we'll lose some of our supplies."

"What way?"

She glanced back at the three trailing kralets. "It is risky."

"Go on."

"We set two kralets free, send them there," she said, pointing to the path angling off from the one they were on, which according to the maps, would rise up and cross to the western side. "Then we hide our scent on this path and keep going."

It's not risky—it is dangerous.

His unspoken response surprised her. Not because he used his mind to speak to her—their way of communicating had become second nature—but that he thought it dangerous. *Why?* "Did you not tell your father you were sure there would be game? What else do we need? We bring all the supplies the kralets and our kraals can carry and we push on." *We will find game.*

His gray eyes held her like two profound jewels. *Because you believe it so?*

Because we must.

"And how do we cover our own scent? The last time we had a lake and a ferry. We have nothing but rocks, snow and ice," he stated in a low staccato stream.

She maneuvered Hero until the kraal was shoulder to shoulder with Mikaal. Her eyes never left his face. "What bothers you? The last time we rode out, you had not even a small degree of the power you now hold. We have done so much since we first left Tolemac for the east. We…you did what no other man has ever done before and you came away from the Island with powers and abilities unheard of. What stops you from believing?"

Mikaal took her words in, rolling them through his mind as he gazed at her. He started to speak but stopped and shook his head. In that instant, something jumped between them, and she knew exactly what. The feeling stunned her. She had never sensed doubt within him.

Reaching out, she grasped his hand tightly. "You blame yourself for what happened with those wolves." Wolves….even the word was dark to her. "You blame yourself for your injuries. You think you did something wrong."

He remained silent. Until that very minute she spoke, he had had no idea why he had closed himself off the last few days, but Areenna's words held true. "I should have been stronger."

"You were strong enough to stop me from being hurt or killed. How much stronger do you need to be?"

He started to speak but stopped. He shook his head.

"It was me, not you, who wasn't strong enough. Do you not see? Mikaal, I hesitated. I did not use the abilities gifted to me. I…" She drew in a deep breath and squeezed his hand again. "What happened was my fault, not yours. Watch!" she commanded him. She drew him into her mind and replayed the attack.

When she finished she let go of his hand and his mind. "Do you not see?"

He had seen the ambush by the creatures, watched every bit of it through Areenna's eyes. When the memory ended, a curtain lifted. She had been right. Nothing had been more important than protecting her, than keeping her unharmed. He had forgotten the most important of the lessons he had learned on the Island and let his need to protect take command.

"How do we cover our own scents and force them to follow the kralets?"

Areenna breathed easier with his words. Gone was the heaviness present moments before. "Look up," she said.

He followed her gaze to the cliffs above, so heavily laden with snow it seemed more like the strands of an old man's beard, hanging from a jutting chin, than snow leaching over the edges of the cliff.

"You would create an avalanche?"

She shook her head. "Not quite, but snow is water. Think of the snow storm in Brumwall."

He remembered well the hours they had spent locked together while she had reversed the snow, drawing on both their powers to fight the storm the Black Sorceress had controlled. "Go on."

"After we send the kralets off, I will bring down snow to block this trail and cover our scent. We will put some clothing on the kralets to add whatever scent we can. They do not seek to catch us, not yet. They will follow the kralets as they follow us now, and her dark…spirit follows the wolf things. We ride through the night. We stop not. By the time *she* realizes what we have done, we will be out of their reach."

"You are so certain?"

"I am. It started after I fought them the second time. I touched the edges of the spirit-thing *she* created. I learned but little, yet I knew its purpose as soon as I touched it. She no longer seeks our deaths. It is us *she* wants, alive for whatever reason."

Mikaal shook his head. "No, *she* will not have us." When he dismounted and went to the three kralets, Areenna slipped off Hero's back and joined him. Together they took the most important supplies: as much food as the single pack animal could carry, along with their sleeping silks, water skeins, and spare clothing. They hung the light metal armor his father had made for them on Hero and Charka's saddles and when they were done, Areenna stepped up to the separated kralets.

Placing a hand on each of their necks, she closed her eyes and drew up her power. Coils of power spread through her until they reached her hands. She pictured the map in her mind and the trail leading up into the mountains and pushed the direction into the pack animals and, using every bit of her abilities, she drew her scent and Mikaal's to the animals, covering them as best she could.

When she was satisfied, she lifted her hands and gave them a silent command. The two kralets started forward.

Mikaal nodded. *Perfect.*

Now the snow, she told him. Together, they led their kraals along the lower trail until Areenna stopped them. *I need your help.*

Over the past months, it had become effortless to join her, and he did so instantly. The warmth and the comfort contained in the joining was a feeling he could never describe, only enjoy and welcome each time. *What do you need from me?*

Your support as I work. Follow what I do, add your power to mine.

Without another thought, Areenna raised her powers to the fullest as she called upon the gift of divining and used the formula she had created to call water. Remembering every step she had used to control the snow during the storm at Brumwall, she wove her hands in circular motions, her palms always pointing to the snow above.

It was hard work, and she drew on the unusual power contained within Mikaal's masculinity. Slowly, the snow above them began to whirl. Chunks of ice fell to the trail just before a huge section of the hanging snow crashed to the pathway, covering a hundred feet. As it struck the trail, another section separated from the cliff's edge and tumbled down.

Enough?

She shook her head.

The snow and ice had formed mounds, some five and six feet high, which covered more than half the distance between them and the trail's junction. He remembered the ambush, how the creatures had climbed the rocks during the attack. He shook his head. *They are climbers. We need more.*

Raising her arms, Areenna called forth the formula. She dug deep within her and within Mikaal as well, building their joined power to a peak and launched them at the mountainside. There was a loud crack as a huge shelf of snow separated from the cliff and poured down, a mini-avalanche landing atop the already fallen snow.

When the mist created by the snowfall cleared, the pile was twice her height. "This should stop them," she said.

"It better."

They mounted the kraals. "We ride through the night, yes?"

"Yes," Mikaal agreed.

<><><>

In the large gathering field outside the walls of Tolemac, twenty-two days after Areenna and Mikaal started on their quest, Roth sat astride his kraal, looking at the lines of soldiers, most of whom were regular citizens of Tolemac. There were four companies, each comprised of a hundred men and women and led by one of his 'Six' groups. Many of those who had volunteered to follow Roth were veterans of the war twenty years past, their grown sons and daughters riding at their sides. While men made up three quarters of the army, a full quarter were women of varying powers.

None of the women marching with them was the equal to the four women who sat on their kraals behind Roth. Yet, each had valuable abilities to aid the men at whose sides they would fight. Layra and Atir's husbands were already gathering their armies, preparing as Roth had asked, while Ilsraeth's husband, Timon, gathered a fleet.

Roth eyed the gathered force, hating the knowledge that too many would die when they faced the Dark One's forces. He thought about saying something, but changed his mind. These people needed no inspiration—they knew what would happen should the dark forces overpower them. None would give up the freedom they had won, and if they had to sacrifice their lives, they would.

Roth raised himself in his stirrups until he stood straight and said, simply, "Thank you."

At his words, the men and women of his 'Six' groups all raised their arms, their fists balled in a silent salute. A low growl emanated from the throats of the four hundred warriors behind them.

Turning his mount, he rode to the four women and stopped next to Enaid. He gazed at her, his lips forming a half smile. "Once again we go to war. What happens from this point on determines all."

Enaid nodded. She knew his words were absolute. They would either be victorious, or cease to be who they were.

XX

THE DAYS GREW shorter the further north they traveled, the sun rising only for a few hours, and setting for short periods of real darkness. Most of the day and night had a pale gray cast, the sky slightly brighter near the horizon while it remained darker above. It was so different from Freemorn and Tolemac, Areenna could only wonder why.

Late on the night at the start of their fourth week of travel, Areenna and Mikaal made camp within a cutout of the mountainside. The trail they had been following since using the kralets as decoys had risen steadily. They were hundreds of feet above the arctic ice fields, which lined the coast of the Frozen Mountains. Only 'Frozen Mountains' were not exactly what the name proclaimed them to be. Yes, they were cold and primarily covered with snow, but many areas of the red and brown mountainside held no snow, only the dead remains of trees so old they seemed to be made more of stone than wood. The land itself was abnormally warm. Intuitively, Areenna knew to stay too long on the bare ground would be somehow dangerous to them. It was as if the ground contained strange poisons killing whatever lived upon it as it had done to the stone-like trees.

Their supplies were nearly exhausted. They had been lucky a few times in finding game. One time they'd come across a lone rabt, which, although scrawny, held enough meat for two sparse meals.

A few days after that, Gaalrie had found a peculiar looking tarq. The only way to tell it was a tarq was because of its horns and hooves; but unlike most targs, this one's horns were larger and curved in a semi-circle ending with the tip at eye level. Its thick coat of wiry hair was grayish brown, its rump white and it had a very short white beard beneath its chin.

After the hunt and, with as much of the meat as they could carry stuffed in bags with snow, they had moved on. Thanks to the snow and cold, the meat had lasted a week.

Wrapped in their fur cloaks, and sitting before the small fire, they finished the last of the meat. They ate silently until Mikaal wiped his hands and turned to her. "According to the map, we will be at the chasm in two or three days and then we must cross the mountains."

"Your father was right. We have made good time since losing *her* creatures. With luck, the crossing will be as smooth."

"You get no sense of the wolf-things?"

She shook her head. "I have no feel of them nearby. Nor that spirit-thing of *hers*. Gaalrie has seen nothing of them either."

Mikaal nodded, stretched and pointed at the sky. *So different from Tolemac.*

So beautiful, Areenna responded. The stars were like a shimmering blanket of gems sewn into a black quilt. Their patterns, woven so randomly, made her believe a woman of great power had created a magnificent quilt in the sky.

She yawned as the toll of the long day of riding settled over her. Before she could say anything, Mikaal spoke. "You are tired. We should sleep."

She nodded and smiled. Sleep had become a troubling time for her, yet it was the most important time of the day. To protect themselves from the cold while they slept, they had begun to combine their sleeping silks. Beneath the protection of the furred cloaks, atop the silks, they would lay next to each other for the added heat of their bodies. When she'd awaken each morning, she had found, somehow during the night they had drawn into each other's arms.

Having him so close was a wondrous comfort, but vastly disturbing, as her body had begun responding to their closeness. While she was well aware of the normal reactions of her body, it was because of who they were and even more so what they must do, that what should have been natural to them had become both a curse and a deep inner need.

"What?" Mikaal asked, seeing her far off look.

Areenna smiled at him. "Nothing, my mind wandered. And yes, I am tired and need sleep."

Rising, he went to their supplies. Areenna followed behind and together they set their sleeping silks on the most level section of the inwardly curved mountainside cutout. Then they put their swords and knives next to the silks.

Ten minutes later, their personal needs taken care of privately, they laid on the silks and pulled the cloaks over themselves. No words passed between them as they lay on their backs, their sides touching from shoulder to hip, until they fell asleep.

<><><>

The scene before her was extraordinary. Large boats filled with the soldiers of the Master rocked on the water beneath. The ships had arrived during the day. While he had not shown himself to her, not communicated with her, his presence was everywhere. *She* took in the powers dancing in the very air itself, breathing in the essence of the great Master with every breath. *She* had been waiting patiently on the Cliffside for him to call her.

Then, at last, from behind, *she* sensed him and, turning, found herself face to face with her Master for the first time in five decades. *She* knelt, her head bowed before him, trembling with the anticipation of his words.

When they came, her body arched backwards. His eyes, burning amber orbs surrounded by a thin circle of red, stared into her very core. Hairless, his skin was the color of a dark gray stormy day. His features were barely recognizable as a man: a nose, short, flat and bent, hovered over the small round dash of a mouth framed by thin lips five shades darker than his gray skin. He was taller than *she,* and slightly bent. *She* could not make out his body beneath the black robes he wore. Elongated fingers and hands peeked out from the folds of his robe, his nails black and more like claws than a man's hand.

"Long have you waited, long have you served. The end is near and we are strong. Stand!" he commanded.

She drew herself upward until *she* stood almost eye-to-eye with him. He reached out, his hand open, his fingers and nails stretched wide. He placed his hand on her head and a bolt of power raced through her. Her muscles tightened and expanded. He filled her with tendrils of his deeply dark power, more so than *she* had ever experienced before. Breathing deeply, her chest expanded with every breath and *she* was renewed.

"Tell me of the two."

Within her mind, a picture of Areenna and Mikaal rose. "They are powerful together. Why this is I know not, Master, but such power as I have never seen. I tracked them to here," *she* said, and drew a mind picture of the Frozen Mountains. "Somehow they have been able to hide themselves with a block I cannot find. My pretty wolves, they tracked them by scent, but they were deceived—"

"You have lost them?"

"My creatures follow them now. I sent them back and found where they had gone. They are four or five days behind."

His anger grew, hitting her like a fist. *She* staggered back but did not fall. "It was not a fault of mine, Master. When they returned from the…Island in the East, they were changed."

"You were warned. You were told." He reached out an open hand and balled it into a fist. As he did so, the power he had filled her with, twisted and constricted harshly, squeezing inward and sending shards of crippling pain through every part of her being. *Master, look within me, see what happened. She* begged, fighting the inner agony he poured through her.

Opening his hand, he released the torturing pain and, with two fingers, drew her to him as if she were no more than a puppet. He pushed her to her knees, and placed a gray and claw-like hand on her head. *Show me!*

For an hour *she* poured out her memories, from the first instance her wraith had met Areenna and Mikaal to Tolemac to the battle within Tolemac's council chamber. *She* showed him the death of the duplicate king, the clone the Master had sent, and the giant snuck *she* had released on them. Then *she* showed him how they had evaded her and how they had grown in powers with every mile they had traveled.

She played out the battles along the road to the Island, and the way *she* had delayed the two most hated ones, Roth and Enaid, in their attempt to help the other two reach the Island. *She* went on, holding back nothing of how the two had defeated her mighty wraiths. When *she* reached the point of their final battle on their return from the Island, *she* revealed how the man had unexpectedly shown unheard of powers and had used fire—long streams of shooting flames—to kill her greatest and most terrible creation.

It was not my fault, my Master...

Releasing *her*, he withdrew his hand from her head. *She* collapsed on the hard stone of the Cliffside, the pain ebbing from her twisted body. *She* lay there at his feet, waiting, wondering if he would spare her.

"Rise," he said.

She gained her feet as quickly as her deformed body permitted and stood before him, her eyes pleading.

We have seen your truth. The fault is of the Circle, for we did not see clearly. We need more. Show me the woman-child first and then the... man.

She brought up a mind picture of Areenna and showed him Areenna as *she* had been as a young child and then as she was today: tall and slender, lean of muscle with skin the shade of golden oak and pale hair framing an oval face. Green eyes sat beneath curved brows, set above a smooth aquiline nose.

Yes, she is the one we have foreseen. She is the one we must have. Show me the man.

The Black Sorceress projected her thought to the Master, building a picture of Mikaal. Gray eyes with black straight hair cut off just above wide powerful shoulders. His features were almost the same as Roth but set in lines that turned Roth's sharp angles into smooth curves. Mikaal was tall and broad, with long dense muscles bespeaking strength and endurance.

We must separate them, understand who he is and destroy him...obliterate any part of him!

"How, my Master?"

Show me where your creatures are.

She sent her senses out and when *she* found the spirit and the wolves that raced along the trail overlooking the Arctic Ice Fields, *she* showed the Master. *They are a few days ahead.*

Good. Turning, the Master went to the edge of the cliff, where he could see his ships anchored below. He spread his arms, the fingers of one hand drawing in the air. When he stopped, he turned both black palms down toward one vessel in particular. His hands turned perpendicular and came close to but did not touch each other. An instant later he turned them to face upward and behind him, ten dark-skinned and hairless things—things that could have been but were not men—appeared. They were tall and wide with heavy muscles and powerful legs. Their eyes, holes buried deep within their faces, were an odd color of amber. Mouths, almost oval, showed ragged rows of teeth. Their noses were flat lumps set on their faces, the nostrils wide and flaring. They wore shirts of dirt-covered rusted chainmail that dropped to mid-thigh and boots of stiff leather. Swords hung at their sides; each carried a knife and two carried axes strapped to their backs.

The Master stepped close to the first of them. He placed his hands to each side of the man's head. When he released the head, the man and the nine with him turned and began running at a pace that would cover miles as fast as a trotting kraal.

His strange almost oval thin-lipped mouth twisted into a smile. *They go to join your wolves but on the far side of the chasm, which is the only way through the mountains. They will be there in time to stop them. Be ready at the rise of the day. We meet then.* He disappeared on the last word.

<><><>

The frosted air, moved along by unseen winds sweeping down from the mountaintop, bit at her skin. Grayish white clouds gathered around the peak, hiding the very top from sight. She could not feel her face or her hands, even though her hands were under the heavy cloak. Areenna looked around for Mikaal, but could not find him. She sought him with her eyes and her mind when a shift rumbled through her. Turning, she found herself staring at a spot carved into the side of the mountain.

It was wide and flat and made of something other than rock. Twice the height of a man, and five times as wide, it was the most unnatural thing she'd ever seen. Then it wavered. Shimmering mist grew before the spot and seconds later, eight figures appeared within the shifting haze; the eight sorceresses of the Island stood before her, their tightly wrapped cloaks hiding what she knew lay beneath—bodies of half woman-half snuck.

Here is where you must come to. In here is what you must find. Here is where your fate and Nevaeh's rests. The words came from a single mind, yet Areenna knew all eight were speaking at the same time.

We are coming. We move as fast as we can, she told them.

There is much danger both following you and coming at you. You must go faster for time is running out; the darkness approaches quicker than foreseen. A Dark Master has reached our shores.

The one in the lead, the one who had tested them on the Island, pushed her arm through the cloak, a long black finger pointing to the shimmering wall. *This is where you gain entry.*

Before she could speak, the Eight were gone. Areenna opened her eyes to find Mikaal lying next to her, his arms around her, his eyes wide and staring at her. "You saw?"

"I saw," he whispered. "I saw where we must go. I saw the shimmering wall."

"I saw as well. And heard…"

We must move faster, she told him. "How do you feel? How is your strength?"

"I am fine. I feel nothing of the attack," he said, rotating his shoulder smoothly.

She joined with him. She found everything was as it should be. His strength had returned; his body healed.

"Are you satisfied, my Princess?" he asked sarcastically.

She reached out to cup his cheek. A month of whiskery growth rubbed at her hand. "Mock me if you will, my Prince, but…"

He smiled. "The lessons of the Island are with me. The fight with those creatures serve well to remind me of such. I will not lie to you with a false need to protect. I am healed."

"Then we can move faster," she said, lowering her hand and sitting up. "What do you make of the dream—the vision?" she asked, still not rising.

He studied her before shaking his head. "I'm not certain. It appears to me this sheet of…metal perhaps, is an entryway inside the mountain."

"Yes, but how do we get inside?"

He cocked his head slightly to the left. "Did you not see the indentation on the side? They showed it to us for a purpose. What other meaning can be taken?"

"We'll see. But now we should eat and be on our way."

Fifteen minutes later, they sat before the fire, sipping cups of morning tea and eating a small amount of the remains of dried dar meat from their meager supplies.

Areenna finished her tea, put down the cup and froze. Above her, Gaalrie cried out. She joined with her and an instant later, called the giant treygone to her.

The bird dropped to Areenna's waiting arms and when she landed, Areenna drew her to her chest. Behind them, Charka cried out and came to them, pressing his head to Mikaal.

Areenna closed her eyes. "We are found. The wolf-creatures are on our trail again and…" She stopped speaking as a whisper of a mind touch brushed through her. Her eyes flew open. "There is something else…something darker, viler than is even *she*," Areenna said and worked her way through the blocking shield she'd erected around them after the first attack. As soon as she did, she caught the faintest trace of a deep dark evil that sent shudders of revulsion through her in heart-stopping waves.

Cutting off her searching thought, she pulled Gaalrie even tighter to her chest. *The Afzareen… A Dark Master… it seeks us now.*

XXI

A DARK MASTER. Enaid stiffened the instant she sensed the evil. She turned to Roth, about to speak when from behind him, Layra, Ilsraeth and Atir turned from where they sat to stare at her.

Rising, she went to them. “You felt it?” The three nodded. “Then it has begun. We must raise a strong shield. One he cannot penetrate. He must not know our strength. We need to come with surprise.”

She looked beyond the three women of power, to the hundreds who were preparing for the day. The forces from Fainhall and Kashold had joined Tolemac’s army. Two days ago, they had received word that Welkold had gathered their forces. Trebor had also sent word that King Libon had dispatched three long-carts of arrows and lances a week earlier. The weapons should reach today. Roth had asked Enaid to send a return message to hold Welkold’s troops until he sent word.

“The shield will hold through the wastelands, but when we enter the badlands—*her* territory—we will be found,” Atir said to Enaid.

Sitting, Enaid exhaled a long-held breath. “What have you seen?” she asked the three.

Ilsraeth shook her head. “Only that there is a Master here. This has not happened for…”

“Before our births,” Layra finished for Ilsraeth. “Only the old legends of their powers have we.”

Reaching out, she grasped Atir’s hand on one side and Layra’s on the other. When they were connected, Enaid began the formation of a powerful block and shield, building it slowly and carefully, drawing upon the offered powers from each of their abilities until they swayed within the grip of the formula Enaid called forth. The powers swirled around them like an unseen tornado and built in strength until it was solid. Then they encircled the army of the three dominions with the shield, and nine hundred souls became invisible to any of power who sought them.

When they finished, Enaid went to where Roth stood. Three steps later, she stopped and turned back. “Ilsraeth, where is Timon?”

The queen closed her eyes. When they opened, she said, "He is a day out. The boats arrive in the morning."

Enaid spun and went to Roth, who stood waiting. "What has happened?"

"Much, Solomon," she said and told him of what she had found.

<><><>

On the early afternoon of the third day after sensing the Dark Master's presence, Areenna drew Hero to a halt. She turned to Mikaal. "The kraals need to rest. We have ridden for three days without stopping for more than a few minutes. Hero needs rest and so do I."

Mikaal strength too was almost gone. "We have one maybe two meals left for ourselves and the kraals. Send Gaalrie to find a place to camp. We must hunt."

Areenna called to her aoutem and asked Gaalrie to find them a suitable place. The treygone rose, her silver, black, and cinnamon feathered body casting a pale shadow over the snow-covered slope of the mountain. While Gaalrie flew ahead, Areenna and Mikaal went on.

"I have had no sense of them for the last day," she told Mikaal. "You?"

Nothing.

I hope that is for the good. She added.

They moved on in weary silence. Each had slept in short spurts on the backs of their kraals, one sleeping while the other stayed alert. Gaalrie had found enough food for herself, but nothing large enough for them to hunt. What remained of their supplies was barely enough to help keep the kraals moving. Neither Areenna nor Mikaal had eaten since last night.

The relentless cold was taking its toll on their bodies and minds, and it was only the heavy fur cloaks they wore that kept them from freezing. Two nights earlier, Mikaal had taken one of their sleeping silks and split it so they could wrap the pieces around their faces. The thinness of the silks allowed them to breathe while the material's protection kept their skin from freezing.

When Gaalrie's call came, Areenna had no idea how long it had been, but at the mind-touch, she grew alert. The treygone had found a place for them.

She shared what Gaalrie was showing with Mikaal, who raised his eyes to stare ahead. She sent Gaalrie onward to seek game, if there even was any in this forsaken and frozen land.

"We are near the chasm as well," Mikaal spoke aloud, needing to talk aloud, to move his mouth and jaw in an effort to shake the cold claiming him.

When Areenna did not respond, he turned and saw her head bent low. He pushed toward her and found she slept. He sent his thoughts to Gaalrie and reinforced Areenna's asking for the giant bird to search for food.

Fifteen minutes later, Mikaal reached the spot Areenna's aoutem had found. It was little more than an indentation in the rock wall mountainside but large enough for them to lay down and be shielded from the cold winds. He drew Charka to a stop with only a thought, dismounted and went to Areenna, who had just raised her head. "I'm sorry," she whispered.

Mikaal laughed. "Are you apologizing for sleeping? Don't. Let's get the kraals and the kralet fed. Then we can rest. Gaalrie seeks game."

Without a single mew of protest, Areenna slid from Hero and went toward the kralet. Mikaal stopped her.

He untied her sleeping silks from the back of the saddle and taking her hand in his free one, walked to the open area where he spread her silks and without a word, pointed to them.

Areenna forced a smile. "Thank you, my Prince." Then, she went to the silks and laid down. "Where are your silks?" she asked just before her eyes closed.

Mikaal stood there for a minute and in that short time, Areenna fell asleep. He called to Charka, who responded by nudging Hero toward him. When they were next to him, he stroked both kraals and went to the pack animal. He removed the last of the grain bags and spread half on the ground for the two kraals. He put three handfuls out for the kralet and took the supplies from its back.

When he took what was left of his sleeping silks and placed them next to Areenna's, there was a tug in his mind from Gaalrie. Instantly he was in her mind seeing with her eyes. What he saw amazed him. Gaalrie was at the chasm. The separation between the mountains was very wide. The trail cut deeply into the mountainside, and the water below was not frozen but raced with the speed of rapids. In the water, almost like a sheet, were fresh, huge silver and red freeshes, their scales casting iridescent flashes in the waning afternoon light, swimming and jumping into the air as they raced against the water's current.

Mikaal sent Gaalrie a quick thought; the bird wheeled, spun in a circle and dove straight to the water. Two heartbeats later the treygone rose skyward, a large squirming freesh in its huge claws.

Mikaal had never seen this type of freesh and only hoped its meat was edible. A few minutes later, Gaalrie was overhead. Instead of landing, the bird flew twenty feet over Mikaal and dropped the freesh to him. The freesh, still fighting in its clawed grip fell hard but did not die.

Mikaal used his knife to end the freesh's struggle while Gaalrie landed on Charka's back and settled herself comfortably. *Thank you, sister.*

He saw she had not moved during the last few minutes. Smiling, he looked from her to the mountainside and his smile died. There was no wood.

He thought about climbing upward in hopes of finding one of the old dead trees but knew he was too tired and was reluctant to leave Areenna alone; instead, he gutted the freesh, scooped up snow, packed it into the freesh and giving into his own exhaustion, laid down next to Areenna, his cloak tight around him. Instantly, he fell asleep.

He woke two hours later, stiff, cold and screamingly hungry. The night was upon them, if the half-light of this strange place could be called night. He turned to Areenna, who was still asleep. He toyed with letting her sleep, but realized how hungry she had to be as well. He leaned toward her and shook her shoulder. She did not respond. He shook her once again, harder. Nothing. He opened the cloak and slipped his hand under the leather tunic, grasping her shoulder. Her skin was icy.

He cut off a sharp surge of fear, closed his eyes and pushed his thoughts to her. He almost withdrew when he caught a strangely fragmented dream of a little girl walking with her mother in a forest. Then she was older, kneeling at the side of a bed. Her mother lay in it, her face drawn, her skin sallow and her body thin and weak. Areenna was crying, pleading for her mother to be healed.

Areenna, he called, *Areenna, you must wake. Come back, come now*, he pushed, forcing his own energy to her. *Wake!*

With his last thought, he went deep into himself, awakening the powers laying within and tasting the hot surge of his abilities roaring to life. He pushed it all to her, willing his own powers to fill her, to warm her and to wake her.

Nothing happened for an unending minute and then a loud gasp echoed from her mouth. Areenna sat upright before the sound died. She grasped her chest with both hands, her breasts heaving, as her wide eyes searched everywhere until they settled on Mikaal.

She knew the minute their eyes met what had happened. Reaching out, she wrapped her arms around him and held him tight, her body trembling with emotion. When she settled down, and her breathing returned to normal, she loosened her hold on him and leaned back.

"How long," she asked.

"A few hours. You were sleeping too deeply. I could not wake you."

You used your powers. I heard you call me, but I could not leave the dream. I...

I understand. It's the cold. It was claiming you.

"It was more. I had dreams from which I did not want to awaken. I was with my mother."

"I know, I saw."

"And you rescued me from them."

"We have food."

"You hunted?"

He smiled. "Gaalrie did. A large freesh. A strange one. How do you feel about eating raw freesh?"

"What else have we?"

Nodding, he stood and offered her his hand. "You need to move about."

She took his hand and pulled herself up. "There are no old trees around?"

He shook his head. "We must eat it uncooked."

Her brows furrowed. "I wonder…"

What?

Your weapon.

On the freesh? There will be nothing left.

You control its force.

He focused on the freesh and then on his hands. He called up his powers and the response was immediate. Flames encased every inch of his hands. He raised them and pointed his palms at the freesh.

"Wait!" Areenna called. She went to the freesh and drawing her knife, cut the head free. She placed it a short distance away. "For Gaalrie," she added and called to her aoutem.

Mikaal took another step closer and began. Having never done this before, he moved ahead with caution. He cut off his first try instantly, realizing there would be nothing left but ashes. He stared at the freesh for several moments before he moved to it, squatted above it and very, very carefully increased the flame. He held his hands a few inches away and watched the fire created by his powers cook the freesh. It took three minutes. The outer skin was darkly crisp, but the scent of cooked freesh was tantalizing.

He separated the skin and pulled a small piece free. He sniffed the strange scent and popped it into his mouth. Then he smiled. *The best I have eaten in days.*

It's the only real food you've eaten in days, Areenna retorted.

Mikaal picked up the freesh and brought it to where they had slept. He motioned Areenna to sit with him and when she did, they ate in earnest. They did not speak, did not smile, and did not look anywhere but at the freesh. When they finished, there was enough left for one more meal, barely.

"How do you feel?" Mikaal asked after using snow to clean his hands.

Areenna, doing the same, paused for a breath. "Good. I feel better, stronger, less tired."

"Then we move on?"

"Yes. We move on."

He turned to where he had placed the remaining supplies he'd removed from the kralet, grabbed the map and opened it. "The chasm is close. If the trail stays true there, the crossing will be level, and we should make it to the western side in two days. There are freesh aplenty in the water. And fortunately, the water in the chasm is not frozen."

Areenna shook her head. “This part of Nevaeh is so strange. How can the water be frozen down there and not in the chasm?”

“You might as well ask how I can have the powers of a woman.”

“The answer to that, we know,” Areenna replied.

“I have been thinking about that. My father has no powers. Why would I?”

Areenna gazed at him. “What brings this question?”

He shrugged. “It comes to me on and off. It’s a puzzle.”

“Your father is the last of the old ones. He is…how did he explain it, he is not mutated.” She paused, seeking an elusive thought. When she caught it, she smiled. “I think it is because he is an old one and your mother is so powerful that when you were created, you were open to your mother’s powers and somehow…”

Areenna stopped. She shook her head. *I don’t have the words. I believe you must accept your gifts because they make you who you are.*

He gazed at her a few seconds before smiling. *Your thoughts are enough.*

Areenna stiffened. She sensed something at the edge of the block she’d created. *They are following, getting closer.*

XXII

"HOW FAR BEHIND?" Mikaal asked.

"A day at the most. We need to go."

Standing, Mikaal offered his hand. She took it, ignoring the ever-constant tingle when their skin touched. Together, they gathered what supplies remained and set them on the kralet.

It took them just over an hour to reach the divide separating the two sections of the Frozen Mountains where they turned to follow the trail westward. The chasm was wide, perhaps a thousand feet across, while far below the water roared along with frothing urgency. Large freesh jumped madly into the air as they threw themselves against the current. They fought to swim eastward where they dove below the frozen artic ice fields, going to a place of which only they knew.

A quarter mile in, riding the kraals single file, Areenna said, "I have never seen the likes of this. So many freesh they almost hide the water."

Mikaal tilted his head upward. The top edges of the mountains on both sides of the chasm reached so high their outlines faded against the dark gray sky. Yet, in the hazy heights, the mountains appeared to come toward each other, the gap between the two sides narrow at the top. When he looked ahead, it was as if he were staring at the walls of a huge tunnel.

He turned in the saddle to look behind. The outline of where they had started appeared even more tunnel-like from where he rode. "I feel as though I am inside the mountain itself."

"It does feel so," she agreed. Her brows knitted together a minute later. "I like it not, knowing those…creatures are moving faster, getting so close. We have nowhere to hide, nowhere to find safety."

Her words triggered a deep response; he closed his eyes and sought it for what it was. He took several breaths and opened his eyes.

"What did you see?"

"The other side of the chasm to where we go. I saw us reach it and know the wolves will stay behind us. They herd us there." He shook his head to clear the foreseeing. "Something awaits us, but of what, I saw nothing."

She started to speak but stopped when she sensed he had turned inward, searching for more of the foreseeing. Instead, she urged Hero forward—Charka and the kralet followed. She called Gaalrie to her. The aoutem dropped to her perch on the saddle horn. She held her thoughts to herself as they moved deeper into the chasm. After an hour of riding, there was a change in the chasm trail and she turned to Mikaal. "The trail is widening and we are descending."

He sat straighter, his eyes alert. He moved Charka next to Hero. "We must find what lies ahead."

Areenna stroked Gaalrie's head with the back of her forefinger. "This is a strange place."

"We need to know if it goes up or down, and whether it ends at water or land."

Areenna sighed. "I understand." She joined with Gaalrie, asking the aoutem to fly ahead, but she also placed restraints upon the bird. "Not far," she whispered and joined with her.

She reached across and clasped Mikaal's hand, pulling him into her mind as Gaalrie flew ahead. Everything appeared the same as the bird flew a dozen feet over the pathway, which descended slowly but steadily. A short time later, Gaalrie leveled off as did the path. It ended in what appeared to be a valley carved into the bottom of the chasm.

Gaalrie flew into the valley, rising and falling as she gave them a view of what should not have been possible. There were trees, plants, and animals. *How can it be?*

Mikaal gave a mental shrug. *The Eight knew we would come this way. They knew we would find food.*

"The wolves?" she said aloud as she called Gaalrie back to them and released Mikaal from her mind.

He understood her unspoken question. If they spent a day hunting and resupplying with what they could find, the wolves would be on them.

"I saw them herding us to the other side. I…" He stopped, his mind searching through the memory of Queen Ammie's training. She had spoken of how a foretelling told only of what might happen. The future was not absolute. *Change something in the present and the future adjusts.*

"We will meet whatever awaits us on the western side of this chasm on our terms and not herded there by whatever *she* has sent. As they ambushed us, so should we return the favor."

Areenna thought on his words and a moment later nodded. "We cannot afford to sacrifice the kralet. We need it."

"Then we must be sure when we strike."

She lifted her arm and Gaalrie dropped to it. Areenna accepted the treygone's weight and held her arm steady. She gazed into her aoutem's eyes and offered a gentle 'asking' of the bird.

Gaalrie spread her wings, and Areenna tossed her arm upward to give the treygone a lift. The bird rose with an easy double flap of its wings. It circled the two riders and rose higher until its gray and cinnamon feathers disappeared against the high walls of the mountain.

We will know soon enough.

They moved forward and down, the sound of rushing water growing loud. Fifteen minutes after she'd left, Gaalrie sent them their answer: the wolves were two hours, not a day, behind.

Another quarter mile further along the path, Mikaal drew Charka to a stop. There was a notch in the mountainside, wide enough for both kraals to get through. Inside the opening, a path rose upward. He wondered where it led. "Send Gaalrie up there," he said, pointing to the notch. "Let's see where it leads."

Gaalrie flew into the notch swiftly and Mikaal joined with Areenna to see through the treygone's eyes. The trail widened slightly and rose steeply but not too much so. As the giant bird ascended, the path it followed lightened as well. After what seemed like intolerable amount of time, Gaalrie burst from the side of the mountain and flew in a circle above the pathway's exit.

Mikaal's sharp indrawn breath echoed around them and matched Areenna's own exclamation. "The mountains almost touch. The other one has a trail as well."

"Yes," Mikaal said with a smile. "Come, we must prepare a trap for the wolves. I have a thought," he said and sent a picture of what he planned.

Understanding his idea, Areenna called Gaalrie back to her. The bird came straight down the sides of the mountain rather than return through the strange pathway. They moved on and entered the valley that should not have been there. Trees and shrubbery flourished everywhere. In the distance, stood a forest.

"How can this be?" Mikaal asked. There was no sun; yet, within the grayness the trees and vegetation held a riot of greens and reds.

Unable to answer, Areenna rode Hero silently, but her eyes scanned everywhere. Craves flew between the branches; she spotted a rabt hole not ten feet from the rocks they rode upon. The temperature kept rising the further in they rode. The breeze blowing over them was now warm, not cold.

Mikaal drew Charka to a halt. Dismounting, he knelt and put his palms to the ground. He snapped them back quickly. "The ground is warm, almost hot, as if there is fire below."

Areenna dismounted, joined him and touched the ground. Instead of drawing her hands back, she dug her fingers into the earth, between small shards of rock.

Closing her eyes, she let go her senses, exploring not around them but under them, feeling for whatever lay below. She remained locked with the earth for several minutes. Then, withdrawing her hands, she turned to him. "You have been to the mountain in Welkold, the one that shoots fire and gives off burning melted rocks like streams of water?"

"Yes." A long ago memory tried to break through. It took a moment but he finally remembered his father's explanation of the mountain in Welkold they had seen when he was very young. At the time, it was smoking and spitting fiery rocks. "Lava," he said. "My father once told me it is called that. It comes from deep within the earth and as it rises, it turns rock and dirt into liquid fire.

"What flows beneath us is the same. It is what heats this valley. It gives life to the trees and plants."

"Without sun, how can they grow and live?"

"I cannot give an answer for what I don't know, but how do we live?" She went silent, her eyes still on Mikaal. *How can there be magic?*

How can we have powers? How can you have the powers of a woman? In these past months, I've come to accept the impossible. We have seen too much to believe otherwise, have we not?

"So we do not question, just accept?" he asked. *Is it so easy for you?*

I see no choice. I believe your father will have an answer.

Mikaal laughed. "He always does, somehow, he knows." Then his features turned serious. "We must find a place." He nodded toward the beginning of the thicker trees. "We go in there and find trees with branches low enough to reach from the kraals, so we do not touch the ground. I will have Charka lead Hero and the kralet deeper into the forest. When the wolves come…"

Areenna nodded with the plan. "You have no bow."

Mikaal smiled again. He drew out the knife his father had given him, and reached into his boot to draw the one his grandfather had gifted him at Brumwall. "Both are perfectly balanced."

Mikaal had spent two days teaching her how to throw a knife. While he did this effortlessly, for some reason she could not master this skill. *Yet,* she told herself.

"Gaalrie saw five. We will have to be fast."

"You said she wants to capture us, not kill us."

"It's what I sensed."

"That is our advantage."

"They are on the downslope. Do not use any powers. We know not what formula *she* has set. If we kill them without such, there is a chance *she* may not be warned."

"Come," Mikaal said and pushed Charka forward.

When they were closer to the thicker stands of trees, Areenna and Mikal dismounted and walked next to the kraals. Each touched the boles of the trees as they passed by, making sure their scent remained. Soon they entered a heavier stand of trees and found several bunched together, their thick branches low enough for them to reach from the backs of their kraals and pull themselves up.

Once settled in the tree and with a quick asking, Mikaal had Charka lead Hero and the kralet deeper into the forest.

Then they waited on their branches for the dark creatures. Areenna, straddling a thick branch, selected three arrows and set them across her thighs. She held the bow comfortably in her left hand. Gaalrie was perched on a branch ten feet above her, directly over her right shoulder.

Closing her eyes, Areenna began to 'feel' the valley. There was much life. Craves and their smaller cousins, smiges, were everywhere within the trees. She found a family of rabts, secure deep within their warren, not fifty feet below her tree. From them she caught ribbons of fear rising out, for they had already scented the wolf-creatures approach.

They are near, she told Mikaal. She notched the first arrow. Across from her, Mikaal sat straighter, the tip of one knife held between his thumb and forefinger.

She watched Mikaal set himself and close his eyes. They snapped open seconds later.

Two come in the lead, more follow. Wait until they are directly below. We must take down the first ones together.

Areenna's muscles tightened when she sensed the wolves approach. Her fingers curled securely around the bow's leather grip. She drew the arrow back and the tension of the gut increased. Just as she reached full draw, the first two heads emerged between the trees. Their snouts were close to the ground, following the mixed scents, their powerful bodies moving smoothly along.

They were halfway to where she sat when the three trailing wolves came into view. These held their heads straight, their nostrils quivering. These were bigger than the ones they had faced weeks before. Their matted furred brown and black coats were shaggy; pieces of melting ice dripped from them. Amber and oval eyes, burning like orange fire, were set within wide and long black furred heads.

As if recognizing something wrong, the lead wolves slowed. Mikaal sent a thought to Charka and the cry of a kraal echoed through the trees. The wolves stiffened and turned in the direction of the sound. They moved cautiously forward.

When they reached the base of the trees below Areenna and Mikaal, Areenna released the first shaft a heartbeat after Mikaal's knife flew from his fingers. The glistening metal struck true and the first wolf staggered, took two more steps and dropped motionless on the ground. A hairsbreadth later, Areenna's arrow penetrated the space between the second wolf's ribs. It fell in its tracks.

Areenna notched her second arrow before the first hit the beast and let it fly at the next wolf. It struck the creature in its right eye. It fell sideways, all four paws clawing at air until it drew its last breath. Mikaal's second knife spun downward, tip over handle in a perfect arc embedding itself in the neck of the middle wolf, severing its spine.

Areenna's third arrow soared at the last creature, who had turned and started to run. The feathered shaft caught its side and blood sprayed out in a sharp stream. The wolf screamed but did not go down; instead, with blood jetting from its side, it fled back along the trail and disappeared into the trees and the undergrowth.

Dropping from the branch, Mikal called Charka back while Areenna shimmied down the trunk. They met at the first of the dead creatures. Areenna sent Gaalrie to search for the wounded wolf before turning to Mikaal. "Do we just leave them here? Let them rot?"

He shook his head. "I have a better idea. Let those who await us see them."

Charka came to where they were, with Hero and the kralet trailing behind him. As soon as the kraal reached Mikaal, it stepped back to stare at the dead beasts, letting out a snort when he did.

"I understand," Mikaal said to his aoutem. After retrieving his knives and Areenna's arrows, he took a coil of rope from the kralet's rigging and looped one end around the neck of one wolf and the other around another. He mounted Charka, dragged the bodies to the edge of the water, and dumped them in. He watched for a moment as the brown and gray furred animal sank. It popped back up, and the current carried it westward. The freesh jumped over or dove below the carcass on their journey upstream.

He returned and did the same with the next two and when he was done, dismounted next to Areenna and said, "It will be a perfect greeting for…whomever."

"The last one is still moving, but slowly. He bleeds his life out as he goes…wait, there are others," she whispered. Closing her eyes, she concentrated on seeing through Gaalrie's eyes. A few moments later, she exhaled and said, "There are more, but they do not move forward." Her brows furrowed, her head tilting sideways. She pushed her senses toward the creatures. "I am having difficulty reading them. *She* holds them back. They will wait and stay further behind."

"Until the next time," he said. Then he smiled. "And we used no magic to defeat them."

She returned his smile. "We did well."

"Now we hunt."

<><><>

It was dark and late. The sky was so thick with clouds no light from the moon or stars reached the ground. Hundreds of feet below the southwestern palisades, the grouping of large boats floated.

Above them, the deformed image of the Black Sorceress stood near the edge, looking not down on the boats, but north and west, trying to peer through the void. *She* held a clay pot filled with brackish green water pressed to her side by the stump of her left arm. Pieces of insects floated in it and with her right hand, *she* crushed them with an old wooden pestle.

As *she* worked, low and unintelligible words poured from her mouth like sand through an hourglass. Then something struck deeply into her mind. The bowl fell from numb fingers. The pestle remained forgotten in her hand as the death cries of a wolf ripped through her.

In an instant, *she* was staring into the chasm in the Frozen Mountains. Her wolf lay on the side of the trail, blood trailing from the arrow in its side across the rocks and down to the rushing water. The mutated beast lifted its head, staring upward as if it could see her. Then, its head fell and it breathed its last.

"No!" *she* screamed and sank to her knees. Hatred for the two who did this, boiled in her mind. Then *she* sensed his presence behind her. *She* spun and knelt at the feet of her Master.

"Master, they have killed my pets. They have destroyed five of the ones following them. We must stop them. We must!"

Rise, he commanded her. *Call back what creatures still live. Keep them well back.*

She did as she commanded, and when *she* faced him, her eyes locked with the flaring circles of his eyes. *She* offered her silent plea. *Guide me Master; show me the way.*

He placed an elongated claw-like hand on her shoulder. *We will create a wraith, not too large. Not to kill, but to follow. They are well blocked. They think they have some advantage with your wolves gone, but your pretty beasts have shown us the way. We know where they are and what they do. We shall know their every move.*

When he released her shoulder and lowered his arm to his side, he pointed to the bowl *she* had dropped. "Of that we have no need." *Join with what I do, create power with me*. He commanded.

When they finished, a wraith stood before them. It was not large; perhaps three times the size of a treygone, but it was powerful. Red eyes—two glowing coals fused within black circles were set above the dagger point of a long, sharp, and hooked beak, which curved over the bottom by several inches. It had four legs, not two, and its talons were curved spikes. Each wing was the length of a man's body, and the long tail whipping behind it held razor sharp feathers so thin they had the appearance of hair and so sharp they could slice through skin and bone.

Follow them, watch them, and always know where they are. I leave now to find them on the western side. You will keep me informed of their movements. I leave behind my ghazi warriors for you to command. The Circle requires the energy of Nevaeh and such we must have. Roth leads his people here as we speak. He thinks to defeat us but my brethren of the Circle are already riding the sea. Stop Roth and his people; hold them.

The last Afzareen of Nevaeh—the last living sorceress protégé of the Circle bowed, before her Master, her eyes locked on the sacred ground where he stood. "I will, my Master."

"Soon the might of the Circle of Afzal will be at the lead of a vast army, its size alone will conquer Nevaeh."

She turned to the black-winged wraith. *She* raised her right arm, her hand open, her fingers pointing to it. *Fly. Find. Follow!*

When *she* turned back, the Master was gone.

XXIII

AREENNA STOOD in the stirrups and scanned the cavern's height, trying to pierce the grayness above. Although it was hard to tell time in the gray light of the cavernous valley, she always had the ability to know the approximate time of day and to her, it was early morning.

Following yesterday's defeat of the wolf-creatures, they had hunted and had enough meat for several days. After hunting, Areenna had sent Gaalrie to see where the wolves had gone. The treygone had flown to the beginning of the chasm but had found no sight of the wolves. Both Areenna and Mikaal had tried to sense them, but neither could. "*She called them away. But why?*"

After a badly needed night's sleep, but before packing their supplies, they had studied Roth's map. Mikaal had explained the full details of his plan, which, if successful, would leave the Dark Ones waiting at the end of the chasm and not where Areenna and Mikaal would be.

Once they'd solidified their plan, and agreed on sacrificing their last kralet, they had packed their supplies and returned to the pathway in the mountainside.

At the junction, Mikaal turned to Areenna. "We need to wipe our scent from here and release the kralet."

Dismounting, she concentrated on the best way to accomplish the task. "Take Hero and Charka twenty feet in. I'll wait here." Mikaal led the heavily laden kraals up the pathway while Areenna pulled the kralet to the western side of the opening and pushed an asking command for it to move away. When the pack animal was far enough from the opening, she back-stepped to Mikaal.

Areenna called up her divining ability. Although she could not see the water, she reached it with her mind and called forth a column of clear crystal liquid. It separated from the stream and rose upwards until it was at the same level as her eyes. She curved it over the edge of the chasm's trail and brought it to where she stood. She released it and the water crashed to the ground and rushed back over the edge, dropping to its origin. She repeated the process three times.

"Our scent is washed from here." She pushed a final asking to the kralet, and the small pack animal started westward on the trail, leaving its scent on the rocks it trod. When it was gone, she mounted Hero and with Mikaal, started upward.

<><><>

The small forces of Tolemac, Fainhall and Kashold, dressed in battle armor, waited in the badlands a half mile beyond the border of the southwestern wastelands. Twenty miles ahead lay the rocky cliffs of the Palisades. Roth sat on his kraal, staring at the barren land before him. He turned to Enaid and the three women beside her.

"You are certain?" he asked.

"They are a quarter mile ahead, over the far rise before us. *She* stands with them, in the flesh." Enaid said.

"As in the old days, *she* thinks herself invincible," Aldimor's Queen Layra declared.

"Then we hold the advantage," Roth replied. He turned to Prince Nevets, who was on his left and nodded to him. "When we move forward, take Kashold's troops and ride the right flank. Come wide when you hear the signal and attack from the rear flank."

"As you ask, My Lord." Drawing his reins, he rode to his troops.

Standing in the stirrups, Roth looked back over his shoulder. The quickly raised army of men and women spread out before his eyes was a mighty sight. Hundreds strong, they stood with spears, swords and bows held in proud readiness. There were six columns of troops: four with Roth's 'Six' groups at their lead, two with Fainhall's men, King Nomis and Queen Eetak at their head, and the one phalanx of the soldiers of Kashold at the right flank.

Although the forces of the Dark Circle outnumbered the troops of Nevaeh, Roth knew his men and women held the main advantage: their minds were free so they could act and react independently. Their foes could not. They were drones controlled to perform exactly as instructed. They could not think for themselves—which was the most important advantage Roth and Nevaeh held—for it had led to their defeat twenty years before.

The night before, in a meeting with the Kings of Fainhall and Kashold, the four Queens and the officers of the armies, Roth had presented his battle plans, laying out the troop movements to the minutest detail. If he were right, it would be how they would defeat the invading forces of the Dark Circle.

With the sun at his back, Roth raised his arm and whirled his hand in a circle, finishing with a finger pointing forward. Behind him, the voices of the officers echoed his hand signal with commands to move forward.

Roth urged his kraal forward. On his right side, Enaid did the same. Irii, her gorlon, padded next to her. Layra and her white gorlon rode next to Enaid. At Roth's left were Ilsraeth and Atir. Ilsraeth's treygone flew above. Her eyes were their scout for the upcoming battle, while Atir's lionesque black rantor loped easily between her and Ilsraeth.

This was a sight not seen for twenty years, the royalty of Nevaeh leading their army. Roth knew this would be no simple incursion; it would be the battle, to set the stage, for their future. "We take no chances. We must weaken them now, stop them today and destroy the Black Witch as well, if we are to have a chance against the ones yet coming."

They crested the hill and found the creatures of the waiting dark forces spread out below them. Standing in the center of the massed forces was the Black Sorceress, her red-rimmed eyes glaring directly at the man leading the Nevaens.

"These are no exiles, they are ghazi warriors," Roth exclaimed.

"Something's wrong," Enaid said the instant she saw the opposing force. "The Master is not there." She turned to look at Atir. "What see you?"

Atir closed her eyes. When they flew open, she shook her head. "I did not see this. He…the Dark Master, he has gone, and with him, he has a force larger then what stands before us."

"He goes north?" Enaid asked.

Atir nodded. "He chases Areenna and Mikaal."

Roth cut their words off. "At this moment, it matters not what he does. We must concentrate on what lies before us." He pointed at the Black Witch, the Afzaleem controlling the dark army of ghazi warriors.

Glaring angrily at Roth, *she* raised her right arm, her thumb and first two fingers were directed at the oncoming riders. With a flick of her wrist, a lightning bolt hurtled toward them.

<><><>

It was afternoon when they reached the top of the pathway. Across from them, separated by fifteen feet was the other side of the Frozen Mountains. Areenna looked left and then right. The spot they were on was no more than twenty-five feet wide and was, as far as she could see, the only place where the divided mountains came close.

It is a long jump for the kraals and harder with riders on their backs.

We will not be on them, Mikaal told her.

"I certainly can't jump across. I doubt you can either."

He smiled broadly and observed the chasm, which was perhaps a thousand feet below. "It's not too far, but I won't chance it. Will you be able to get Hero to jump?"

Areenna nodded. "He will do as I ask. But how do we cross?"

Instead of answering, Mikaal went to Charka and removed the thick coil of rope attached to the saddle. He tied one end to the saddle's cross bar and unrolled the rest. He stepped before Charka and put both hands on the side of his head and pressed the kraal's forehead to his own. He picked up the end of the unrolled rope and wrapped it around his wrist.

The large blue-coated kraal back-stepped almost to the opening of the pathway and without a moment's hesitation launched himself into a gallop. When he reached the edge, he leapt effortlessly up and across the chasm. He landed sure-footed and was able to stop before the rope ran out and Mikaal pulled over.

He went to Hero and tied the rope to the smaller kraal, drew him back until the rope was taut and said to Areenna, "Have him hold strong."

She laid a hand on Hero's neck and pushed her asking to him. When she was done, she said, "He is ready."

"Are you?"

Areenna touched the rope, testing its tautness. "You are sure?"

Instead of replying, he smiled.

Then I am ready, My Prince. With her bow slung across her shoulder and back, the quiver of arrows left attached to Hero's saddle, she grasp the rope he drew down for her. She took a deep breath, her muscles tensing.

"Wait."

She froze. "What?"

He went to Hero and freed a coil of rope. It was as long as the first, but less thick and much lighter. He tied one end around her and the other around his own waist.

"If I fall you do as well," she pointed out.

It is but a precaution. If you fall, I will hold you. If not, we go together.

You are gallant, My Prince.

No, I am selfish. You are a part of me now.

Areenna could not reply. She closed her eyes beneath the rush of warmth spreading through her. "I will not fall," she promised.

"I know," he said. "Go!"

With a deep inhalation, she pulled herself up. As she did, both kraals backed up just enough to keep the rope tight. She started off, hand over hand, refusing to look down, staring only at Charka as she crossed the opening and the rushing waters below. She moved as quickly as she could and was across in a minute. When she stood on her feet, she turned back.

When Areenna's feet touched down, Mikaal grasped the rope and pushed off the edge. His weight, so much more than Areenna's, pulled the kraals forward for an instant, but Charka drew back and the rope straightened. Without hesitation, Mikaal crossed, hand over hand and reached the other side in less time than had Areenna.

When he stood next to her, the rope around his waist gone, he went to Charka and untied the rope from the kraal's saddle. "Bring Hero," he said to Areenna.

She turned and gazed at her kraal. She formed the asking, drawing a full mental picture of what the kraal needed to do. The kraal back-stepped as far as he could and charged forward.

Mikaal had picked up the rope and braced himself in case the smaller kraal did not make it. Even though he knew he could never hold the animal's weight, he would not willingly let Hero fall. His caution was unnecessary; the kraal leapt across the opening as if it had been nothing more than a small ditch.

Once Areenna had Hero at her side, Mikaal said, "And now we move as fast as we can. We have added more distance to this journey."

And given us a better chance to reach the mountain, she responded.

<><><>

The flashing crack of lightning burst at the oncoming troops of Nevaeh. Roth, his kraal moving forward at the pace of his footed troops, remained in the lead. The four women flanking the High King joined together to create a shield so strong the lightning struck it and flashed harmlessly, fading into a shimmering nothingness before its force could touch a single man or woman of Nevaeh.

Ahead of him, the dark soldiers of the Circle moved toward them, splitting around the tall unmoving sorceress like a swarm of black writhing insects while *she* sent blinding bolts of *her* powers at the oncoming mass. From the rear of the charging vileness of the dark swarm, a rain of arrows rose skyward. The sheet of dark bolts raced across the sky, holding for a moment before curving downward and speeding toward the oncoming forces of Nevaeh.

From within the Nevaen forces, the women warriors—those with varying abilities—used their special powers to stop most of the arrows. Some men carried shields and were able to deflect the shafts, but there were screams as well, as those few arrows able to get through struck their targets.

The instant the arrows fell, Roth raised his left arm, his hand clenched into a fist.

Behind him, the archers of Tolemac paused, knelt and released their arrows. The volley flew high and true; hundreds of quilled acont shafts soared toward the onrushing forces. The last surviving Afzaleem sorceress stood firmly in the center of her army and destroyed many incoming arrows, but more of the dark swarming ghazi warriors of the Circle fell than had Nevaens.

Then, the two armies met with a roar of voices and the clash of metal upon metal. Roth, strong in the saddle, swung his sword in half arcs, slicing away at anything moving toward him. The four women, their hands covered with the light of their powers, struck. Bodies fell in a path before them. Behind Roth and the four queens came two of his 'Six' groups, at the head of their platoons of fighters, their fierceness in battle never seen by the dark forces.

The fighting grew fierce, the soldiers entangled, each side pushing deeper into the other. The sound of metal upon metal, of sword and spear meeting flesh, and the haunting screams of the injured and dying filled the air, shaking the very ground they fought upon.

Roth charged the black warriors, their misshapen bodies and faces hidden within leather and rusted metal armor. They formed a solid wall against him. Enaid, at her mate's side, her sword in one hand, her other glowing with the force of her powers.

Roth and Enaid fought, his sword and her abilities blending to form the tip of a cone so strong it cut through the invaders like a battering ram. Yet, for every foot gained, more black forces filled the void created by the Nevaen's weapons and powers.

The battle grew in ferocity; the Black Sorceress sent streaking bolts of killing power at the Nevaens while the women sorceresses of Roth's army retaliated in kind, powers fighting powers even as sword met sword.

The battle wore on; the ground turned black and deep in the blood of the fallen. The echoing cries of the wounded blended with the sounds of crashing weapons until everything became a blur of sound and light.

An hour before the sun reached midway into the sky, Roth and Enaid dismounted and, side by side, battled the vileness. They fought their way through the horde to within a hundred feet of the Black Witch who had surrounded herself with a thick barrier of ghazi soldiers.

"The fight lasts too long. They will consume us if we do not stop *her* now," Roth shouted to Enaid as he cut down the warrior before him, slicing through his armor as if it were paper. The fighter fell before the High King, his torso split in half.

Roth's arm ached from the fighting, his legs cramped, but he held himself strong. Behind him, centered within the groups of 'Six', Atir, Ilsraeth and Layra fought.

Roth raised his left hand and pumped his fist twice. In response, the three 'six' groups moved to him, the other sorceresses joining instantly with Enaid. Roth raised his arm again and with his index finger whirled it in a circle.

The sound of a hundred kraals charging from the right side echoed loudly as Prince Nevets led his men in a flanking charge. "Now!" Roth called to Enaid.

Enaid buried her sword tip in the ground and raised both hands, palms facing the armored vileness before her. The three queens, now joined with Enaid, pushed their most powerful abilities to her. Streaks of blue, gold and red raced from the hands of the queens to encircle Enaid in a brilliant sphere of pulsating light.

Enaid stood tall, her head back, her eyes locked on the enemy before her as she accepted the rush of power and was soon encased in a globe of flickering rainbow light. She released the built up powers and a stream of blue lightning erupted from her palms. The black-armored soldiers before her disintegrated, leaving the ground as empty as if nothing had been standing there.

The instant the dark things before him disappeared, Roth charged forward, his broadsword in one hand, a long dagger in the other, slashing as more armored dark soldiers desperately lunged to fill the gaps and block his path. Enaid, at his side, slung bolts at those who would come before them. Behind them followed the Sixes, their swords flashing and black warriors falling.

The Black Sorceress stood straight, glaring at the hated ones as they rushed toward her. Her hatred fed her anger and exploded toward Enaid and Roth in dark jagged waves of malevolence.

When the Black Witch released her explosive force at the two in the lead, the three queens went to their knees. Digging their hands into the earth, they drew every modicum of power possible and created a blocking shield to stop the Black Witch's attack.

"No!" the deformed mouth screamed. Drawing a swarming mist around her, the last sorceress of the Afzaleem in the lands of Nevaeh pushed her body upward, stretching every fiber of her being until *she* had doubled in size.

Roth and Enaid, knowing *she* would use this defense when trapped, had prepared everyone for it. "Now!" Roth shouted.

The three queens stood quickly, raised their arms and hands toward Enaid and released a stream of iridescent wavering light. Enaid, shimmering within the dancing light, inhaled and drew the power within. In the heartbeat following the vanishing of the iridescence, she exhaled sharply. From her hands, two violet shafts rocketed toward the sorceress.

The repulsive form of the dark misty sorceress turned toward the shafts, *her* single hand flared and one of the shafts burst midway between them, but the second flew true and exploded against *her* abdomen.

The Black Witch flew backwards. As *she* fell, two of the Sixes swept around Roth and Enaid, cutting off the dark-armored ghazis who had raced to protect their fallen sorceress. The Sixes destroyed everyone before them while Roth and Enaid ran to the sorceress, who was struggling to *her* feet.

She made it to one knee. Roth was almost upon her. Enaid, instead of attacking, sent a stream of pure white energy at Roth's right hand. His sword glowed and when he reached the Black Witch, he leapt high and swung.

The sword arced through the air and descended in a blur. The glowing edge of the metal—a metal not born of this earth and created three thousand years before—struck at the juncture of neck and shoulder and sliced completely through.

Before the severed head could fall, the body of the last sorceress of the Afzaleem dissolved into a pile of gray black ashes, all dissolved except for her head, which lay on the ground, her red-circled eyes staring upward at Enaid, unending hatred still spewing from them.

Enaid stepped past Roth to stand over the head of her most despised enemy—the sorceress who had murdered Areenna's mother, the Black Witch who had killed more of her people than she could ever contemplate—and held her hands over the still aware head and released every last remaining strand of her powers.

There was a loud crack and the head ripped apart. An instant later, it too dissolved into ashes blacker than a starless midnight sky.

"It is done," Enaid whispered.

Roth came next to her and took her hand in his. Looking around, saw the army of Nevaeh had overrun the invading troops. There was no mercy asked nor given as the Nevaens made certain the last of the ghazi breathed no more.

"We have succeeded, My Lord," Enaid said.

Roth looked over the battlefield, at the fallen enemy mixed with the dead and wounded of Nevaeh. "For now," he whispered. "What comes next lay with Areenna and Mikaal."

"Highness," came the voice of Noslen, the captain of the Sixes. Next to him walked the Master Boatsman, Timon.

Roth turned to him, his eyebrows raised.

"Some of their boats are gone," the Captain said.

Roth turned to Enaid. "We cannot catch them by foot."

Timon stepped forward. "I have eight boats and two hundred men. We can follow."

Enaid exhaled slowly. Her eyes flicked across each face, ending with Roth. "There is no choice."

XXIV

IN THE MORNING, five days after leaving the southern palisades, and two days after the death of the Black Sorceress, the small fleet of the Circle of Afzal dropped anchor at the mouth of the chasm of the Frozen Mountains.

The Master stood on the platform at the bow of the lead boat and stared into the channel cut between two mountains of the divide. Kneeling on the platform next to him was one of his ghazi. The Master secured a claw-like hand to the ghazi's head, his long nails digging into the poor soul's scalp as he fed himself with the life energy of the hapless soldier. When he had pulled enough, he released him and the ghazi fell forward on the platform.

The soldier was not dead but so drained of energy he would not be able to move for hours. Ignoring him, the Master pushed his senses deep into the chasm, searching for the two. There was no choice. The Circle knew who they were, knew what they could do if they were not stopped. They had foreseen this when the *Before Man* had defeated their Afzaleem twenty years ago. They had known the dangers and had taken steps to regain their foothold, but the last Afzaleem had failed to destroy the girl and her complement. The Masters of the Circle of Afzal had no choice but to come to Nevaeh themselves.

Off to his left, something bobbed in the choppy waters. He leaned forward and saw the decomposing body of one of her wolves. He raised one clawed hand and drew the lifeless body out of the water. He studied the creature for several seconds before turning his eyes to the mouth of the chasm.

He sensed nothing of the two, not even the block the Master knew they used for hiding. He wrapped his arms about himself and a whirlwind of grayish black mist appeared around him. An instant later the mist rose skyward and like a lance thrown into the mouth of the chasm, it sped within, leaving behind only his shell.

The Master's essence scoured the chasm, deeper and deeper until he was certain they were not there. Swirling above the rushing waters, he sought the wraith he and the Afzaleem witch had created.

The Master found it sitting on a ledge, hundreds of feet above the water, staring in the direction the two would come from, obeying both its Master's orders to await the two and track them.

The Master's formless shape settled next to its creation and searched for any remaining essence of the two. It took only a few minutes to find the body of the wolf that had crawled away to die. When he finally discovered the barely readable trail of the kraals, he followed it to the pathway leading up from the chasm.

The mist rose and surrounded the wraith and when it did, the Master pushed into the blackness of the wraith's simple mind and placed a mind picture of the two and of where they had gone. *Find them! Track them!*

<><><>

Areenna shivered beneath the furred cloak. The further they traveled, the colder it grew. She glanced at Mikaal, who rode on her right, slightly ahead. He sat straight, his face, like hers, wrapped within silks to help against the cold. She was tired and hungry and for the last couple of hours had begun to doubt herself and her ability to handle everything, from the cold to the hunger to the repeated self-questioning of what she was doing.

For the past eight months, everyone spoke of her as the woman chosen to save Nevaeh. Chosen by whom? By the stars? By the earth? By some sort of invisible force? She had done too many things someone her age should never have done. Even if she were to accomplish what everyone hoped and expected, where would that leave her?

She glanced at Mikaal again, at his straight back and proudly held head, taking in the strength and power surrounding him like a beautiful robe, and for the hundredth time wished…

Her self-doubting thoughts ended when something touched her mind and quickly withdrew. She chased after it but lost the trail. She knew it was not of the dark but had been unable to tell what or who it was.

She spent a few minutes searching but found nothing. She wondered if it was a trick of her mind brought on by cold, hunger and doubt. She had lost track of the days and wasn't sure if it had been a week or a month since they had jumped the chasm. Their food supply was exhausted. The trail, if such it was, was layered with ice and awkward to ride. To their right, the vast expanse of arctic ice fields stretched on as far as she could see.

We are near the end. Mikaal's thought interrupted her reveries.

In the distance ahead, she saw the mountains were curving to the left. She turned in the saddle and realized they had been angling to the left for a while. *A good sign*, she replied.

A few days…three or four and we should reach the double-peaked mountains.

If we survive. We have no food. The kraals must eat too, she responded. She took her hand from around Gaalrie, who rode on her lap beneath the cloak. She reached down to run her numb and frozen fingers along the last of the grain bags. There was barely one meal left for the kraals. The bag holding their own food was completely empty.

Then the mind touch came again. *Join with me* she called to Mikaal. He instantly fit within her mind and mingling his power into her own, chased after the touch. This time she was able to follow it. She withdrew quickly, stunned at what she had found. At the same moment, she asked Gaalrie to fly ahead and opened her cloak. The treygone lifted into the freezing air and disappeared a moment later.

There is a woman ahead, a woman of power. Who I know not, but not of the Dark Ones. She studied the lingering feel of what little remained of the woman's essence, turning it around in her mind, reading as deeply as possible.

"She is in trouble. Injured I think," Areenna said aloud.

Mikaal turned to Areenna. "How is it possible for her to be here? Why?"

Something inside of Areenna snapped with his question. Her back stiffened and her eyes spat sparks of pure anger at him. When she spoke, her voice blasted through the silks protecting her face. "How is it possible? Why is she there? Do I know everything? I don't know what is or isn't possible. I don't know where I am…or even who I am any longer. I've spent most of this year riding on the back of a four-legged beast seeing and doing things so strange not even the children's stories my father told me when I was growing up could come close to the reality I now live. I have killed creatures and men. I have found terrible powers within me and met people and things who should never be but are. What I cannot do, is answer questions when I have no answers!"

He didn't need to stop Charka, who sensed a sudden change in Mikaal and even as the blue-coated kraal stopped, Mikaal was off the saddle. He pulled Areenna from Hero's back and drew her close to him. He held her tightly with one arm and with his free hand, pulled the silks from her face.

Accepting the glaring anger pouring from her eyes, he kept her tight against him. Wisely, he did not speak, neither with word nor with thought, but simply held her to him. Her eyes changed and tears spilled down her cheeks. Still, he held her silently. She buried her face against his fur-covered chest and let out the emotions that had built so quickly, the emotions she had been hiding for far too long.

They stood together for several long minutes until Areenna lifted her head and whispered, "I am sorry."

I am sorry, she repeated silently.

Sorry for being alive…for feeling? Or, sorry for being afraid of not knowing what lies ahead?

She favored his words with a barely visible upturn at the corners of her mouth. "No, for acting like a child."

"I'm afraid, My Princess, you are anything but." With that, he kissed her.

The kiss was nothing like the one she had stolen when he was healing and asleep. This kiss branded her lips. More than the touch of his mouth was the sense of his becoming a part of her. It was as if they had become one person, one mind.

When the kiss ended, she drew away from him, shaking her head. *We cannot*!

Kiss? Who made this rule? Who says we cannot?

She cut him off from her thoughts. "We must stay focused. We must hold to what we have been sent to accomplish."

"And a kiss prevents such?" he asked. The sarcasm sliced sharply through her.

"Yes," she said. The softness in her voice was a counterpoint to his sharpness. "It changes us, makes us react differently. Please, there is so much... It is hard for me. Do you understand?"

"I don't want to understand," he said, his eyes locked on hers. "But I will do as you need me to. Do you understand?" he snapped.

Before she could speak, a mind picture replaced Mikaal's face. Gaalrie had found the woman. She watched as the treygone flew over a section of the trail piled high with snow and chunks of ice. Areenna saw an arm and part of a head sticking out of the whiteness.

"We must go. Gaalrie has found the woman and she needs us." Without a backward glance at him, she mounted Hero and moved forward. Behind her, Mikaal shook his head and jumped on Charka's back. It took a half hour to reach the small avalanche, and when they did, they saw the same as had Gaalrie.

Throughout the ride, Areenna had been unable to sense the woman, for she had put up a block. Though weak and easy to find, it held strongly enough to stop her from sensing more than her presence.

The block tells me she fears us, Areenna told Mikaal.

Why? She knows us not.

Perhaps for that reason. We will find out soon enough.

Jumping off their kraals, they ran to where the woman lay buried. Mikaal, his hands, covered in fire when they reached her, used the fiery coating to melt snow as he dug. Areenna's hand went to his shoulder before he got too far.

Wait. Mikaal stopped at the instant of her touch.

Stepping back and spreading her arms, Areenna called forth her abilities. The heat flared deep within her, centered just above the joining of her legs and like flames spreading through dried grass, it raced through her body until reaching her fingers.

She called on the divining, and drew the snow and ice off the woman, slowly at first so as not to move any chunks of ice supporting the heavier snow above it. When the woman was almost free, Mikaal reached into the opening Areenna had created and pulled her out.

I have her. Nodding Mikaal, she moved her hands. Whirls of snow and ice rose. With her right hand, she sent the column of snow to the right, where it cascaded over the side of the mountain and fell to the ice field below.

She turned to Mikaal, who was kneeling and holding the woman. Her eyes were open, staring at Areenna. The woman trembled, shaking not as much with the cold, as with fear. Areenna stood still, her eyes fixed on the woman. She was small, no bigger than a twelve-year-old girl, but her face was that of a forty-year-old woman. Her eyes, larger than normal and browless, were the color of dark straw. She had never seen such eyes before.

She glanced at Mikaal. *Exile?*

He shrugged. *Out here?*

"We will not harm you," Areenna said, coming close to the woman and kneeling next to her. "Are you injured?"

The woman's pale eyes danced between Areenna and Mikaal. Her breathing slowed and she nodded. "My leg," she said and pointed to her left calf.

Areenna bent closer, reached down and feeling along the woman's calf until she reached a point two-thirds toward the ankle. "Broken, but not too bad."

"Can you heal it here?" Mikaal asked.

The woman's lips were almost blue. Standing, she took off her cloak and spread it on the trail, fur down. "There is no choice. Put her on it," she told Mikaal.

Mikaal lifted the woman from his lap and gently placed her on the cloak. She cried out only once, when he laid her down.

"Slice her leathers," she directed Mikaal. He split the leather using the bone handle knife, and peeled it back to expose the injury. Areenna knelt beside her. Before she did anything, she glanced at Mikaal and thought of her earlier words. *This is perhaps the most important gift I have received; it gives, not takes*.

Areenna locked eyes with the woman. "Will *you* trust me to help you?"

The woman held Areenna's gaze for a moment and nodded. Areenna closed her eyes, placed her hands over the cracked bone of the woman's calf, and called on her healing gift. Everything went black. The only thing visible was the glow around the woman's calf as Areenna placed her hands carefully over the skin.

Holding the leg gently, she pushed the flow of energy directly into the bone and slowly manipulated her ability into melding the bones together. As it always did when caught within this power, time stood absolutely still. Her ability flowed through her, heating her body and hands as she mended the leg.

Finally, she drew her hands back and inhaled sharply. In spite of the freezing air, regardless of her having no cloak, the powers Areenna had called forth had warmed her to the point of sweating. Opening her eyes, she found the pale ones of the woman fixed on her. Bending closer, Areenna placed her hand on the side of the woman's head. *Can you sense me?*

The woman lifted a six-fingered hand and covered Areenna's with it. *I hear you.*

You need not fear us.

I know that now. How be you here? You look not like exiles.

Areenna realized this was a woman of strong power, unexpectedly so. The rhythm of her words held a strange, older feel. *We seek a place*, she explained and brought up a mind picture of the mountain with the two peaks.

"You go to the mountain," the woman said aloud, a tone of reverence filling her words.

"We do," Mikaal answered for them both. "You know it?"

She nodded. "No one is permitted there. To tread upon the mountain is to find death."

"We have been sent to the mountain."

Sent? This cannot be.

Sense you deception within me?

The woman's eyes glazed over. She lifted her hand and raised it to Areenna's chest. Then, she placed it over the girl's heart and closed her eyes. Three seconds later, the woman's eyes sprang open. *You speak with truth.*

"Why are you out here alone?" Mikaal asked.

"To gather herbs as I have done for most of the years of my life."

"In the ice?" Mikaal asked, shaking his head. "Where can herbs live in this desert of ice?"

The woman smiled at Areenna. *Men see only what is before them. It is truly sad.*

Mikaal mentally stiffened, having forgotten he had joined with her before.

The woman shifted and winced. "Many herbs thrive here. They grow without sunlight and live beneath the frost."

"Where do you live?" Mikaal asked, looking the woman over.

"My village is a half day from here. You will be welcomed…and fed. My name is Sirod," she said.

Smiling at the woman, she replied, "I am Areenna, he is Mikaal."

Mikaal's eyes flicked to Areenna. *Welcomed or…*

"Your face tells me you doubt me," Sirod said to Mikaal.

He studied her face, swept his eyes across hers before saying, "There are those who seek us, those who would reward you for our capture."

Sirod stiffened. "I am Woman of the Village. What I say is bond, to myself and to my people."

XXV

STANDING AT THE rail of Timon's boat, Enaid studied the remains of the Dark Master's fleet. It had been several days since the Black Sorceress's death; in those days, much had happened.

Following the battle, the four women of power had spent the rest of the day and most of the night within the midst of the forces of Nevaeh, taking care of the wounded. While the healers had tended the wounded, Prince Nevets and King Nomis had worked with their people to bury the dead. Roth and Enaid had walked to a place away from the others, where they could talk freely.

"We must follow the Master. We cannot allow him to stop Areenna and Mikaal. They are strong, but his forces will overrun them. There are too many, no matter how strong Areenna and Mikaal have become."

"There is only one way to get there quickly— by water," Roth had stated.

"Timon and his fleet are here now. Ilsraeth goes to meet him."

"We will do the same." Roth swept his hand toward the men and women spread across the distance. He glanced up at the disappearing moon, heralding the dawn of a new day. "Today they will rest while we work with Timon. Tomorrow we go north."

They had met the Master Boatsman two hours after sunrise. His fleet of small boats had numbered twenty, each with full crews. The boats had been small and could not have carried a sufficient number of their forces: they decided instead, to use the abandoned ships of the Dark Ones. When they'd gone to the ships, they found the sails slashed and the tillers removed. It had taken two days to mend a single set of sails and for Layra, who had a finely tuned sense of search, to find a rudder in shallow enough water for Enaid to raise from the bottom.

To Roth, what the Master had done to his ships had led him to realize he had no plans to leave Nevaeh.

Now, at midmorning on the third day, they were ready.

Enaid turned to Roth, who stood behind her with Timon, watching the loading of the men and women and the necessary supplies to keep them alive. "I sense no bad weather before us," she said.

Timon motioned to the large ship. “That ship will be enough to worry about without dealing with weather. At least the stench of those things—I cannot call them men—is almost gone,” he added with a shake of his head. “The rudder is seated and working and the sails will hold well. With a good wind and a bit of luck we’ll be there in a few days. It is a clumsy vessel at best. How it made the crossing, I cannot understand.”

Roth placed a hand on Timon’s shoulder and squeezed. “Luck will have nothing to do with it. Your strong hands on the wheel is all we need.”

The Master Boatsman did not respond for several seconds. “Your Highness, I hope your words lend truth to my hands.

“Solomon… I have no doubts. And now, Timon my friend, it’s time to go.”

<><><>

“I should have expected this,” Mikaal said when they passed through the mouth of a huge cavern. Mikaal on Charka and the two women on Hero entered a valley not unlike the one they had found inside the chasm. A warm breeze washed over them, and Mikaal drew Charka to a halt.

“It is like the other valley, but not,” he said, rising on the saddle to take in what lay ahead and around him. The cavern was huge, and he could see no signs of its end. It was lighter than in the other valley as well, with the hazy pale gray light of the frozen lands encasing everything. He looked up but saw nothing above them. There were trees and shrubs in abundance; strange tress with pale yellow leaves. The shrubs held yellow leaves as well. Mikaal closed his eyes and let his senses range. He found rabts and other small animals, but no larger ones; of birds, there were none.

He turned to the women just as Areenna opened her cloak to let Gaalrie free. The treygone rose upward in lazy circles, her cinnamon and silver wings spread wide to catch whatever the updrafts. As the aoutem flew, Sirod, sitting behind Areenna said, “A narrow road will be on the left, a short distance ahead. We take that.”

Connected to Gaalrie, Areenna sent an asking for the treygone to find and follow the road, while next to her, Mikaal said, "Your villagers, your people, they will not attack us?"

Before she could answer, he started them forward again, ignoring the look of disdain that had crossed her features.

"What purpose would serve such an act?"

"To protect themselves. To help you," he said to the woman while pushing his thoughts to Areenna. *She speaks strangely.*

"What would a village fear from two who still hold the vestiges of youth?"

"You would not want to know." He had spoken quietly, but each word carried with it the loudness of a thunderclap.

Mikaal!

Mikaal mentally shook himself. The woman cocked her head to the side when she gazed at him and he knew she was trying to figure out his sudden mood change. "How far to your village?"

"Not far, a short distance after we reach the turnoff."

"It is around the next bend," Areenna said as Gaalrie swooped over it and flew in the direction of the village.

"Your…bird. You can join with it?"

"You do not know of aoutems?"

"The word is unknown to me," Sirod said.

Areenna hesitated before saying, "I was fourteen when my body changed from child to woman and my abilities grew strong and I found Gaalrie as a hatchling. There was a connection between us, as it is with most women of power from where I come. We bonded to each other and we became sisters. Aoutems are… They are a part of us and we become a part of them."

Behind her, Sirod leaned forward to press her cheek against Areenna's back. "So different are we, yet the same we are as well."

A few minutes later, they reached the turnoff to the narrow road. A few trees were scattered alongside the road ahead; but more spread from there. While the leaves were more yellow than green, the trees appeared to thrive within the cavernous valley.

Mikaal, join with me. He did and found himself joined as well with Gaalrie, who was flying high over the village. The village was comprised of many buildings, all with roofs of yellow leaves. It spread out from a center square with the small buildings forming rings around the square. Mikaal instantly saw the beauty of it; the construction of the village was purely defensive. There were six rings of buildings—homes he was certain—each was staggered off-center to the one in front, so one had to zig and zag to get to the square. This would slow an attacking force to give the defenses time to build.

Mikaal understood whoever had designed the village, had been a Master of wartime defense. It made him think of his father and of what Roth would say about this village.

Gaalrie circled the village once more and Mikaal continued to look it over. Off to the side was a larger building. Its purpose was not evident. He saw people walking in the streets between the buildings as Gaalrie made her final turn and started her return.

When Gaalrie rejoined her, they were halfway to the village and passing cultivated fields. It took fifteen minutes to reach the first ring of houses. Areenna's reaction on seeing the houses was surprise. Every house was the same. Each was a single story rectangle with a peaked roof made of woven yellow leaves and windows of glass.

The buildings...look closely Mikaal. They are not wood; they are the same as the building in the cavern where you healed. It is the same wood but not wood.

They are the descendants of the ones who had lived there.

Why choose to live here? They could have gone to Welkold or Lokinhold and not have lived...here.

The unanswered question lingered in their minds as they rode deeper into the village. When they neared the center, the villagers were gathering in the square. Areenna watched them come toward her, Mikaal and Sirod. While a few appeared to have normal bodies, there were many, who did not. Their mutations were not visibly severe, yet there were those like Sirod who had malformed hands or extra fingers. Some had twisted bodies while others carried their differences on their face, in the set of their eyes or a strangely formed mouth, yet all appeared healthy and vital.

The square was not large, perhaps a hundred and twenty feet across. In the center was a small platform standing a few feet above the yellowish grass. The platform was made of the same strange wood-like material. Other than the platform, the square was empty of any decorations.

"Stop here," Sirod said when they reached the far side of the square, in front of a slightly larger building. A young girl, perhaps eleven or twelve, raced out from the building and came to where the kraals had stopped.

Just before she reached the animals, Sirod dismounted, making sure her good leg was the first to touch the ground. When she stood and turned, the girl raced into her arms. "Mother, I was worried for you. I knew you had been hurt," she said, hugging Sirod.

"Here now I am, with thanks to these two who helped me," she said, releasing her daughter and turning with her to Areenna and Mikaal, who stood next to Hero.

"My daughter Neleh," Sirod said in introduction. "This is Mikaal and Areenna."

Neleh took two steps toward them and bowed her head formally. "My thanks to you for helping my mother."

The powerful aura surrounding the child caught Areenna by surprised. While she knew none other than a woman of power could see the aura, it burst with colors so magnificent she couldn't imagine any man or woman unable to see its beauty. Purples and pale blues, amber and gold swirled around the child like a cocoon. *Do you see it*? she asked Mikaal.

How could I not?

"No thanks are to be given. We did only what was needed," Areenna said to the child.

The girl, instead of speaking, studied her with a growing intensity. Then her eyes, the same pale wheat color as her mother's, glazed over. She stood like that for several seconds before shaking her head. Then she smiled. "You are different. You have great powers."

"And you as well, I sense," Areenna responded.

Their conversation ended as the villagers surrounded them. Sirod told them of how Areenna and Mikal had rescued her. When she finished, Sirod bade them to go about their business or return to their homes. Areenna and Mikaal were her guests and to be treated accordingly.

Then she turned to Neleh. "Where is your brother?"

"He is working in the cold stores building. He will be home shortly."

"Fetch Lemel now."

Without a word, the child raced off. "Come," Sirod said. She started forward, but stopped. "We have no place for your animals."

Areenna glanced at Mikaal and he nodded. "They will stay in this area. Is there grain to feed them? I saw yellow cob in the fields. Is there stock here?"

Sirod nodded. "I will see to it when my son returns." She turned and limped toward the building. Areenna and Mikaal followed behind.

Two hours later, while the kraals ate chunks of cob ears, and Gaalrie sat on the roof of the house eating a freesh Sirod had given her, Areenna and Mikaal, finished their first meal at a table since leaving Welkold. In the time before the meal, Areenna and Mikaal had taken turns bathing in heated water before changing into their last unsoiled clothing.

The house itself was comfortably warm, yet Mikaal had found no evidence of a heating fire anywhere. Nor did they have nightmoss to light the interiors; rather, they used some sort of liquid to burn within wall hanging lanterns. *Everything is different here. The people, the way they live*, Mikaal pushed to Areenna.

Yes, but it is good too. They seem happy here.

"The food, it satisfies?" Sirod asked.

Mikaal laughed and pointed to his plate, which was as clean as if it had not been touched. "Wonderful," he said. "Tell me, how do you keep your home so warm? I see no heating fires."

Sirod nodded. "When our ancestors came here and built our village, they were able, somehow—exactly how I cannot explain for it has been long forgotten—to open holes within the ground to allow heat and steam to rise and warm our homes. We use it for other purposes as well."

"How is the heat directed into the house?"

Sirod's son Lemel spoke. "I can explain," he said. "I am apprenticed to the smithy. We work on the buildings to ensure the heat always works. The weather is the same, at all times, and to keep the chill from within, heat must flow. Each building is above what we call 'vents'. These vents go into the hollow planks in the house. The heat goes through them. Only in the drying room is heat released freely. The heat comes from deep beneath the ground. It is always there. Do you understand better?"

Mikaal nodded. Lemel, of all the people he had seen so far, appeared to have no visible mutation, except for his size and eyes. Barely taller than his mother, he showed no physical differences from Mikaal, other than his eyes, which were the same pale color as his mother and sister.

"What liquid burns in your lanterns? I have never seen such before."

"It is the fat of huge freeshes, some as large as this house. We store the fat and when we need it, turn it to liquid for our lanterns."

"Thank you for the explanation." Then to Sirod he said, "You have lived here all your life?"

"My entire life, yes."

"You and the others are not exiles—" Mikaal asked.

"—Why think you such of us?" she interrupted.

Her words caught Areenna off guard. *Careful,* she warned Mikaal.

She speaks strangely, he told her again. *I am not stupid.* "I have never heard of any people living in the Frozen Mountains," he said to Sirod.

"Why would you? We have been here since the beginning."

Areenna leaned forward. "Since the beginning? The beginning of what?"

Sirod gazed thoughtfully at Areenna before answering. "Of our history. When else could such be? Thousands of years—how many I can say not. The very roots of our history bespeak terrible things done by horrible people. My ancestors fled their lands and homes as their world fell apart. For years they traveled across seas and through many lands before reaching this place."

"Why?" Areenna asked after digesting Sirod's words. "Why come here?"

In the soft glow of wall lanterns, Sirod turned to Neleh and nodded her head. Neleh took a deep breath before saying, "Our ancestors were chosen to come here."

"Why?" Areenna asked again, puzzled by the child's words.

"We protect and wait."

Areenna shook her head. She glanced at Mikaal, who stared openly at the young girl, his brows furrowed in thought. "Wait for what? Protect whom?"

Neleh's eyes roamed Areenna's face. "We wait for she who comes. We protect the path to the mountain of two crowns."

Our mountain, Mikaal shot at her. *There is danger in this.*

Perhaps. We will worry when necessary. We need to learn more.

We do. He turned to Sirod. "How could you possibly stop a large force from going to the mountain?"

"How matters not, Mikaal," Sirod said softly. "What matters is the deed."

Silence built around the table until Areenna asked, "She?"

Neleh spoke. "She who comes. She who is the deliverance from the evil consuming all."

"But you do not know who she is?"

Sirod leaned forward. "By name we know her not, by her mark we will know her. I am Woman of the Village, as I have told you. My mother, her mother before her and all their mothers were Woman of the Village. We all carry her mark." Sirod motioned to Neleh with her six-fingered hand.

Neleh stood and without any modesty took her top off to expose skin the color of tanned hide and barely formed breasts. She turned to show everyone her back. Centered over her spine, at waist level, was a dark brown and circular birthmark. Within the birthmark were lighter lines forming the shape of a crookedly angled six-pointed star.

Areenna's breath caught in her throat. "You both have the same mark?"

While Neleh drew on her top, Sirod leaned forward and pulled at the opening of her collar. The threads holding it closed opened and she parted the garment to expose the area between her breasts. On the skin was the same circular birthmark.

What is it? Mikaal questioned.

This is not possible, she told Mikaal. "What is expected of this woman who carries the mark?" she asked Sirod.

Sirod reached out and placed her hand on Neleh's shoulder after the girl sat down. "She is the one who frees us. She is the one who will bring life to our world. She is the one who will rid us of the Dark Ones—she will defeat the Circle of Afzal."

Mikaal stiffened. "How do you know of the Circle?"

Sirod met his challenging gaze. “As I told you, my ancestors were not born of this land; they crossed the sea to escape the Circle while the end came to their world. They were instructed to flee their homeland and come here.”

Images of the eight sorceresses of the Island rose before Areenna and she knew these people had been part of their plan from the very beginning. “You have been waiting for so many years.” *They have been here since the creation of Nevaeh,* she told Mikaal.

Sirod nodded. “It is why we survive.”

Mikaal, t*he Eight foresaw this. They knew we would come this way.*

You are she?

She did not reply to his thought; rather, she stood and walked around the table. When she reached Neleh, she said, “lift my top,” and turned her back to the child.

Neleh’s hands went to the leather of the tunic and pulled it upwards. Loud gasps sounded when the skin at the exact center of the small of Areenna’s back showed the identical birthmark the two women carried.

XXVI

THE BIRD-SHAPED creature of darkness flew in concentric circles, moving northward, slowly and carefully searching for the two. Many days it had traveled without locating them, many nights it had flown and discovered nothing.

Late on the day before, as it flew over the trail separating the mountain range from the ice fields, it had seen something and dipped lower. Landing on the ice-crusted trail, it had found two discarded leather bags, a few kernels of grain embedded in the ice. The bags carried the scent of the two and their kraals.

As soon as the creature had continued its search, it sent a message to its Master.

The next day, having finally reached the curving end of the mountain chain, it followed the high, heavily angled mountainside toward the west. It would continue on, forever if necessary, until it tracked down its prey. It had no thoughts of its own—no desires. It was conscious of nothing other than the command of its Master. Its purpose was the sole reason for its existence: to find the man and woman, and let its Master know where they were.

And so, the mindless creature, a beast requiring no food, no drink, and only air currents to fly upon, continued its search, while hidden beneath the mountains itself were the two it hunted.

<><><>

"You are she," Sirod whispered after staring at the birthmark. "We have been waiting so long for you."

Areenna turned, her tunic falling back into place. From the corner of her eyes, she caught Mikaal watching intently.

Areenna started to speak when a wave of exhaustion washed over her. She grasped the table for support, willing herself to stay strong and think clearly. But she could not. Shaking her head, she tried to speak but a curtain of dull red rusted mist fell across her eyes and the room and the people in it disappeared.

Before her stood the speaker of the Eight. Her black face and haunting eyes glowed from beneath the dark cowl about her head. A long-fingered hand pointed at her. *For these three millennium past have waited these people. They have lived, suffered, and stayed strong to await you. When you have found what you seek, found what you must, much death and blood will follow. You cannot stop what comes, only deal with it. These people will be your defense as you will be their salvation.*

The Speaker paused to point to Mikaal. *As you are hers.*

What is it? What have you sent us to find? Areenna asked.

The sorceress of the Eight, her black skin aglow, stretched out to touch Areenna. When her fingers reached her chest, there was no sensation of being touched; but, a breath later, something opened within her mind. A warmth grew centered within her head. It bathed her in the feel of the mind touch of her mother. *What you cannot expect is what you will find. Fear it not. Listen to what I speak next: the mother is ill and dying, we call the child soon. See to it you transfer the gift of thrice. The powers of the mother the child holds now.*

As quickly as the mist had come, it was gone. Areenna grasped the side of the table, her legs weak, her mind and body filled with the lingering touch of her mother. Sirod and Neleh caught her and eased her onto a chair before Mikaal could get around the table.

When he reached her and grasped her face between his hands, he saw her eyes had focused, and she was returning to them.

You saw?

I did, the Speaker of the Eight. Mikaal affirmed.

Did you hear her clearly, her words of the seeking?

She told us what we seek is something we will not expect.

Areenna shook her head. *No, what we cannot expect, not will not. There is a difference.*

"Who was she?" Neleh asked, breaking into their silent conversation.

Areenna turned to her, her eyes wide. "You saw her?"

The young girl nodded her head once, her wheat-tinted eyes wide. "Who was she?" she asked again.

"Who?" Sirod asked, looking from Neleh to Areenna.

"The Old One. Was she the one of the Island?" Neleh asked.

At that, all three looked at the child. Areenna spoke first. "What know you of the Island?"

"That all women of power must go there, they must learn."

Areenna turned to Sirod. "How can you go to the Island?"

Sirod drew her daughter into her arms and as she spoke, stroked Neleh's hair. "There is a place, far within this valley, forbidden to any but women. When called, we go there. Then we are not there, but another place, an island covered in reddish mist with strange things that once were. So it has been since the beginning."

Do you believe? Mikaal pushed his thought to her.

Without hesitation. Aloud, to Sirod, Areenna said, "We have much to discuss."

<><><>

It was cold, colder than most of the men and women of Tolemac and Fainhall had ever experienced for more than a short time. Roth knew these warriors could handle the cold as long as they did not freeze. Still, when the winds turned into bitter blades lashing whip-like across their skin, it was enough to force most below deck, jammed arm to arm, front to back as they sailed the great ship of the dark forces steadily toward their destination.

Shifts of ten men worked the deck at all times. Four women worked near them.

The women had a single responsibility: to make sure the men did not freeze.

No simple task for the four women who surrounded a hatch, below which, two large ovens roared with fire. They'd built racks above the ovens and upon these racks were layered the cloaks and leathers of the warriors within. While not strong in ability, not like Enaid or Ilsraeth, the women used their combined powers to protect the clothing from the cold. This was the only means of keeping those who worked the deck from freezing. Most men lasted a bare quarter hour in the icy wind before having to change out of stiff and frozen leathers and over-cloaks to put on freshly heated garments.

In the center of the ship was the small and well-protected wheelhouse. Roth, Timon, Enaid and Ilsraeth stood within, unaffected by the winds racing across the deck. Their aoutems—Irii the golden gorlon and Ilsraeth's black rantor—lay on the floor by the women's feet. Timon held the wheel as he had for most of the three days they had been at sea, relieved for short spells by Roth, while Enaid and Ilsraeth gave them as much energy as they could raise with their abilities.

"The winds are strong. A curse to our people but a blessing to the ship," Timon said, his hands wrapped in cloth as he fought to hold the wheel steady. The seas had been relatively calm until that morning when they'd reached the colder air. As the day had progressed, the cold had increased proportionately. Ahead of them, small blocks of ice bobbled in the waters, none too big to damage the ship, but some large enough to cause Timon worry.

Of the four queens, the women of strong power who had fought the Black Witch and the Master's army, only Enaid and Ilsraeth remained. Layra and Atir had returned to their dominions, where they would help their husbands rebuild the armies they had disbanded twenty years before and await word from the High King.

"This gray is maddening," Timon snapped, "I cannot see the coastline clearly."

"But we can," Ilsraeth said.

"And we will guide you," finished Enaid.

"The coast continues in the same angle we have been following. It stretches ahead without obstruction," Ilsraeth assured her husband.

"How far to the chasm?" Roth asked. "Can you see such distance?"

"I can attempt it, but it will drain my strength quickly." Enaid reached across to Ilsraeth, who took her hand. Their minds joined and their powers melded together. Enaid dropped her hand to Irii, who had stood and was now pressing against her leg. She grasped the short coat around her aoutem's neck. On her other side, Ilsraeth did the same with her rantor.

Suddenly, Enaid was above the ship, bodiless yet floating. She moved forward, cautiously, as she regained the feel of being without body. When she was ready, she raced forward toward the land and the chasm.

Look, Enaid heard Ilsraeth's sudden command.

She turned from the coastline to look ahead. The instant she did, she saw one of the large ships. *Only one.*

I sense no Master.

Nor I. Where did the others go? Her strength ebbed as she spoke. She had to draw back. To stay would be too dangerous to her and to Ilsraeth.

Returned to her body, Enaid shook herself to clear her vision.

"The chasm is a half day ahead, but only one ship is there. The Master has gone ahead with his troops. He has left perhaps a hundred behind."

"Damn," Roth snapped. "We will bypass the ship. We cannot afford the time to destroy them. We must get to the mountain."

Roth's words went unheard as a wash of pale light swept across Enaid's eyes. Following that, she saw the ship they were on change course and go to the coast where two people stood waiting.

"Master Timon," she called softly, but all heard it. "You must go to the coastline, here, and quickly. Three people await us."

"Here, now?" he asked incredulously.

"Here," Enaid answered. "It needs be done now."

<><><>

"I must speak with Sirod alone. Then we can all talk. Can you go with Mikaal to check on the kraals? Areenna asked Neleh.

Neleh nodded, but her eyes never left Areenna's face. "If that is your need of me," she whispered. She grasped Mikaal's hand and led him out. When the door closed, Areenna turned to Sirod.

"Does Neleh know of your illness?"

Sirod cocked her head to the side, which was her habit when caught off-guard. "I am not aware of such. She is a strong one. She may know."

"Do you know the cause of this?"

Sirod shook her head. "I have seen a dozen in my lifetime die as I am dying. Something grows within me, here," she said and tapped her left breast. "It is a slow death; I have perhaps a year at most."

"May I join with you? May I look to see?"

"You can, my cousin."

Areenna paused, her hands half raised to Sirod's head. "Cousin?"

"None but those of my female lineage ever bore the mark as do we both. I doubt not, we are of the same blood."

Areenna nodded, understanding her only choice was belief. The mark was not a discoloring of the skin as she had always thought. While she had never seen such a mark on her mother, after seeing the marks on the two, she was certain it had to have been somewhere on Inaria's body.

She finished placing her hands on Sirod's head and joined with the woman. She called up the healing ability and searched. Sirod's garment was thin enough so it was not necessary to remove it. As Areenna traced her hands over Sirod's body, she watched from behind closed eyes, seeking for what caused the illness. It took several minutes before she found it. Her hand was at the side of Sirod's breast when the skin beneath her left hand began to glow. With her right hand, she cupped the woman's breast.

She concentrated on the glowing ball, feeling it, sensing it, trying to determine how to help. She pushed the ability through her arms into her hands and fingers. The heat grew rapidly, almost burning as she tried to penetrate the thing growing inside. The growth within Sirod had protected itself by deflecting the energy back at Areenna.

Lowering her hands, she opened her eyes. "I cannot heal it."

Sirod smiled at her, cupped her cheek with a calloused yet gentle hand and said, "You were not sent to heal me, Areenna, you are meant to heal our world."

"If I cannot heal you, how can I—"

"—no," Sirod interrupted. *My healing is not for you. I know my journey here is over, but I will live on within Neleh, as my mother lives on in me...as your mother lives on in you.*

Areenna tried to form words but could not. Tears welled in her eyes and Sirod smiled at her. With one hand, the Woman of the Village stroked Areenna's hair and gently pulled her head to her breast and held her there. *Feel not sad for me. I understand my journey in this life. You must do the same. Be strong, Areenna, be strong for me, but even more so for Neleh. She will need your strength to grow.*

Areenna drew back to meet Sirod's eyes. "Neleh will be called soon. They... they want her to be gifted."

Sirod blinked several times before she whispered, "So soon…" She took a deep breath. "It shall be as asked."

<><><>

"She is sad," Neleh said.

Mikaal, who had been stroking Charka's powerful neck and being nuzzled while Neleh stroked Hero's wide flat nose, stopped moving to look at the girl. "Your mother?"

Neleh shook her head. "Areenna. She is sad because she cannot heal my mother."

Mikaal stepped away from Charka and knelt before the girl. "You know of this?" he asked, reaching out to draw the girl toward him.

Her eyes locked with his. Her large wheat-shaded oval eyes gazed into him, not at him. "I have known since it started. My mother knows this not, and I speak not of it until she is ready."

Mikaal had a sudden flash of memory. It was the first time he had seen Areenna at the school and how she had answered Master Thrumweld's question to the shock of the others[1]. Neleh reminded him of Areenna in many ways.

"You are very wise for one so young," he told her. He smiled inwardly, realizing he was only a few years older than she was. Before he could say more, Areenna's call touched him. *We are ready.*

"We should return now," he said, but Neleh was already walking to the building.

Did you call Neleh?

No, came Areenna's reply.

I think she knows.

Knows what? About her mother?

Yes… and about me, about you.

[1] See Born To magic, Tales Of Nevaeh, Volume 1

XXVII

AREENNA WAS MORE tired than she had realized. The day had been long and having used her healing ability twice in a day added to her weariness. All she wanted was sleep, but there was more to do this night if they were to leave in the morning.

When Mikaal and Neleh returned, Areenna talked about the village, drawing out Mother and daughter to get the history of their people. After learning what they could to understand their uniqueness, Areenna turned the conversation to the twin-peaked mountains.

Sirod's knowledge was deep and she spoke for a long time, describing the trail leading to the mountains and the two paths available to reach the peaks. "One is on the northeastern side, the other on the western," she said, after summing everything up.

"The northeastern slope is the more difficult; it is steep and somewhat narrow," she explained. "The western slope is easier but will take another day to reach. The trail to it is dangerous as the ice fields end and the sea begins. The waters are treacherous and often wash over the trail."

"You have been on the northeastern trail?" Mikaal asked.

"Many times. I go every year to make certain all is undisturbed."

"Can we join? Can you show me the trail?" Areenna asked.

"Yes."

She clasped Sirod's hand and reached out with her mind. When they joined, Areenna saw the snow-covered slopes, and the groove of a trail cut deeply into the mountain and was as narrow as she had said. Areenna gauged the width and judged it wide enough for the kraals, barely. She was surprised to note how close they were to their goal, and how far they had come.

She continued to watch Sirod's mind pictures showing the trail to the top, and around the first peak. Then she descended toward the second, shorter peak and finally reached the spot on the mountain near their destination. From this high vantage point, Areenna could see the base of the mountain and the miles of land stretching toward the sea that expanded endlessly west. Yet, the area at the second peak was hazy and unclear. Areenna sensed something—not Sirod—clouding the view. She wondered if the Eight had set it in that way in Sirod's mind.

She broke their joining and drew back. Glancing at Mikaal, she asked silently if he had seen. He nodded.

"Thank you Sirod. We will go as you suggest, by way of the northwestern trail." Areenna yawned.

She shook off the wave of tiredness that followed, but Sirod said, "You must sleep."

"I have more to do." Areenna stood and turned to Neleh. "Come here," she said to her.

Neleh left her chair without question and stood before Areenna. "When I was your age, I was sent to a special school to learn many things. You do not have the chance to do this, but you are already older than your years. It is time to learn more. Will you trust me to help you do this?"

Neleh gazed at her and, without touching Areenna, silently said, *you are a woman of great power. Why would I trust you not*?

Areenna knelt before her. "As are you, Neleh. I sense great strength in you." She raised her hands and put them to either side of the girl's head. *Are you ready?*

When Neleh nodded, Areenna closed her eyes. *What I do now is to gift you three times with abilities. These are for you to carry to your tests on the Island.*

Instead of answering, Neleh opened herself completely to Areenna—opened her mind and her heart and drew her within. There was a calmness within the child, so deep and so soothing it caught Areenna by surprise. She breathed slowly, accepting the unexpected tranquility of the girl. While floating with the serenity of Neleh's mind, Areenna identified the gifts for Neleh.

The first was the simplest, the gifting of truth sensing. For a girl of her years, this would be invaluable. The second gift was the one of her own mother's ability—the lifting. This gift would serve both as a tool and as a weapon. Areenna prepared the third gift, but before she could transfer the power, Neleh interrupted her.

The girl's eyes turned upward, disappearing and leaving only white showing. A heartbeat later, her eyes were normal again. Neleh raised her hands and covered Areenna's with her own. She shook her head from side to side. *She says it must be from him.*

She? From him?

The…the sorceress; she told me it must be from Mikaal.

You know about Mikaal?

I know he is not like other men. I know he has the powers of women.

Areenna turned to Sirod. "Do you trust me? Do you trust Mikaal?"

"What need have you to ask? You know such is true," Sirod responded.

"What happens next cannot be spoken of, ever," Areenna said.

Sirod nodded without speaking.

Areenna dropped her hands from Neleh's head and stood. She turned to Mikaal, who was staring openly at the three. *The third gifting must be from you.*

If there had been a time for laughter, it would have been now, but laughter was the last thing called for as Mikaal's mouth dropped open, and his eyes widened with disbelief. *Me…how…I….*

It is a gift, she told him, *given from your own abilities to Neleh. You…push it to her. If she is able, if her powers allow it, she can accept your gift. Be prepared,* she warned. *Her mind is unlike any I have ever touched.*

Stay with me.

I cannot during the gifting; however, I can stay with Neleh and help her understand what you give.

Mikaal drew in a deep breath, walked the five feet and knelt before Neleh. He started to speak, but the child stopped him by taking his hands and placing them where Areenna's hands had been a minute before. She covered his hands with hers and closed her eyes.

Mikaal entered the calmness of the child's mind. He drank in the peacefulness, let it soak through his every fiber and when he was done, concentrated on his own abilities. Within seconds, he knew exactly what gift to give—fire.

When he finished, he heard Areenna instructing the child while all he could do was float within the strange calmness. Even now, it lingered on within him after he had parted the joining.

"You must not use this gift or the lifting until your full power comes. Do you understand?" Areenna asked. When Neleh nodded, Areenna continued. "Very soon, your body will change and you will start to become a woman. When that happens, your mother will begin your training." Turning to Sirod, she added, "Be ready, for I sense she has matured faster than most. The changes will be upon her soon."

Sirod's eyes darted between Areenna and Neleh. "I understand. It was so with me. I was the same age as she is now. There is a difference, though. She already accesses more power than did I at her age."

"This is a good thing. As soon as the first flow begins, her training must."

"It will be as you say." Sirod shifted her gaze to Mikaal. "Can you tell me how… how Mikaal gained a woman's power?"

"I cannot explain how, only that he was born to it as were we."

Again, Sirod's head tilted sideways as she digested Areenna's words. "It is beyond my understanding of how, but of the darkness there is nothing. I speak of this to no one as you have asked."

"Thank you," Mikaal and Areenna said at the same time.

Sirod smiled at them and seeing Areenna's eyelids begin to droop, said, "It is time for sleep. Come."

Standing, Sirod walked to the far side of the room and opened a drape, exposing two beds. Take one; Neleh and I will share the other."

"We do not wish to impose—"

"—it is settled and time to change from the day's clothing."

"We thank you for your generosity," Mikaal said as Areenna picked up the traveling bag with her clothing and went to the other room, closing the hanging drape behind her.

Sirod smiled at him. "Generosity it is not; rather fulfillment."

Mikaal's brows furrowed. "How so?"

"We have waited for centuries, always on guard, always with patience and today, to be the one… The honor is the fulfillment of my…our people's purpose. To know we have carried true what our ancestors had foreseen and tasked us."

He reached out, took her hand and squeezed it gently. There were no words needed.

Sirod glanced at Neleh, who had been standing silently near. "May I ask for a favor?"

"If I have the power to grant it," Mikaal said with a nod.

"Neleh's father was a good man, but he was taken from us when she was but four. The ice he hunted the large freesh upon was weak. It cracked while he fought with the freesh. He fell through. I know not if you and I shall meet again, but I would ask, even though you leave us in the morning, you accept Neleh as her guardian."

The speaker of the Eight... She said Sirod's people will be our defense and we their salvation. It is strong within me, a sense of returning here. I believe we must do so, Areenna whispered in Mikaal's mind.

No sooner had the silent words filtered through his mind than his precognitive ability flashed and he saw himself with Neleh, walking along a road in Nevaeh, not in the Frozen Mountains—when was unclear.

Neleh's, pale eyes locked on him. "It is an undeserved honor," he said formally.

"Come," Sirod said, rising to her feet. She motioned Mikaal to kneel before her and the same to Neleh. They knelt there; Mikaal's left side pressed to Neleh's right. She placed one hand on Mikaal's head and the other on Neleh. A spark leapt from her hand to him. It traveled through him and moved to the child. A few seconds later, Sirod lifted her hands. From outside came the sharp call of Charka as Mikaal's aoutem felt the bonding of man and child.

<><><>

It was almost midnight. The large ship, once again speeding on the sea with the three new passengers safely aboard, swung wide when it passed the chasm so it would not be seen by the Dark Master's ship. After picking up the three, they'd learned that upon completing her testing, Akassia' instructions were go to where they'd waited for the ship.

After she had returned to the western Landing, she'd found Laira waiting for her with three more kraals. The Eight had called Laira to the landing as well. They'd ridden non-stop to Welkold, alternating the kraals they rode for the ones they had not. There, Prince Trebor had joined them, such being part of their summoning. "All we know," Akassia had said, "is that we are needed and will learn what we must do when the time comes."

"When we started away from the Landing, three more women were arriving. Have you ever heard of such?" Laira had asked.

Enaid had not, but she had foreseen this happening. An hour later, the three went below for much-needed sleep, leaving Enaid to watch the waves crash from the ship's bow. Roth stood next to her while Timon guided the ship as only he could. Ilsraeth had stayed below to talk with the three until they fell asleep.

Staring at the white cresting waves, an unusual warmth formed deep within her, in the seat of her power. The warmth spread, turning to heat and filling her with a slow moving fire that did not burn; rather it flowed in a soft and secure way—then it was gone. In its wake, came the unexpected understanding of what had happened.

She turned to Roth, put her hands on his shoulders and turned him to her. "Mikaal…he has become guardian to a woman child."

"How can this be?"

"I know not," she said, "only that he and Areenna are safe. They are near their destination, and he has become the guardian of a child of power."

<><><>

Somewhere between midnight and dawn, Areenna's eyes opened. She was on her back. Mikaal lay next to her. The heat from his skin touching hers was as close to fire as possible, yet it mattered not, as the spot in the center of her forehead vibrated with warning.

She concentrated on the sensations, seeking the disturbance. Above her, on the yellow thatched roof, Gaalrie stirred and joined her. She searched slowly and carefully, never rushing, moving cautiously, and drawing quickly back when she touched the outer reaches of a hovering darkness. The instant she did, she knew it for what it was. While scarcely grazing its essence, bile had risen into her mouth; the bitter coppery taste was all she needed to understand what had awoken her. A wraith.

Her intuitive ability for time told her it was an hour before daybreak. She was undecided if she should wake Mikaal. She thought about the wraith. It was perhaps a day behind. She knew it moved slowly, seeking them in every crack, every crevice along the trail. She would let Mikaal sleep until daybreak. Then they would have to go, and go fast. She could not let the wraith find them. This wraith had a different aura than the others she'd faced and was certain if the wraith caught sight or scent of them, the Dark Master would know instantly.

<><><>

Daybreak came swiftly and with it, Areenna told Mikaal about the wraith. She had spent the time between finding the creature and Mikaal's waking, to work out a way to hide from its seeking. Only she knew this would be impossible on the narrow trail leading up to the mountain peaks.

In just under an hour, the four had eaten a filling meal and Neleh had gone outside to feed the kraals. When the others went outside carrying their small bags, they found themselves facing a crowd of people standing in a semi-circle around the kraals.

"My people wish to thank you," Sirod said.

"Thank us?" Areenna echoed in question. "For what do they do so?"

"For what you do, for what you will do," she said in a low voice.

Areenna regarded the faces of the people standing there, all so different, each not perfect, each emanating a warmth she drew within her. The connection between them was older than she could imagine, yet new to both she and them. While she had grown up with the fealty of the people of Freemorn, this was different. There was a sensation of something so familiar, so deep and so old she was humbled.

Do you feel it, she asked Mikaal silently.

So strong I... but he could say no more.

A man stepped from between two others and walked to them. He was old, very old. He had a face framed by silk white hair and lined with deep wrinkles; his eyes were the light blue of the palest of crystals. He walked with a limp from a leg that was both shorter and wider, a walking stick aiding his short journey. When he stood before Areenna and Mikaal, he dipped his head. When he raised it, he gazed deeply into her eyes.

"This is Racso, Elder of the Village," Sirod said.

"For your coming, we offer welcome. For what you will do, we offer ourselves and will await for your call. Our village is yours, our people at your service."

Areenna reached out and took his hand in hers and, slowly, Areenna, Princess of Freemorn, knelt before the elder and placed his hand on her forehead. She remained kneeling for several seconds before she stood. When she was upright, she saw twin trails of tears rolling down the elder's cheeks. Looking around, she realized the villagers spread out behind him had knelt when she had.

She took in all their faces and tried to find the right words to say but could not. Instead, she simply said, "Thank you."

The elder bowed his head again, turned and walked to his people. "We have placed food on your animals," Sirod said, pointing to the kraals. Each had four heavy skeins hanging from straps placed across the kraals. "Four bags have crushed cob for your animals, the other bags contain salted freesh. The freesh will keep you strong. Tasteless though it is," she said with a slight smile.

Rather than speak, Areenna pulled the older woman into her arms. *I have no words to thank you.*

Words are as unnecessary as thanks. "But leave now you must, for I sense your anxiety."

Releasing Sirod from the embrace, Areenna glanced at Mikaal, who nodded, already knowing what she was about to ask.

"There comes something dark behind us, a wraith," she told Sirod. "It will come to the village perhaps later today or tonight, tracking us. It seeks to tell the Dark Master where we are, where we go. It will find our scent and follow us. Do not challenge it. I think the villagers will not see this dark thing, but you and Neleh…"

"Concern yourself not, if you are certain the villagers are in no danger," Sirod said. "We leave soon after you. I sensed the change coming to Neleh the day before you arrived. She will become a woman in the next day or two. We must go to where this will happen. But only if you are certain my people will be safe."

Areenna turned to Mikaal. *Can you see? Can you call your ability for this*?

It happened yesterday. I will explain later, but for today, tonight, they are safe.

Areenna turned back to Sirod. "They will not be harmed," she said.

"Then we go to do what must be done for Neleh. Travel swiftly Areenna." She turned to Mikaal, stepped before him and placed her hands on his shoulders. *You, Man of Power, stand strong by your woman's side, for I see you and she are not of two but of one mind.*

She lowered her hands and stepped back, "It is our custom to bless those who go forth. Allow us this honor which has been handed down from before the beginning of our time here," Sirod said, both manner and voice gentle.

When Areenna and Mikaal nodded, the villagers moved forward. Neleh stepped before Mikaal, and Sirod before Areenna, their right hands on each one's chest. Behind them, they spread in a semi-circle of expanding rings; the villagers put a hand upon the shoulder of the person before them until each connected to another and finally connected to Sirod and Neleh.

When the energy of the villagers flowed forward, Sirod said, "Venture forth you do, and within you carry the strength of each of us. Fear not what crosses your path, know we stand with you."

When Sirod finished speaking and drew her hand from Areenna, Neleh did the same. "Travel swiftly," Sirod said, repeating what she had said moments before. She turned and walked away. The villagers all did the same, moving off in different directions without speaking.

Only Neleh remained. Looking from Areenna to Mikaal, her wheat-colored eyes were large and luminous. "I know I will see you soon." She went to Mikaal and slid her arms around his waist, pressing her head to his chest.

The calming warmth so deep within her spread over him. She stepped back without speaking and started away. Behind her, Charka cried out and reared slightly.

Neleh froze. She turned and the large blue-coated kraal walked up to her and nuzzled against her chest with his long triangular head. Neleh laughed at the touch and pressed her head to his as she had with Mikaal. A moment later, she followed her mother.

Areenna waved toward Neleh and Charka. “I have never seen such before. It was as if…”

Mikaal nodded. “It seems Charka has become her guardian as well.”

“So it does,” Areenna agreed as Gaalrie descended from the thatched roof where she had watched the proceedings and landed on Areenna’s shoulder. Areenna ran two fingers across the cinnamon and silver feathers of the treygone’s head before sending her aloft to lead the way to the mountain.

XXVIII

A DAY AND a half after leaving the village, eating the salted freesh, which was as tasteless as Sirod had said but powerfully nourishing, and drinking melted snow and ice, they reached the opening of the narrow trail leading to their destination.

The ride had been monotonous with nothing to break the long stretch of ice and snow-covered mountainsides. Even Gaalrie, who was always more comfortable flying than anywhere else, had ridden on Areenna's saddle bar, her cloak covering everything except the treygone's head.

Because the trail from the village had been narrower than the one they'd taken when getting there, it was impossible to camp; there was not enough room on the trail between the mountainside and the drop-off to the ice field below for all to sleep. Even the kraals needed space to move, for when they slept they, like people, shifted and stirred.

While a poor way to travel, there had been no choice; but when they turned off the trail, they found a large area separating the entry from the even narrower ascending trail.

Mikaal inspected the area. "We should camp here for a few hours before moving on. The rest will help gain us back strength."

Yes, Areenna agreed gratefully and dismounted. Gaalrie remained on the saddle bar. The treygone, having been asleep on the bar for the last several hours, was fresh and strong and she sent an asking.

The treygone stretched her wings, her body arching much like the way a person would stretch upon waking. Then the large bird was aloft, floating above them. From Gaalrie's eyes, Areenna saw the trail they had been upon—saw it receding until it faded into the grayness that was so much a part of the frozen north.

There is nothing behind us, yet. I sense no darkness.

Good, Mikaal sent back as he pulled their sleeping silks and knelt on the ground where he would spread them out. As he had been doing for weeks, whenever they made camp in the ice and snow, he called up his ability to create fire and bathed the ground in flames. It took only a few minutes for the snow to boil away and reveal the ground beneath. Three minutes longer and the ground was not only dry, but the first few inches of earth was softer.

He spread the silks and called Areenna, who put out crushed cob for the kraals. Mikaal sent an asking to Charka, to keep Hero within the opening while they slept. Then he laid down and Areenna came next to him. Gaalrie circled lazily above them.

Sleep claimed them both within moments of their heads touching the silks.

<><><>

Two ships bobbed on the choppy waters off the coastline of the Frozen Mountains. The Master stood at the bow, staring out at the mountain range. He saw not the ice and snow; rather, he hunted for his creature. When he finally caught a snatch of its emanations, he followed it to its source. The wraith was flying over the ice fields, moving slowly above a trail.

The Master entered the creation and took control, making it drop to the trail. He pressed its head to the ground and cast out his sensing. It took only an instant to find the traces of kraal. Mixed with it, was the 'feel' of the woman he must destroy and the man... For him, there would be no death. He needed to understand how this…abomination had come to be.

He pursued it until he was certain this was the trail they were upon was not an old scenting. As soon as he was sure, he withdrew from the creature and returned his essence to his body upon the ship. He twisted from the waist and raised both hands. The ships turned toward land. He knew, somehow, his creature would find them soon and when it did, he would be ready.

<><><>

Gaalrie's sharp cry woke Areenna and Mikaal instantly. The overwhelming sense of danger sent by the treygone sped them to their feet. *What?*

Areenna, her eyes closed cast out her senses. Her eyes sprang open an instant later. *The wraith*! *It comes. We must stop it before it can tell its Master.*

"How," he asked aloud.

"By surprise. We need to catch it off guard. It has not found us yet, but it's only minutes away. We…" She paused, her mind racing.

"We must take it down," Mikaal finished for her. "If you are right, if it is but tracking us, we have to stop it before it can give us away."

Areenna forced herself to think logically. "I think I know how. It will take both of us and perhaps our aoutems as well. This wraith is different." She pushed her idea to him.

Closing her eyes, Areenna called up her powers. Next to her, Mikaal did the same. The heat came alive, erupting into channels of superheated fire, which leapt from deep within. Flames burst around Mikaal's hands, Areenna's turned bluish white as the light dancing madly over her skin.

Seconds later the wraith appeared above them. It flew slowly in small circles, stopped, veered to the right and flew up. Then it flipped over in mid-air and started away.

It saw us! It runs!

Stop it! Mikaal responded.

Areenna released the blue light at the retreating creature. The light sped faster than the eye could follow. Commanding her ability, she surrounded the beast with the light. She closed both hands into fists and caught the flying monstrosity within a blue globe.

A loud wailing scream of anger reached them from the distance, as Areenna drew her arms and hands back. The wraith, caught within the bubble of light fought against Areenna's power but could not break free.

Mikaal, acting in tandem, projected a shield around them, stretching it to contain the wraith as well. When the shield solidified, he added a full block as Areenna had taught him. No dark magic could get in, and nothing could get out.

Struggling against its capture with every ounce of dark and vile energy, the wraith fought Areenna, but it could not stop her from bringing it closer. With an unexpected shift, the wraith turned within its shimmering prison to face Areenna and Mikaal. It pushed toward them, this time trying to tear through the imprisoning bubble.

Sparks erupted across the surface of the globe as it fought, its red eyes glowing in anger.

It has powers, Areenna warned Mikaal.

Mikaal, his ability rising in orange red flames, was ready to release the fire when Areenna stopped him. *This is no simple wraith. We must learn about it. We must bring it down.* Even as her thoughts reached Mikaal, the globe shredded. Sparks erupted when the wraith's large talons ripped through the shimmering light.

Mikaal did not hesitate. Twin streaks of fire shot from his hands and struck the wraith's wings. The mist-like appendages exploded, falling and twisting, as it fought for its existence. Its loud keening wail echoed along the mountainside while Areenna worked quickly to rebuild the globe. Just before the wraith hit the ground, Areenna managed to slow the creature's fall. Still, the wraith, for all its misty countenance, hit the earth with a thunderous crack.

Before the echo faded, Areenna raced to where it lay, its life source fading. Areenna knelt beside it, gagging, but doing her best to stave off the putrid waves of evil rising from its misty black feathers. Knowing what she had to do, and disgusted at the need, she pushed herself into the wraith's tiny mind.

Five seconds later, the creature stiffened and dissolved into a pile of ash. Areenna's stomach clenched, she vomited as the last dregs of the beast's mind separated from her.

Then Mikaal's soft mind touch soothed her, as if he were holding her in his arms. He pulled her up from her knees. Lifting and turning her to him, he drew her into an embrace, held her close and patiently waited for her tremors to subside.

Finally, taking in a deep breath, Areenna stepped back. "They know we are here," she said.

"They? The Black Witch?"

She shook her head, her eyes distant. "No, the Dark Master. It was only him. It was as if she is no part of the creature." She shook herself free of the thought and joined with him to show him what she had discovered within the wraith's mind.

It had to find our scent to follow us. The Master will not be able to track us now that this...thing is dead.

No, Areenna responded, *He has no need. The wraith found us before we pulled it into your shield and block. We need to go.*

"No. We need sleep. A few hours will make no difference. He knows where we are, but not where we go, not exactly. We need to be strong, not exhausted."

She started to argue but held back and took stock of their situation. She admitted to herself she was tired, more so even than she'd realized; this last short battle had drained her even further. She nodded. "As you say."

<><><>

The Master roared in anger. Behind him, two of his followers, deformed as all of them were, trembled at the sound. He turned toward them, but the red-ringed eyes saw them not. Rather, he heard the cries of his creature when the block surrounding the two dropped. Seconds later, came the death throes of his wraith. Even that was cut off the instant the block was rebuilt.

The Master closed his eyes and concentrated. The last image his creature had sent was of the two standing within a crevice on the side of a mountain. He knew this would be their path up and across the mountain. To where he had not learned, but their goal was somewhere on or within the mountain; there could be no other destination.

Make ready the landing, he commanded the trembling figures kneeling a few feet from him. Rising quickly, they raced to the hatch while the Master spread his arms and opened his hands. The ships moved toward the shoreline, where in the faint distance rose a high double-peaked mountain.

<><><>

Areenna and Mikaal awoke at the same moment. They'd slept for four hours, not two, and wakened with much of their energy restored. After eating a quick meal of tasteless freesh, and with the stars shimmering mightily above them, they mounted their kraals and headed up the mountain.

Climbing the steep and narrow trail in the semi-darkness of the northern night was slow work. Most of the time, they rode one before the other. When the night began its transformation into day, they were able to see more of the mountain they'd been ascending, and the trail that was clearly the only possible way to go. The snow and ice covering appeared to be less than it had been below. At midday, they passed a lone, disfigured and bent tree—leafless and long dead, a single gnarled branch pointing upward—which appeared more like a road marker than a tree.

Areenna glanced back and up. She estimated they had climbed perhaps a third of the distance. Gaalrie, flying above, continued to show them the way, as she flew higher into the upper reaches of the mountain. *Go*, she told the treygone and sent a mind picture of the place they sought.

Gaalrie lifted higher and in a few minutes disappeared from their sight. Areenna joined with Mikaal and together they navigated the meagre trail while watching through Gaalrie's eyes, as she followed the pathway toward the top.

When Gaalrie reached it, Areenna saw the top of the mountain rose to a sharp peak. At the base of the jagged and rocky final peak were small flat areas and jutting rises. She asked Gaalrie to go lower and when she did, Areenna was able to see several valley-like passages between the short and sharp rises.

Two thirds of the way to the top, they were forced to dismount and walk, as the trail became too steep and slippery to ride upon. While they climbed higher and Gaalrie flew above them, Mikaal caught glimpses of what Gaalrie saw. It was just as Sirod had shown them with her mind pictures, but clearer through the treygone's eyes.

By nightfall, they reached the base of the mountain's peak, where the trail split just after a flat open area. "Left or right?" Areenna asked staring at the way the pathway curved around the high peak. Up close, the crown was formidable, rising at least three hundred feet above them in a jagged triangular formation, looking not unlike the jagged and roughhewn tip of a spear.

"At least we don't have to climb that," she said, staring at the ice-sheathed sides of the mountain's highest point. From where they stood in the small and flat clearing beneath the crown, the path forked. The path to the left, wider than the one to the right by half again, sloped gradually downward between the crown and a jagged line of what she could only call smaller bumps in the mountain. Except, these ‘bumps’ rose high above her head. Strangely, the snow was only a few inches deep on the path. Just beyond the smaller rises, the ground widened. To the right, the trail rose upward, narrowing further.

“Left,” Mikaal replied after studying the terrain.

Areenna looked from Mikaal to the crest. The mountaintop was more like a sheet of ice than something created of rock. Areenna yawned and shook her head to push away the claiming exhaustion.

You are tired and it’s getting late. We should camp there, he said, motioning toward the area just past the smaller rise where it widened.

So close…

It will be there after we rest.

Areenna drew her eyes from the crest to look at him. “As you say, My Prince,” she said.

A half hour later, with the kraals fed and themselves as well, they went to sleep beneath a lean-to of silks, wrapped in the warmth of their fur cloaks and lying close to each other to stay warm in the icy air. Gaalrie, who perched on the big kraal’s back, slept in snatches but was ever aware, and always on guard.

<><><>

Areenna awoke first and slipped from the lean-to. She walked to the edge of the crest and peered downward. In the lighter gray of the early morning, she was able to see the trail’s descent clearly. Her sense of anticipation soared, and all she wanted was to get across the crest and to their destination.

She turned toward the lean-to and sensed Mikaal still asleep. Taking advantage of this rare privacy, she walked a short distance away and tended to her personal needs. Returning, she pushed a thought to Mikaal, who emerged from the lean-to, smiled at her, and sought his own moment of privacy.

Five minutes later, they breakfasted from of their dwindling supply of dried freesh while the kraals ate cob, and she pleaded with Gaalrie to eat some of the freesh. The bird finally ate a strip of freesh. The feeling the treygone sent back to Areenna made her gag.

"That wasn't nice," she scolded Gaalrie aloud.

Mikaal shook his head, a smile firmly fixed on his lips. "I agree with Gaalrie."

"She had to eat."

"Agreed, but she doesn't have to like it any more than we do."

Without further hesitation, Areenna and Mikaal mounted their kraals and began their descent. To their right, the sun broke from the horizon, but as it had for the past weeks, the sun did not rise upward; rather, it moved westerly. Still, it was a sight they had not seen on the trail ringing the mountain range.

At midday they were halfway toward the second crown, which they saw rising ahead of them. With her eyes locked on the top of the lower peak, Areenna sent the giant treygone toward the rocky projection. Floating on a soft updraft, Gaalrie banked slightly and dipped down toward the second crest. As she flew, Areenna and Mikaal saw an impossible sight—a green plateau between the two mountain peaks.

At the far end of the plateau, which ended at the second peak, they saw the concave and shiny opening the Speaker of the Eight had shown them in her vision. With a gasp, Areenna ended the connection with her aoutem, but not before asking Gaalrie to return.

"You saw?" she asked Mikaal.

He nodded. "The grass before the entrance, yes."

"Strange, is it not? And why could we see that not, when Sirod showed us this place?"

He shrugged. In the last three quarters of a year, he had seen so many strange and unbelievable things that even the sight of green grass in the snow and ice did not surprise him.

Areenna laughed when she caught his thought. "So far have you come that nothing surprises you any longer?"

"Many things surprise me. You do, every day. But the grass, no. It is a marker to tell us we have found what we seek."

"I surprise you, do I?" a warmth, gentle and sweet, spread through her.

Instead of answering, Mikaal pushed Charka on. The going was slow but steady and soon they reached a level point on the trail to find themselves staring down at the valley separating the two peaks. The second peak, the lower one, was still high enough for clouds to ring the highest point. There was just enough peak visible to make out its white crown against the gray sky. Areenna sighed, thankful they would not have to climb the peak.

What lay below the peak, the swath of green cutting through the plateau and leading up to the place they sought was a welcome sight.

Finally, Mikaal said to her silently, as he dismounted and stepped before the large blue-coated kraal. He put his hands to both sides of Charka's long muzzle and pressed his forehead to it. He drew the warming comfort his aoutem offered and returned his own to him. He dropped his hands and turned to Areenna just as Gaalrie landed on Hero's saddle bar.

Areenna stroked her aoutem's head, dismounted and stretched her body. "I feel like I have spent my entire life on his back," she said, continuing to twist and stretch the kinks that had grown with each mile ridden.

"We will be there soon," he said, staring toward their haze-covered destination. "We need to be moving. It's getting late."

"A hard taskmaster you are," she said with a smile and sensed the anxiety bubbling within her was doing the same to him.

"Only as hard as you have taught me to be," he replied, but he did not return her smile.

What bothers you?

I don't know. Something feels wrong. But it is not here, not of now.

A premonition?

I see nothing. It is a feeling only.

Then we need to be wary.

"Always," he said aloud. "And we need to be on our way."

They mounted and started downward, Mikaal leading and Areenna following behind with Gaalrie once again beneath her furred cloak. The descent was slower than they'd expected. The trail more slippery than it had been on the upslope.

It took them three hours to reach the point where the mountainside met the valley created between the twin crowns. They started forward, moving quickly toward the place they had been seeking for months. As they rode, Areenna became aware of something she had not sensed on the trail. *Rabt*, she told Mikaal.

Mikaal joined with her and he too sensed the presence of not a single rabt, but many. He took in the expanse of green grass and smiled. He would hunt later.

When they were three-quarters to their goal, Areenna drew Hero to a halt. Mikaal stopped next to her. *What?*

She shook her head. *Wait!* She looked around but saw only grass and snow. She closed her eyes and sought for anything in the area. She found no life. Then she sent Gaalrie aloft, and through her eyes, sought for what her senses could not find. Again, there was nothing.

We are alone. There is no one near. Yet there is something.

Mikaal nodded and urged Charka forward. As they closed the distance, the air grew slightly warmer. Moving nearer, but not too close, they inspected the entrance.

A strange low vibration began to pulse within Areenna. At that exact moment, the wall of the entrance glowed softly. "It is…crystal," Areenna said, staring at the wide sheet, which was perhaps twenty feet across and ten feet high. Streaks of stone ran up and down in strange patterns. When they were closer, she saw piles of gravel at the base of the crystal sheet. Dismounting together, they walked cautiously to the entrance.

Bending, Mikaal picked up some gravel. His eyes went from his hand to the strands still on the door and knew they were the same rock. It only took a second to realize what had happened.

He held his hand out to show Areenna the gravel. "These rocks were somehow bonded to the surface as camouflage. Look," he said, pointing to a jagged and uneven strand of rock that ran from the top to the bottom of the crystal sheet. "The same." He dug a fingernail under the edge of a strand and pulled. A few pieces came loose. When they hit the ground, they crumbled into gravel.

"A façade to hide the entry, to make it look like the mountain." Areenna ran her fingers over the crystal. The pulsing inside her grew stronger at the touch. "It's warm." She tapped it with her knuckle, but there was no sound. She pressed her palm to it and closed her eyes. There was a slight vibration. She dropped her hand and drew her shortsword. The metal of the weapon Roth had created for her glowed even in the grayness of the coming night. She grasped the pommel, turned it so the top of the pommel faced the sheet of what seemed like some sort of metal and tapped it. The sound was clean and crisp, not like metal upon metal, but not unlike it either.

Within her, the pulsing quickened. *Do you feel the vibration?*

Mikaal closed his eyes and joined with Areenna. He shook his head. *In you, yes. In me, no. It is only for you.*

Areenna nodded toward the entrance. "The question now is how do we open it?" With that, she sat on the grass before the door.

Mikaal stood there for a moment before sitting next to her. "How does sitting here open it?"

Instead of speaking, she took his hand in hers and placed their clasped hands on her lap. "Come with me." She drew him into her mind and pushed them both toward the crystal entrance. She sensed along its surface, trying to push through, but could not. *Blocked*! She moved them up to the top, seeking a crevice to push her senses through but found nothing, nor was there anything at the bottom or sides.

Can you use your mother's ability, the one to move objects...the one you gifted to Neleh?

She studied the crystal. *Move it how? Up, down, to which side*?

His brows furrowed and his eyes narrowed as he scoured the crystal wall. He looked up and shook his head. Then down and again shook his head. It seemed wrong to raise or lower the sheet. He focused at the point where it touched the right side of the mountain. The side curved off less than three feet from the crystal's edge. The left side of the mountain was long enough, and its slope less severe than the right. *To the left.*

She had followed his thought pattern and understood his conclusion. *I will try.*

She settled herself and called forth her power. With it came a strong increase in the strange pulsing, which vibrated throughout her body. Without moving, she pushed her ability toward the crystal, grasping its surface and forcing a bond between her mind and the gleaming facade. She pushed with every bit of her ability. Nothing happened for long hard fought seconds, until finally, there was a give and the crystal moved. It moved barely the width of a hair, but move it did.

She pulled her ability back, pushed it deep into the source of her powers and let it rejuvenate. While she did, she called Gaalrie to her.

When the giant treygone landed on her shoulder, it settled gently. *Bring Charka.*

Mikaal called his aoutem, who came to his side and, as gracefully as the large kraal could manage, Charka went to his knees and lowered his body to the ground, pressing against Mikaal.

When all four were settled and joined together both in mind and body, their energy and life forces melding together and burrowing deep inside her, Areenna took a deep breath and released her ability. This time there was no gentle feeling of the crystal; rather, she pushed a stream of power so strong the crystal vibrated loudly, emitting a screech, as it began to slide to the left. Areenna's body reacted in turn.

Sweat beaded over her brow despite the cold air rushing across her face. The cry of the crystal vibrated through her until she was pulsing in tune with it. Colors swam through the crystal, swirling and churning. Reds and blues, violet, yellow and greens raced through it in ever changing rainbow streaks. With her body vibrating and the colors flashing faster across the crystal, Areenna drew all her strength, all the energy of the others into her and pushed. The crystal's sound changed and rose higher until a note, like the peal of a bell, resounded through the plateau echoing off the mountainsides. When the sound ended, the entry opened another few feet.

Exhaling sharply, her power drained, Areenna sighed. She turned to Mikaal, and saw his eyes focused intently on the space between the crystal and the mountain.

"Mikaal?" *Mikaal!*

It took him a moment to respond. When he finally turned to Areenna, there was a strange look in his eyes. "Don't you feel it?" he asked.

The colors and sound of the crystal still ringing in her ears made it impossible to concentrate. "What?"

"There are two people inside... They are not alive; they are not dead."

XXIX

AT THE BASE of the mountain, two miles inland from the coast, the Dark Master stood on a platform built by his slaves. While he silently surveyed the forces spread out before him, seven hundred dark, mutated and armored ghazi soldiers of the Circle knelt silently, awaiting his commands.

Another hundred human warriors stood off to the left of his soldiers. These exiles of Nevaeh had been living in the northwestern outlands; men and women who had rejected their domains, and most criminals, recruited and subverted by the Black Sorceress. All called by the Master while he had sailed to this very spot.

The Master turned toward the mountain and the twin peaks, his senses projecting upwards, seeking the two who had so far eluded him with their blocks. As he searched for them, his body began to vibrate when the chiming sound Areenna had released raced down the mountain's slope and reached him.

He took in the sound, held it to him and when the sound vibrating within him ended, he smiled. He had them and with them, the prize the Circle had been seeking, the prize that had been stolen from them twenty-five hundred years before. Tomorrow he would have all, and the Circle of Afzal would be once again complete.

He raised his arms and pointed to another group of eighty or so of the semi-human ghazi who were off to the right. *Prepare to move. The rest remain here. Be ready for those who follow behind. Stop them*!

"You!" he shouted aloud this time, looking at the controlled and mind-locked exiles. "You are to come with us. Prepare yourselves. We leave soon." His eyes lingered on the Nevaen exiles and the mutated wolves who roamed within their ranks.

He turned back to the mountain, focusing on the lower peak. Leaving now, they would be near the lower peak by morning. *We have you...*

<><><>

Areenna, with Mikaal at her side, moved toward the opening of the entrance. As they approached it, she sensed what he had spoken of moments before. There were two inside the mountain, neither dead nor alive but somewhere between.

The feel of them was strange. Coming across this type of ghostly mind touch worried her. She gripped the pommel of her sword, not for protection but for the feel of something solid within her grasp.

They reached the opening and stopped. All they saw was darkness—the inky, black darkness of the unknown. Surprisingly, the scent of the air was fresh and clean. There was a hint of moisture in the cavern's air, and she realized water flowed somewhere in the mountain, giving the air its freshness.

With her right hand on her sword, she took Mikaal's in her left and glanced at him. His features were tense; strangely, his mind closed to her. Not closed, she realized; rather he was focused so intently on the interior it was as though he'd put up a block.

"What is it?"

Mikaal shook his head, unaware he was blocking her. "I don't know. There is something...different. A darkness but not of evil."

Releasing his hand, she called forth the ability to create illumination. A half dozen bubbles of white light rose from her open palm and floated through the opening. They moved forward, and the ceiling above them took on a glow. The nightmoss, so long deprived of any form of light, was absorbing her illumination and soon glowed above them.

The nightmoss grew brighter as the bubbles went deeper, revealing the extent of the cavern. In the distance, two objects floated four feet above the floor. They walked cautiously toward them, and Areenna's powers burst within, unleashing a fiery heat. Next to her, Mikaal reacted to her surge of power and his abilities sprang forth.

Coming closer, they studied the two long boxes floating a few feet above the floor. Between them floated something long and thin. *What?* Mikaal asked, staring at the sight. In the way Areenna had taught him during his training, he sent his senses ranging to the objects.

There are two bodies in the boxes. I like this not.

She put her hand on his arm. *They are the reason we are here. There is no other explanation. Come.*

He studied the boxes for several seconds. Then he moved forward, drawing his longsword as he walked. Behind him, Charka call out. He joined effortlessly with his aoutem and catching Charka's emanations, relaxed. The kraal sensed no danger.

They reached the floating containers and saw from the sheen, they were made of the same crystal as the entry wall. The thing floating between the boxes was some sort of staff, carved of a pale wood with a simple curved handle. Mikaal glanced at Areenna and back at the black boxes. "It is the same crystal, yes?"

Areenna sheathed her sword and with both hands, reached toward the box on her right. Mikaal caught her arm and held it back. *Are you sure*?

Areenna searched his face, seeking the cause of his doubt but could not decipher it. She nodded once. *Absolutely.*

Mikaal released her hand. "May I join with you?" he asked aloud.

Without responding, Areenna drew him in, took a step closer and placed her hands on the box. The crystal came alive, not with sound, but with color. The container, as she now knew it was, changed from black to dark purple to red and to blue before even that color faded and the crystal became clear.

Areenna gasped at the sight of a woman floating within the crystal box. Her skin was the color of a tawny dar. Her white blonde hair, the exact shade of Areenna's own, hung in long shimmering waves. She was naked, her arms crossed over her breasts, her hands on each shoulder. Her chest moved not at all, but Areenna knew this woman was not dead, yet she lived not either.

Look at her face. She is Bekar of the Highway. [2]

Mikaal saw what Areenna saw. It was Bekar, yet, his instincts told him she was not Bekar. *No.*

The other box, he said to her. She placed both hands on it, but nothing happened. She raised her brows in question. Mikaal studied the box, pushed his senses along its surface and found something undefinable. He placed his hands atop Areenna's warm skin. At his touch, the black of the box changed and new colors wove through the crystal. The colors faded and the crystal turned clear, revealing a dark-robed figure afloat in the clear crystal container. They could make nothing of it, its face, hands, and feet hidden by the folds of the robe.

Arrow-like, a chill raced through Areenna; she intuitively knew what he was. "A Master… a Dark Master," she whispered.

They stepped back from the crystal container. "I don't understand," Areenna whispered, looking from one crystal box to the other. "Who is she…who is he?"

"Not just who, we have to learn why they are here to understand what's expected of us."

"You're right." She stepped back and cast another glance at the boxes. "There is powerful magic here. I need to study it."

"It's late as well," he told her, looking at the entrance and the deepening grayness outside. "We should set up our camp and—" He smiled, "—hunt rabt."

Areenna, her attention fixed solidly on the floating boxes, nodded absently.

Do what you must; I will take care of the rest. Mikaal went outside, where he found Charka and Hero grazing on the long grass. He stopped after a few strides to find a dead rabt laying on the ground and heard, above him, the flapping of Gaalrie's wings, as she descended toward him, another rabt in her talons.

She deposited the furry body at Mikaal's feet and landed next to him. Reaching down, he scooped up the large bird with one hand, lifted her to his chest and stroked her head. *Thank you, sister.* He received a rush of warmth from her before releasing her skyward.

Looking around, he sought a place to camp but realized the best place would be in the cavern, not outside in the cold. He called Charka,

---

[2] See Born To Magic, Tales of Nevaeh, Volume I

sending his aoutem an asking to bring Hero. Then he picked up the two rabts and returned to the entrance where he dropped them and went inside. Charka and Hero followed, barely squeezing though the narrow opening between the crystal and rock.

Outside, Gaalrie hovered above, watching and waiting. Mikaal sent a thought to Areenna's aoutem. *Scout, seek, hunt*, he asked the bird while removing their supplies from the kraals.

Behind him, Areenna sat cross-legged, eyes locked on the crystal container holding the woman. She had been pushing at it since the moment Mikaal walked outside, trying to find something, anything to guide her. Thus far, she had failed.

With her frustration rising, she willed herself to calmness. *There has to be a way*! Knowing this as surely as she knew anything, she brought up the remembered visage of the Speaker of the Eight. She built her image as she had last seen her on the Island, with the long gray robe covering her snuck-like lower body, and the black face with the pale blue eyes glowing even though shaded by the folds of her cowl. *Why have you sent us here? Who are they?*

A shimmering mist grew before her eyes. The crystal boxes vanished. The image she had called forth floated before her. The sorceress' hands, their long black fingers clasped together, rested across her chest. *Patience, Child. Rest tonight, prepare for tomorrow. You will know more then.*

The image faded. "Wait," she cried aloud, but the Speaker was gone.

Prepare for what? Exhaling loudly, she stood and turned to Mikaal. He had spread their silks halfway between her and the cavern's entry. Charka and Hero were inside, but not Mikaal.

She went out into the rapidly falling night and found him cleaning a rabt. She looked for Gaalrie but did not see her and sent out a questing thought. It took only a moment to join with her treygone, who was flying over water on the northern side of the mountain, seeking her own dinner in the last dredges of the gray-lit day.

She flew with her until Gaalrie spotted a small flock of seabirds skimming low over the choppy water. As Gaalrie selected her target and dove, Areenna withdrew from the aoutem's mind.

Looking up from the rabt, Mikaal saw Areenna staring at the sky. “Gaalrie hunts.”

“I know. Real food,” she added with a smile. “What can I do?”

“Gather small rocks.”

“For what?”

“How else can we cook? There is no wood.”

“In the cavern or outside,” she asked, understanding what he needed.

“It makes no difference. There will be no smoke, except from the meat itself, only fire.”

She went near the entry, to where the peak rose from the plateau, and picked small hand-sized rocks from the ground.

Areenna made three rock-carrying trips into the cavern where she dropped them a few feet from the entrance. Then, as she arranged them into a pile for cooking, Mikaal joined her. He laid the rabts on the ground and studied the neatly arranged stones for a few seconds.

“We need two arrows and two large stones.” He built a mind picture of what he wanted to do. “The arrows are of acont wood, they will hold up to the heat.”

Knowing what she needed, Areenna went outside where she found two large rocks, which would be perfect. Then, using her mother’s lifting ability on the deeply embedded rocks, she drew them from the ground and moved them to the fire. By the time they were in place, Mikaal had the rabts spitted and was heating the stones.

Fifteen minutes later, with the kraals outside grazing on the grass, the stones were white hot and the rabts roasted above them.

<><><>

Two hours after midnight, when the Dark Master and his force reached the foothills of the mountain, and the trail leading to its lower peak, Roth, Enaid, Ilsraeth and Timon stood at the prow of the large ship. “How many? Roth asked.

Ilsraeth, who had been searching the Master’s forces, opened her eyes. “A half a thousand at the least. More I believe. They wait two miles inland.”

"There are no ghazis waiting near the shore?"

Enaid shook her head. "The land is clear."

Roth turned to Timon. "How close can you bring this boat to the shore?"

Timon studied the vista and pointed to an area to the right. "That spot is the only place where the water and land are almost level. I know not what lies below the water, but it will give us our best chance. It will take a strong wind to push this box of a ship to the edge of the land and get the bow upon it. We want no water-soaked warriors. The cold will kill them."

"Can you and Ilsraeth give us the wind to speed us to land?" the Master Boatsman asked the women.

"Wind we cannot raise, but fill the sails with power we can do. And push with water as well," Enaid said.

Turning from the others, Roth looked down at the deck. Noslen, Captain of the Sixes stood at the ready, awaiting Roth's command. Roth stepped down the short ladder from the prow and motioned Noslen to him.

"My Lord?"

"Prepare the Sixes to lead. Have all our people ready. When this boat reaches shore and all are on land, we move. This gray night may or may not hide our approach, and the fight will be anything but easy."

Noslen smiled. "Easy is not what we seek, Highness. Nor do I think those…things will find us easy to stop."

"When we reach their main body, we will be heavily outnumbered," he cautioned.

Noslen drew himself to his full six and a half foot height. He smiled. "Nevaens they are not. We will not fail you."

Roth placed his hands on Noslen's shoulders. "My concern is that you live to fight on."

"I will do my best," he responded.

Roth could not help but smile. "Of that there is no doubt. Prepare. We move with speed."

Noslen offered a slight head bow, spun and headed toward the groups of Sixes waiting behind him. Roth rejoined the other three.

Reaching Enaid, he asked, "How many women of sufficient power do we carry?"

"Thirty-four. Seven of whom fought with us twenty years ago, in our last battle. I have had them work with the others. They are ready."

"Good. Have them lined on the railings to aid the Sixes and protect our people when we land. Once this is done, we go."

Enaid started off, but Laira stopped her. "We must go our way when we land." As Laira spoke, Akassia and Trebor came to the bow.

"To what purpose?" Enaid asked.

To aid Areenna. The Eight...they charged us with this duty on the Island.

Wait until all our people are on land. When the fighting begins, circle around, stay as distant as possible, Enaid cautioned the three.

A quarter hour later, Enaid and Ilsraeth stood behind the sails and called forth their extraordinary abilities. The sails billowed and the huge ship lurched forward. Ilsraeth, containing the forces of their joined abilities, pushed on the sails while Enaid turned to the stern and called forth the divining, pulling the very sea itself up and against the wood of the stern, adding more force to their charge to land.

The ship lurched forward, moving faster than ever before while Timon held the wheel, guiding it to the exact spot needed to get the troops off the ship quickly. As the boat hurtled landward, an explosion of activity erupted as the captains called their fighters together.

Lined on the right side of the ship stood thirty-four women of power, each ready to protect the forces of Nevaeh should it be necessary. The Six groups stood behind them, ready for the moment the ship touched land. Near the steps leading up from the lower deck, two hundred men and women-warriors prepared for battle. Rope ladders hung from the side of the ship and ropes meant for the Sixes hung between them.

Watching the land draw near and dressed in battle armor, as was everyone on the ship, Roth stood at the bow, his sword grasped tightly in one hand. He thought about the centuries that had flowed behind him and of how he knew this was the beginning of the end. One way or another, from this point on, Nevaeh would either survive and grow, or wither and become enslaved to the abhorrent rulers of the Dark Circle.

"Where are you?" he called aloud to Mikaal and the one person who held the ability to create victory with his son: Areenna. Two breaths later, all thought vanished from his mind as the ship rushed toward land.

Back off, Enaid told Ilsraeth when they were a hundred yards from the edge of the land. The sails fell flat, the powers pushing them gone, but the ship did not slow, rather, it sped forward. The sea, under Enaid's control, propelled the ship onward. When they were a hundred feet from the edge of the rocky shoreline, Enaid shouted to Timon, "Left! Hard!"

Without hesitation, Timon spun the wheel left, turning the boat leeward. When the side was perpendicular to land, Enaid closed her eyes and drew up the water beneath the ship. The ship rose a half foot above the level of the land. Enaid did not slow the water; rather, she pushed the icy seawater over the land and when the ship was inland enough, set it gently on the ground.

As the ship settled on land, the Sixes, with perfect timing, grasped their single ropes and went over the side, sliding down the ropes even as the warriors behind them raced to the railing.

The instant the Sixes moved, Roth gave the command for his army to follow. Twenty streams of Nevaen warriors descended the ladders. Still at the bow, Roth forced himself to wait. As much as he needed to be at the forefront of this battle, he knew he had to wait to make certain there was no attack by any hidden ghazis.

Eleven minutes after they landed, the army of Nevaeh had formed its ranks. With the Six groups in the lead, Roth, Enaid, Ilsraeth and Timon, went with them in a distance-covering jog.

<><><>

Shortly after daybreak and two hours after waking, Areenna and Mikaal were mind-joined and sitting before the twin containers. They'd been there for almost an hour, testing ways to unlock the secret of what lay floating within the crystal walls.

I am lost with this. I have no idea of what to do, she told him.

You saw the Speaker last night. She said we would know today. We must wait.

I like this not! Something is wrong, but what...

No sooner had her thought raced through Mikaal's mind than his vision blurred. When it cleared, he was standing on the steep western mountainside. Coming toward him were fifty dark forms wearing armor and carrying swords and battle-axes. They were ascending quickly toward the lower crest… and toward them. As the scene unfolded and Mikaal watched the dark force reach the plateau and charge at the cavern, behind them, a black-robed figure moved slowly; the emanations, drifting so foul from it that even within the vision, Mikaal gagged.

The scene shattered and Mikaal broke the joining with Areenna and rose to his feet. He had five minutes at the most. He raced to where his armor lay and drew on only his upper armor, freed his sword and long knife and turned back to Areenna. She was running toward her armor too.

He grabbed her, held her by her shoulders and said, "No matter what, do not leave the cavern."

Her head jerked back, her green eyes flaring. "I will fight with you!"

"You saw the Dark Master is with them. He controls them. You must hold him back while I fight his slaves."

"Mikaal—"

—It must be this way. There is no choice. You must close the entry. Turning, he went outside. When he was ten feet from the crystal wall, he pushed the tip of his sword into the earth, slipped his knife into its sheath, and summoned his powers. As the heat roared to life deep within his core, he called to Areenna. *Where are they?*

Areenna closed her eyes and joined with Gaalrie. Her eyes flew open. *They are here, now!*

He turned back to the entrance and raised both hands. Areenna joined her powers with his and together they released their combined abilities. The crystal sheet screamed in protest. Colors erupted across the surface. The chiming of the crystal was ear shattering as it sealed itself, locking Areenna, Charka and Hero within.

Charka's cry of anguish, at the separation, hit Mikaal hard. He had no choice but to ignore it. Mikaal turned to face the oncoming ghazi-slaves, pulling the sword from the ground but leaving his knife sheathed when the first of the dark mutations charged him.

As the ghazi neared, a sudden wash of power, alien and putrid, attacked his mind. Areenna, behind the crystal door, pushed her powers at him, surrounded him with her shielding ability and freed him from the Dark Master's attempt at control.

Mikaal called forth his primary weapon. While his right hand gripped the longsword, his left rose, fire spewing from his palm. The first line of attackers erupted in fire, yet they did not scream; rather, they kept charging until the fire disintegrated their bodies.

Behind them, more rushed forward, carrying their axes and swords high as they charged him. While he fought, he sensed Areenna was in battle as well, fighting the Master even as she held her shield over him.

Release the shield! I hold my own, he added as one of the Master's people burst through two burning slaves and charged directly at him. Although the creatures' arms were afire, he swung the battle-axe at Mikaal's head.

Mikaal turned sideways. His sword whistled through the air and met the oncoming soldier at the joining of the shoulders and neck, severing his attacker's head. Completing the swing brought him to face the others moving toward him, slower now, more cautious.

The attackers spread out in a semi-circle, moving forward to encircle him. He released another stream of fire. This time it struck an invisible wall. The Master had rejoined the fight.

Areenna!

XXX

WHEN THE CRYSTAL was sealed, Areenna could only stare at it. She exhaled loudly, closed her eyes and pushed herself to Mikaal. She joined with him to fight the Dark Master's attack. Without thinking, she created a shield around Mikaal, freeing him to face the oncoming semi-human ghazi fighters.

Within seconds, the Master struck at her. She held him off and, in turn, fought back, all the while seeing the battle outside raging through Gaalrie's eyes. The revolting strength projected against her was even viler than the power of the Black Witch. The force of the magic attacking her was the very essence of depravity, sucking out the light from her very core. Above all, she knew she had to occupy the Master to keep him from Mikaal.

Reacting to the vileness of the attack, she fought harder, bringing forth all she had learned from her mother, from Enaid and from every woman of power who had shown and given abilities to her. In doing so, she created a barrier so solid the Master of the Circle of Afzal stopped his attack.

In the pause, she heard Mikaal's call to her and from Gaalrie's eyes saw him surrounded by an ever-closing ring of the dark soldiers. "No!" she screamed and sent Gaalrie to Mikaal's aid.

The moment she made the connection with Gaalrie, the Master attacked again, this time sending a terrible force at her. Although nothing physical could reach her, this was anything but. Like a fist slamming into her abdomen, the force struck hard and knocked her back. She landed hard on the rock of the cavern floor and slid another dozen feet, her head hitting the hard rock floor.

Pain spread everywhere. She cried out. Before she could rise, a giant unseen hand wrapped around her torso, its fingers squeezing the breath from her lungs. Her thoughts, already spinning from the fall, faded; she could barely take in a breath. Just before her mind shut down, she reached inward and grasped a spark—the spirit of what made her herself— and called upon the powers the Master was suffocating.

Her powers responded instantly. She drew out Mikaal's weapon first. Fire shot from every pore of her skin. The unseen hand jerked from her body. She pulled the flames from her and sent them outside, out past Mikaal, out past the charging mutations and directly at the Master.

In the same moment, Gaalrie struck the face of the soldier closest to Mikaal. When the treygone ripped her long talons across his face, his scream reached through the crystal barrier. Through Gaalrie's eyes, she watched two black-armored fighters behind the fallen one, race over his pain-twisted body in an effort to reach Mikaal.

The Master raised both his black long-fingered hands and closed them into fists. The flames attacking him went out and his troops overran Mikaal.

Near her, Charka screamed in agony.

<><><>

Just before the first armored warrior reached Mikaal, Gaalrie attacked, ripping her talons across the man's face. Blinded, the man fell screaming. Mikaal swung to his left and split open the armor and chest of another. He drew his knife and spun around. The circle of ghazi stopped short.

From behind came the rushing of feet. He turned just in time to catch the first one on the tip of his sword. He pushed up, and pulled it free as another struck at him. The thing fell while Mikaal feinted at another onrushing warrior, sidestepped, and plunged the long-bladed knife into the man's throat. He spun again only to find the others charging forward in a massive rush. No sword swung, no axe fell as they piled atop Mikaal, ghazi upon ghazi, crushing him until, mercifully, he lost consciousness.

◇◇◇

Even as the flames winked out of existence, she lost contact with Mikaal. She rejoined Gaalrie, who flew above the battle now and saw the armored mutants pile atop Mikaal. “No,” she whispered.

The Master struck in that moment. Not a physical blow but one directed at her mind. Like pincers, he drove at her, squeezing her head, trying to penetrate her mind and take control of her thoughts and body.

She fought, pushing against him, holding him back as best she could until a new force built within her, a force both familiar and strange. Together, they pushed back the Master’s power.

The staff, projected the Speaker of the Eight. *The staff,* the ancient sorceress repeated. A picture of the object floating between the two crystal boxes filled in her mind. *Yes.*

With one last effort, she pushed the Master’s attack from her and with the help of the Eight of the Island, set a shield around herself, gained her feet and ran to the crystal boxes. There, she reached out and grasped the floating wooden staff.

A flash, like lightning, burned into her hands. A surge of power filled her with an incredible energy. Turning to the crystal entrance, the staff held firmly in both hands, she stared at the crystal and pushed herself to see through it to the outside. The horde of semi-human warriors were retreating and of Mikaal, there was no sign. She could not feel him or see him, yet she knew he was alive.

Then, on the far side of the crystal entry, standing before her was the Master.

His black robe and cowl hid his features; yet she could see the burning red rings around his amber eyes. Staring at her, the wall of solid crystal between them, he pulled the cowl back and revealed his face. It was almost the face of a man… almost. Hairless, his eyes were wide-set and oval. The irises tinged with a red circle separating orange irises from the white. His nose was a small flat piece of skin with two small holes for breathing. His mouth was a small oval, nearly circular, and the exposed teeth were yellowish brown.

Mine he is now, your…man. His mind and body mine to control. I will have you as well. Mistake this not. Your powers are futile against me. For you and your kind, it is the end.

Areenna's hands clenched into fists. *Never will I allow such. I will find you and I will take him from you and together we will destroy you!*

He smiled, his oval mouth twisting. *Yes, come find me.* A gray swirling mist rose from the ground to surround him. An instant later, he was gone.

Areenna closed her eyes and exhaled her long held breath. The emptiness within her grew into a cloying, anguished void. Opening her eyes, she looked at Charka. He was next to the wall, at the edge of where the crystal sheet would open. He stood there shaking, a low groaning sound bubbling from his mouth.

She went to him and, still holding the staff in one hand, stroked his elongated snout as she sent him a calming energy she did not feel. A few moments later, he stopped trembling. Areenna pressed her mouth to his head and held it there.

We will find him, brother; we will bring him back.

In turn, she accepted a surge of warmth from the kraal, a sensation of absolute trust in her. Turning from Charka to the crystal entrance and intuitively using the staff, she pushed at the crystal. It responded immediately with a flare of color and opened without a sound. She stepped through the entrance and surveyed what lay before her. There were at least ten dead lying in a circle where Mikal had stood. In its center lay his longsword and dagger.

She picked them up, hugged the cool metal to her chest and sent out another questing thought to Mikaal. There was no answer. She called to Gaalrie, who swooped low above her. *Find them, track them, and watch over Mikaal.* When Gaalrie rose skyward, she returned to the cavern and using the powers she drew from the staff, sealed the entry.

She stood still for several seconds before going to the two crystal boxes. When she reached them, she turned to face the woman within.

Areenna could not stop comparing her to Bekar, whom they had met on the old highway in Northcrom. She studied her intensely. The pale skin, the white blonde hair, and the beautiful features combined to tell her this was no woman of Nevaeh, yet somehow, Areenna knew she was.

She studied the crystal box, looking at the seams. Slowly, carefully, she reached for what appeared to be a small notch on the top and placed her hands near it. The instant her fingers touched the crystal, a powerful surge burst between her and the box and she froze. She tried to move but could not. Whatever it was, it had paralyzed her.

She reached for her abilities but a strange vision caught her and drew her from the cavern. She found herself standing in a thicket of woods unlike any she had ever seen and a shimmering vision of the woman in the crystal box stood before her.

The breezes lifted the vision's long hair, tossing it randomly. "You did well, Child," she said.

"I don't…" Areenna looked around, trying to understand where she was.

"You will understand," the woman said. "I have waited for you and him for millenniums as I told you on the old highway."

"Who are you? Bekar you are not." She stepped closer to the vision and peered into her eyes to find they were the same as her own—sea foam green with silver flecks. Areenna gasped with understanding.

"Yes, Child of my childrens' childrens' children. For more than a hundred generations, for well over two thousand years, have I lain here. You are correct. I am not Bekar."

Areenna'mind was a swirling storm of random thoughts. Everything she had done since the day she'd left for the Island rose up within her, attacking her, making her head hurt and her mind cry out for help. Then, slowly, she rebuilt her composure, settled her mind and drew herself tall. "How do you still live? How come you? How were you on the old highway?"

She smiled sadly. "I am but a memory placed within this cavern for you, my body sustained within the crystal for this singular purpose. I am not Bekar of the highway, although she too is my descendant and your ancestor and as such a part of me. When I lived, I was called Ailish."

"Ailish…" She whispered, the old tales of her childhood rising quickly. "You are… but a legend."

"As I should be, Child. A legend, a memory, a reason to survive. I have been kept here, hidden from all while they waited."

"They?" As she spoke the word, understanding came. "The Eight," she whispered. In her hand, the wooden staff glowed.

Yes, Child, we are here, came the all too familiar thoughts of the eight women of the Island.

Why did you not do this on the Island? Why did you send us here?

Because the staff and he are here, the Speaker of the Eight said.

Although she was staring at the vision of Ailish, she saw flashes of others, of the black-skinned half-women half-snucks from the Island. *He*?

Sit Areenna, I will show you. Ailish reached out and grasped Areenna's head. The instant she did, Charka cried out.

<><><>

A wave of vertigo drew her into a maelstrom of sound and color until she grasped harder on the staff to stop from falling. Transported yet again, she stood in an unfamiliar cove cut within the walls of the southern palisades. They were familiar but different, taller, reaching higher above the water than in present time. When the familiarity of the palisades grew on her, she realized where she was.

This is Nevaeh, millennia before your birth. The lands were still shifting, the oceans changing, and even as the lands were changing, the people adapted and transformed from what they had once been and were becoming what you are now. Our magic was growing, and our women were learning more control and developing stronger power with its use.

The Circle of Afzal had conquered all the lands of the world except for Nevaeh. We were the last left to stand against them. For centuries, they sent their slaves against us and while our people had stopped them, the costs were high, and we were on the verge of failing. The Masters believe every living being is theirs to do with as they please—they take it as their right to bring everyone under the control of the Circle, to accept only the Circle's ideals.

It was at this time the Circle sent a huge fleet with tens of thousands of their subjugated mindless ghazi soldiers to overrun Nevaeh and enslave our people. For the first time, all the Masters were upon the ships. They are terrible in their power. They use their slaves as food, not to eat their flesh but to consume the very life force within each. They have subjugated them, turned them into mindless creatures with but a single purpose: to bring more slaves to the Circle. The Masters believe themselves omnipotent, to be above all others. Watch!

The vision who was Ailish pressed her hands tighter to Areenna's head and a new scene unfolded within her mind's eye. Off the shore of the southern palisades, riding upon the sea were hundreds of huge ships. The night was cloudy and moonless and she was floating above one of the ships.

Below her, a twisted man crossed the deck—she knew intuitively he was the Master whose body lay in the crystal box. A dark clinging mist surrounded the Master and, caught within the memory of thousands of years before, she followed the Master's limping rush toward the railing.

Reaching the ship's side, he climbed the railing and jumped into the sea. The whirling gray mist covering him, held him above the water and carried him to the shore, where he walked west. A short time later, he climbed to the top of the palisade. Once there, he walked east.

When he disappeared in the distance, Areenna looked down at the ships. On the ship below her, the one the Master had jumped from, two more Masters stood at the bow. Behind them a hundred followers moved in a frenzied pattern until the ship lurched forward toward the notch in the palisades where the first Master had gone.

The ship skimmed over the water, picking up speed on its race toward shore. Both Masters had their arms raised. The sails billowed fully, propelling the ship faster. Four minutes later the ship ground to a stop, its bow embedded in the gravel-like sand of the cove's shore.

Cries and shouts rose from the deck as the Masters urged their creatures over the sides. Once everyone was aground, the Masters led them up the side of the palisade. When they reached the top, they formed into ranks and started after the first Master.

She watched them follow him while Ailish's voice filled her mind. *These are the fifth and last generation of Masters. Each generation before them became stronger, their magic more powerful, and each generation longer lived. The Master you first saw, the one with the staff, is he who now lies within the crystal. He is a direct descendant of Afzal Mahmud Tarek, the creator of the Circle. These Masters retain their life force by draining that of their people.*

Like our sisters of the Island, there are eight Masters. As time passed, they became equals; no one single Master ruling the others. They were always of one mind, one purpose: to make all subservient. However, this one Master was different. We know not why he was so, we can only guess, but for whatever reason, he was different.

As the grandson five times removed from the grandfather, he held the sacred possessions of Afzal, and among those possessions was a book. This book, called the Koran, was the writing from which the Circle of Afzal drew its beliefs.

This Master spent decades reading and studying the Koran, and one day he discovered his ancestor had twisted the meanings of the writings. What Afzal Mahmud Tarek had taken to signify they were supposed to make everyone believe as they did, was not what the writing had intended. No, it was just the opposite. The original book spoke of peace and the joy of life. It spoke of compassion and understanding, of love and acceptance, not war and subjugation.

This Master, within the revelation of the Koran's true meaning, understood what he needed to do. While the other seven Masters planned the conquering of Nevaeh, he worked out a plan to stop it...forever.

The staff, Ailish continued, *handed down from one descendant to the next, became more and more an object of power, made so by the generations before it. However, this Master learned the staff could be more. He believed it could bridge all, stop this endless war of* annihilation, *if the deepest powers of Nevaeh, the powers of the Masters' opposites— the Eight women of the Island—could merge with it.*

He believes when he and the Eight join together they will have the ability to turn the staff into an instrument so powerful it will defeat the vast forces of the dark powers.

Areenna shook her head. She raised her hands to her head and covered Ailish's with them. *He never reached the Island, did he*?" Areenna dropped her hands to her sides.

Reached the Island he did, for I was there when he stepped upon the Landing. They had summoned me to be there when the Master, Jalil Ben Afzal arrived. We entered the ruins together and together met with the Eight.

I watched them gather around the Master and each place one hand on the staff and the other on the shoulder next to them. A force built around them so powerful it caught me within its embrace, and I too became connected to the nine who held the staff. A bolt of lightning flashed, not from the sky to the earth, but from the staff itself. It rose into the clouds and when it struck them, a strange golden rain fell upon us. The lightning continued to touch the clouds, and as the golden rain poured down, the nine holding the staff glowed within the misting droplets.

A trembling started within me and grew stronger. The nine cried out in one voice, and the rain stopped. The lightning withdrew from the sky and returned to the staff. The trembling within continued and I realized what it was. The staff linked me to the nine of them, and the powers they were pouring into the staff passed through me as well.

I know not how long this lasted; when it ended, I fell unconscious to the floor. When I awoke, the Speaker of the Eight brought me to my feet. She told me the dark forces were across the water, at the western Landing. They were preparing to attack the Island. They knew what the renegade Master had done and wanted him and the staff.

They charged me with keeping the Master safe and taking him to a place of hiding. When the other Masters discovered Jalil Ben Afzal's defection, they'd ordered their fleet to the Island.

They would attack the Island, but without the eighth Master, the Circle would not be able to overpower the Sorceresses; yet, the Masters would sacrifice every one of their army to get the Master and the staff, so important were they both to them. There was only one way to prevent the attack: the Master and I had to get away.

The Eight placed a vision of my destination, and the route to get there. Then the Master and I went to the landing and boarded the skiff. Once they were certain the Masters had seen us board the skiff, the Master raised his staff and created a fog to surround us. The Speaker of the Eight told me to raise both shield and block, to maintain it until we were far away. The powers within me had grown stronger since my joining with the staff. I did as instructed, and the Eight came together and created a vision of a skiff with myself and the Master seated within it. Then they sent us off, our skiff hidden with the fog, the other skiff barely visible.

Instead of crossing to the Landing, we headed toward open sea. When we passed the tip of the Island, the illusion still shrouded by fog, we turned to circle the Island. In that moment, the seven Masters sent a huge wave upon us—at the vision, to force it back. Because we were turning, our skiff was sideways when it struck. The small skiff rose and was tossed madly about. It almost went over, but the Master stopped it from rolling. At the same moment, from behind me came a terrible crash. When I turned, I found the Master laying upon a shattered bench. A long thin piece of wood was sticking out from his back.

The Eight came to us, projecting their minds and abilities to me, as I pulled the long wooden spike from his back. Having the healing ability, I stopped the flow of blood but did not have the time to heal him fully, nor could I spare the energy without dropping the shield and the block.

Thankfully, we rounded the tip of the Island while the other Masters continued to drive the vision skiff toward them. Four hours later, I pulled to the shore and returned to healing the Master. When he tried to move, he could not. The wood had not just shattered inside of him; it had broken his back and he had no movement below his waist. Later I learned the healing had not fully taken because there was more of the wood inside him.

I could do nothing, and he asked for nothing. He accepted what happened and was grateful we had escaped. In one village of Northcrom, they made us a rolling cart so the litter I carried him on would not be necessary. From there, with the aid of many Nevaens, we moved north to the tar fields, west across the Arctic Ice fields to the twin-peaked mountains the Eight had sent me.

It took almost a year to reach our destination. We met many people who aided us along the way. We met too, many agents of the Dark Masters whom we fought and defeated. When we reached the mountain, the Master used his staff to create the cavern and the crystal door. He was sick, the infection from the wound had grown and slowly spread through his body. His magic and mine slowed the infection but we could not stop it.

The Speaker of the Eight appeared to me. She told me what came next but also said it was my choice to accept. My daughter was Queen of Fainhall, married to the King. My husband had died in battle six years before, and my son ruled Morvene with his queen.

All was as it should be, and I knew, without me, there might be no future for my children or any Nevaen. I accepted my role and told the speaker of my decision. When I did, the Master called me to him. I knelt next to Jalil Ben Afzal and he took my hands in his. He raised them to his lips and kissed each one.

He said nothing, but I understood. He was dying.

Then the sorceresses of the Island joined with the Master and their vision essence surrounded me. Then each put a hand on me and pushed into me, the vision of the eras ahead.

When they finished, they moved the Master to the center of the cavern and placed him on the ground. They had me lie near him, and after I did, they stepped back to form a circle around us.

The cavern glowed with light. Above me, two balls of pure energy rose rippling and stretching. I was falling asleep, yet I was able to see everything. The crystal formed around me; yet, through all the time, as I lay here...through all the generations of my children, I was granted the knowledge of all that has transpired until the moment you entered this cavern.

The images faded and Areenna was back in the cavern. "You went into the crystal even though you knew you would never come out?"

The wavering image of Ailish nodded. "Why would I not? I am a woman of power. It was my duty to ensure Nevaeh lived on, and to save my children. Did not you and your complement come, as the Eight foretold, and I have not come out as well…so to say?" She smiled gently at Areenna.

"The stories I have been told of you… How you fought the invasions, helped stop the Dark Ones from overtaking us, those were true?"

"They were. It was not myself alone, but all the women of power who were with me. Our powers were not as strong as are women's now, if what I see within you holds true with others."

"Hold true, yes." She drew in a shaky breath. "You sacrificed yourself to wait for me," Areenna said.

"All I did was but what my ancestors did for the hundreds of years before my birth, when women first discovered their powers—it was the beginning of magic in Nevaeh. My maternal ancestor was the first woman to learn how to use her ability and she taught others. She was the first woman called to the Island.

So long ago.

Areenna turned to the second crystal container. “He too no longer lives, only his memories?”

Ailish met and held Areenna’s eyes for several long moments before saying, “No. Jalil Ben Afzal lives.”

XXXI

TRAPPED WITHIN THE deepest recesses of his mind, Mikaal struggled to find himself, but could not. Bogged down and held hostage within a strange cocoon-like prison, he was unaware of anything other than the sucking black void within which he was suspended. He had no physical sensations: he knew not that he lay upon the cold ground.

His last memory was of being overwhelmed, of body upon body piling atop him until he could not breathe. With the loss of his breath came darkness and within the darkness, a terrible cold murky grip fenced in his mind. Trapped by the unrelenting fog, he pushed his senses hard and found…nothing.

He tried to move his legs but could not feel them. He called out to Areenna, but no sound issued, nor could he send her any thought. He stopped fighting and took stock of himself.

He suddenly remembered the Dark Master. No sooner had the thought birthed than he was aware of a stealthy probing within the shadows of his mind. Fingers of thoughts so alien his body convulsed and twist in agony, probed his mind, yet he was aware only of the inky horror seeking to infiltrate and control him, not the pain racing through his nerves and muscles.

Anchoring himself with the knowledge of who he was and the abilities granted to him, he raised a block, fighting the relentless tendrils seeking a pathway to control his mind and ultimately control him. He pushed at the fog while he struggled to erect the block.

An instant later, the tendrils were gone and he lost consciousness.

<><><>

The sky was turning from dark gray to a lighter shade when Roth stopped the Nevaens a thousand yards from the massed ghazi soldiers. His experienced eyes told him there were, as Enaid had said earlier, more than a five hundred of the creatures—he would not call them men.

He signaled Noslen to him. "Divide our fighters into three. We strike with a three-prong attack to separate them. You are with me. We will lead the center. Have the two other Sixes lead from the flanks."

Noslen dipped his head slightly. "As you command." Moving quickly, Noslen went to the three Six groups and gave them Roth's instructions and battle plans.

The next minutes found the Nevaen troops shifting to the positions Roth had ordered. Forming into three columns of warriors, and with Noslen and Enaid to his left, Ilsraeth and Timon to his right, Roth gave the command.

The columns moved forward, slowly at first, and as they neared the enemy, changed to a slow run. Ahead of them, in the closing distance, the ghazis roared their battle cries and charged the oncoming Nevaens.

When the two armies met and the clash of metal rang loudly, Laira, Akassia and Trebor trailed behind the right flank. The moment the armies met, Laira and Akassia joined the other women to protect their vastly outnumbered force.

The fighting was fierce, no quarter asked, none given. Blade met blade, and as lances penetrated armor, the forces of Nevaeh moved relentlessly forward, stepping over the bodies of the fallen. The gray sky darkened above the battlefield, turning the rocky ground into shiny, blood-soaked black pools.

<><><>

On a small and level ridge above the battle, the Master watched the clash of the two forces while his followers prepared the camp and placed Mikaal within a tent. A few hundred feet below, between him and the fighting, a hundred of his ghazi waited for any who might get past his larger force.

Turning from the battle, the Master walked to where Mikaal lay and motioned to one of his slaves. The ghazi came to him quickly, removing the pack he carried. The Master searched through it and found what he sought. Although he had placed a powerful block around Mikaal, he found the power of the young male strong enough to break through should he rise to full consciousness—an event he could not permit. He needed Mikaal under his absolute control. He could not claim the staff without Mikaal. He needed his concentration uncluttered, for he had to learn how this male had gained his powers. After that, the boy would have to die—no males with powers other than the Eight Masters could live.

He removed a glass vial, pulled the stopper and poured two drops of the potion into Mikaal's mouth. He waited a full minute for it to take affect and when it did, the Master released the block, knowing his prisoner's mind would remain locked until he decided it was time.

He returned to the rock he had been on minutes before and projected himself toward the battle, where he saw his ghazi army cut by two-thirds. Of the Nevaen army, only fifty or so were dead.

He studied the scene. The front line of the Nevaens was solid. Behind the first line were the women, each utilizing their abilities to fight the opposing force while the front line used sword and lance. He stretched his arms forward and wide, his fingers pointing not at the armored soldiers but at the women on each end. He released twin spheres of dark power. The two women fell instantly, their bodies ripped by spasms until they lay unmoving.

When the women of power went to the aid of the two, he sent a command to his followers to withdraw quickly. The front line of his forces stopped, turned and raced away. When there was distance between the two forces, he sent a sheet of flames across the ground to separate them. At the same time, he ordered what was left of his army to join the other ghazi above the foothills.

The battle had moved swiftly in their favor. The left and right flanks had converged, driving the ghazi between them, forcing them closer together and giving them less room to maneuver. Enaid, standing in the center of the line of women, projected her abilities at the enemy's front line. Using stones the size of a fist, she battered the armored filth who fought the warriors of Nevaeh. Ahead, Roth stood with Noslen and Timon, their swords never stopping as each fought two or three of the malformed semi-human creatures at a time.

At the edge of Enaid's mind, came the cries of two women struck so severely they died within seconds. Instinctively, she reached her hands to the two women next to her. *Shields!*

Without further thought, the three women combined their powers and raised a shield around themselves and the Nevaens. "Hold!" she cried aloud. Ahead of her, Roth froze and turned to look at her. At the same instant, the ghazi turned and retreated and a wall of fire flared between the two lines of warriors.

Roth held his sword high and shouted the command to reform their ranks. The cry echoed up and down the lines of armored men and women. The soldiers of Nevaeh stopped moving and waited for the next command. Roth left the line and went to Enaid.

"What happened?"

"The Master. We must regroup. He sees the battle going badly and gathers his forces to him. He has more planned. There is something else I sense, something about…Mikaal," she said, her son's name a mere whisper coming from her lips.

"What?"

Enaid shook her head as she tried to sense her son but found only emptiness. "I know not, but there is…darkness and he is in grave danger." She reached out and grabbed Roth's arm, her fingernails digging deep into his muscles. "The Master has Mikaal."

Behind them, in the sudden lull, Ilsraeth ran to where one of the women lay, but her ministrations were of no use. She returned to Enaid and shook her head. "Dead. He killed them both."

Enaid released Roth's arm. "Have two of the strongest women build a shield. That is their only duty. The shield must hold. Send them to the rear for protection. We cannot afford to lose another woman of power."

Ilsraeth went to the other women. When she was gone, Enaid turned to her husband. "We must set aside our concern. There is more going on here than a simple battle. The Dark One… the Master can disappear from us at any time, yet he chooses to stand and fight. There is a reason he recalled his forces." She paused in thought. "He is above the foothills, on the mountain. He has set them to block our way so we cannot free Mikaal." She paused, her eyes widening. "Areenna… Where is she? What has happened to her?"

Staring into the haunted eyes of his wife, Roth knew what he must do. He signaled Noslen to him.

When the captain of the Sixes reached him, Roth said, "I have a request, which you can accept or decline. There is no command."

Noslen's brows furrowed, his eyes searched Roth's face. "My Lord?"

"The Dark Master has captured Mikaal. He holds him in a place, halfway to the peak. I need you and your men to get to him. Will you consider this?"

Noslen's brows furrowed even deeper. His eyes questioned further. "My Lord…Solomon, there is no choice in this. How could you think I—"

Roth cut him off. "—to send you into the mouth of such danger is something I cannot command."

"Had I known, I would already be there."

<><><>

"He still lives?" Areenna echoed.

"He has waited for you and your complement. Only the two of you, when joined with the staff can release him and unlock the full power within the staff." Ailish paused before silently saying, *only then can you stop this war of annihilation. You must find Mikaal and bring him back here.*

Everything clarified for Areenna. With the sharpness of a finely honed blade, the understanding of what must happen next pierced her mind. She connected with Gaalrie, who was halfway down the mountain. The treygone, flying over a small camp, lifted higher and circled.

Areenna saw a dozen of the dark soldiers; some standing and others seated around a tent but could not see what was inside. She knew, intuitively, Mikaal was there. *I have found him*, she told Ailish.

Turning, she took three steps when Ailish said, “The staff must stay. It is too dangerous to take with you. Without Mikaal, the staff is not strong enough to stop the Master. No, if the Master gains possession of it… No” she repeated, “it is too dangerous.”

Areenna moved to where Ailish’s vision shimmered, and when she was between the two floating crystal containers, she lifted the staff and released it. It did not fall; rather, it rose until it was once again floating between the crystals.

Be strong, granddaughter, Ailish said and vanished.

Areenna stared at the space where Ailish had been. She had so much she had wanted to ask and wondered if Ailish would appear to her again or if she was gone forever. She shook away the sad thought and focused on her task.

Five minutes later and dressed in full armor, the bow and quiver secured on her back, she stepped outside. She took three long strides and saw Charka raise his head. His eyes locked on her and she froze. Her mind went blank. Then, as if every bone in her body turned to water, she fell to her knees and gave an anguished cry.

How can I do this alone? How can I face a Dark Master and steal back the one person who has become my world? How can I protect him... protect Nevaeh? The questions spewed forth like lava from a volcano. Tears overflowed her eyes until anger took charge; a cold red anger directed solely at herself. With it, self-loathing at her weakness boiled dangerously.

She tried to fight the strong emotions, wrapping her arms about her and bobbing back and forth on the ground, torn apart by her inner struggle. Then, a strange white mist surrounded her, settling around her like a second skin. It was warm and gentle and her tears stopped as quickly as they had started.

You do what you must, came an unfamiliar mind thought that she knew instinctively was coming from the Master within the crystal. *You have the strength of all Nevaeh. Contained within you is the power of all the women of Nevaeh. You are Areenna, Daughter of Inaria who was the daughter of Alegna who was the Daughter of Ennazus—daughter are you of all the descendants of Ailish. You cannot and will not fail unless you so choose. Know, Areenna, whatever path you walk, be it foreseen or not, it will be the correct choice for you. I am at peace with whatever be your decision.*

Something warm pushed against her head and brought her back to the world. She opened her eyes to find Mikaal's aoutem staring down at her. She lifted herself off the ground, shook her head and went back into the cavern.

She strode directly to the crystal box holding the Master and stared deep into the crystal. *How could you know I would come*? She turned to the other crystal box. Naked, suspended in the center, Ailish floated within the shimmering mist of the crystal. Areenna pressed her face to it, as if she were trying to get inside the box.

As she concentrated, the waviness of the crystal cleared, and now she was staring at Ailish's body. Her eyes traced her ancestor, and her breath caught. On the top curve of her shoulder, was the circular mark with the star in the center—her birthmark, Neleh's birthmark, Sirod's birthmark and her mother's as well.

She knew everything Ailish had told her was true. She was Ailish's many times removed granddaughter. She understood, too, there was but a single path open to her: no matter what 'they' choose for her, she could not do what was expected—not while Mikaal lay prisoner to the Dark Master.

Drawing herself straight, she walked outside only to find Charka blocking her path. He lowered his large head and pressed his snout to her forehead. There was no mistaking the kraal's emotions.

She ran her hand along the side of his head. *Yes Charka, we go to free him.* She told him, knowing anything less would cause the aoutem pain; this separation was hard for the kraal.

The large aoutem sidestepped and Areenna walked forward; Charka followed behind. When they reached the path down the western slope, Areenna called to Gaalrie, telling her they were coming.

<><><>

Roth scanned the sky. The gray was turning dark and night would be on them again. They were at the base of the mountain, unable to go up.

They had tried three different times and each time the ghazis above them showered the Nevaens with arrows, killing some and wounding others.

Finally, Roth called an end to their attempts and gathered the remnants of his people together with orders to eat and rest. While his people followed his instructions, he strode about the outer edges of their camp unable to keep his eyes from the heights. "Noslen's Six team is in place near the ridge," Enaid said from behind him. "The woman you sent with them has relayed the message."

"They will be ready when you are close. They will let no harm come to Mikaal," she told him. "You cannot doubt this."

He shook his head. "It is not doubt; it is fear. Fear that he will kill Mikaal rather than allow rescue."

She cupped the side of his head with her hand and stroked his skin gently. "This cannot be what he plans. Mikaal is different from anyone else. He controls magic as they do. He is a great danger to them, but they will want to know how such is possible. No, they will not kill him…not until they learn everything about him."

He started to speak, but Enaid cut him off. "Do not forget Areenna is there, somewhere. Akassia, Laira and Trebor as well. Solomon, Areenna will never willingly let anything happen to Mikaal. They are one person in many ways, and in the future, they will become more so. You know it already; you have seen the evidence with your own eyes.

"What are you saying?"

She smiled. "What did you tell me, years ago in Morvene?"

He took in the smooth lines of her face, the gentle expression within her eyes and joined her with his own smile. "It was the morning of the day after I had arrived in Morvene. I was leaving the inn, and going to the main keep, when I saw you walking toward me on the street. I watched every step you took and knew I would never again look at another woman."

"And you stepped in front of me and said those exact words."

"I did. Of course I had no idea who you were."

Enaid laughed. "But my brother did so explain."

"With the tip of his knife at my throat."

Enaid laughed. "Which you took from him, spun him around and slammed him to the ground, his knife at his own throat."

"And I woke up later lying on a bed in your father's keep with him ranting on about exiling me."

"It was the least I could do for my future husband, making you comfortable until I could convince my parents you meant neither me nor my brother harm," she said lightly.

Roth's brows furrowed as he shook his head. "They're to become—"

"Their feelings are silent for now, they have no choice. I can tell you, absolutely, Mikaal feels toward Areenna as you did and do toward me. And Areenna...doubt her not, My Lord."

Roth exhaled slowly. More of the night's darkness had fallen while they'd talked and he could now see fires rising in the high distance, as the Master and his ghazis settled in for the night.

"Let us call council," he said.

Ten minutes later, Roth sat in the center of a small circle comprised of Enaid, Ilsraeth, Timon and four captains. He laid out his plans and listened to the various comments, which he encouraged. When everyone finished speaking, Roth replayed the plan, this time incorporating several of the suggestions.

When he was done, everyone stood, went to their sections and gave the orders. In a quarter hour, guards manned the perimeter and the rest lay in their silks, resting as best they could for shortly the battle would begin again.

Just as she was drifting off to sleep, a knife-like pain cut through her head. Enaid groaned and was still. Roth sat quickly and turned to her. In the dancing firelight, he saw her face was as white as the silks upon which she lay. He pulled her to him, shook her gently, but there was no response.

Lowering her to the ground, he raced to where Ilsraeth and Timon slept. Waking Ilsraeth, he said, "Something has happened to Enaid."

Ilsraeth was on her feet instantly and with Timon and Roth running behind, she raced to Enaid. She dropped to the ground next to the fallen high queen, put her hands to each side of her head and tried to gain entry to her mind.

She looked up at Roth. "It's Mikaal. She is trapped with him."

◇◇◇

An hour after she'd left the plateau, and as the day ended, Areenna saw the light of fires far below. Gaalrie had already shown her where Mikaal was—at the camp where the closer fires burned. Her aoutem had also shown her other things. At least fifty of the Master's followers were at the camp, and three of the wolf-creatures they had fought on their journey here.

She joined again with Gaalrie and asked her to descend to the base of the mountain and show her how many of the ghazi camped below. As she descended again, Charka staying close behind, she tried to reach Mikaal but failed. Yet, she sensed something and slowly realized there was no block on Mikaal; it was something else, something far worse. Whatever it was, it held his mind prisoner. It was an unnatural thing—a potion, she assumed, knowing only those of dark power would use such.

She had heard many stories about the days before Roth had come, of how the Afzaleem sorceresses, who could not control a woman of power, would create potions to take over one's mind and bend it to their will.

Her concern mounted. If Mikaal was under the influence of a potion, she feared what the Master could make him do. Her pace quickened along the downward trail. Suddenly, as if blades were striking into her head, pain seared through her. She fell to her knees, her hands pressing the sides of her head until she created a block. It took several tries for her to catch her breath and when she did, the pain dulled somewhat but did not leave.

The Master was doing something to Mikaal, and he was fighting him back, even under the might of the potion. She tried to stand, but the attack had weakened her. Reaching behind, she grasped Charka's leg, using it to gain her feet. She turned to him and pressed herself against him, wrapping her arms around his neck and hugging him tightly. Each drew strength from the other and together, they willed their strength to reach Mikaal.

Minutes later, the pain finally gone, she heard Gaalrie's silent call and joined with her. Below the treygone, beneath the Master's camp, a few hundred feet above the foothills, was another ghazi camp with several hundred of the malformed creatures.

She sent Gaalrie to range further and when the treygone did, she discovered another encampment. This one made her breathe easier. The people gathered there were not ghazi but Nevaen. Roth had come. Hope sprang quickly but died when she could not reach Enaid. *Why?*

Find Enaid, she told Gaalrie.

Gaalrie flew low over the camp. She circled once and dove to the ground, landing next to Ilsraeth. Areenna watched as the Queen of Northcrom tended Enaid. She saw that neither Roth nor Ilsraeth had realized Gaalrie had landed.

When Gaalrie hopped on Enaid's chest, Ilsraeth reared back, startled. It took a few more seconds for Ilsraeth to recognize Areenna's aoutem. When she did, she stroked the treygone's head. Areenna, through Gaalrie's eyes, turned to Ilsraeth. "Something has happened to Enaid. And to Mikaal," Ilsraeth said to Gaalrie.

Areenna called Gaalrie back.

From behind came footfalls. Spinning, she drew her sword and called up her powers as several dark forms rose up.

XXXII

IT TOOK ONLY a second to recognize Laira. Stunned, Areenna looked at her two companions, whom she recognized as well. Akassia and Trebor held still under her gaze, frozen to the spot and staring at her sword.

Areenna lowered the weapon. "What are you doing here?" Her voice was barely audible yet her heart beat calmer now with the presence of her three friends.

Laira stepped forward. Her ret slid out from beneath her cloak to raise its head to Areenna. It did not hiss at her. "We were sent here by the…the woman of the Island."

"Sent," she whispered. "How so?"

"She told us we would be needed here. That you would need us."

Areenna reached out and caught Laira's shoulder. She dropped her sword to engulf the young woman in a tight embrace. "Truly, help I need. How strong have you become since the Island?"

My mother says I am stronger than she is, Laira said in the silent talk of women.

We will need the strength. "And you," she asked Akassia, releasing Laira from her hold, "How did you fare on the Island?"

Akassia grasped Areenna's left hand. When their skin met, a flow of energy raced through her. *She said I have one purpose for now. To heal. When I asked more, she said I will know how and what I must do.*

And you will. Aloud Areenna asked the three, "Are you prepared to fight?"

Laira cocked her head to the side. "Tell me."

It took only a few minutes to sketch out the situation. When she finished, Trebor spoke. “How many are in the camp?”

“At least fifty...most likely more. And there are wolves.” Their blank expressions almost made her smile. “Terrible creatures. They are bigger than a rantor, and covered with fur. They’re the most vicious animals I have ever seen and they’re controlled by the darkness.”

“Do they die?”

Areenna nodded. “Mikaal and I killed many. He was injured doing so.”

Trebor nodded “What do you propose?”

Areenna studied Trebor in a different way than she had before. Since they had been in the school together, Trebor had grown into a large man, tall, strong, and broad. She knew exactly how to use him, and why the Eight had sent him. As she was about to respond, Gaalrie cried out and dropped to her shoulders. “Laira, have you a writing cloth?”

The young sorceress reached into her tunic and withdrew a soft linen. Areenna took it, transferred a message and gave it to Gaalrie, who closed her talons around it. *To Ilsraeth.*

When Gaalrie flew off, she turned to the others. “Mikaal has been given a potion to control him. We must get him out, no matter the cost. If the Master controls him, he will control Nevaeh.”

<><><>

Gaalrie dropped to Roth’s camp, alighted next to Enaid and Ilsraeth and released the cloth. The Queen of Northcrom scooped up the message. Looking at Roth, she said, “I know what must be done. Mikaal is under the control of a potion. The Master is trying to take his mind, to drain it and control him. Enaid is a powerful woman and because of Mikaal’s abi—” Ilsraeth cut herself off. When she was certain no one but Roth and Timon were near she said, “Because of his abilities, the connection between mother and son is strong and different. It is what caused this.”

Closing her eyes, Ilsraeth bent her head and created a block to encase her and Enaid. Building the block was time consuming. It took several minutes and a lot of determination.

When she completed the block, she sank to the ground, exhausted. Timon, who had been standing with Roth, knelt by her side and wrapped his arms around her. Ilsraeth leaned against him and took several breaths. As she did, Enaid's eyes flickered open.

It took another minute for Enaid to gather herself and try to sit up. Roth reached down to her and grasped her hand, helping her to a sitting position. She traced the contours of his face. "So far away was I. So dark a place, so…vile."

Ilsraeth handed her a cup. "Drink," she told her. "It will help."

Enaid drank the water and tasted herb within it. "The Master tries to control Mikaal. He attempts to learn about him, about how he…how he is what he is."

Then she saw Gaalrie by her feet. *I am myself,* she told the treygone, knowing Areenna would know as well. Gaalrie took to wing and Enaid turned to the others. "We must free him soon. The Master is strong. Mikaal fights, even unconscious he fights, but the darkness will get through."

Roth stared at the mountain and at the hazy glow of the fires above and thought of Noslen. "We cannot go now. The advantage they hold by their position will defeat us if we move as an army. No, we will need stealth, and stealth means moving slowly." Roth hesitated. "There is a way, but I need to think this out."

"Take not too long, my Lord," Enaid whispered.

<><><>

The four lay on the ground, ignoring the way the leeching cold sucked heat from their bodies, intent on inspecting the small campsite below them. The main camp of the ghazi was an eighth of a mile beneath.

Areenna took in the dark figures, the wolves, and the tent where Mikaal was. Of the Master, there was no sign. Akassia had created a block to surround them and knowing too well the danger of trying to sense the Master, she continued to look around.

"We are fortunate," she whispered. "The Master is not here. He must be at the lower camp with his…men."

"There are still too many to fight," Trebor said.

Areenna cast her eyes below once more. There was an area to the right, where the mountain appeared steep enough to warrant no guards. *Was it too steep*? She called to Gaalrie, who responded with a wave of gentle warmth. She asked her to fly low over the steepest part of the mountainside so she could see.

Gaalrie dipped low, and Areenna saw the slope littered with half buried rocks. If she handled herself well, she could use those to keep herself balanced. *Thank you, sister.*

"Here is what we must do," she said. Two minutes later, her explanation finished, she surveyed the three faces whose features told her she was insane. Instead of trying to convince them with more words, she laughed lightly.

"Trebor, after the two guards at the entrance to the tent are dealt with, wait no more than a minute and ride Charka to the tent. I will need your strength and the kraal's to get Mikaal out. He will be unconscious and unable to help. Do you understand?"

Trebor looked down at the camp. "I do," he whispered.

"Akassia. Maintain the block around the three of you, no matter what."

"I will," Trebor's betrothed said.

"Laira, your task is harder. When Trebor rides, you must disrupt the camp. What is your most powerful weapon?"

Laira smiled widely. "It was the first ability I discovered during my mother's training. It…it was not a weapon, but an ability to move small objects, like sand and dirt and pebbles. I can manipulate and increase the speed of what I move. I can create a dust storm, or blind a person by spraying sand or dirt into their faces."

Areenna studied the positions of the dark-armored figures. "The ground is hard and damp. Are you sure you can use the dirt?"

Rather than respond, Laira turned her eyes to the camp. Areenna sensed the power rising in Laira and watched the edge of the camp. Between two ghazi, a small whirlwind, no higher than a few inches, rose and shot upward into the mountainside. Neither ghazi moved.

"There is no problem," Laira said.

"When the two guards are dealt with, aim your first attack on those closest to where we escape. Work both sides but stop when we get out and concentrate on the ones behind us."

"It will be done," Laira said, solemnly.

Areenna's heartbeat quickened as she called up her power. It grew quickly. "I will signal when I'm ready. Go to the trail, Akassia. Do not let the block fall."

She started up, but stopped. "There is one more thing I must do."

She went to the path, the three following behind, and stepped close to Charka. Placing her hands on the sides of his head, she pressed her forehead to his and built a mind picture of Trebor mounting and riding him to the tent below. *For Mikaal.*

His response was immediate and she released him. "Wait for my signal," she repeated. It took her ten minutes of careful walking to make certain she did not kick any rocks, for they would slide on the patchy snow and tumble down to the camp below. She could not afford to give them any warning.

Once settled on her route, she drew her shortsword and closed her eyes. Gaalrie flew above, to give aid when the time came. She sent an asking to Charka, and the kraal responded by rearing soundlessly on his back legs.

She moved down the slope where Gaalrie had shown her, although it was steeper and slower than she had thought it would be. Her need to reach Mikaal pushed her relentlessly onward. She worked her way along the side of the mountain, stepping from rock to rock and securing her footing with every downward inch she traveled.

Moving fast, her fingers digging into the frozen ground or grasping partially sunken sharp-edged rocks for support, she crept lower along the mountainside. Her scratched and cut hands left droplets of deep red blood to mark the trail with her descent.

Frustrated because it was taking longer than she'd planned, her anxiety reached a fever pitch while her sense of danger screamed out warnings with her every breath. Only when she was at the edge of the camp, and after she forced herself to calm down, did she call upon her gifted ability to hide. She was gone from sight in an instant.

Moving past the first guard undetected, she took five strides and stopped to look around. On her right was a single guard; to her left, twenty feet from the tent was a string of ghazi guards. They stood six feet apart, their eyes fixed on the trail leading up from the foothills, for all knew the only attack could come from the foothills below.

There were two guards at the tent's entrance. They stood with less than a foot between them. Areenna moved forward, her pace slow as she worked out how to take them. The sword was in her right hand; she reached to her side and drew the long knife.

She stopped three feet before them. Drawing in a deep breath, she braced one foot behind her, tensed her muscles and charged forward, sword and knife held level before her.

The sword hit the first guard in the throat a half second before the knife did the same to the guard on the left. The metal went deep into their throats but she did not pause; she kept pushing forward and burst through the tent's split flap to land on her knees. The two guards were unable to call out because of the steel piercing their throats. They both bled their lives out on the floor.

Areenna dropped her hiding ability and took several breaths. She pulled her weapons free, sheathed them, and went to Mikaal's side. He was pale, as if the blood had drained from him. She pushed against his shoulders but he did not react.

Outside, the ghazis, blinded by a storm of small rocks and dirt from Laira, roared in anger. Charka's cry cut through the night, as the pounding of his hooves reverberated on the ground. Shifting, she reached under Mikaal's shoulders and dragged him to the front of the tent and through the flap to the outside.

Bootfalls came from her left and before she could draw her sword, one of the ghazi was on her. Her power flared and she released a stream of energy. He stopped as if he'd hit a wall, blew backwards and knocked into the guard behind him.

She grasped Mikaal's shoulders again, knowing she had to raise him high enough for Trebor to grab as two more ghazi came forward, the one in the lead holding a short fighting lance.

A loud cry echoed from above and Gaalrie struck the first guard. She did not fly by; instead, she impaled his face with her long talons. The ghazi fell screaming and fighting to free his face. Before he could grasp Gaalrie, the giant treygone released him and leapt at the second guard. This time she ripped her talons across his eyes, blinding him.

From behind her came the chilling sound of a wolf's low growl. Trebor vaulted from Charka's back, sword in hand. The wolf launched itself at Areenna; Trebor's sword swing sliced the wolf's chest open.

Too much time, Areenna thought as two more wolves slunk forward. A dust storm rose around them. Laira ran forward, her arms spread wide, creating the whirlwind around them. Trebor took Mikaal from Areenna and lifted him stomach first over Charka's back, and turned, his sword at the ready. The dust storm settled when Laira went to Charka to hold him steady. The two wolves crept forward.

Ghazis came rushing around both sides of the tent. The wolves charged. Areenna dropped her sword and slammed her palms together, projecting her unique ability. The powerful waves of energy hit the wolves and lifted them into the air. They flew backwards, slamming into the charging ghazis.

It was not enough to stop the oncoming rush. The ghazis came closer, and Trebor stepped in front of Areenna, bracing himself as the first of the oncoming guards came at him swinging a flat blade axe.

Trebor dipped below the blade and rose quickly, his sword slitting the other's armor as he buried it in the ghazi's chest.

Another ghazi was on him and caught Trebor's shoulder with his blade. Trebor dropped his sword, his arm numb. Areenna sidestepped and with a wide swing, sliced through the man's sword arm. He screamed and fell. Two more charged.

Areenna prepared herself for the attack. Trevor, on one knee, reached for his sword when something whizzed by Areenna's ear and a knife blossomed in the lead guard's throat. He fell in his tracks; behind him came more.

"Surround them," came an order. Areenna turned to see Noslen and his Six-group racing toward her. Behind them ran Akassia.

"Get Trebor," she ordered Akassia. "Get Trebor and Mikaal out. Go now before the way is blocked."

Trebor turned to her, but she shook her head. "Get Mikaal to safety. Do it now!" she shouted and turned back to Noslen.

"Go with them Princess. We will hold them."

"You cannot without me," she said simply. Suddenly, blue-white light covered her hands. She released the light at the first of the charging ghazis, who exploded and disappeared.

"Bows!" Noslen shouted. In the space of a breath, the six men pulled their bows and drew arrows. The first volley flew and six ghazi fell. Areenna drew up more power and sent lances streaking at the still charging dark soldiers.

A half-second later, a hammer blow struck her chest. Doubling over, her breath driven from her lungs, she gasped for air and fought to regain her breath. *The Master is coming.* She grabbed Noslen's hand. "We must go, now!"

"Back," he ordered the Sixes. They did not turn and run; instead, they back-stepped, firing arrows as they moved. The ghazis, mindless enough to charge forward, fell one atop the other.

The Master struck again and this time, a wall of fire encircled them. It flared skyward, cutting off their retreat. High above, Gaalrie screamed.

XXXIII

FOR THREE HOURS, a hundred and thirty Nevaen men and eighteen Nevaen women climbed the steep slope of the mountain. Not a sound issued. They moved carefully and by spreading across the face of the mountain, they rose inexorably closer to the lower camp.

They were within two hundred yards when Enaid grasped Roth's shoulder and leaned close to his ear. "The Master is there," she whispered. "He senses something. We must be ready."

Roth nodded. He turned left, then right, each time signaling to the Nevaens. Every man and woman freed a weapon and prepared to climb the last yards. "Have the women ready," he told Enaid.

She stopped moving. She sent a message to Ilsraeth on her left and another to a woman to her right. Each relayed the message on to the women next to them. Less than a minute later, she nodded to Roth. He moved first, and the lines of Nevaens continued upward.

They were ten yards from the camp when the first of the ghazi guards spotted them and raised a cry while throwing a short lance at one of the easy targets. The lance struck a Nevaen warrior, burrowing deep into his shoulder.

Roth rose, whirled his sword over his head and pushed himself toward the ledge of the camp. The Nevaens followed. The wounded man pulled the lance free and, ignoring the pain, charged with the rest.

A stream of fire erupted above them and struck down at Roth. Enaid, already filled with powers, released a shield to stop the flaming bolt while Ilsraeth released a wave of dark red energy across the ridge that struck the ghazis standing ready to repel the advancing forces.

The ghazis, those not killed but knocked backwards, retreated out of the blistering force of the attack, allowing the Nevaens to reach the ridge and form ranks. They surrounded their Master and prepared to defend him. The Master stood a full head above his slavish followers, his dark robes fluttering in the predawn breeze.

Roth, with Enaid still at his side, signaled his troops to form the ranks he had outlined before leaving their camp. The troops moved forward to face double their numbers. The archers released a wave of arrows at the ghazis. The arrows exploded harmlessly, blocked by the Dark Master's powers.

At Enaid's command, all the women of power combined to attack the Master. The shield he had raised glowed orange yellow around him, drawing in and surrounding him like an impenetrable solid ball. The energy of the women crackled across the shield, hissing and popping ineffectively.

No one had expected this attack to reach the Master; rather, it had forced his attention on the women, allowing the Nevaen troops to attack the ghazis. The fighting grew frenzied. The Master joined in the defense, sending streaks of lightning at the oncoming fighters. Half the women changed their energies to shields, protecting their fighters while the other half continued the assault on the Master.

Roth charged forward, heading directly for the Master. With him came one of the Sixes. Behind them were another twenty Nevaen warriors. They met the front lines with swords, knives and axes, tearing into the mindless creatures and cutting a swath to where the Master stood. Unbelievably, Roth saw the Master encircled by more troops, not ghazi but Nevaen exiles, all with weapons ready.

The Master, turning toward the onrushing troops, raised his hands directly at Roth. Next to him, Enaid cried, "Down!"

Without thought, Roth dropped to the ground and his Sixes did the same, as the Master unleashed a powerful wave of bloody crimson power. The fighters behind Roth, those unlucky enough to have not dropped instantly, received the full force of the lethal burning power. A dozen died instantly, another five burst into flames.

"No more!" Roth screamed. He jumped to his feet and charged the Master.

<><><>

The high-walled circle of fire trapping Areenna and the Six disappeared. When it did, Areenna saw ghazis standing there, their weapons at the ready. Before Noslen could order his men forward, Areenna stepped in front of them, her hands already encased with blue-white energy. Without hesitation, she slammed her palms together.

The waves of power were so strong they became visible as they exploded from her palms. The twenty odd remaining ghazis flew in every direction. Some died instantly from the force of the power; others spilled over the edge of the campsite to tumble down to the ridge below.

"Back!" she ordered the Sixes and together, they ran to where the others waited. The ground erupted with fire as the Master attacked. Reaching the others, Areenna sent a silent asking to Charka, who carried Mikaal across his back.

The kraal gave a low cry and started up the mountain, careful not to move too quickly so Mikaal would not fall. "Up," she told everyone, "Hurry."

Concentrating forcibly, she sent out a call to Enaid. *I have Mikaal. We go to the peak.* Then she ran after Charka. When she reached him and Mikaal, she grasped Mikaal's lolling head between her hands. *I have you. You are safe*. She knew not if she could reach him through the potion; but, touching him, having him free was all that was important.

Go quickly, the Master follows you, came a dart-like thought from Enaid.

Turning, Areenna ran to Trebor and Akassia. "Mount the kraal, ride fast," she ordered Trebor. "There is a cavern at the peak. Go inside and wait for us."

Trebor started to argue, but Areenna cut him off. "You cannot run with your wound. Do as I say."

Without further words, Trebor went to the kraal and, mounting behind Mikaal, urged Charka forward. The kraal took off with a lurch and sped upward. As the kraal climbed the mountainside, Areenna gathered the rest to her.

"We must move fast. I will trail behind. The Dark Master is coming and we must get to the peak. Go! Shields," she shouted to the two women.

Noslen and his men surrounded the two women and everyone ran. She waited until they were twenty feet ahead before following. She ran, her eyes skimming everywhere, desperate to find something, anything to stop the Master. To her left, a hundred feet above the trail was an enormous bolder protruding from the mountainside. *Was it big enough? Can I move it?*

Realizing she had no choice, she knelt down, dug her hands into the rocky ground of the trail and built her moving ability, the one inherited from her mother. She had never attempted to move something as big as this boulder, and could not guess its weight. Yet, she knew she had no choice. When she had enough power, she focused on the boulder and tried to extract it from the ground. Perspiration beaded her brow, sweat poured into her eyes, stinging and blurring her vision, but she did not stop. The boulder moved a fraction of an inch. The slight movement of the huge rock was enough for her to believe she could control the boulder.

A wave of darkness struck her. It was not a weapon, simply the forewarning of the Dark Master's approach. Time was running out. Digging deep within herself, she pushed her ability to its furthest edge. The boulder moved again. Small rocks, dislodged by the movement tumbled down the mountainside.

She blinked sweat from her eyes, and saw the Master walking toward her. Behind him was a horde of...Nevaens. Surprised, it took her a valuable moment to realize they were not Nevaens, but exiles under the Master's control.

She renewed her efforts. A loud cracking echoed down. Following the sound, small rocks, snow and dirt slid down the mountainside when the boulder came free. Areenna controlled the massive rock with what remained of her strength, moved it directly over the Master and released her hold.

The Master froze and raised his hands seconds before the monstrous rock reached him. Light flared, waves of violet power shimmered around the Master. The boulder froze above the robed figure and the exiles.

<><>

Roth charged forward, his anger so strong he no longer cared what happened to him. He needed to get to the Master and end its life. He made it ten feet before there was a huge explosion above him and bodies rained down the mountainside.

The Master gave vent to a scream. A gray mist rose quickly and surrounded the Master and the exiles. Three seconds later, he was gone, his ghazis undefended, and the exiles nowhere to be seen.

Roth did not stop his mad charge and when he reached the first of the ghazi, he slashed at anything near. The Nevaens, seeing their High King charging forward reacted by following him, their shouts coming as fiercely as their swords meeting the flesh of the Dark Master's puppets.

The battle lasted three minutes. When it was over, only Nevaens stood. Roth, his breathing strained, drew his anger down. Next to him, Enaid closed her eyes and a moment later, heard Areenna's silent message about freeing Mikaal.

Go quickly, the Master *follows you,* she responded and turned to Roth. "Areenna has freed Mikaal but the Master chases them."

Roth turned from the carnage. "Then we chase him." He called Elyk, the leader of a Six group. "Come with us. Bring the other Six."

"Tend the wounded. We go to the peak," Enaid told Ilsraeth.

Timon, who stood next to Ilsraeth, sheathed his sword. "I go as well," he stated flatly.

Roth nodded.

<><>

Areenna and the Master stared at each other. He stood still. She sensed he could not release the boulders and fight her as well. Taking advantage of his situation, she ran. Almost exhausted from the fighting, Areenna ignored her screaming muscles and moved as fast as possible while the Master dealt with the boulder.

Behind her, the Master's anger surged and faded. She could almost hear him laughing. Then his thoughts hit her hard… *Run, run. I will have you soon, Sorceress. You and he will be mine.*

She almost responded, such was the vileness carried within his thoughts, but somehow she stopped herself. She would not allow him to know she'd heard him, not allow him to know where she was.

There were shouts behind her and she glanced back. The exiles were slipping past the Master, who continued to hold the rock aloft.

She pushed herself harder, made her legs pump faster. "Faster," she urged when she reached the Six and the two women. "He has more fighters—Nevaen exiles, not the mindless ghazis. We must reach the peak before they catch us."

The sky had lightened further and the crown was visible a thousand feet above. At this point, the trail narrowed and the sides of the mountain rose higher above the trail, creating a bottleneck and squeezing them into a single line. Next to Areenna, Noslen turned to two of his men. "Lag behind us. Slow them. They will not be able to move quickly through here."

The men stopped to let the others pass, pulling their bows from their back, and notching arrows. Once the others were through, they began to follow, but slower, one looking forward on the trail, the other walking backwards behind him, watching for signs of the exiles.

There was a loud explosion below. The waves of the Master's dark force washed over her. She knew it could mean only one thing. The Master had destroyed the boulder. She shuddered at the depths of power he controlled. "Faster," she pleaded.

The time it took to reach the lower peak seemed eternal to Areenna. Her only concern was to get Mikaal into the cavern and find a way to cleanse him of the potion. Nearing the peak and the plateau leading to the cavern, she joined with Gaalrie, who had been shadowing her throughout the fighting. With a gentle asking, she sent her aoutem to watch the trail behind. When the small group reached the plateau, Gaalrie whirled and skimmed over the mountainside toward the oncoming exiles.

Gaining the somewhat level ground of the plateau, Areenna saw the exiles two-thirds of the way up the trail. The Master was still following behind.

Areenna caught up with Charka, as the kraal moved toward the cavern. "Call your men back," she shouted to Noslen. "There is enough time."

Slipping two fingers between his lips, Noslen sounded a sharp staccato whistle. A few second later, he turned to Areenna. "Where?"

"In there," she said, pointing toward the far side of the plateau and the crystal sheet of its entrance.

The small group raced across the plateau and Areenna called Gaalrie back. The treygone flew back to her and they all reached the entrance and went inside. Noslen, standing in the cavern's opening said, "They come."

Areenna stopped to look back. The exiles were pouring over the ridge and running toward them. Noslen and his men sent a wave of arrows at the oncoming exiles and Areenna went to the two floating crystal boxes and grasped the staff suspended between them.

The instant her fingers went around the ancient wood, a spark of power filled her hand and spread through her body. She returned to the entrance. The exiles, two hundred feet away, were rushing madly at them. "Inside!" she ordered the Sixes.

Without hesitating, she raised the staff and closed the entry. Noslen, the last man of the Sixes, barely squeezed inside before the crystal sheet closed against the mountainside. With the door closing, the ceiling of the cavern came alive with nightmoss. Areenna sank to the ground, her chest heaving.

Noslen stood next to Areenna and as she fought for breath, he reached down to grasp her shoulder. "Will this doorway hold?"

Areenna drew in one more deep breath and stood. She favored Noslen with a wry shadowy smile. "For eternity if need be," she whispered.

Noslen laughed. "Let us hope we wait not so long." He paused, his eyes inspecting her. "You're unharmed, My Lady?"

Across the cavern, Akassia and Laira were taking Mikaal from Charka's back. "I am fine," she said, "but he is not. Put Mikaal between the two boxes," she called to the women.

She reached them as they lay him on the ground and knelt by his head. Bending low, she took his head in her hands and pressed her forehead to his, pushing her mind to him. She pushed and pushed again but could not penetrate the barrier the potion had created.

She wanted to scream her frustration aloud but held back. She had not stopped moving or fighting since the Master had taken Mikaal. Now, with the crystal entry locked in place and the small group temporarily safe for the present, she had to stop her mind from racing and concentrate on what was next.

She stroked his face gently, her stomach tight with her need to bring him back. *I cannot lose you, not now, not ever!* She drew back. His eyes were open and unblinking. *I will find you,* she told him silently. *Fight, Mikaal, fight*!

All too aware of the faces staring down at her, her mind raced frantically. Laira and Akassia were closest, Noslen and his men behind them. Trebor sat off to the side, holding his shoulder. *Think*! She commanded herself. *How do I break through?*

She met Akassia's eyes and a spark of memory surfaced. "What did she tell you, the Speaker?" she asked Akassia, as she released Mikaal and stood.

"She said I have one purpose for now. To heal. She said I will know how and what I must do."

Areenna looked from Akassia to Mikaal and back at the young sorceress Princess. "And do you know?"

Akassia's face ran through a gamut of expressions until she closed her deep umber eyes. When they opened, she glanced from Mikaal to Trebor, who sat silently off to the side. "I know what is needed," she said and came forward.

Areenna stepped out of her way, opening the path to Mikaal, but Akassia went to Trebor instead, where she knelt at his side. "Help me remove his armor."

Two of the Sixes came to them and carefully unhooked the chest armor from the back plates and pulled them free. They used their knives to cut off the padded leather tunic, which had already become stiff with Trebor's drying blood. When they reached for the blood-soaked undergarment, Akassia stopped them. "Leave it."

She placed her hands over his eyes. When she lowered them, Trebor's eyes had closed and his chest rose and fell evenly. Areenna watched Akassia's every movement closely, her insides roiling with anxiety for Mikaal. A soft yellow glow formed around her hands when she placed them on the wound. The young Princess held as still as a statue and two minutes later, the glow faded and her eyes opened. "It is done."

Trebor's eyes remained closed when Akassia stood. "He will sleep for a while." Then she went to Mikaal and knelt behind his head, her knees together. Areenna watched the young Princess lift Mikaal's head and place it gently on her thighs. Her hands remained at the sides of his head, her palms cupping his ears. Her eyes rolled back, she exhaled softly. The yellow glow spread across her hands and floated over Mikaal's face.

Every muscle in Areenna's body tensed. Her nerves vibrated. She balled her hands into fists to stop them from trembling. Time stretched. Akassia remained in the healing trance for many long minutes until she suddenly opened her eyes.

Areenna's breath caught when she saw Akassia's eyes as the same yellow as the glow over her hands. "I need help," Akassia whispered.

"What need you?" Areenna responded without hesitation.

Akassia's features went distant. Her eyes rolled in their sockets. "You, and Laira, at my sides."

Areenna knelt next to Akassia while Laira did the same on the other side. *One hand on me, one hand on Mikaal*, came Akassia's next silent words. The two women did as asked. Areenna placed her hand on Mikaal's chest directly over his heart while Laira grasped Mikaal's upper arm. Akassia closed her eyes. The bonding was instantaneous and electric. Akassia's breath exploded from her mouth. She jerked her head back and turned to Areenna. *There are two blocks. This cannot be. He…beneath the potion, he holds his own block.*

Areenna eyes flicked to Laira, who knew about Mikaal, and back to Akassia. *Will you trust me?*

Akassia blinked. *I will.*

I will explain all, after. Rid him of the potion and I will lower his block.

When Akassia nodded, Areenna said to Noslen. "Take your men and stand by the entry, look not back at us regardless of what you hear."

Without the slightest pause, Noslen dipped his head and said, "My Lady," and with his men strode to the entry where they spread out evenly and stood facing the crystal.

When the Sixes were set, Areenna sent an asking to Charka and Gaalrie. Charka shifted from where he stood next to Hero and moved to them. He lowered himself to the ground by Mikaal's feet and laid his head across Mikaal's legs. Gaalrie gave vent to a low whistling cry and hopped next to Areenna. Lowering herself, she pressed along Mikaal's side, resting her head atop Areenna's hand, the one covering Mikaal's heart.

When Akassia seemed caught by the strangeness of seeing the kraal on the ground next to Mikaal, Areenna reached across and touched her shoulder lightly.

The young Princess shook her head. "Join with me."

XXXIV

ENAID GRABBED ROTH'S shoulder. "Hold."

Roth followed her command and with a raised arm, halted the others. Behind him, the remains of his force were thirty strong. The rest of the Nevaens were far behind.

"What do you see?" he asked Enaid.

"Areenna and Mikaal are safe for now, but he is still under the control of the potion. The Master and his exiles wait above. It is not clear. But…" She closed her eyes and shook her head. "There is danger." She worked out the warning until she understood. "From here, this pathway is between the sides of the mountain." She paused, her eyes flicking back and forth over the trail ahead. "The sides rise high and it narrows. I sense much danger ahead." She pointed to where the path tapered and the rock sides rose above the pathway.

Roth followed the direction of her finger and saw, in the growing light of the day, how this part of the trail was ravine-like, cut through the mountain by years of water running down the surface. It was a perfect place for an ambush. "I see it. What choice is there?"

"Caution…not choice, Solomon. There is no need to charge blindly upward. We must find another route."

He shrugged. "How?"

Reaching down, she stroked Irii's head. The Gorlon had not moved from her side since the start of the fighting, except to defend her and take down an enemy. She knelt, pressed her head to his soft coat, and asked her aoutem to seek a way.

The gorlon jumped to the rock closest to their left, its huge claws digging into the hard ground. She moved slowly, cautiously, and made it another twenty feet before she slipped, caught herself and returned to push against Enaid's thigh.

"We wait," Enaid said, running her hand along Irii's head.

Roth signaled everyone to rest. While he studied the ridge of the mountain's lower crest, Timon came over to him. He did not speak; he just stood next to Roth, one hand on Roth's shoulder. Roth glanced at the Master Boatsman.

He went back to sudying the trail, which was not quite the width of two people and the mountain's slope. A moment later, he said, "The choice is made for us. There is no other way but this trail."

<><><>

Twenty minutes after they'd begun, the three women remained kneeling around Mikaal. The energy created by them had centered within Akassia, whose hands stayed on Mikaal's head. The soft yellow healing energy had grown into a golden aura, surrounding his head and her hands and pulsing alternately with deeper and lighter colors in rhythm with the beat of his heart beneath Areenna's hand.

Joined with Akassia, Areenna experienced everything flowing from Akassia's hands and head while Akassia worked to break through the potion's blocking power.

From somewhere close, there was a hovering at the edge of Areenna's mind. She separated a part of herself from Akassia and sought it out. When she touched the sensation, she stiffened at first before cautiously opened herself to it.

Her perception was of an entity almost but not familiar. She chased it and froze; the true realization of who it was, striking her hard. White, the color of snow, and an underlying calmness, rolled through her mind. She exhaled slowly, her knowledge becoming a certainty. Without words, without thoughts, she knew what to do.

Accepting the gentle waves washing to her, she drew in the presence of the Master locked within the crystal and released Akassia's shoulder. She raised her arm, her hand open, and the staff flew into her palm. She placed the staff atop Mikaal's body, from his chin to his thighs, and again settled her hand on Akassia's shoulder.

The yellow glow expanded, wavered and turned into a white clinging mist. The white shifted, flowed and enveloped each of the women surrounding Mikaal. The three glowed white, and soon the white mist covered Gaalrie and Charka.

Now, she told Akassia.

Akassia was not gentle this time. She collected the healing power within the core of her body, growing it and raising it and, like a sculptor forming a work of art, created a weapon of healing. Then, she released it against the potion the way an arrow shot at an enemy. The healing, a shimmering silver perfectly formed lance, struck the block around Mikaal's mind. The lance shattered into a thousand pieces and each small splinter of power entered his bloodstream. Mikaal's body arched. Every muscle tightened, twisting his limbs madly. Every being surrounding Mikaal reacted the same. Their bodies stiffened, twisted and froze and a blinding explosion of color and light burst within the cavern. When the outburst ended, the only light in the cavern came from the low-glowing nightmoss.

Akassia fell backwards, unconscious. Laira was bent over, breathing is harsh gasps, while Areenna held herself together, her hand still on Mikaal's chest, as she fought to calm herself. The two aoutems were steady. Charka's head on Mikaal's legs had not moved and Gaalrie continued to press against Areenna's hand.

"See to Akassia," Areenna said to Laira, who responded with a quick nod.

She looked Mikaal and saw him blink. Seconds later, awareness returned to his eyes. Areenna's tears welled and a single drop spilled onto his cheek where it splattered and rolled off. Bending, she kissed him for several long seconds.

"What happened?" Mikaal asked in a dry and husky voice.

Areenna gave vent to a relieved half laugh at the sound of his voice. "What do you remember?"

Mikaal's brows furrowed. He shook his head. He started to speak but could not get the words out. *Water…*

Areenna went to their supplies, pulled a full skein from the pile and brought it to him. After he drank, he said, "I remember smelling the stink from the ghazi piling on top of me. Then everything went black and something tried to invade my mind. I fought it."

Areenna sighed. "That was yesterday. Much has happened. I will explain later. Can you stand?"

He tried to move and grabbed at his head, as bolts of pain ripped through him. "My head," he whispered.

"It will pass," she said. "The…the Dark Master gave you a potion. The headache is from that." She straightened herself and took his hands in hers to help him sit up.

Once his head was up, the pain receded. He tried to shift and realized something was pressing down on his legs. It was Charka. As soon as his eyes met his aoutem's, a flow of warmth ran through him and the pain faded further. Charka pushed his moist snout into Mikaal's face. "I'm fine," he told him. "Let me up."

Charka clumsily righted his large body. Mikaal followed and when he stood, he stretched, but froze when he saw Laira working on Akassia, and Trebor leaning unconscious against a wall. "How…" *What happened*?"

Before she could respond, his eyes went distant and he stiffened. He shook his head. "They are outside, waiting."

He turned and saw Noslen and his men still facing the crystal entry wall. *What happened after they took me*?

Rather than explain, Areenna drew him into her mind and let him discover the answer for himself. It took but a short time for the flashing scenes of her memory to play out.

When it finished, he reached out and took her hands in his. *How many times must you save me*?

How many times must you get yourself into trouble?

His mouth half open. A second later he laughed. "Point taken, Princess."

"He is unharmed?" asked Akassia, as she gained her feet with Laira's help.

Turning to Akassia he said, "I am unharmed. You released me?" When Akassia nodded, he smiled at her. "Thank you for that and for helping Areenna."

Next to Akassia, Laira held her aoutem. The ret was wrapped around her forearm, its head pressed to her skin, its tail wrapped around her wrist. Mikaal went to her and gave a slight head bow. “And you as well, Laira.”

She replied with a nod. Then he turned to the Six. “Noslen,” he called.

The captain of the Sixes turned and, seeing Mikaal standing, smiled broadly. “Welcome back, My Prince.”

“How many are there?”

Noslen shrugged. “They are exiles, not ghazi. There are many—more than we can handle alone.”

“How come you are here? My father?”

Noslen nodded. “We came with him on one of their ships. King Roth took the main body, attacked the Master and the ghazis and sent me after you.”

“And now?”

Noslen shrugged. “We are trapped here. When the time is right, when you are ready, we fight.”

Mikaal studied Noslen, traced the lines of his rugged face and slowly nodded. “Fight we will. And fight as they have never seen before. I promise you that.”

Noslen’s response was a broad grin.

Mikaal turned back to Areenna and the others. Trebor was finally awake and Akassia helped him to his feet. Mikaal walked to Areenna. *We will have to fight our way out.*

We will. First, there is more for you to do. But...

The doubt filling her last word caught him short. *What?*

Areenna glanced at the Sixes quickly and then at the two crystal boxes suspended near them. *After they took you, I... Join with me.*

They merged and Mikaal’s mind filled with visions of what had happened since his capture. It took another minute for him to absorb Areenna’s tale.

“Ailish,” he whispered.

Ailish told me you are the one who has to free the Master.

Mikaal’s eye locked on the floating crystal coffin. *Ailish? Free him? How can he still live?*

He does. Ailish has said so, but only you can do this. I cannot.

You worry Noslen and the others will know about me if I do so?

Areenna nodded but spoke not, either aloud or silently.

Mikaal studied the crystal boxes and the staff, which again floated between them. He glanced to Noslen, who stood watching everything. He thought about when Trebor had seen him do magic, and of Neleh's knowledge of his abilities. Laira already knew about him from the Island. What he was certain of, was how hard it would be to hide his powers in the fight soon to come. *Everyone will know, eventually; in this, I think we have no choice.*

"Then it will be best to prepare him," Areenna said aloud.

When Mikaal walked to Noslen, Areenna watched carefully. She was unsure of what the captain's reaction would be, but she was ready to do whatever might be necessary and so she watched his every step.

When he drew Noslen aside and whispered in the captain's ear, every muscle in her body tensed. She watched Noslen's reaction closely. Noslen's face stiffened, his shoulders arched back and heat surged within her. She held back, waiting while Mikaal spoke. Then Mikaal turned his back to her, blocking her sight of Noslen. Noslen back-stepped, startled. Mikaal spoke again, and slowly, Noslen's shoulders settled and the lines of tension eased from his face.

Mikaal stopped talking and grasped Noslen's shoulders with both hands. When Mikaal released him, he said something else and Noslen nodded in response. Mikaal turned and came back to her.

"And?"

Mikaal gave her a half smile. "His first response was to ask if my head was injured because he could not believe I believed what I was saying."

"And?" she repeated.

"I built fire in my hands."

"Shock him, did you?"

Mikaal nodded. "He is strong of mind and loyal beyond doubt. No matter what he feels, what he believes, he accepted."

"The others?" she asked, seeing Noslen now talking with the other men.

"They are Sixes. They will do what Noslen says."

"Then it is time. We cannot stay here forever and if what Ailish told me is true, we must get this Master to the Island." *How is your strength?*

I will manage. He took her hand and walked them to the suspended crystal containers. The one in which Ailish floated was clear as glass; the

Master box was cloudy and barely showed the twisted outline of the ancient Master.

Lead me, he asked Areenna.

She joined with Mikaal but did not draw him to her; rather, she went into his mind and carefully showed him the next step. He lifted one hand and placed it on the crystal box. He grasped the staff with his other hand. Areenna put one hand on Ailish's container and one on Mikaal's shoulder.

When she touched him, the staff flared orange-red and the box holding the Master came alive with color. A burst of colors twisted through the box, individual streaks separated and flowed faster with each passing second until the box glowed with an ethereal life of its own. A half-minute later the colors swirled, faded quickly, and the crystal cleared.

Areenna and Mikaal took in the long black hair, the grayish brown skin and the robes covering the Master's body. A strange sensation arose, followed by the soothing sound of music, more so than of thought. Within the soundless music, came the knowledge of what Mikaal must do next.

Mikaal's hand tightened around the staff. He drew it toward himself and, as the staff moved, a white mist issued from it. The mist snaked along his arm like tendrils of fog, staying close to his skin, moving along his body until it covered him in white.

Carefully, he placed the staff against the crystal. When it touched the box, the white mist drifted from his skin and surrounded the box. Soon the mist reached into the crystal, covering the Master.

The knowledge of the next step seemed to come from the staff itself. Mikaal stepped back, raised the staff and slammed it against the crystal. The box shattered; pieces of crystal flew everywhere. Then, the Master stood before them, his eyes open and staring.

"Hurry," he whispered and collapsed.

XXXV

ROTH LOOKED OVER his shoulder to Enaid. "Are there any women with birds?"

Enaid shook her head. While unusual for not one aoutem to be a bird, it had happened. She surveyed the resting Nevaens and the women of power. Lying next to one was a white rantor. It was smaller than most, only the size of a large gorlon, but she'd seen it during the fighting. It had handled itself with precision.

"A rantor can climb this," she said to Roth, "and a white one will blend with the snow." Without waiting for a response, Enaid went to the woman, crouched by her side and spoke. When Enaid finished speaking, she, the other woman and the rantor came toward him.

"What service is needed, Highness, of myself and Salis?" the woman asked.

"We need a scout, one who can climb the side of the mountain unseen and gain us the information of what waits above."

"I am Nasus of Kashold. I serve my Queen, Kali, as advisor," she said in introduction. "My rantor, Salis, can do what you seek. He is sure-footed on all terrain."

"Thank you Nasus, for your service," Roth said formally, bowing slightly to the woman. "We must learn what awaits on the ridge above. Both Enaid and I suspect ambush before we can reach the ridge. There is no other way to get there, except by this narrow trail."

Instead of speaking, Nasus took a knee and drew her aoutem close. She pressed her head to its head and pushed an asking. The rantor drew back, raised a huge paw and placed it on her shoulder. Its turquoise eyes locked with Nasus's and a moment later, the big cat turned and started up the mountainside. It did not appear to move fast, yet it ate distance with each clawed step.

"We will know shortly, My Lord."

"Your aoutem is a powerful hunter?"

Nasus's smile lit her face. "Like no other, Salis is. He makes up in ferocity and cunning what he lacks in size."

"Have him stay atop when we go. You stay close to Enaid. When it is time, she will give you word. Have your rantor take out as many of the enemy as he can while we fight from below."

"It shall be done," Nasus said simply, despite the worry that flashed across her eyes.

Roth nodded, thinking, *it has to be.*

<><><>

Mikaal dropped to the Master's side and lifted him by the shoulders. His eyelids were open, but his eyes had rolled back and only the whites showed. "Areenna, help him."

Having remained frozen to the spot since the crystal box had disintegrated, leaving the Master standing before Mikaal, Areenna broke free of her trance and took a step toward Mikaal. She froze when another power took control of her body. *No, this is not for you. She must do it,* said Ailish from within her crystal box, *as Mikaal, who is a man of power, was the only one who could release him from the crystal, only she can heal him.*

Then Areenna was free of Ailish's presence. She turned and said, "Akassia, this healing is for you. He is the one whom the Eight sent you to heal. Quickly."

Startled, Akassia reluctantly dropped Trebor's hand. She came over to where Mikaal held the ancient Master and knelt at his side, but her eyes never left Areenna. "I know so little of healing," she whispered, her self-doubt much too evident in her eyes.

"You only think such. You healed Trebor. What you did for Mikaal, I could not. Within you is a powerful healer: trust in the women of the Island and doubt not your ability. They would not have sent you if they had not prepared you. Although you know it not, your ability will guide you. You must trust such to happen, just as it did with Mikaal."

Akassia touched the Master's face and stiffened. Areenna's breath caught when Akassia turned to her, her eyes glazed with a golden glow. "Lay him flat. Take his hands and do not release them—both of you."

Mikaal carefully laid him down, took his hand in both of his, and clasped it tightly while Areenna did the same on the other side. Akassia swept her eyes over him and hesitated as the golden glow faded. "I don't know where to begin, he is so…broken."

Areenna leaned toward her. "Start anywhere, look for what is the worst and begin there. Give yourself over to the healing. It is the only way."

With her eyes locked on Areenna's, she placed her hands on his chest. The instant she did, the golden glaze spread across her eyes, and she was blind within the healing. Her hands glowed as she traced slowly over his body. When she finished, she opened her eyes. "His heart is failing," she told Areenna

"Begin there."

Akassia again bent over the ancient Master and went to work. Her hands stayed centered over his heart. She remained motionless for five solid minutes before she lifted her hands. When she did, his eyes opened and Mikaal saw their pale blue shade. "Rest easy," Mikaal said.

I have been resting for too long. Squeezing Mikaal's hand, he closed his eyes.

Lowering her hands, Akassia continued tracing his body. She stopped every so often and the glow around her hands grew brighter. When the glow dimmed, she moved on. Finally, she drew her hands from him and said, "Turn him over, be very gentle."

While Mikaal turned the Master over, Akassia pulled at Areenna's arm. "A knife."

With her brows furrowed, Areenna drew the long knife from its sheath. "Why?"

Akassia pointed to a scar in the small of his back. "There is wood lodged into his spine, it is…melded to the bone. It must come out."

"You mean to cut it out?"

"I… No, to open the skin only. When I start the healing, you must cut the skin deep enough to open, but not so far as to do damage."

Akassia returned to the healing trance and Areenna placed the sharp tip of the knife at the scar. She touched the edges of Akassia's mind and as soon as the girl began to push the healing, she opened the scar with a single cut. Blood welled from the wound. The glow around Akassia's hands deepened and the bleeding stopped.

Areenna watched the wound and the way Akassia's hands appeared to be working, her fingers making strange cutting and slicing motions. Then, minutes later, the broken piece of wood appeared in the open skin. It rose higher until Areenna could grip the wooden fragment with her thumb and forefinger.

It took another minute for Akassia to lift the long slice of wood completely free from his spine and when she did, Areenna pulled it out.

Akassia spent another quarter hour in the healing trance before she ended it and sat back. "He will need to rest."

Mikaal started to pull his hand back, but the Master held it tight. *Stay. Tell me of the situation. It is bad?*

Areenna knew the question was for Mikaal, not her, and remained silent within their joining.

Bad, yes. Impossible? No. The Master *who took me is very powerful,* Mikaal responded.

He is Fasil Abdul-Mu'eid who was once my second. He now is the strongest voice of the Eight Masters.

Eight Masters? You are not a part of them?

My son has taken my place. Afzal Ben Jalil. They do not yet know I am alive. Nevertheless, he will know the moment the crystal entry opens. They want the staff of Afzal. This must never happen.

With his free hand, Mikaal touched the staff, which was now just a simple piece of wood. No spark issued from it, no white glow surrounded it.

Then we must not allow it.

Without releasing either Areenna or Mikaal's hands, the renegade Master pulled himself to a sitting position. "I need time before I can aid you," he said aloud, his words sounding strange in Mikaal's ears, the thick accent making the way he spoke unfamiliar.

Jalil Ben Afzal, the direct descendant of Afzal Mahmud Terak, the founder of the Circle, looked from Mikaal to Areenna, his eyes both sad and kind. "I need time to heal, time to regain my strength. It will take both of you to stop him. He is powerful, cunning, and has only one goal—to complete the domination of every living being on our world, and Nevaeh is the last. If he gains the staff, he and the other Masters cannot be stopped."

"You, with your complement, are the only two who can stop the Circle from conquering Nevaeh."

Areenna, both hands still gripping his hand, shook her head. *We are not like you, or the Eight women of the Island. We are... just people.*

He nodded, and smiled. *Yes, just people you are, and just people you are not. Both of you are...more.*

Before Areenna could reply, Jalil pulled his hands free and grasped the staff. "You must use the staff when you face him. It will protect you and he...the Master you must stop is very powerful, and you must both believe in the powers you have been granted. Without such belief..."

Areenna took the staff. When her fingers closed around the old wood, a spark snapped between her skin and the wood. A vibration hummed beneath her fingers and entered her body.

"Good. It is as I have foreseen; you have accepted," said Jalil Ben Afzal. "It is time."

◇◇◇

"It is time," Roth said, looking back at the gathered Nevaens.

Nasus had just finished her report. Her aoutem had found things exactly as Enaid had predicted. There were two dozen exiles armed with bows lining both sides above the trail's end.

Hidden beneath the edge of the ridge, the rantor now waited for Nasus's command.

Roth started to signal when he saw Timon running up the trail toward him. Two hours earlier, Timon had disappeared after telling Roth he needed to look for something. Behind him followed a group of Nevaen soldiers, carrying planks of wood.

When he reached Roth, he pointed to the soldiers. "We found wooden planks in the encampment and rope enough to make a shield of sorts to protect attack from above." Turning, he motioned to the soldiers, who put the wood down and began lashing the planks together.

"Once again, my friend, you have come to the rescue."

"We'll see," Timon said with a shrug.

Roth glanced at the lightening sky and knew the sun, for as little as it would ride the sky, would be up soon. "You're ready?" he asked Enaid.

"I am, we are," she said motioning to the small group of women standing behind her.

He stepped toward them, Enaid at his side. He gazed at each one in turn, and at the aoutems as well. "You will follow the wood shield we are building. Stay far enough behind to be out of range, but close enough to use your abilities." His eyes swept over each woman. "You are the only protection we have."

Each woman's face was set in determined lines as they listened to their King. None spoke.

At Roth's signal, eight men lifted the long wooden shield parallel to the ground. Roth motioned two of his 'Six' groups to go under the shield. The twelve men barely fit, but they managed. Roth took a breath and gave the signal.

The men beneath the shield led the way. Roth, Enaid and Timon were between the shield and the women. The rest of the Nevaen warriors followed.

<><><>

Areenna and Mikaal stood at the crystal entry. Behind them were Akassia and Laira with Trebor between them. On each side of the women were three of the Sixes. *You are ready*?

As ready as I can be, Mikaal responded.

We must be joined and stay so. It is the only way possible.

Instead of words, he sent a rush of warmth to her, as if embracing her physically. Areenna responded in kind. Mikaal and Areenna joined and their powers flared. She glanced over her shoulder at the Master and nodded.

The crystal wall made no sound, no color changed as it opened—not slowly as it had for them, but in one quick moment to expose them to those who waited.

Her first sight was of the Dark Master standing in the center of the massed Nevaen exiles. When the crystal opened, the Master drew himself to his full height and spun to face Areenna, his deformed face the color of cold, burnt charcoal. Her powers flashed and the staff vibrated in tune with swirling heat within her and Mikaal.

Areenna created a shield around them and stepped forward. When she and Mikaal cleared the cavern opening, a dark purple flash exploded across the shield with the Master's first attack.

Mikaal's longsword was in his right hand, his left encased in fire. He raised his left and let loose a stream of fire directly at the Master. The flames struck an invisible wall.

The Master spread his hands and circled them once. Then, he pushed his hands toward them. Flames rose and shot toward Mikaal and Areenna. Areenna raised the staff and before the flames were halfway to them, they were gone.

"Forward," Mikaal said, knowing there was more than magic to come. He raised his sword and charged. At his side, Areenna lifted the staff with her left hand, her right hand enveloped with the blue-white light of her most powerful ability. As she ran next to Mikaal, she sent two bolts of blue lightning—one at the oncoming exiles, the other directly at the Dark Master.

XXXVI

"READY," ROTH WHISPERED just loud enough for the men carrying the wooden shield to hear. He turned to Nasus, who stood at the head of the women. "Now!"

Nasus closed her eyes. Within the space of a breath, came the loud cry of a hunting rantor followed by two bodies crashing downward.

"Go!" Roth commanded and raced forward. Enaid was at his side, her powers flaring as she raised a shield to protect them from the Dark Master. There was another scream, this one issued from the mouth of a falling exile, as the rantor created havoc above.

On the plateau, the Dark Master, in the midst of his attack on Areenna and Mikaal, turned and with a flick of one hand created an avalanche of rock, snow and dirt. The shifting earth careened down the sides of the trail. The landslide the Dark Master had so easily created caught three of his own exiles.

The moment the surge of dark energy struck, Enaid shouted for everyone to stop. "With me," she added to the women and drew on her abilities. Aided by the women, Enaid pushed at the falling rocks, forcing them to drop straight and not roll down upon her people.

She poured every ounce of her powers at the mass of earth—not to stop it as had the Dark Master earlier—but to direct its fall, slowing the debris until it settled on the trail without rolling down on them. The result was not good. Their way to the top was blocked.

Taking in what had just happened, Roth screamed his rage and charged the pile of earth, jumping onto a large boulder, grasping at another and pulling himself up. His Sixes raced behind, clawing for handholds and footholds as they followed their King.

"Shield them!" she ordered the women. "Use your bows," she told the Nevaen soldiers even as she pulled her black wood bow from its hitch on her back and slotted an arrow.

The arrows flew quickly, striking some of the exiles, who leaned over the side to fire at the climbing men while others ducked back out of the way. The white rantor took two more down. "Keep shooting! Keep them away from the ridge. Protect Roth. Protect our men!"

<><><>

At the instant Areenna released her bolts at the Dark Master and the exiles, the Master turned toward the trail and dislodged the avalanche. Areenna's first bolt struck the oncoming exiles and cut a path through them, their bodies flying in every direction. The second bolt sped toward the Master, who turned back just in time to raise his shield and stop it. The blue lance of power struck the shield and spread out across its face—its force so powerful the Master staggered within his own bubble of protection.

Areenna sent another volley of energy at him, but this time he was prepared and, roaring out his anger, sent two streams of killing energy at Areenna and Mikaal.

Without thought, Areenna raised the staff. A stream of dazzling white spread before them. When the streaking death reached them, it hit the white misty barrier and disappeared.

The exiles ran forward, their weapons raised, their faces distorted with the projected fury of their Master.

Taking in everything as if she were an onlooker and not part of this battle, Areenna recognized the impending danger. "Circle with me!" she shouted. Turning her back on the onrushing enemy, she raised the staff and slammed it into the earth. It hit the ground, stopped for an instant and then its tip went down a half foot. The ten with her circled the staff shoulder to shoulder and prepared to defend themselves and the staff. *To the center, grasp the staff,* she directed the two women.

The Dark Master stood surrounded by his exiles. She watched him order a third of his exiles back to the trail to stop the Nevaens while sending every other exile except those protecting him to attack Areenna.

When they stood next to the staff, Areenna released her grip, turned and reached for her sword, knowing her bow would be useless in close fighting. Her hand stopped an inch before she touched the sword. There was only one chance. She raised her hands, drew back her arms and shoulders. "Drop the shield… now!" she shouted. Akassia and Laira released their shield before Areenna's words died.

Drawing up the power the Eight had gifted her with and combining Mikaal's incredible powers too, she slammed her hands together and sent out a massive surge of energy. Before it reached the exiles, the Dark Master responded with a sweep of his arm. The rippling force stopped before it reached the first exile.

Without hesitating at her failure, Areenna freed her sword and prepared for battle. "Shield!" she told the two women.

The shield went up. Areenna hoped against hope it would be enough protection from the Dark Master's powers, as they fought his distorted minions. All thought left when the exile leading the charge reached them and swung a long axe at her head.

She stepped forward, ducked beneath the axe and plunged her sword into his chest. He fell as she stepped back into the circle and blocked a sword stroke from the next onrushing fighter.

Next to her, Mikaal fought two more. She swung at another, slicing his arm. His sword fell from numbed fingers and the two exiles behind him pushed him down and stepped over him. The small circle of defenders was being pushed back as the overwhelming force continued to press against all. She joined with Mikaal, and working together moved their swords in patterns eyes could not follow. Their swords, blurring in wide sweeps, took down exile after exile.

Yet the oncoming rush of the Dark Master's fighters continued. To her left, one of the Six fell and they closed the circle. Another fell, two away from Mikaal. *We cannot withstand this for much longer,* came Mikaal's thought.

We must, Areenna shot back. *We have to hold.*

On her left, Trebor stumbled under an attack. From within the circle, Akassia screamed. Laira, seeing Trebor fall to one knee, raised her arm. Her aoutem leapt from her arm and struck Trebor's attacker in the face, its long teeth sinking into an eye. The exile screamed and grabbed at the ret. Laira's aoutem bent in half and plunged its inch long razor-sharp teeth into the man's hand. He screamed again and Trebor, regaining his feet, put his sword through the exile's heart.

The Dark Master's troops forced them into a tighter and tighter circle within which they could now barely move their arms to defend themselves. Then, exploding within her head came a single word: *Hold!*

Areenna recognized the touch instantly. *Hold,* the silent voice repeated. In the face of the oncoming madness of the exiles, Areenna raised her sword, reversed it and jammed it tip first into the ground. Next to her, Mikaal did the same. With one hand on their swords, they clasped their free hands together. When their hands and minds joined, Areenna's blue-white light melded with Mikaal's yellow orange fire. Then, a sheet of flames, not yellow, not red, not orange but deep blue, encircled the remaining Nevaens with a barrier of pure energy.

The Dark Master's fighters stopped short. Behind them, the Master drew himself to his full height, his mouth forming words no one could hear. From around him, came mist twisting like a rising whirlpool.

Hold, came Enaid's insistent thought.

The energy needed to maintain the wall was draining them and Areenna's powers began to fade as the Dark Master released the gray mist at them. The gray mist did not simply strike the protection Areenna and Mikaal had created, it snaked along the ground weaving through the exile warriors before it rose from the ground to create a second wall. Slowly, the mist, particle by particle touched the blue wall of fire. A heartbeat later, both the blue and gray were gone, and those who remained in the circle were without protection. A loud roar came from the throats of the exiles who charged forward.

We cannot hold. Mikaal's thought came, and with it, all the emotions he had been containing since the day he had met Areenna. Those emotions burst through to her, caught her unprepared, and, strangely, rebuilt her waning strength.

I will not lose you, she told him. *Not now, not ever*! She swung her sword at the face looming before her. The exile ducked beneath the blow and countered. As his sword descended at her head, she knew she could not stop it. Then, suddenly, the exile lifted into the air and pitched backwards. A long wailing scream poured from his mouth.

From the corner of her eyes, she saw another attacker almost on top of Mikaal. Before she could move, Gaalrie descended and struck the exile, knocking him forward, impaling him on Mikaal's sword.

Then the impossible had happened; the shouts of oncoming fighters filled the air.

On the plateau across from them, Roth and the Nevaens emerged, fighting the exiles at the mouth of the trail. Two of the Sixes stood on high rocks, firing arrows at the exiles attacking Areenna and Mikaal. To her left, Sirod and Neleh, with the small women of the village, were on the western slope of the mountain, attacking the exiles with their powers while the men of the village fired arrows. *Join us*, came Neleh's thought.

Areenna and Mikaal pushed themselves to her and the four were one; seconds later, Akassia and Laira joined. Instinctively, Areenna took control and drew all their powers to herself. She reached back and grasped the staff. It came out of the ground without her pulling it free. When her hand went around the staff, she channeled the incredible amount of power within her and, pointing the staff at the Dark Master, released a storm of hellfire.

The force exploded from the staff in giant waves, knocking away anything before them and arrowed toward the Dark Master. In the heartbeat before it reached him, the gray mist reappeared and surrounded him. Before their powers could strike him, the Dark Master and the gray mist were gone.

Is he dead? Mikaal asked.

Areenna could not sense him at all, yet there was something. She focused on the ground where he had stood, feeling for anything. *He lives*, came the voice of the Speaker of the Eight. *He hides now. However, we foresee he goes to his ship in the dark.*

And we follow, Mikaal told the Speaker.

A strange silence fell over the plateau. Within it, Sirod and Neleh walked toward them from the left while Roth and the Nevaens came from straight ahead. From within the cavern, flowed the gentle warmth of Ailish. *I am now complete. Trust in the Master Jalil; he is the means to survival and freedom.* Then Ailish was gone. Mikaal's arm went around Areenna and drew her close. “It will be all right,” he whispered aloud.

Areenna shook away the certainty she would never see or hear Ailish again and looked at the village’s two women of power. *How did this happen*?

Neleh broke away and ran to Mikaal, who picked her up and held her close. Areenna smiled at Neleh and Mikaal. Sirod walked toward them and said silently, *we went for Neleh’s training. It was…it lasted only a day and she was done. Before we returned, they told us to come here at this time. No reason was given; that we would be needed was all we were told.*

You were. You saved our lives.

Sirod reached Areenna and put her hand on her shoulder. *As you will save ours.*

Before she could respond, voices rose and the rest of the Nevaens arrived on the crown’s plateau. Roth was almost to them and behind him, Enaid ran to catch up, her thoughts to Mikaal and Areenna moving faster than her feet. *We were not too late.*

<><><>

A half hour later, with the wounded attended to, Areenna, Mikaal, Roth and Enaid stood at the very edge of the plateau, looking down at the foothills. Areenna said, “We must go after the Dark Master. We have to stop him.”

Enaid, her eyes closed, said, “He hides in the foothills. He will go to his ship.”

“He has no ghazi left to handle the ship. He cannot get away,” Roth added.

“He can,” Areenna said. “The power he controls…I have never seen the likes of it before. There is no time to explain what has happened. Mikaal and I must go after him.” She held up a hand to stop Enaid and Roth from speaking. “No one else can do this. Enaid, join with me.”

When Enaid did so, there was an instantaneous sharing and a half minute later, Enaid staggered back and grabbed Roth’s arm for support. “Ailish,” she whispered. “I…and a Master…”

Areenna signaled to Neleh. When the young girl came to her, Areenna knelt before her. *What powers were you gifted on the Island?*

Neleh opened her mind and Areenna saw all. *Good. I will need your help.*

Mikaal, she called. *Come with us. We must clear the way.*

"Enaid, we will need you as well," she told the High Queen.

They crossed the trail and with Areenna holding the staff of Afzal, Mikaal on one side and Neleh and Enaid on the other, they began. Using her mother's gift, and aided by Mikaal's strength, Areenna lifted the first boulder, after which Neleh and Enaid took control and moved it to the high ridge. When she started working on the second huge rock, something touched her mind. She stopped and turned. Coming toward them was Akassia and Laira, supporting between them, the Master Jalil.

Again, silence descended across the plateau. Every head turned to watch. When the Master reached Areenna, and his gentle touch caressed her mind, she handed him the staff. He stepped forward, the staff raised even as Akassia and Laira continued to support him.

He stood there for several long moments; the staff raised high, his mouth forming silent words until sparks erupted from the staff. The white mist grew, not from the flaring staff, but the very ground itself. The white billowing haze lifted and enveloped him, wrapping around him before spreading to the two women supporting him. There was a sudden flash followed by a low whooshing, like air released from an old wine skein. On the trail below, the rocks turned to dust.

The white fog withdrew quickly from the three and the Master turned first to Areenna and then to Mikaal. "You must try to stop him before he can get to the ship and to…them."

Mikaal's brow furrowed. "Them?"

Master Jalil's eyes locked on Mikaal. "The other Masters are on the sea. They all come. Without him, they weaken." He collapsed, half dragging the women to the ground.

"Get him to the cavern. Tend to him," Areenna told Laira and Akassia.

Areenna gazed skyward. *Find*, she asked Gaalrie, sending a mind picture of the Dark Master. She watched the giant treygone wheel and dive, flying parallel to the mountainside in search of the Dark Master.

"Call Charka and Hero," she said to Mikaal, who she realized, was already doing so.

Neleh stepped close to Mikaal. "I go with you."

He dropped to one knee. "You will stay here. You are not ready for this."

I am!

You chose me as guardian. You will listen. I need you to stay here. Neleh, you are strong. You will know if and when to use your powers.

Her pale yellow eyes welled with tears. *I am afraid for you.*

Mikaal smiled at her. *Fear for me not, little one, I have Areenna to protect me.*

You will protect him? Neleh asked.

Areenna opened her mind to the small sorceress. *He is my life.*

Neleh smiled hesitantly. *"I know. Neither do I want to lose you.*

Tell her to come to me, came the call of the Master Jalil. Areenna stiffened. "Go to the cavern, your purpose here is not yet done. Go, Child, you are needed."

When she was gone, Mikaal nodded to Areenna and mounted Charka while Areenna did the same with Hero. The staff lay on the ground, where Master Jalil had dropped it. She stretched out one arm and the staff flew from the ground to her open hand. Once she got hold of it, she nodded to Mikaal and they started after the Dark Master.

Even before they moved, Areenna was already seeing through Gaalrie's eyes, watching the Dark Master, who had reached the foothills of the mountain. Gaalrie flew higher to give Areenna a further view. She saw one long ship on the ground. On the water, hundreds of yards from shore rode another ship, which she knew awaited him. Like broken branches after a storm, the small landing boats of the ghazis littered the shore.

In the far distance, a thick darkish gray fog blanketing the horizon was rolling toward shore. *We have little time,* she warned Mikaal, sharing the sight of the ships and the fog.

Once past the narrowest section of the trail, they pressed the kraals to a faster pace. Using the staff, Areenna cleared the trail of ice and snow to allow the sure-footed kraals a faster and safer passage.

"Can we make it in time?" Mikaal asked.

"We have to," Areenna said. By the time they reached the foothills, Gaalrie had shown them the Dark Master was almost at the shore.

"We must slow him," Mikaal shouted. *We have to stop him from reaching that ship.*

How?

◇◇◇

In the cavern, laying on a sleeping silk, Master Jalil held Neleh's hand. Sirod knelt behind her daughter. Surrounding Jalil were Enaid, Roth, Ilsraeth, Laira and Akassia. "So many of Ailish's line," he whispered. "So strong are you." He turned his gaze to Roth. "You have done all we have foreseen and more. But there is still much to accomplish, Solomon Roth. Know you of whom you were named after?"

Roth, fairly certain of what the Master meant, played innocent and said, "My grandfather was named Solomon," he said.

Jalil's weak smile broke his beard. Teeth, shades whiter than the beard, peeked from beneath strained lips. "I speak of the old book, of the old Kings."

"I know you do," Roth whispered.

"Such is good. In the coming months, you will have to show the wisdom your namesake was said to have had, for what comes will be the hardest on Nevaeh and on you." He turned his head to Neleh and Sirod behind her. "You have done your duty well. It is time for you and for all your people to become part of the people of this land." He stiffened, his eyes rolling up and all that was visible were the whites. His grip on Neleh's hand tightened.

Neleh's eyes widened, her yellow irises deepening. "He…he sees them, I see them," the girl whispered. "The dark one has reached the shore. Areenna and Mikaal are too far back to stop him."

"Use your gifts," Jalil Ben Afzal whispered to Neleh.

◇◇◇

They rode as two, but their minds were one. Even as Areenna asked how, a plan emerged. They both knew there was only one way. At the end of the foothills, they drew the kraals to a stop and called Gaalrie back.

Mikaal dismounted but stayed next to Charka. Areenna did the same and stood next to Mikaal. Gaalrie rolled and, like an arrow shot from the sky, sped toward Areenna. The giant treygone dropped to the saddle bar of Areenna's kraal before hopping to Areenna's shoulders.

Facing each other, Areenna took the staff and dug it into the hard ground. Mikaal grasped the staff, fitting his hand so it was below hers, yet touching Areenna's skin. The staff vibrated within the joined grip and their powers roared forth. Their eyes locked on each other, their minds opening fully, and they joined as never before.

Areenna felt the blood pumping through his body, stood with the solid muscles of his legs and breathed through his lungs while Mikaal did the same. There was no time for modesty or for hiding thoughts, as each mind melded with the other.

Then another mind joined them: a woman-child. *Neleh.*

He escapes! Neleh opened her vision to them.

The Dark Master stood in one of the small boats. His hands spread wide, the gray mist that had carried him now moved the small boat into the water. The distant fog had edged closer and was engulfing the ship furthest away.

Areenna's first thought was fire.

Fire erupted around them, flames shooting to twice their height. Together, they took control of it. They raised it from the rocky ground, formed it into a ball and sent it hurtling toward the Master.

The fireball struck the Dark Master and the boat and…disappeared as quickly as it struck.

The gray mist wrapped around the Dark Master while propelling the boat toward the first of the large ships. The fog rising from the ocean hid the far ship and flowed quickly toward the second ship. The Dark Master glared back and raised one hand. A shockwave struck savagely, knocking Mikaal and Areenna off their feet.

Laying on the ground, her back screaming from the jarring fall and gaging on the vileness within the dark powers, Areenna raised her shield in time to stop the second wave of the evil Master's attack. Mikaal gained his feet, picked up the staff, grabbed Areenna's hand and pulled her up.

When they again stood together, their hands on the staff, Areenna's strong shield pulsed as the Dark Master sent wave after wave of deadly energy at them. Areenna sensed a deadly change; he no longer wanted to capture them. Now, he wanted them dead.

The water. It's the only way!

Yes, Areenna responded. Their powers were so connected the thought itself created the formula needed.

The Staff of Afzal glowed white when the combined abilities of the two flowed through it. Areenna took charge of their abilities and directed her power to where it must go. On the water, between the Dark Master's small boat and the large ship, a huge wave formed. The blue waters turned foamy under her control and soon a huge wave rose high.

Together, Areenna and Mikaal controlled the wave, urging it even higher. The seawater spiraled skyward; the tip of white cascading foam grew broad. Curving forward but not cresting, the wave turned into a wall of water, a hundred feet above the sea's surface.

Through Neleh's vision, they watched the Dark Master turn in the boat and raise both hands at the water. Directly in front of the boat, the water split into two, leaving an opening for the boat to escape.

No! Mikaal screamed silently.

Areenna gripped the staff tighter and drew up a spout of water in the exact spot where the wall had split. This time she turned it into a spinning waterspout and sent it crashing onto the small boat.

We cannot lose him, came Areenna's frantic thought.

A wave of energy washed through them, built within them and blossomed, lifting the very essences of their minds from their bodies and projecting them high above the water to a floating place made of shimmering golden light. Yet they stood on something solid even though they were floating above the vast sea.

From here you fight, came the mind-voice of the Speaker of the Eight.

They looked down from the golden place on which they floated and saw the small boat bobbing in the water. The Dark Master was gone.

There! Areenna cried and pointed to a speck on the water. Between the boat and the fog-shrouded ship was the Dark Master, his body moving just above the water.

Areenna released a stream of energy, not from her hands, but from where she floated bodiless above the Master. The bolt struck. He spun and fell into the water, only to rise and send another wave of blackness at her mind, not her body.

Mikaal projected a shield. The energy struck hard, flashed violet and faded. The Dark Master disappeared.

A heartbeat later, the Master's face floated before them. The small oval mouth opened showing yellow brown teeth. Red-ringed eyes glared at them. Rage spewed from the now dark ocher orbs, and the Master gave vent to a scream. Mikaal started to project himself in front of Areenna, to protect her. He stopped, instinct holding him back. At that exact moment, on the ethereal projection they both rode, Areenna enveloped his consciousness within her entire being just as the Dark Master's rage struck.

Areenna fought back, defending them both with her every ability. *You will never defeat me! You are mine!* He sent a massive wave of power at her. Blinded by the awful energy of his fury, and ripped from the golden air she floated within, Areenna was spinning with Mikaal still wrapped in her protective aura. She fell into a whirlpool of darkness, grasping at anything to hold herself back. There was nothing, and she spiraled down, tumbling helplessly into a darkness so devoid of life all she could do was to scream soundlessly.

◇◇◇

"No!" Neleh cried in the cavern. Her back arched. Her hands rose and yellow-white lightning-like bolts discharged from her hands to strike every woman in the cavern. Caught by her power, she pulled the women's energy into her and sent it to where Mikaal and Areenna fought the Dark Master.

◇◇◇

Mikaal swelled within the protective circle Areenna held him in, expanded with a power so strong he drew himself from her protection and in the next instant was back in his body, standing next to Charka. Areenna lay at his feet, the staff on the ground next to her hand. He grabbed the staff, held it up, channeling the lava-heated blood flowing through his veins into the staff, and projected it at the Master.

He dropped the staff when it struck, knelt and pulled Areenna into his arms. He pushed them into a joining and wrapped his shield around them as he pressed her head to his chest.

◇◇◇

Slipping away, Areenna was lost in the dark void. Her mind pulled from her consciousness, emptying her of…herself, until something grabbed her, stopped the draining of her mind, held her, caressed her and brought her back.

Areenna opened her eyes and found Mikaal's face above her. His features were drawn, his skin the color of carna milk and his eyes frantic.

"You… you stopped him from taking me. How—"

"—no, not just me," Mikaal whispered. "I was caught, but not like you. Neleh…it was Neleh who freed me so I could free you."

Areenna took several deep breaths to steady herself and joined with Mikaal to see what had happened. "The Dark Master?"

Mikaal shook his head. "Gone. We… we could not stop him."

Areenna sat. "Neither could he stop us. You remembered the lesson of the Island."

He nodded. "I can only protect you, if you are protecting me. But we have failed," he said, his voice bitter. "He joins the other Dark Masters. All of Nevaeh will soon be at war."

"Failed, no, no, for we still live…and we have learned a weakness," she whispered.

"Weakness? I saw none."

Strangely, she smiled at him. "Because you cannot see yourself. You are his weakness, you and I. In the last moment before you stopped him, as he was draining my mind, there was a connection. It lasted but a heartbeat yet I saw clearly his weakness. They know you make me who I am. You give me strength and increase my abilities. For the first time he and the others are afraid. That is the weakness of the Circle of Afzal—fear of you and me together."

◇◇◇

It took them two hours to return to the plateau of the lower peak. When they were a short distance away, Mikaal drew Charka to a stop and motioned for Areenna to do the same.

Her eyes roamed his face, moving from feature to feature. *What bothers you?* Areenna asked silently.

He does. Master Jalil. I want to trust him, but something is stopping me.

Areenna struggled with Mikaal's words. She went deep inside herself but found nothing to make her doubt the old Master. She thought back to the first touch from Jalil and the subsequent ones. "All is as it should be," she said. *Our minds met his. There was no deceit.*

"Did you join with him?" Mikaal asked aloud. *As you do with women of power?*

I... She shook her head slowly beneath the realization of Mikaal's truth. *It was not mutual. He joined with me.*

As he did with me.

"But why? He has lain there for thousands of years. Would someone as powerful as a Dark Master willingly imprison himself in crystal not knowing we would release him?"

"But he did know. There had to be a foretelling. What if this is the Dark Ones' plans to finally conquer Nevaeh?"

Areenna shuddered at Mikaal's words. "What of Ailish? She was open. She drew me into her. It was not me."

"He could have deceived her as well."

Areenna thought about what they had said and came to the only conclusion she could. *Careful must we be on this. Challenging him will be dangerous.*

Not as dangerous as accepting without question.

Areenna closed her eyes and pushed herself to him. They joined instantly. Heat flowed through her, and she almost pulled away; but instead, she let his warmth wrap around her, as if it were his arms. Then, ignoring what was happening, she asked, *Neleh?*

As soon as she thought the name, they touched the young woman's mind. She was unresponsive, lost within a healing. *She heals the Master and we cannot stop her.*

XXXVII

FROM WHERE SHE sat upon Hero, when they emerged from the ravine-like trail, there was nothing but devastation. While they had battled the Dark Master, the remainder of the Nevaens had reached the summit of the lower crown. The wounded lay on silks while the uninjured men and women tended them. A full half of the Nevaens were injured, some severely. How many had died fighting the evilness she did not know—what she knew was however many it had been, it was too many.

While she'd listened to the old stories of the battles against the Dark Ones, this was the first time she had been in full battle. The effects were numbing. So many hurt, so many dead, and what lay ahead was…unthinkable.

The bodies of the dead exiles and ghazis were gone, to where she cared little. The devastation wrought by the dark continued to assault Areenna's emotions. Several of the Nevaen women, some still in battle armor, walked among the badly injured to tend whomever needed their help. Beyond where the injured lay, fires burned and food cooked, and the remainder of the Nevaen force sat or milled about. The men from the village lend aid wherever necessary.

Roth stood near the cavern with Timon and Noslen at his side. The three turned to watch her and Mikaal's progress through the plateau but did not move. When they reached the cavern, Areenna and Mikaal dismounted.

How do we do this? Mikaal asked.

Together is the only way.

With the staff in her right hand, she clasped Mikaal's hand with her left and entered the cavern, took three steps inside and stopped dead.

Before them, the Master floated a few inches above the ground. Sitting cross-legged at his head, her hands set on each side of his face, was Neleh. At his feet, sitting the same way with her hands on his ankles was Akassia. Laira was on one side and Enaid on the other. Their hands were touching him as well.

To the side, stood Ilsraeth, Queen of Northcrom. Unlike the four women surrounding Jalil, her eyes were open and unfocused.

A sense of darkness hung within the cavern. An insidious black malevolence crept along their skin. Tentacles of evil sought to capture their bodies and mind. Without thinking, Areenna and Mikaal created a shield that broke them free of the darkness.

"There is much wrong here," Areenna whispered aloud. Still tightly joined with Mikaal, she turned to look into his eyes. *We must break through their trance.*

How?

She drew on her power, drew Mikaal's as well and explored the minds before her. Carefully, she tested the borders of the four minds surrounding the Master and found them completely locked. She pushed herself to Ilsraeth and found a solid block so powerful she knew the queen was under another's control.

It comes from Jalil? Mikaal questioned.

I...I cannot tell.... Releasing Mikaal's hand, she went around the Master to where Enaid knelt. She put a hand on Enaid's shoulder and attempted to join with her mind. Nothing happened.

She moved to Neleh and did the same. The result was identical—nothing.

When Areenna's hand lingered on Neleh, something faint touched her, something distant. *Do you feel it?*

Barely. What is it?

Whom, she corrected and pushed herself harder than ever before. It took almost a full minute before she recognized the mind feel, so weak was it. Releasing Neleh's shoulder, she spun to face Ailish's crystal box.

Thinking of how Mikaal had released Master Jalil from his crystal tomb, she went to the floating haze-filled box. Mikaal walked next to her, understanding her intention.

Are you certain?

Can you think of another way?

Mikaal looked from the floating crystal to Areenna. His eyes searched her face while his mind sped through every possibility. "No," he whispered aloud.

They stopped before the crystal. Unlike the last time, when she had seen Ailish within, its surface was now so cloudy there was nothing to see within, yet there was no doubt it had been Ailish whose mind she had touched a moment before.

She raised the staff, held it against the box. Nothing happened. *Mikaal*?

His brows furrowed, his eyes questioned.

Then she remembered. He was her complement. The Eight of the Island had so said. '*Your Complement*,' Ailish had said. '*He was born to be your complement*,' Enaid had said too. Suddenly, she understood exactly what that meant. He was the masculine half to her feminine. His magic complemented hers. His powers were the hidden part of her, the part she could not access because she was a woman. The knowledge of what it meant burst forth with a startling clarity. He was not just her complement; he was more. His male strength—not the strength of his body, but the strength of his mind—and his powerful abilities, so different from hers, did not detract; rather, they added to and increased the strength she had been born with, deepening it beyond imagination and making her complete.

In that moment of realization, she knew what had to do. "Grasp the staff," she said aloud. "Your hand over mine."

"You said she was gone when she returned to the crystal." *Can we bring her back*?

We can but try. There is no other choice.

She will never be able to return to the crystal, he stated.

Areenna closed her eyes and took a shuddering breath. When she opened them, she sent her senses into the floating container. Nothing changed. The same low vibration was there, one of almost feeling but not, held steady.

A low cry from Gaalrie echoed within the cavern. The giant treygone landed on Areenna, her talons locking on the leather covering her shoulders.

A sensation of strength filled her and Mikaal as well. *Gaalrie...she senses the same as we.* Areenna said.

With Mikaal's hand still covering hers on the staff, she raised the ancient wood high and swung it downward at the crystal. *Forgive me, Ailish.*

The staff descended and the world ground to a stop. A flash of white leapt from the staff and flooded the cavern, turning everything within into a blur. It took an eternity for the staff to reach the container. When the wood and crystal met, there was a flash, followed by an explosion that sent thousands of shards of crystal careening through the cavern. Yet, the slivers of crystal evaporated—not one touched a living being.

Ailish stood before them. Her eyes wide, her mouth a bare line cut between nose and chin. Slowly, she crumpled to the stone floor.

Mikaal dropped to the ground next to her. He slipped his hand beneath her head to cushion it from the cold stone floor. Her eyes, the same green as Areenna's, focused on his face. A smile tugged at the corners of her mouth. *So strong you have become.* She told Areenna, who knelt at her side as well. *You understood.*

Areenna shook her head. *Understood, no. We sensed a wrongness about Jalil.*

It is not Master Jalil: it's the others. The Eight Masters have joined minds. They attack Jalil. They hold him and the women prisoner.

Releasing her ability to sense her surroundings, she tried to go beyond the cavern, but struck a solid wall. *I cannot see out.*

I am dying now. Ailish told them. *You must take what remains of my powers. Both of you, but as one.*

Areenna shook her head. *I have the healing I can—*

—No. My body, my mind is alive only for the purpose I have now accomplished. You must take what remains of my powers and of me before they fail. Do not allow my sacrifice be for naught. Be strong, children of my children.

Ailish slowly reached out and grasped Areenna's hand. She placed it over her heart. She did the same with Mikaal's hand, placing it on top of Areenna's. *Now*!

Under their hands, Ailish's body arched. Unlike other transfers of ability, this one was extremely gentle. There was no flash of power; rather, heat built slowly, growing stronger with every heartbeat beneath their fingers. With each rise and fall of Ailish's chest, the heat built until their hands glowed with vibrant shades of orange and red. The glow moved upward long their arms, into their shoulders and spread throughout their bodies. Then the heat moved upward through their faces and into their minds. Their vision blurred beneath red and orange flashes. The heat, like a stoked furnace, roared madly once more.

Areenna gasped, her mind reeling from what had just happened. Her hand was still beneath Mikaal's and saw Ailish was no longer there. All that remained of the ancient woman of power was an outline of white ash.

Tears rolled down Mikaal's cheeks and she realized her cheeks were wet with tears as well. Without a word—silent or aloud—Areenna and Mikaal stood and as they did, Areenna released Mikaal's hand and transferred the staff from her right hand to her left.

When she raised it, Mikaal placed his hand on the staff. *Fire,* he said.

Light, added Areenna.

Areenna's blue light rose, not from her hand, but from her entire body. At the same time, Mikaal's fire joined the shimmering blue light, turning the red of the fire and the blue of the light into a deep sapphire of shimmering shifting flames. Together, they pushed their combined powers at the block holding everyone within the cavern prisoner. The blue fire struck the barrier the Dark Ones had created, and there was an explosion of light. The block crumbled and the malicious darkness fled.

Together, one mind one thought, Areenna and Mikaal chased after the malevolent tendrils, unwilling to let them flee, until the darkness stopped its retreat and released a bolt of pure evil at them.

When the force struck their wall of blue fire, they raised their hands and, together, released a stream of white light at the oncoming blackness. There was another flare as the powers met and, strangely, Areenna and Mikaal were no longer in the cavern— rather, they were suspended high above the twin peaks of the mountain.

The Nevaens were frozen in place. In the distance, two thousand miles away and floating on the sea, a huge armada of ships sailed toward Nevaeh. On the lead ship stood the eight Masters of Afzal—all were looking up at them.

Fasil Abdul-Mu'eid, the Dark Master, the leader of the Circle, The Master whom they had been unable to stop on the sea, raised his arms. A swirling blackness rose from his hands and streaked toward them.

Areenna and Mikaal reacted with blue fire, but just before the two powers met, another force grabbed them and they found themselves standing in the cavern exactly as they had been before breaking free of the block.

This is not the time for your battle, came the voice of the Speaker of the Eight. *You are not yet strong enough. You must learn more of yourselves. Understand what Ailish has sacrificed; understand what she has given you. Only in such a way can you defeat them.*

Everything was exactly as it had been. Master Jalil floated in the air, the four women still holding him. Ilsraeth stared vacantly. "We must free them," Areenna said aloud.

Not yet, said the Speaker. *Accept my words and follow them carefully.* This time the Speaker waited for both of them to agree before she joined with Areenna and Mikaal. When she did, thoughts and pictures, instructions and lessons streamed through their consciousness until finally, the Speaker withdrew and their minds were their own.

So much to do, Areenna thought.

So short a time to prepare, Mikaal responded to her thought.

Again, without either consciously directing a thought, they went to Ilsraeth, one on each side. Areenna placed her hand on Ilsraeth's chest while Mikaal did the same on the queen's back. A half a heartbeat later, Ilsraeth blinked and gasped. Mikaal caught her before she fell and eased her to the cavern floor.

"Rest," Areenna said. "Regain your strength."

Ilsraeth reached out and stroked Areenna's cheek but did not speak.

Areenna rose and went to the others, Mikaal following behind. They repeated the process with each of the women until all were free. Areenna and Mikaal knelt on each side of Jalil. Areenna placed the staff on the Master and their hands on his back. The staff flared white for a second. When it cleared and Jalil opened his eyes, Areenna and Mikaal lowered him to the ground.

<><><>

It took most of day for the five women and Master Jalil to regain their strength. It was late in the day, barely an hour before the darker gray of the Northwestern sky took control of the night, when the leaders of Nevaeh gathered about a fire just outside the cavern.

Roth and Enaid sat together as did Ilsraeth and Timon to their side. Areenna and Mikaal sat on the other side of the High King and Queen and next to them were Neleh and Sirod. Master Jalil, who sat quietly between Laira and Akassia, completed the circle. Trebor was, of course, next to Akassia.

Mikaal and Areenna explained to them all that had happened. When they finished their explanation, Roth asked. "What you saw was not of now?"

Areenna shook her head. "It is hard to explain. Time seemed to stop outside the cavern. We saw you and the Nevaens here on the plateau, but you were frozen. When we saw the ships of the Dark Ones, the Master we fought was with them. He could not have reached them so quickly. Not even he has that amount of power."

She paused for a moment to moisten her lips. "It was a vision of the battles to come. It came from Ailish's powers."

Mikaal took over, speaking the moment Areenna stopped. "We saw ships, perhaps forty. They will be here soon, a few months at the most. There is not much time to prepare. We must also bring Sirod and Neleh's people with us."

Roth, his eyes sweeping from Mikaal to Sirod and Neleh, said nothing.

"Our ship is grounded and severely damaged," Timon said.

"They left one ship in the water. It is large enough, is it not?" Areenna asked.

Timon paused in thought. "You are certain?"

Areenna nodded as did Mikaal.

"These ships are clumsy, but they are large. They can hold six, seven hundred with ease, much more if necessary. We have not nearly that amount. We can manage."

"How long will it take to bring them here?" Roth asked.

"Two days to reach the western edge of the mountain, where the sea meets the land," Sirod responded. "But we need a few days to prepare our leave taking."

"They give up much," Enaid said.

Sirod smiled gently, her eyes on Enaid. “They gladly go to start a new life knowing they have fulfilled the purpose our ancestors placed upon us.”

“They will be a great benefit to Nevaeh,” Areenna said, looking first at Sirod and Neleh, and then at Roth. “I would ask you to allow them to settle in Freemorn. They will find a welcome home in my father’s dominion.”

Roth nodded. “A good place to start.”

“There is more you have not spoken of,” Enaid said, looking at Mikaal.

“Much more, but we need time to understand,” Areenna said.

Mikaal reached out and took Areenna’s hand. “We must go to the Island again. We have work to do there. Master Jalil go with us.”

“It will take you too long,” Roth said.

“No,” said Master Jalil, speaking for the first time. “We do not go with you by ship. There is another way, but only for those born to the powers.” Jalil paused to look at Areenna and Mikaal. He favored them with a slight smile before turning back to Roth. “You must gather all the forces you can. There will be those who will not join, not many, but some. They are already corrupted. Afzal will land at two points. The southeast shores and the southwestern.”

He closed his eyes for a moment. When he looked at Roth again, he exhaled slowly. “For now, that is all I see.”

“So be it,” Roth declared.

<><><>

Areenna awoke an hour before daybreak. Turning on her silks, she stretched out her arm to Mikaal but found his silks empty. She reached out with her mind.

Here, he responded.

She closed her eyes and joined with him. He stood at the edge of the plateau looking west. Rising, Areenna walked to where he stood. Charka was next to him, the kraal’s head pressed to Mikaal’s arm. Gaalrie was perched on Charka’s saddle.

She stopped next to him and took his hand. As always, the spark leapt between their palms when they touched, and a rush of warmth spread through her. "We are almost done," she whispered.

"Yet so much is still before us," Mikaal replied.

She searched his face. A strange feeling settled over her. There was a heaviness wrapped around Mikaal. It took her a moment to understand the doubt she sensed was the weight of Nevaeh's future pressing upon him. "All that matters is that we do it together."

"What comes will be hard."

Areenna gave a short laugh. "What else could it be?" Her smile turned into a frown. She stared deeply into his eyes. *We have changed again.*

We have. We are closer.

We are one, she corrected.

Almost.

She closed the few inches that separated them, slipped her arms around him even as he did the same with her. Their mouths met and their minds joined. The kiss deepened into something far more than a simple kiss. When it ended and Areenna drew back, her breath came in short spurts, which matched the sudden pounding of her heart. She could not help but feel the thundering of his blood as well.

"Soon," she whispered.

He nodded, his eyes never leaving her face. He stepped back, breaking the embrace. "So much is expected," he said. "So many have pinned their hopes on you."

Again the heaviness spread. "On us."

"No, Areenna, on you. It has always been you."

"What bothers you?"

He shrugged. "The future. The Eight of the Island, the Master Jalil, even the Masters of the Circle are manipulating us. Each day I feel more like a pawn."

A sad smile quirked the corners of her lips. "I understand; it has been the same with me since I touched Duke Yermon's hand in Freemorn—since we fought the first wraith *she* released upon Yermon and us—and on the Island when the Speaker commanded us to take this journey."

He started to speak. She stopped him with a single finger across his lips. *Listen but speak not. They manipulate us because we are the hope the people of Nevaeh need. You, you are my hope. Without you, I am nothing. Without you, the Masters of Afzal win. Without you—*

—Do you not have this backward? Without you, all is lost.

No, Mikaal, without you I am lost. It is the two of us, not just me. As to the manipulation, how else can we reach the point we must attain? I know what they do, but what they know not, is that when the time comes, we will end the manipulation. You and I have a purpose. What it ultimately is, I know not, but when it is time, we will know.

The gray of his eyes deepened to the color of steel. He raised his hands and grasped her face between them. "So certain are you?" he asked aloud.

She sighed. "As certain as my love for you. As certain as I know our children will change not just Nevaeh but the very world itself."

Before her last word was finished, everything around them vanished. They rose bodiless; below them was the plateau, in front of them rising through a cloud was the Island surrounded in reddish mist. A shimmering vision of the black face of the Speaker of the Eight floated before them.

So finally, you begin to understand the truths of who you are, the truths of your lives...and not just your lives, but everyone's. The Speaker's eyes flared red when they locked with Mikaal's eyes. *Remove doubt from your mind, Man Child, for you serve a greater purpose.* The red flaring eyes faded and turned a softer shade of amber. *And you, Child of Power, how else would you have grown into the woman you are without the manipulation necessary for you to become? Being born to magic means nothing! It is the understanding of your power, the learning of your abilities and the acceptance of them that makes you a woman of power. Come to us soon. There is much to learn and more to do before they arrive.* The Speaker's face dissolved, replaced by another vision—it was of a huge fleet of ships sailing toward Nevaeh.

This vision disappeared as well, and Areenna and Mikaal were once again standing on the plateau, Mikaal's hands still clasping Areenna's face. Reluctantly, he lowered his hands, stepped back and shook his head. His lips twisting with a terrible semblance of a smile. "What choice is left?"

The End

The Dark Masters

Tales Of Nevaeh

Volume II

AUTHOR'S NOTES

Dear Reader,

Thank you for your support! Without you, my stories would sit on a bookstore shelf, a warehouse, or in a database somewhere in a 'cloud' waiting for you to find them. I don't write because it's a job, I write because it's my passion. I hope reading and enjoying the worlds created by writers is your passion.

I hope as well, you have enjoyed this second book in the *Tales Of Nevaeh* series, *The Dark Masters*, as much as I did writing it, and I would love to hear from you about your reading experience.

If you enjoyed this book, and would like to lend me your support and help spread the word about *The Dark Masters*, please tell a friend and share it with the world by writing a review. Nothing fancy, just tell the world what you think—even just a sentence or two would be appreciated.

Reading your reviews, and receiving emails from you, means a tremendous amount to me. And I would like to thank you in advance for your help in spreading the word about Areenna and Mikaal and the people of Nevaeh.

I have included below, some convenient links for you.

Thank you for taking the time to read *The Dark Masters,*

David

Amazon: http://bit.ly/TheDarkMasters
Goodreads: http://bit.ly/GoodreadsDarkMasters
Email me at david@davidwind.com

ABOUT THE AUTHOR

David Wind

When my first novel was published in 1981, I had no idea where I was headed. published thirty-seven novels, thirty-three with traditional publishers, but in 2007, I decided I wanted more freedom than the traditional publishers would allow and began a new phase in my life as an Independent Author.

I live and write in a small village about thirty miles upstate of NYC, and share my house with my wife, Bonnie and our dog Alfie, an apricot poodle. Our three children have ventured out into the world on their own (or so they think). Our son Zach works on the CBS show 48 Hours. Our daughter Devon, her husband Russell and my grandson Sawyer live in New Jersey where Devon teaches Special Education. Alana, our youngest daughter, is a Pastry Chef in San Francisco.

In 2008, I published *Angels In Mourning*, my 'homage' to the old time private detective books of the 50's and the 60's. I used to love to sneak them from my parents' night tables and read them as a young boy. Angels, is a modern day take on the old style hardboiled detective. In April of that year, *Angels In Mourning* won the Amazon.com Book of the Month Reader's Choice Award.

My Fantasy, *Queen Of Knights*, reached #2 on the amazon.com bestseller lists for historical fantasy and medieval fantasy, and my sci-fi of parallel worlds, *The Others*, received wide acclaim.

Born To Magic, the first book in the Tales Of Nevaeh series reached #1 in several Amazon best seller lists.

I am currently working on the third volume of the *Tales of Nevaeh.*

My novels have been translated into 11 languages and published in 15 countries.

David's Links

David's Amazon Author's Page: http://amzn.to/1AKYcyR
Twitter: http://www.twitter.com/david_wind
Facebook: http://www.facebook.com/authordavidwind
David's website: http://www.davidwind.com
Goodreads Authors Page: http://bit.ly/1v1IE6B

◇◇◇

Available Novels by David Wind

***Born To Magic*, Tales Of Nevaeh, Volume I**
Queen Of Knights
The Others
The Cured
Angels In Mourning
The Hyte Maneuver
A Conspiracy Of Mirrors
As Peace Lay Dying
CO OP
Shadows
And Down Will Come Baby

Short Stories

***Prelude To Nevaeh**, Tales Of Nevaeh:* the back-story of how Roth reached Nevaeh and the start of his life there.

The Guardian At The Edge Of The World – Published in André Norton's ***Witch World 2*** anthology, TOR Books

◇◇◇

For more information about David Wind, please visit http://www.davidwind.com